Praise for L. R. Braden

Winner of:

The Eric Hoffer Book Award for Sci-Fi/Fantasy

The Imadjinn for Best Urban Fantasy
(multiple books)

First Horizon Award

The Colorado Authors League Awards
for best SF/F and best Paranormal

"I absolutely can't wait for more. This series never disappoints and just keeps getting better with each installment. I highly recommend it!"
—Richelle Rodarte, Booksirens reviewer on
Of Mettle and Magic

"The best yet . . . L. R. Braden is one of my favorite fantasy authors."
—Ann Klausing, bookseller, Books-A-Million on
Casting Shadows

"Great new series, intriguing characters, excellent world and character building!"
—Bonnie Scherr, Librarian and NetGalley Reviewer on
Demon Riding Shotgun

"A series that has burrowed its way into my heart and made a home there. I love fae, vampires, and shifters, and this series has all of that and more wrapped up in an adrenaline-fueled package."
—J. D. Brown, author of the Ema Marx series on
Courting Darkness

Other Titles
by L. R. Braden

The Magicsmith Series

A Drop of Magic, Book 1
Courting Darkness, Book 2
Faerie Forged, Book 3
Casting Shadows, Book 4
Of Mettle and Magic, Book 5
Chaos Song, Book 6
Lies and Illusion, Book 7

The Rifter Series
(set in the Magicsmith Universe)

Demon Riding Shotgun, Book 1
Personal Demons, Book 2
A Demon Faerie Tale, Book 3
Dancing with a Demon, Book 4

Chaos Song

The Magicsmith - Book 6

by

L. R. Braden

Magical Realms Press

This is a work of fiction. Names, characters, places and incidents are either the products of the author's imagination or are used fictitiously. Any resemblance to actual persons (living or dead), events or locations is entirely coincidental.

Magical Realms Press
PO BOX 24
Broomfield, CO 80038

Print ISBN: **978-1-968414-11-5**
Copyright © 2022 by L. R. Braden
Published in the United States of America.
Previously published by BelleBooks

We love to hear from readers!
Contact us at:
MagicalRealmsPress.com
LRBraden.com

Cover design: Debra Dixon
Interior design: Hank Smith

This book is dedicated to Faolan Maedoc Graff

2011-2021
May the road rise up to meet you
and the wind be always at your back.

Chapter 1

THE AIR BURST from my lungs in a painful *whoosh* when my back hit the mats.

"Again." Sarah Nazari was bouncing from foot to foot as though she had infinite energy to burn. Sweat slicked her golden skin and dampened her tank top. Her long, black hair was twisted into a thick braid that made a tempting target, but I knew from experience that trying to hold it was like grabbing the tail of a viper.

I groaned and rolled to my knees, wiped a few sweat-slicked strands of auburn hair off my forehead, then slowly drew up to standing. I'd given up sparring with human partners after a magically imbued tattoo—courtesy of my fae grandfather—shifted my nature enough to make me stronger and faster than a regular human, but I still wasn't anywhere near as strong or fast as a werewolf.

"Take it easy," I panted. "It's just a workout."

Sarah swept my legs before I could blink. I was back on the ground.

"You think the fae will 'take it easy' when they invade? Or the PTF when they turn on us? Or any of the other baddies you're likely to come up against who want to mount your severed skull as a prize on their wall?"

I cringed. "Very graphic. Point taken."

She offered me her hand. I took it gladly, letting her pull me up.

"Now"—she took up an offensive stance—"come at me again."

A growl that wasn't nearly human enough for my liking came from behind me, bringing up memories of jagged teeth rending muscle from bone on a moonlit mountainside the night I learned werewolves were real.

Sarah's fist connected with my cheek. I went down to the mats again.

I blinked to clear the tears from my eyes and readied myself for Sarah's comments about my wandering attention, or the fact that I hadn't even tried to block that punch, but she was staring at something over my head. I twisted to see.

Across the room, near the free weights, two of our newest werewolf recruits were locked together, and their match didn't look like a friendly round of sparring. The muscular calves of one of the combatants elongated and grew an extra joint as the underlying skeleton shifted to something other than human. I winced at the pop of bone. Black fur sprouted from the man's dark-brown skin. The second man, shorter and wider than the first, sank too-sharp teeth into his opponent's shoulder. His eyes were wild and bright, irises bleeding out to devour the white around their edges.

I tensed and muttered, "Stupid Weatherly being right."

I'd spent the better part of the past two weeks trying to convince Deputy Director Weatherly and Governor Anderson's liaison, Mrs. Daniels, that werewolves were safe to work with despite their volatile natures. As the newly appointed Deputy Director in charge of Paranatural Relations, it was my job to match our more magically inclined agents with human partners. So far I'd only created three successful teams—well, functional teams. The rest had resulted in one or both members requesting reassignment. An altercation like this was not going to improve my retention rates, and if we ran out of humans willing to work with our paranatural recruits, that would effectively put an end to our alliance.

Sarah was halfway across the room, fists balled, by the time I scrambled to my feet, but she wasn't the first to reach the fight.

"Knock it off." A lanky teenager in running shorts and a sweaty gray T-shirt shoved between the combatants. He braced his forearm against the chest of the man who was now furry from the waist down and pressed his other hand against the bare chest of the sharp-toothed man, who snarled like a rabid dog and immediately clamped his too-long jaws around the offending arm.

"Look at yourselves," the newcomer commanded in a voice that seemed too deep for his wiry frame. "You're behaving exactly like the brainless beasts we're trying to convince the world we're not."

Blood trickled from the wound on his arm, and the half-wolf strained against him, but the man stood rooted to the spot as though no force in nature could displace him, let alone a couple of quarrelsome werewolves. The half-wolf was the first to calm down. He shrank back onto fully human legs. The second man, panting and wiping the blood from his mouth and chin, stepped back.

The young man in the middle lowered his arms. "Hit the showers and cool off."

He looked first at one, then the other, leveling his cloudy blue gaze like a weapon. Neither of the older men seemed to have any fight left in them as they slunk toward the locker room. The remaining man exhaled, his shoulders sagging as he visibly relaxed. He looked at his injured arm.

Snapping to my senses I called, "Just a sec." I jogged to the first aid box mounted to the north wall and came back with an antiseptic pad, some gauze, and tape.

"I'll heal," he said with a smile when I tore open the antiseptic pad.

"I know, but in the meantime you're bleeding all over the gym." The blood around the bite marks was already starting to thicken. Knowing werewolf healing, he'd be right as rain in an hour. Still, no harm in being careful. Once the wound was clean, I wrapped it in gauze and stepped back.

Sarah had watched the entire exchange from her position in the middle of the room. Once my ministrations were done, she came to stand beside me, hands on hips, dark eyes narrowed.

"You're Faolan, right?"

The man nodded, meeting her gaze.

"From which pack?"

"Florida," he said. "You?"

"Sarah Nazari, from here. You handle yourself well. Had much experience breaking up fights back in Florida?"

He shrugged. "I was an enforcer."

Sarah's stance shifted slightly. "Same."

The two continued to stare at each other until the silence became awkward.

I cleared my throat. "Thanks for diffusing that situation. The last thing we need is a full-blown fight in the PTF gym."

He smiled and moved his gaze to me. "Happy to help. Now if you don't mind, I think I'll hit the showers, too." He backed up three steps before turning away from Sarah.

When he disappeared into the locker room, I nudged Sarah. "I need to talk to you about the escalating violence among the werewolves."

She pulled her gaze away from the locker room entrance. "Isn't that something you should discuss with Marc? He *is* the werewolf liaison after all."

For now. I'd had more than a few discussions with Marc about how to handle the increasing tension between our werewolf recruits, but I wasn't very happy with his recommendation. Mostly, because it included him stepping down as liaison.

"I'm looking for a second opinion."

She shrugged. "Shoot."

The doors at the west end of the gym opened, and four men took up positions on the basketball court.

I waved Sarah toward the women's locker room. "What do you think about forming a separate pack within the PTF?"

She pulled up short, then hurried to catch up as I continued talking.

"Rather than identifying by territory like a traditional pack, the members would be defined by their enrollment with the PTF."

"Who would lead it?"

I pulled open my locker and grabbed a towel. "That's one of the things I'm a little worried about. Marc says we should select a new alpha for the pack, and we should do it in 'traditional werewolf style.'"

"So it's a fight for dominance."

"But the new alpha will also take Marc's place as the werewolf liaison. I'll have to work with them every day, not just for the benefit of the pack but of the whole PTF. I feel like I should have some say in selecting a good fit."

"Marc disagrees?"

I tugged my sweaty shirt over my head. "Sort of. He says the best alpha will make the best liaison. He seems to think the jobs are one and the same."

"And it's not just the alpha you'll need to consider. Creating a PTF pack would probably solve your infighting issues, but an internal pack could also act as a deterrent for joining."

I frowned. "How so?"

"Well, take me for example. If the PTF becomes its own pack, I'll no longer be a member of Marc's, but my husband has no interest in joining the PTF. He's not a soldier and has no desire to become one."

"So you'd be mates in different packs. Is that even possible?"

She shrugged. "Anything's possible, but it's certainly something to consider."

"Would you withdraw from the PTF if we insisted on an internal pack?"

She pursed her lips and was silent for a moment. "I doubt it. I love my husband, but my primary drive is to serve and protect. That's why I became a cop. Since paranaturals aren't allowed to be police officers, and I can't exactly go back in the closet, this is the only place where I have the opportunity to serve a larger community. Gil will understand that." She tossed her sweat-soaked shirt in her locker. "How we'll work out the logistics though . . . that's another matter entirely."

"Right." I grabbed my shampoo and headed for the showers, still unsure what the best course of action would be.

PROTESTERS FLAPPED their signs in my face when I pushed through the front doors at the end of my nine-to-five—mostly slogans about sharing a bed with freaks and monsters, complete with some pretty graphic imagery. I briefly toyed with the idea of telling them that I shared my literal sheets with a blood-sucking vampire, but why add fuel to their fire? Three weeks ago, if I'd approached this building, I would have been arrested on sight. Now I was supposed to be running the place. Well . . . co-running it. The term *Paranatural Task Force* had taken on a whole new meaning since my appointment as co-director of the Colorado facility. It hadn't come as any surprise that not everyone was thrilled with the change.

Clutching my purse tight to my side, I bulldozed through the mob and made a beeline for the rusted blue Jeep at the far edge of the parking lot. Fingers of orange twilight lit the undersides of swollen storm clouds against a navy sky. There would be rain in Denver tonight and probably snow in the higher country where I lived.

Denver to Nederland was a long commute, especially when I was expected to do it every day in rush-hour traffic. I sang my lungs out to the radio as I inched along Highway 36 toward Boulder and wondered how I'd gotten roped into this lifestyle. I wasn't an office worker. I wasn't a suit-wearing, report-filing, decision-making boss. Hell, I'd been fired from my last job for flakiness.

Half an hour later, I rolled past the remains of that lost job—a visual reminder of how much my world had changed. The bookstore founded by my friend Maggie was now unrecognizable as the cozy space we'd created where patrons sipped lattes and browsed books amid displays by local artists. Plywood filled the windows, scrawled with messages of hate and ignorance. At least Maggie wasn't there to see it. She and Hortense, my ex-tutor for all things fae, had their hands full at a secret camp out east—curing a group of drug-addled kids from a goblin fruit addiction. Maybe by the time they got back, the world would be a better place.

I snorted at my own optimism and turned the corner. People didn't change that quickly.

Mounds of grayish-brown slush appeared at the sides of the road as I wound along the curves of Boulder Canyon. Ice clung in patches along the banks of the river that traced the rock walls. The bare branches of the town's cultivated trees gave way to the wild spruce and pines of the evergreen forest. The last stretch of road to my mountain property was a layer of packed ice that wouldn't thaw till mid-April. The Jeep's engine rumbled with the effort of the climb.

I pulled to a stop next to a yellow Volkswagen Bug buried under a mound of snow and cut the engine. I stared at the unused car for a moment, guilt and grief twisting my heart. Then I shook myself, grabbed my bag, and headed inside.

The smells of cooking enveloped me as soon as I opened the front door—such a difference from when I lived alone and dinner was a frozen meal in the microwave. It was Kai's night to cook, and he stood on the far side of the long counter that separated the living room from the kitchen. The sleeves of his gray shirt were pushed up to his elbows, and a blue apron embroidered with the slogan *ROMAINE CALM AND CARROT ON* was slung around his neck. Since he rarely wore his glamour at home these days, Kai's eyes were their natural galaxy-spiral kaleidoscope, and his ears tapered to blunt points that marked him as fae.

My second roommate, the owner of the abandoned Volkswagen, had her back to the living room when I walked in. Emma was wearing a rust-orange sweatshirt, and her hair was a layer of dark, close-cropped fuzz coating her skull. My chest tightened at the sight. Before her coma, Emma's hair had been an ever-changing fashion statement that matched the bright flamboyance of her temperament. Now both had been stripped back to bare practicality.

I swallowed the lump in my throat and closed the door against the cold. "Hey guys."

Emma turned. Her elbow knocked a glass of water off the counter. She gasped and reached for the falling glass. Her fingers brushed the rim but closed on empty air.

Kai ducked out of sight. He reemerged holding the unbroken glass. "Just a few drips. No harm done."

Emma stiffened her jaw with a forced smile. Her face turned toward me, but her clouded eyes didn't focus. "Welcome home, Alex."

Her voice trembled slightly, but if she wanted to downplay the loss of her sight, so would I. It was the least I could do . . . seeing as how the magical backlash that cost both her sight and her magic was my fault. She'd merged her magic with mine, acting as my paladin—both battery and bodyguard— so I had the juice to stand against my demon-corrupted father and his sorcerer rebellion. We'd taken him down together, but she alone had paid the price.

I hung my bag and coat on the hooks by the door and said with my own forced smile, "Dinner smells great. What are we having?"

Kai grinned. "Ambrosia salad, candied carrots, honey-glazed ham, and sweet potatoes."

"Plus chocolate cream pie for dessert." Emma indicated the contents of the glass mixing bowl she'd been stirring when I entered. "It's my mother's secret recipe."

My teeth ached at the thought of so much sweet food. Still, it was an improvement. I'd implemented the "well-rounded" rule after the second time Kai served ice cream for dinner. "Need any help?"

Emma's smile faltered. She shifted her weight.

Kai glanced at her then at me. "Emma and I have it covered."

The corners of Emma's lips turned up. She lifted her chin. We were all trying to get used to Emma's new normal, she most of all. While I worried about her trying to pretend nothing had changed, I also understood her need not to feel like an invalid, so I was doing my best not to treat her like one.

"Then I think I'll pop over to the studio for a bit."

Kai glanced at the clock on the stove. "We'll be ready to eat in two hours."

The oversized shed that served as my studio was a short walk from the main house. I took a deep breath of the cold evening air, shivered, and un-locked the door. The overhead lights took a moment to warm up, so the room was a bit dim when I first stepped in, but a quick scan told me everything was as it should be. The knot in my chest eased.

It had taken me weeks to get my creative sanctuary back in order after the PTF raided it in their search for me. Every tool was now in its place—every hammer, drill bit, burnishing compound—but I couldn't help seeing the space as it had been when I returned after clearing my fugitive status. That sense of violation still clung to me.

I walked past tools, cabinets, benches, and the cold forge, and stopped in front of a collection of metal sheets leaning against the back wall—dozens of sheets in a variety of materials, each as tall as my chest and wider than I could spread my arms. This was the material from which I would make my newest, and most ambitious, sculpture. A space had been marked and prepped for the installation just to the right of the PTF main entrance, where it would be impossible for protesters, agents, or any other visitors to miss. There was little there at the moment besides leveled dirt and a few anchored strips of rebar, but these sheets were about to become the six walls spiraling toward the center of my design. My fingers itched for the handle of my hammer. I smiled and exhaled the tension I'd been carrying around all day. *This is where I'm meant to be.*

Pulling a sheet of brass from the pile, I propped it against a workbench, pressed my palms to its shiny surface, and stared at my reflection. Then I reached for the fae magic pooled inside me and tapped into the imbuing ability that was my birthright.

The feelings of violation surrounding my studio intensified, mingled with self-doubt, guilt, and fear of all the changes happening around me. There was also a sense of triumph and pride. And there was hope, bright and warm, shining like a beacon in the storm. Sinking past my surface emotions, I drew on feelings of loneliness, isolation, abandonment—memories I'd spent most of my life avoiding. Tears pricked at the corners of my eyes. I sniffed to keep my nose from dripping. Imbuing was a bitch because I couldn't access the magic without feeling the emotions . . . but art was all about connection through shared experience. I couldn't ask people to face the pain of being alone if I wasn't willing to face it myself.

Easing my magic into the metal, I tied my feelings to the core of the material, locking them in place. When I was sure my emotions had been successfully merged with the metal, I released my magic and took a step back. My palms left two perfect, sweaty prints on the surface. I took a ragged breath and reminded myself that I was not alone these days. I had friends. I had a family. I was accessing those uncomfortable feelings for a purpose. I was making a point.

I moved the brass sheet to an empty space beside the original pile and grabbed a fresh one. Setting it on the workbench, I began the process again.

After five sheets, I was ready to cry from the emotional drain, and an aching hunger was tearing at my insides. Propping the most recently imbued sheet with its companions, I wiped the sweat off my forehead, grabbed a granola bar from the emergency stash in my workbench, and plopped down on a stool for a breather. The granola bar was gone in seconds. Imbuing really took it out of me.

I could have tapped into my practitioner magic to save a little strength, but then I would have had to deal with the whispers of the demons who lived in the Rift—the incorporeal energy from which practitioners drew their power. Best to leave that for more dire circumstances and days when I wasn't already thinking of my father's fall to necromancy.

I pulled an open sketchbook toward me, studying a rough sketch and the subsequent scribbles of my failures. The image showed a large stone in a silver setting that resembled the wavy rays of a stylized sun hugging the gem. I'd seen that pendant around James's neck dozens of times before discovering it was a fae charm imbued with the power to protect a vampire from sunlight. The pendant had been traded and later destroyed, but not before I managed to imbue James directly with the ability to walk in daylight. Unfortunately, I'd also promised a certain master vampire that I'd make her more of the pendants in exchange for a favor I desperately needed at the time.

I sighed and tapped my pencil against the sketch. As far as I could tell, the shape of stone and setting didn't matter, but I was determined to recreate the pendant as faithfully as possible. Not that a convincing replica would save me from the wrath of the vampire I owed it to if the damn thing failed to protect her from the sun.

The door behind me creaked. A wisp of frozen breeze tickled the back of my neck, making me shiver. A bright flash of panic surged through me, then I recognized the familiar resonance humming in my chest. I inhaled deeply. The wind carried the scent of raspberries, nutmeg, and copper. The corners of my mouth twitched up.

James's fingers settled over my shoulders, and the vague thrum of our connection snapped into focus. His emotions surged through our link—happiness, worry, attraction. His breath warmed my cheek as he examined the drawing from over my shoulder. "Any progress?"

"I don't suppose you could convince Victoria to postpone my deadline?"

His chest pressed against my back. "It would be a waste of breath. Remember, she thinks you've already cracked the secret to making these." He gestured to the drawings.

I sighed. The master vampire of Denver would come to collect at the end of the month, and despite weeks of experimenting, I had no day-walking amulet to give her—not even one, let alone the five I'd promised.

"What do you think she'll do when she realizes I lied?"

James's hands slid down my arms, then around to circle my torso. "Whatever her response . . ." *you won't face it alone*. The second part of James's answer was a voice inside my head. Time and the various changes we'd both undergone had altered our link so that most of what we shared was inarticulate emotions or flashes of thought, but when we were touching, direct communication was still possible.

I leaned into him, closed my eyes, and let some of the tension in my muscles bleed away, soothed by the gentle rise and fall of his chest. He didn't actually have to breathe, but it was important to keep up appearances.

That thought sparked an unpleasant memory. Weatherly had cornered me that morning to discuss the status of our new paranatural registration procedures . . . and why James had yet to submit for testing. Weatherly's weaselly voice rang through my head. *If you want paranaturals to be treated as equal citizens, let them follow the rules like everyone else. Being your boyfriend does not exempt him. If he hasn't come in on his own by the end of the week, I'll issue a warrant for his arrest.*

James's arms tensed, responding to the change in my emotions. "What is it?"

I sagged, my moment of quiet comfort gone. This conversation was going to suck, but there was no point putting off the inevitable.

"Weatherly asked me when you'd be in for testing." James went still behind me, no longer mimicking human. I pressed on. "Once you're registered, you can take the position Director Harris offered you. The unnamed paranaturals deserve a seat at the table . . . and maybe being stuck in an office all day wouldn't suck so much if you were there with me."

"Because misery loves company?"

"Something like that." I slipped off my stool, twisted around in the cage of his arms, and pulled his hips against mine. I ran one hand through the short strands of his once lusciously long, black hair. This close I had to look up to see his face clearly. His naturally olive complexion had grown darker now that he wasn't restricted to shadows and the night. He met my gaze with the cobalt-blue eyes I was still getting used to. Emma wasn't the only one adjusting to a new normal. When I'd used my magic to change the core of James's being, allowing him to walk in daylight, the change had produced some . . . unexpected side effects.

"If more time together is what you want, you should reconsider participating in the spring exhibition at the gallery." He brushed a strand of hair away from my face and trailed his fingers down my neck and over the swell of my breast. "I'm sure I can make space for you."

"Because I have so much free time between my new job, my public sculpture, and the day-walking amulets I promised Victoria."

"Because misery isn't the only thing that loves company." His lips traced my jaw, and I inhaled his kiss when his mouth met mine.

My pulse quickened. My breath became a series of short gasps. Then

Weatherly's threat jumped to the forefront of my thoughts, tainting my enjoyment. I braced my hands against the smooth fabric of James's silk shirt and created a few inches of space between us. My fingers brushed bare skin over his collarbone, marking another subtle change. James had given up ties in favor of leaving the top few buttons of his shirt open.

"I'm serious." My voice was low and airy. "You need to register properly with the PTF."

He frowned. "You know I can't officially support the PTF until an alliance is approved by the vampire council. And even then, submitting myself for PTF testing. . . ." A wash of anxiety swept over me, and for a second I thought I saw a flash of silver in his eyes.

"You're not technically a vampire anymore."

"Walking in daylight doesn't mean I can ignore the council's wishes without consequence. It's not loyalty that keeps the vampires in line."

"Yeah, yeah, big bad boss monsters . . . I get it." I slipped my hands around his waist. "But you don't have to register on behalf of all vampires. We've created a category for miscellaneous paranaturals. Just tell them you're strong and fast—"

"And feed off humans to survive."

I gave him a flat look. "Maybe leave that bit out."

James stepped back, widening the gap between us. His emotions grew muted. "I won't submit for testing."

I closed my eyes. "If you don't, Weatherly will arrest you and you'll be tested anyway. It will all go much smoother if you come in voluntarily."

"Smoother for whom?"

"Everyone. If you fight the PTF agents who come to collect you, someone is going to get hurt. And how will it look if the Deputy Director in charge of Paranatural Relations can't even get her own boyfriend to play by the rules. Or have you forgotten that I work for the PTF now?"

"*With.* You work *with* the PTF. At least that was the plan when you began this alliance."

"Same thing."

"No, it's not, and it's not our only option. The wheels of this experiment have been put into motion, and while your participation may grease the gears, you're not necessary for the machine to function. I have full access to my funds and stores again. We can leave. Go anywhere in the world and live off the grid, far from politics and prejudice, off the radar of the PTF, the fae, the vampire council, and anyone else who wants to tell us how to live our lives. We could be well and truly free."

I crossed my arms and paced to the side of the room. "You're talking about becoming a fugitive again. Leaving my home, my friends . . . undermining everything I've spent the last few months working toward."

A swell of frustration burst from James's side of the room. "And what about what I've worked for?" He swiped a hand across my workbench, scattering sketches and pencils.

I hugged myself, staring at the mess. It wasn't just James's eye color that had changed, or the olive flush of his skin, or that he'd trimmed his jet-black hair so short it barely brushed the tips of his ears, or that he'd given up wearing ties. James's moods had become more pronounced . . . and more volatile. Sometimes I'd catch him singing to himself or staring into space with a smile on his face. Sometimes he'd fly into a rage over seemingly nothing. He was still basically *him*, but the calm, collected man I'd known for years had been replaced by someone wilder.

James planted his palms against the thick, oak tabletop and took a deep breath. "I apologize. I just. . . ." He shook his head. "You wanted to open a dialogue between the paranatural races and the humans of the mortal realm. You've done that. Do you intend to spend the rest of your life babysitting them?" He narrowed his cobalt-blue gaze at me. "I know you, Alex. Life as a public official will never make you happy."

"Neither will a life in hiding."

"Even with me?"

I hugged myself tighter. "Please don't make me choose."

He stared at me for a long moment, those deep-blue eyes assessing, but we'd both slammed closed the doors of our link. He couldn't read me any more than I could read him.

"I should go."

"But"—I took a step forward and waved a hand in the direction of the house—"family dinner."

"I'm not hungry." He walked out, shutting the door quietly behind him.

I stared at the closed door for one minute . . . two . . . five. . . . Then I started collecting my scattered supplies. I lifted the sketchbook James had given me when we were on the run—the one in which I'd developed the concept for my current work—and ran a finger over the leather cover. I flipped to the first page and stared at my likeness, rendered in charcoal, above James's scrawled signature. The woman in the drawing was beautiful. I couldn't help but think that her features were slightly softer than mine.

Snapping the book closed, I tossed it on the workbench. I couldn't turn my back on the fledgling partnership I'd created between paranaturals and the PTF, but I couldn't force the man I loved to do something he was so clearly afraid of doing either. I rubbed a hand over my eyes, switched off the lights, and locked the studio. By the time I stepped into the clearing in front of my house, there was no sign James had ever come to visit.

Chapter 2

"I SEE YOU HAVEN'T lost your charm."

I spun into a low crouch halfway across the open, ice-crusted lawn and raised my fists to a defensive position, calling my practitioner magic at the same time. The edges of my vision filled with roiling gray fog.

Chase stepped out from behind one of the frosted pines at the edge of my driveway. He moved with cat-like grace, doubtless carried over from his feline form. Vertical pupils split his luminous green eyes, and the faintest stripes rippled through the long silver braid that dangled over his shoulder and down to his waist. His long-sleeved shirt and skin-tight jeans weren't unreasonably out of place in the Colorado night, but he stood on the snow with bare feet. Shifters hated wearing shoes.

Releasing my magic, I raced forward and wrapped my arms around his lithe body, squeezing for all I was worth.

He grunted on impact and returned the hug. "Nice to know you missed me." His hands slid down to my butt.

I shoved him hard enough to make him stumble. "Not that much."

He chuckled and hooked a thumb in the direction of my empty driveway. "So what's got ol' fang-face stomping off in a huff this time?"

I blew out a breath that turned to steam and shook my head. "Never mind him. You're just in time for dinner." I took his hand and pulled him toward the front door. "Did you manage to get all the fae kids back to their homes?" Goblin fruit was only addictive to mortals, so unlike the children Maggie and Hortense were babysitting, the kidnapped fae hadn't needed time to recover—at least not physically. Chase had volunteered to get them all back to their appropriate realms.

He nodded. "All the lost lambs have been returned to their families . . . or as near to family as I could find."

"That's good." *At least* something *has gone smoothly.* I pushed through the front door and dragged Chase into the warmth. "Hey guys, look what the cat dragged in."

Emma glanced up from setting the table, unfocused eyes searching.

I winced at my poor choice of words and announced, "Chase is back."

"Oh." Emma clapped her hands together. I could tell she wanted to run over and give him a hug just as I had, but instead she walked slowly across the room, trailing her fingertips along the furniture.

Chase caught my gaze and lifted one eyebrow in question.

I mouthed the word "burnout."

His eyes widened. The color drained from his rosy cheeks. When Emma reached him, he accepted her hug and gently squeezed her back.

She stepped away with a smile. "I'll go set another place at the table."

An ache tightened my chest like a noose around my heart. "Don't bother."

She turned to face me, confusion puckering her expression. Her eyes didn't focus, but sometimes the way she moved made me forget she couldn't actually see me. "But James—"

"He isn't coming." I said it more harshly than I'd intended.

Chase cleared his throat. "Well, I'm famished." He tugged Emma's elbow, turning her toward the dinner table. "Shall we?"

The two of them settled at the table while I washed my hands at the kitchen sink. Kai pulled the ham out of the oven and carried over the loaded serving dishes.

Chase eyed the food and snorted. "I see your sweet tooth hasn't worn off yet."

I took my seat. "I doubt that will ever happen."

"Maybe not in *your* lifetime," Chase said. "But we all grow up eventually."

I filled my plate and lifted my fork. Then I looked across the table at Chase and Emma and realized how much I had to catch him up on. I pushed the food around my plate, wondering where to start. "A lot has happened since I last saw you."

"So I've heard. Quelling a sorcerer rebellion, fighting your supposed-to-be-dead father, renovating the PTF . . . you've been busy."

I stared at him, my mouth hanging open.

Amusement danced in Chase's eyes. "The shifter spy network is among the best."

Kai snorted. "It helps when you can literally be a fly on the wall."

"One thing I wasn't able to discern from the rumors. . . . How in all the realms did you convince Lord Bael to call off his invasion?"

I lifted one shoulder in a half shrug. "Blackmail."

He slapped the table hard enough to make the silverware jump, threw back his head, and laughed.

Kai's knuckles went white on his fork. A tendon strained in the side of his neck as he watched Chase get his mirth under control.

Chase wiped a tear from his eye. "I'm sorry I missed that."

"It was a risky move," Kai said.

Chase's green gaze swung to him. "And I heard you renounced your knighthood."

I was afraid the fork in Kai's hand was going to snap in two. "How are

Jynx and Ava?" I said to divert the conversation.

Chase's bantering expression closed down. "Well enough. Ava is restless to learn Targe's fate. I'm worried the two of them may do something stupid if they don't get word soon."

My breath lodged like a physical lump in my throat. Ava's uncle Targe had been one of several fae who'd been captured when the PTF raided Crossroads—a local fae-friendly bar—looking for me. The last time I saw Targe he'd been in an iron cage with magic-dampening manacles on his wrists. "I've been trying to negotiate the release of properly registered fae with the PTF, but it's slow going. The governor is against letting any fae out of holding. The fae and humans may not have officially gone to war . . . but there's no real truce right now either."

"The calm before the storm." Kai stabbed a chunk of sweet potato. He studied the skewered vegetable. "Everyone's in a holding pattern while they assess their relative positions."

Chase shook his head. "That won't last long."

"It should last a year," I said. "Bael gave me his word."

"That the Court of Enchantment wouldn't attack," Kai amended. "The humans made no such promise."

"But without paranatural backup, the humans have no chance against the fae. The Purists may be bullies, but even they won't start a war they can't win."

"Except that you've taken it upon yourself to fold paranaturals into the human arsenal," Chase said.

"For peacekeeping, not war. We'll only—"

"Don't be naive. You may be able to handpick assignments while the paranatural troops are limited to Colorado and under your direct command, but if your experiment is successful, those troops will be dispersed throughout the world, and the people pulling their strings will be the same people you've been fighting up till now."

"I realize that, Chase. I'm not an idiot. But what would you have had me do? This alliance was the only way to prevent an imminent war that would have decimated the mortal realm. That may not mean much to you since you've got another world to go home to, but it means a damn lot to me."

"You have another world that would welcome you as well."

I opened my mouth to argue, but Chase held up his hands in a placating gesture. "But I take your point. It's easy to criticize from the sidelines. And for the record, I happen to like this realm. I'd rather not see it ruined."

"Then you'd better hope Alex makes a good impression tomorrow." Emma set her fork next to her empty plate.

Chase arched an eyebrow. "What happens tomorrow?"

Kai smirked. "What happened to the efficacy of your spy network?"

Chase glared at him.

I rolled my eyes. "Put 'em away boys." I focused on Chase. "Weatherly and I are meeting with a delegation from the Unified Church so they can assess what we're doing."

Chase frowned. "I'd think they'd have their hands full with recovering from the attack in Rome and opening their new facility in Singapore."

I shook my head. "I still can't believe they're moving their headquarters."

"I think it makes a lot of sense," Emma said. "The original Unified Church was only in Rome because the Catholics hoarded most of the information on practitioner abilities. Picking a place like Singapore will put the different religious groups on more even footing."

"I guess." As an agnostic, I had never put much thought into how the various world religions balanced their beliefs to make the Unified Church work. The fact that humans weren't alone in the world seemed to be enough for them to set aside their more esoteric differences and focus on the goal of staying top dog as a species.

"Regardless," Chase said, "since when does the Church have jurisdiction over the PTF?"

"Not jurisdiction per se, but their opinion carries a lot of weight. They could pretty easily sway public opinion of our experiment one way or the other, so I'd like to convince them that an alliance is not only feasible but in everyone's best interest."

"You won't convince the Purists."

"True, but not every member of the Church is a Purist. That's only a small faction."

"A small, *loud* faction."

"Every religion has zealots. We can't judge the whole by the outliers any more than all the werewolves should be judged by the violence of a single rogue who lashed out under extreme stress."

He tipped his head to one side. "Since when are you a fan of religion?"

"Since I met a woman who had more reason to hate and fear the church than anyone I've ever met and still kept her faith. Religions aren't the problem. People are. That's who we have to convince, and that's why tomorrow's so important."

"And you're going to do *brilliantly*." Emma nodded with conviction, emphasizing the last word.

I wish I were that sure.

Emma's fate, along with that of countless other paranaturals, could well depend on my not making an ass of myself tomorrow. And I was pretty sure Weatherly was going to do his best to trip me up.

Chase bumped Emma's arm with his elbow. "Speaking of brilliant, you seem to be adapting quite well."

I shot a kick at him under the table.

"Ow!" Emma wailed.

I cringed. "Sorry."

She glared across the table at me. It was a bit disturbing that she could still do that without knowing exactly where I was, but then I guess the kick kind of gave me away. "I don't need you to protect me, Alex. I'm blind, not broken. I can handle talking about it."

Heat crept into my face.

"Humans rely too much on sight anyway," Chase continued as though I hadn't just received a verbal beatdown. "Smell, sound, even taste. There are many ways to be aware of your environment."

Emma shrugged. "I can't say any of my other senses quite make up for losing my sight. Being blind definitely sucks, but we've had the best doctors and magical healers look at me. My sight isn't coming back." Her voice hitched, and a sheen of moisture glittered at the corners of her eyes. She cleared her throat. "All I can do is try to get used to it."

"From what I've seen of practitioner burnouts, you're lucky to even be alive," Chase said. "What about your magic? Can you still use it?"

I stifled a groan and focused on shoveling the last of my food into my mouth to keep from speaking. I knew Chase cared about Emma, but it was like he was intentionally poking every bruise he could find. When a practitioner burned out as Emma had, even if they survived, they lost the ability to channel magic.

She shook her head. "Sometimes I almost think I can feel the energy, especially when I'm around Alex. At first I thought maybe it was because of the way our magic merged when I was acting as her paladin, but nothing's come of it. Now I'm thinking it's like when someone gets an arm amputated but insists they can still feel their hand. So yeah, that sucks, too."

"You know what doesn't suck?" Kai asked. "This chocolate pie."

The corners of Emma's mouth curved up.

Kai cut us all slices, and we dug into the moist, rich dessert.

Once the last crumbs were licked clean, I cleared the table while Emma and the boys moved to the couch. Kai grabbed a remote and flicked on the TV—his second favorite mortal luxury after sweets. Scenes of a California beach piled high with garbage filled the screen as a disembodied voice cut in halfway through an explanation about a massive wave that had washed the trash ashore.

Kai pressed another button, and the news was replaced by a cartoon with lots of flashing lights and scantily clad women piloting huge robot samurais in space.

I shook my head and started the dishwasher. "Keep the volume down," I said as I headed for the hallway. "I'm going to bed."

Chase peeked over the back of the couch. "Want company?"

The question was meant to be teasing . . . or maybe not. It was hard to tell with Chase. Either way, it hit me like a punch to the gut. I forced a smile and a laugh. "Not from you."

I washed up, climbed into bed, and ran a hand over the empty sheets beside me. Somehow I had to convince James that getting tested and properly registered was the right course of action. I closed my eyes. *I'll call him when I'm done with the delegation tomorrow . . . assuming I'm still in one piece.*

THE MIDDAY SUN shone from a turbulent sky, flashing through gaps in clouds that seemed in a hurry to be somewhere else. The intermittent rays failed to ease the cold sting in the air as I shifted my weight from foot to foot at the edge of the PTF parking lot and twisted my hands together in nervous anticipation. In deference to the occasion, I'd foregone my usual ragged jeans and T-shirt for a long-sleeved cotton blouse with buttons down the front, tucked into the nicest pair of slacks I owned—the ones usually reserved for funerals and court appearances. Unfortunately, the outfit didn't make me *feel* any more respectable or confident. In fact, it made me feel like a liar.

Shouts voiced by the ever-present protesters cast a blanket of white noise over the area, but at least I didn't have to deal with them getting right in my face today. Sawhorses draped with orange tape and guarded by PTF security officers blocked off the path to the main entrance. Only three people shared the sidewalk with me between those borders.

Deputy Director Weatherly—who up until my appointment as co-director had been happily running the Denver PTF office all by his lonesome—stood to my right. He wore a pale-gray suit, had a *GQ*-cover haircut, and was currently staring straight ahead through his frameless glasses as though the angry crowd on either side of us didn't exist. On the far side of him stood Cynthia Daniels, a middle-aged weasel of a woman appointed from the governor's cabinet to oversee our work, voice Governor Anderson's opinions, and, I was pretty sure, undermine my authority at every opportunity. My only ally was David Nolan, a college friend turned security expert who—along with a few strings pulled by my Uncle Sol—had made enough of an impression during the sorcerer rebellion to get appointed chief of security at this facility. Unlike me, David had adapted nicely to his new position. With his rebellious curls trimmed, and wearing a dark suit tailored to the contours of his wide shoulders, it was hard to recognize the goofy slacker I'd known back in college.

All three stood like statues, chins raised and hands clasped—loosely, not like the coiling death grip I had. Daniels was a politician, and, as a PTF assistant-director, Weatherly wasn't far off. They were both used to crowds and cameras, smiling and giving speeches, and they wore their hand-tailored suits like a second skin. David, for his part, had shifted to intimidating bodyguard mode.

A long black car pulled into the lot and circled around until its rear door was lined up with the sidewalk.

David pressed a finger to his ear. "Look alive."

The four security officers David had put on crowd control raised their arms and pushed back against the protesters who, upon seeing the car's arrival, had surged forward, raising signs and voices higher in an effort to be heard.

"Couldn't we have brought them in the back?" I muttered under my breath.

"They're here to see the situation in its entirety before making a recommendation to the Church to either back or oppose your experiment." Daniels glanced sideways at me. "Best not to appear secretive right off the bat or they might think you've got something to hide."

I tightened my jaw to keep from responding with something that would only get me in trouble.

The driver of the car opened the rear door, and a man in black-and-red bishop's robes stepped out. He had salt-and-pepper hair, narrow brown eyes, and a double chin. A thick silver cross hung from his neck. He took one look at the gathered crowd and stepped aside. The second person to emerge was a plump, middle-aged woman. She wore a simple black dress, black-framed glasses, and a teal hijab. She, too, looked at the mob, then she moved to stand beside the priest. Her back was slightly stooped, and she barely came to the man's shoulder. The final delegate wore no shoes. His tunic-like shirt hung to the knees of his loose white pants, and a saffron scarf draped his neck. A red bindi marked his forehead.

The three delegates walked down the path together. They kept pace, shoulder-to-shoulder, so no one delegate seemed to lead. I wondered if that was some rule imposed by the Unified Church. As I was learning, maintaining balance in an organization full of people with opposing views was no easy feat. I glanced to my side and noted that Weatherly stood slightly in front of the rest of us. I thought about stepping even with him . . . but then what? I was already way out of my depth.

The calls of the protesters rose to a fevered pitch as the Church's ambassadors passed. David's officers had their hands full keeping the path clear.

"Honored delegates," Weatherly pitched his voice just shy of shouting to be heard over the crowd. "My name is Peter Weatherly, and I'm the director of this facility. Thank you so much for joining us here today."

Each of the three nodded to Weatherly, then the two men turned their gaze on the stocky woman in the middle. She took a step forward and said, "We thank you for hosting us. Please let me introduce Bishop João Silva." She indicated the man on her right, then turned to her left. "And Pandit Aarav Khatun." She faced forward once more. "I am Odella Ali of the Ulama. Together, we will be assessing the requirements and arrangements of this new paranatural branch of the PTF. Once satisfied we understand your operations, we will report back to the Unified Church to make our report to the council."

Khatun stepped even with Ali, pressed his palms together, and bowed his head. "Understand that our role here is to observe and report, not to judge."

"Though I'm sure you won't object to any insights we might share," added Silva, lifting his chin. "Our organization does have a fair bit of practice at working with paranaturals, after all."

I took a deep breath and managed not to bunch my fists. What the Church had done to practitioners like my father was about as close to "working with paranaturals" as kidnapping people and shipping them overseas as slave labor. Their reaction to the less human forms of para-naturals had been even worse. Still, arguing the point in front of an already agitated mob of protesters was not the way to change things. Proving that paras and humans could work and live together equally . . . that's what would ultimately make the difference.

I forced a smile to my lips. "It's a pleasure to meet all of you. My name is Alex Blackwood, and I'm the Deputy Director in charge of Paranatural Relations. If you have any questions about the paranaturals we work with, please let me know and I'll do my best to answer." I turned to my left. "This is David Nolan, our head of security."

"And I'm Mrs. Cynthia Daniels, here to represent Governor Anderson. The governor wanted me to convey his deepest apologies that he could not be here to greet you personally. He hopes you'll accept an invitation to dine with him this evening once your respective duties are finished."

"We'd be delighted," said Silva.

The other delegates nodded politely.

As a member of the Catholic Church—the group responsible for training and controlling practitioners under the old rules, and therefore the group who'd suffered the most from the recent sorcerer rebellion—I was fairly certain Bishop Silva would stand close to if not entirely in the Purity camp when it came to the treatment of paranaturals. Most Hindus leaned more toward the One Earth philosophy—that the world belonged equally to all—but that was no guarantee Pandit Khatun would be an ally. And Ali was a complete mystery. Many Muslims fell on both sides of the argument.

Of course, the final say would rest with the Church council, which was made up of more than thirty religious leaders from different faiths and denominations . . . but these three would be representing us to them, and their recommendations would hold weight. It was my job to make the best impression possible—to convince them that a partnership could not only work but was to the benefit of all the peoples of our world.

I let out a shaky breath. *No pressure.*

"If you'll step this way." Weatherly turned to indicate the front entrance. "We can tour the facility. Then we'll retire to a conference room for lunch and to chat in more detail about our operations."

The three delegates preceded him through the door. He cast me a strange look behind their backs before following.

I frowned and leaned closer to David. "What's he planning?"

But David didn't hear me. He was moving away to help one of the security guards physically restrain a hysterical woman screaming about her husband's tragic demise and how magic was to blame.

Glaring at Weatherly's back, I followed the group inside.

We checked in at the reception desk so each of the visitors could receive an access badge, then Weatherly led the way down a hallway lined with offices. "These are for analysts, clerks, and the workers who handle the day-to-day of keeping this place running." He waved a hand to indicate the offices branching off the beige hall. "They're all human."

I clenched my jaw. Weatherly and I had argued more than once about paranaturals joining in a non-field agent capacity. He felt a paranatural's talents would be wasted behind a desk. Since I couldn't convince him otherwise, I'd tried to circumvent him. He'd buried my proposal in paperwork and red tape. I sighed at the memory. Weatherly had years of practice navigating the bureaucratic procedures of the PTF, while I was still learning the rules.

At the end of the hall, Weatherly pressed the button to call the elevator, then faced the group with a smile. "I've taken the liberty of gathering our werewolf agents in the gym for your inspection."

My heart stuttered. My mouth went dry. "You what?"

Weatherly beamed at me, projecting a mask of innocent helpfulness. "I thought it would be nice for our guests to see how your new recruits are shaping up."

I stepped closer and hissed, "You know the werewolves get antsy when they're all together."

His expression morphed to mock surprise. "Surely they wouldn't lose their tempers from something so simple as a little meet and greet?"

"If you think there might be some danger," Daniels said loudly near my shoulder, "perhaps we shouldn't risk the delegates' safety."

Everyone waited for my response.

I glared at Daniels and Weatherly. Of course I couldn't back down now—

that would confirm that the werewolves were too dangerous to be allowed near humans, which would undermine this entire alliance. I just hoped the wolves could hold themselves together long enough for the Church's inspection.

I gritted my teeth in a feral smile. "There shouldn't be any problem. This just wouldn't have been my first choice for introductions. Most of our werewolf recruits are still adjusting to their new environment, and meeting so many new people all at once might make them a bit . . . nervous." I turned on Weatherly. "Which I would have been happy to explain to my co-director if he'd consulted me on this matter. I *am* the one responsible for overseeing them, after all."

Ms. Ali pushed her glasses a little higher on her nose and turned to Weatherly. "Is it common for you to take on the duties of your co-director?"

"Ms. Blackwood is new to the PTF, and to positions of authority in general," Weatherly replied. "Whereas I've been running this facility for several years now. I try to help her where I can, and if I overstep my current role, it's entirely out of habit."

I pictured punching Weatherly right in his smug face as I said, "Although consulting me would have been the reasonable thing to do, since easing interactions between humans and paranaturals is what I'm here for."

Khatun turned to me. His smile was kindly, but his gaze was sharp. "Yes, how are you settling into your new role here?"

I looked from one unfamiliar face to the next, wishing I had Marc's natural aura of authority or James's easy charm to fall back on. Lacking those, I lifted my chin and lied. "I'm fitting in just fine."

David trotted up the hall as a *ding* announcing the elevator's arrival, and the delegates turned to file on board.

I shot him an accusatory look that stopped him short.

He raised his hands in mock surrender. "What'd I do?"

I stepped close and whispered, "Did you know Weatherly called all the werewolves to the gym?"

He shook his head and scowled. "First I'm hearing about it. How long have they been in there?"

"I don't know."

He looked at the group loading into the elevator and pitched his voice even lower. "Should we abort?"

"And let Weatherly win?" I stepped into the steel cage.

David wedged in beside me.

Weatherly pressed the button for the basement. He hummed softly as we started to move. It was all I could do to keep from wrapping my hands around his throat and squeezing until he turned blue.

Chapter 3

THE DOORS LEADING to the gym were closed. The room beyond was suspiciously quiet. I chewed my lower lip and prayed the silence was because the werewolves understood the gravity of the situation and were standing at attention like well-trained soldiers.

David took the lead. I followed close on his heels, figuring I might need to divert the delegates depending on what I found when I walked through the door. We had a total of ten werewolves in the PTF, and so far I'd managed to avoid having them all in the same place at the same time. Despite my arguments to the PTF board of directors that werewolves were more human than beast, and therefore able to control themselves, there was no denying that violent tempers and short fuses seemed to go hand in hand with their dual natures, especially when dealing with stress, strangers, and small spaces.

All ten werewolves were present. I was sure Weatherly hadn't given them any choice. They were scattered around the room in little clumps. Sarah and a wiry fellow named Xander, who'd also come from Marc's pack, claimed one corner. Opposite them, on the far side of the boxing ring, sat three wolves sent to us from the Appalachian pack—an Asian-New Yorker named Jasmine who was missing her right arm; Noah, the wolf-footed problem child from yesterday; and "Old Bill," whose mannerisms placed his change sometime during the Civil War. Faolan, who'd transferred from Florida, sat alone, as did Tarlo, a Chippewa-Cree from Montana, and Liam, the stocky Texan who'd fought with Noah. Marshall and Maddie were from California—a brother and sister with suntanned skin and bleach-blond hair, who'd been changed together during one tragic camping trip.

Along with the usual gym smells of sweat and cleaner was the undeniable stink of stress, and if I could smell it, the odor must have been suffocating to the more sensitive noses of the werewolves. Some of the wolves crouched, most stood. None were sitting. Tension hummed through the room like a guitar string ready to snap. Every eye focused on me when I walked through the door. They would have heard us coming as soon as we stepped out of the elevator.

I cleared my throat. "Sorry to keep you all waiting. We've got visitors from the Church who'd like to meet you, then you can all get back to—"

"Line up." Weatherly's shout made me jump.

I glared over my shoulder, noting that in this instance he'd chosen to remain behind me. *Coward.* "I'll thank you to leave the instructions to me."

The werewolves looked around the room at their companions, at the delegates, then back to me, clearly unsure what was expected of them.

"If you'll all gather here in the middle of the room." I indicated the space in front of the boxing ring. "This should only take a moment."

As the group drew together, the tension ratcheted up. The large man from Montana with bronze skin and long, black hair was already nearest the middle of the room. He stood front and center and glared at anyone who came close. The two men who'd come to blows the day before eyed each other as they closed in.

I shook my head. If we didn't find some way to unify these wolves as a group, they'd never be able to work together.

Sarah stepped up beside Tarlo. A low growl issued from his throat. The woman who'd come to us from New York shoved the California brother. He reacted by sweeping out Jasmine's feet and knocking her on her ass.

"That's enough," I shouted and stepped forward.

Only about half the werewolves bothered to look at me. The rest were focused on the conflict, muscles tensed for action.

"It seems you have some discipline issues," said Ali.

I turned to face the delegates, hating the way the hairs on my neck rose with the werewolves at my back. "No more so than among any new recruits learning the ropes. As I mentioned before, many of these people haven't received any training or even met each other yet, so dumping them all together was—"

"They all signed up to be PTF agents," said Weatherly, "and agents follow orders. What if we need to send one of these creatures to back up a unit they haven't worked with before? It seems a werewolf would be just as likely to attack their fellow agents as the enemy."

I bunched my fists. "By the time they're ready to deploy they'll have had extensive training and know what to expect, just like any human agent." I gestured behind me. "Most of these guys have been here less than a week. Are you telling me human troops never get in fights at boot camp?"

"Human fights don't carry the danger of a werewolf outbreak." Weatherly pointed to Jasmine, who was crouched in front of Marshall with her teeth bared. Teeth that didn't quite fit inside her still-human mouth.

"Indeed," said Khatun. "I feel it may be prudent to withdraw now."

"I've seen enough," chimed Silva.

I opened my mouth to argue, but Mrs. Daniels—who hadn't actually stepped into the room—called from the open doorway, "If you'd like to move on, we can view the testing chambers. Much safer."

The delegates wasted no time in exiting the gym. Weatherly shot me a grim smile as he backed out of the room. He didn't turn his back until he was safely in the hall.

I spun on the werewolves and growled in my best impression of Marc, "Get back to your rooms and cool down." I raised one finger. "If I hear about even one fight, anyone involved will find themselves in a holding cell for the rest of the week."

Sarah pushed Xander toward the back exit, and the three from the Appalachian pack followed suit. The others shuffled out in a more cautious way, trying to keep from exposing their backs.

I ground my teeth and let out a long shaky breath.

David leaned into me, bumping my shoulder with his. "Cheer up. That could have been much worse."

I nodded, but couldn't speak past the anxious knot squeezing my chest. A few more minutes and those wolves might've gotten completely out of control. Had Weatherly been hoping to get one of the delegates killed? That would certainly shut down any possibility of endorsement by the Church, but surely even he wouldn't go so far as to risk someone's life? Then again . . . it wouldn't be the first time a Purist had killed to make their point.

"Come on," I grumbled. "We need to keep Weatherly and Daniels in check, or they'll convince the delegates this experiment is some evil plot to overthrow the world."

"If it is, you're not doing a very good job."

I chuckled. "No kidding."

We caught up to the rest of the group in the first of a series of chambers designed to test the limits of paranatural abilities. I shivered and hugged myself as I stepped inside. The last time I'd been in a room like this, I'd had to watch as Kai was nearly torn in half. Marc, Garrett, and I had argued to abolish the tests, but Weatherly had pointed out that the tests were mostly for fae and undocumented paranaturals. Paranaturals like James. Maybe he was right to resist submitting for testing. Goodness knows I wouldn't want to be at Weatherly's mercy. But if the alternative was life as a fugitive. . . .

"Earth to Alex." David passed his palm in front of my face.

"Hmm? What?"

"I asked if you'd managed to get your werewolves calmed down?" Daniels said.

My werewolves. Not PTF agents. Not beings anyone here wanted to take responsibility for.

"They're returning to their rooms and regular routines. If you'd like, I can arrange one-on-one interviews with a few of them." I shot a scathing glare at Weatherly. "Which is how these introductions should have been handled in the first place. It's clear the humans in this organization need quite a bit more education on how to deal with paranaturals as more than prisoners."

Bishop Silva tapped a finger against his plump cheek. "Do you expect paranaturals to receive special treatment?"

I took a breath, considering my words. "Not *special*, but reasonable. Most paranatural groups have their own cultures and traditions. We should respect those and learn to work with them as much as possible."

Khatun scrunched his nose. "I can't say I'm eager to come face to face with any of them again."

"Where exactly are the werewolves being kept?" Ali asked.

Speaking of humans in need of educating. . . . These three probably imagine we keep the werewolves in cages until it's time to unleash them on an enemy. That's how the Church handled practitioners, after all. I cleared my throat so my irritation wouldn't show in my voice. *Be diplomatic.* "Right now all the werewolves and the three practitioners we have on staff are staying in a nearby apartment building owned by the PTF."

"Guarded?" Silva asked.

"It has twenty-four-hour security," David said. "Plus two trained paladins provided by the Church who live in residence to suppress any unauthorized magic."

Silva nodded. "I'm glad to hear the remaining paladins are being put to use. I was concerned this new branch might give its sorcerers free rein."

I sometimes wondered if people like Silva understood that sorcerers and paladins were, at their core, the same—powerful practitioners trained in a specific discipline. The Church seemed to believe that since paladins were never taught to project and manifest their magic, as sorcerers were, they were less dangerous. I thought it more likely that paladins just played meek as a matter of self-preservation.

"We understand the dangers of magic," I said. "Not only to the public but to the practitioners themselves. We've taken precautions to ensure that *everyone* remains safe."

Mrs. Daniels sniffed and lifted her chin. "It seems to me that the safest way to avoid contamination of a practitioner's soul is simply to prevent them using magic."

"Easier said than done," said Silva.

"As a practitioner myself"—saying those words out loud still made my heart pound—"I find knowing how to safely channel magic works better than avoiding it until there's an emergency. Then you end up using it blindly."

Khatun nodded. "Knowledge is often the key to control."

"And practice is necessary if we wish these forces to be effective in the future." Ali raised an eyebrow at Silva. "I believe our training programs also required sorcerers to practice their arts, under the supervision of paladins of course."

I resisted the urge to make a tally mark in the air . . . barely.

There was a knock at the door. We all turned. The petite blond woman peeking around the door frame shrank back.

"Sorry to interrupt," she said.

Weatherly frowned. "What is it, Judith? We're in the middle of our tour."

"Yes, sir. But I've just received word from Director Harris. She'll be arriving on the roof any moment now, and she's requested that Ms. Blackwood join her."

A look of consternation crossed Weatherly's face—apparently I wasn't the only one caught off guard by this visit from our boss. "Only Ms. Blackwood?"

Judith nodded.

Weatherly shot me an accusatory look, as though I'd somehow orchestrated his exclusion from the summons to embarrass him in front of the delegates. Or maybe he thought I'd asked Harris to come as backup, since she definitely fell on the pro-paranatural alliance side of the fence.

The truth was I had no idea why Harris had come. I wasn't any more thrilled to leave the Church delegates to Weatherly and Daniels than he was to be left out of this mysterious meeting, but the look of doubt and worry on Weatherly's face gave me a warm, fuzzy feeling.

He turned to me and snapped, "Best not keep her waiting."

"Should we postpone the rest of our tour?" Ali asked.

I opened my mouth, but Daniels was faster—damned politician. "We needn't change our plans for Ms. Blackwood. She can join us again if and when she becomes available. In the meantime, perhaps Director Weatherly can show us how this test works." She indicated a panel set beside a steel table lined with restraints.

I glared at the back of Mrs. Daniels's head, taking silent note of the fact that she'd used Weatherly's title but called me *Ms.* Blackwood.

Judith bobbed with impatience, clearly unwilling to step into a room that any sane person would have registered as *torture chamber*.

I nudged David in the ribs, holding him back while the rest of the group gathered around the testing controls to listen to Weatherly's explanation. "You're going to have to be the voice of reason here. Don't let Weatherly and Daniels steer the conversation."

"I'd need a bulldozer to stop them."

I patted him on the back. "Do your best."

Pressing both hands against the tightening knot in my abdomen, I turned my back on the group of strangers who would very soon decide if the Church would become an ally or an enemy to my cause, and followed Judith back to the elevator.

REGIONAL DIRECTOR Everly Harris was in charge of all aspects of the PTF in the western half of the United States. She had an office in Washington DC, as well as every major PTF hub in her jurisdiction, including Denver. Since helping me gain approval for this experiment, I'd seen her exactly once. She'd wished me luck and left me with Weatherly like a parent throwing their kid in the deep end and assuming they'd learn how to swim. Not exactly the partnership I'd been hoping for, but if I wanted people to take me seriously I couldn't expect her to hold my hand.

Judith and I took the elevator all the way to the top, stepping out into open air. Sunlight glinted off the metal sides of Harris's chariot, and a strong downdraft knocked me back a step as the helicopter touched down in the white circle painted on the PTF's wide, flat roof. My hair lashed around my face, straining against the scrunchy that struggled to hold it. I shivered and hugged myself, wishing I had my coat.

Harris dropped from the open side of the helicopter. Her dark braids succeeded where my ponytail had not, so she looked as prim and proper as usual when she joined me at the elevator. She was wearing a navy-blue suit and a white blouse that stood out against her russet-brown skin. The gale eased as the helicopter's blades slowed and the whine of the engine cut off.

"Thanks for joining me, Alex. Let's talk in my office."

"You know the delegation from the Church is here today? You pulled me away from their tour."

She pressed the button for the elevator and stepped inside. "What I need to talk to you about can't wait."

We rode down one floor, then stepped out. Harris turned on Judith before she could exit with us. "Thank you, Judith. That will be all."

Judith tucked her chin at the dismissal and retreated to the back of the elevator. Harris was already walking away.

I trotted to catch up. "What's the emergency? And—not that I mind—why wasn't Weatherly invited?"

Harris pushed into her office, flicked on the lights, and circled the desk. Opening her briefcase, she pulled out a laptop and plugged it in. "I trust you've seen the news?"

"Um. . . ." I closed the door behind me. "Which news, specifically?"

She glanced up and gave me a look that screamed, *Are you kidding me?* "The trash."

"Oh, yeah, I did see something last night about a bunch of trash that washed ashore in California."

"It wasn't just 'washed ashore,' it was dumped there, and it's not just California. I've spent the morning in conversations with various fae representatives, and, while I never received an official statement, I learned that a sect of water fae living in the Pacific Ocean has seen fit to"—she cleared her throat—"'return the property humans have misplaced in their waters.'"

The knot in my stomach turned to ice. "You think it's an attack?"

I'd managed to convince my grandfather, lord and ruler of one of the largest and most influential fae realms, to stand down from war for one year in order to give peace a chance. The fae inability to lie made me fairly confident our agreement would hold. That bargain didn't prevent any of the other realms from attacking, but none of them had the firepower to overthrow the mortal realm on their own. Being long-lived, most fae were patient and cautious, so why start a fight while their heaviest hitter was side-lined?

"I'm not sure what it is," she admitted. "But the undersea fae's new recycling program isn't the only problem." She turned her laptop to face me and hit the space bar to play a queued video.

For a second I didn't know what I was looking at. The screen seemed to be filled with grainy beige static. Then a piece of metal flashed by, and I realized what I thought was static was actually dust and dirt. I squinted, trying to make out other details. "A sandstorm?"

"This footage was taken just outside Black Rock Desert in Nevada. It hasn't made the news yet, but I'm sure someone will pick up the story before the end of the day."

I gestured at the screen. "What story? It's a bunch of dust and—" My words evaporated as my mouth went as dry as the desert I was seeing. Shadows swooped through the storm. A dense wave of debris hit the camera, then the air cleared slightly as the dust particles slowed their dance and began to settle. A towering silhouette loomed in the image—talons, feathers, a curved beak that tapered to a dagger point.

I licked my lips and finally found my voice. "A griffin."

"At least three," Harris confirmed. "That's the closest anyone's been able to get since the storm began this morning."

"It's a desert. How did you even know they were out there?"

"A rancher near Quinn River Crossing lost his entire herd of cattle. Since then, two more ranches have been swallowed by the edge of the storm. We've evacuated the area, but the desert has already expanded by nearly twenty miles." She closed the laptop. "We don't know if the sandstorm and the trash tsunami are related, but their timing can't be a coincidence. And it's not just us. I don't have detailed information from the other regions yet, but there are reports of over a dozen disappearances near the Black Forest in Germany since yesterday, volcanic instability in Iceland, and of course the garbage dump is affecting Canada, South America, Mexico, Japan, Russia, and several islands in the South Pacific."

"So we're looking at chaos on a global scale."

She crossed her arms and nodded.

Cold dread swept through my muscles. My limbs felt numb and heavy. "Why tell me?"

"I'm being stonewalled by my fae liaisons, but from what I gathered before they stopped returning my calls, they're as concerned as we are. The official treaty was broken on both sides. At this point, the only reason we're not at war is that neither group is certain they can win. If that's changed, we need to know. *Now.* As of this moment, you're my best source of information regarding the fae."

The numbness continued to spread as the weight of responsibility settled over me. I rubbed one hand over my jaw and neck, blew out a noisy exhale, then said, "It can't be Enchantment. Bael gave his word to hold back for a year, and natural disasters aren't his style. The shadow walkers and shifters are content with the status quo in the mortal realm, and again . . . not their style. I'd say you're looking at some kind of nature fae. Maybe even elementals." I shuddered, recalling my encounters with the elementals who guarded the fae reservations. "But elementals don't usually engage in politics. They each have a specific place they protect. They don't wander, and as long as the natural balance is maintained in their area, they're content just to watch."

"What about the elementals who guard the reservations? They attack any human on their land."

"Because that's the established natural order. Humans don't belong in those places."

"So what if someone convinced an elemental that humans didn't belong elsewhere . . . or anywhere?"

I pursed my lips, dredging up the history lessons my fae tutor had drilled into me over long uncomfortable hours of study. "Elementals don't think quite the same way as other fae, but they're not stupid. I can't imagine someone could trick them into fighting all the humans in the world. Otherwise the fae would have wiped the floor with humanity during the last war." I shook my head. "Elementals are all about balance, and, like it or not, humans are a part of the ecosystem of the mortal realm."

"Could an elemental be coerced in some way? Ordered to attack by a stronger fae?"

"The dragons used to lead the Elemental Court, but since the near genocide of their species. . . ." I shied away from that train of thought and the fact that it had been my own fae grandfather, Lord Bael, who had orchestrated the massacre of the dragon home world. "Even before that, I don't think there was an Elemental Lord in the same way there's a lord over each of the other courts, and I'm not sure any other species of fae would be strong enough to control an elemental against their will."

The image of a beautiful, terrifying woman with cerulean skin and indigo hair flashed in my mind. Being a siren, Shedraziel had the unique talent of controlling the minds of weaker beings. A talent she'd used to inflict pain and suffering on countless innocents. But as the general of Bael's army, she was bound by the same deal that prevented him or any member of the Court of Enchantment from threatening Earth until my year was up.

Harris uncrossed her arms and began to pace back and forth behind her desk. "This is the type of situation the Church's sorcerers would normally have been sent to handle."

"I can have six paranatural teams ready to go by the end of the day. Double that tomorrow."

Harris shook her head. "So far none of the disturbances have affected Colorado."

"If war breaks out, it's sure as shit going to affect us."

"And *if* that happens, your troops will be called into service. Until then, any paranatural agents registered with the PTF are to stay within state boundaries."

"Why bother coming to me if you're going to tie my hands?"

"I need someone to investigate . . . just not a PTF agent. I need you, off the books, as a private citizen."

I took a step back and stared at her, struggling to make sense of her words. "You're firing me?"

"Think of it as a leave of absence. Your job will be waiting when you get back . . . assuming you're successful and the PTF is still standing."

"I'm *barely* keeping Weatherly and Daniels from tearing this experiment apart. Now you want me to walk away and leave the fate of the paranatural community in their bigoted hands?"

"Isn't that why you insisted on having dedicated department heads for each paranatural group? Plus your soldier friend who was put in charge of security. Surely they can pick up the slack for a time?"

I thought about yesterday's scuffle and that morning's fiasco in front of the delegates. If the fae were attacking, the paranatural recruits would need to be ready to fight. The experiment I was supposed to have a year to work the kinks out of had just become sink or swim, and Harris was asking me to walk away from it. "We need to establish an internal werewolf pack within the PTF, which will also mean breaking in a new werewolf liaison."

"What? Why? You're the one who said Marc would be the best person for the job."

"Do you really want me to go into the details of werewolf hierarchies right now?"

Harris pinched the bridge of her nose. "How long will it take to get this new pack sorted out?"

"I'm not sure, but I should be here to oversee it."

"Then it'll have to wait until you get back. The fae threat takes priority."

"What about the Church delegation? Weatherly has been questioning my mixed allegiance from day one. How's it going to look if I abandon my post and run to the fae at the first sign of conflict?"

"I don't care how it looks. I care how it turns out. What happened to the woman willing to go to any lengths—to ally herself with monsters and kidnap a PTF director—to save the world from war?"

"I did my world-saving. I just got home . . . to my friends, and my studio, and all the things I fought for. I'm trying to rebuild my life." I hugged myself, desperate to hold on to what little security I'd been able to claw from the chaos of the past few months. "There's got to be someone else."

Harris shook her head, the multi-colored beads at the ends of her many braids clacking together. "There isn't, and you know it. I need you to make contact with the griffins, the undine, and any other fae who might be responsible. Whether it's multiple groups stirring up trouble, an organized rebellion, or some mastermind pulling the strings . . . you're our best shot at getting to the bottom of this."

"I don't even have any connection to the Undine Court."

"But you have contacts among the fae, which is more than I can say right now."

Her words reminded me of Chase's return and our conversation about Ava's uncle and the other imprisoned fae. "Maybe if you hadn't refused to release the legally registered fae in your holding facilities—"

"We've been over this. It's not my call."

"Releasing the fae who were willing to play by your rules might go a long way toward easing hostilities. All those prisoners have relatives who want to see them, and if you wait too long, they may decide violence is the only option."

"You think this may be some elaborate prison break?"

"I didn't say that. I just . . . a lot of fae who might otherwise opt for peace have reason to feel frustrated right now. If someone is stirring up trouble, do you really want to make it easy for them?"

"We don't negotiate with terrorists."

"And you wouldn't be. Whoever is responsible for these disturbances hasn't made any demands." I caught her gaze. "This may be your only chance to make the choice before they force your hand."

She braced her fists on her hips and looked at the ceiling.

"If that's not incentive enough, consider this: What you're asking me to do isn't part of my job with the PTF. You can't order me."

Her gaze snapped to me like a magnet.

I took a deep breath and pressed on. "I'll investigate these disturbances for you if, and only if, you agree to release the fae being held at your Genoa facility."

"You'd bargain with the fate of the world?"

"Wouldn't be the first time. And as you said, there's no one else. So that's the deal. Take it or leave it."

She gave a rueful chuckle and shook her head. Then she held up a single finger. "*Only* the fae who were legally registered before their capture."

"I can live with that." I stuck out my hand.

She gripped my fingers and gave one stiff downward tug. "Remember, once you cross the state border, you won't be a PTF official anymore, just a registered halfer traveling for leisure."

I rolled my eyes. "Leisure . . . right."

"If you get in trouble out there, with either the human authorities or the fae, I won't be able to help you."

"So keep my nose clean. Got it."

"And report back quickly. There's no telling how fast this situation could spiral out of control."

Chapter 4

I PAUSED TO TAKE a deep breath just outside Harris's office. The sounds of distant conversations and the hum of electronics filtered through the hall, washing over me as white noise. I closed my eyes. Another mission—danger, uncertainty, the weight of responsibility. . . . Would I ever be done fighting? I shook my head, thinking of the people who'd lost their lives, or been changed like Emma, the last time I led an "off-the-books" mission. Sure, we'd delayed a war and paved the way for negotiating paranatural equality, but that didn't ease the writhing guilt in my chest or the parade of faces in my nightmares. Yet, even looking back, I couldn't see a better way. Nor could I see a clear path forward.

Stay and try to solidify the position of paranaturals among the PTF while relations between humans and fae crumble to chaos, or abandon my project at this fragile stage and risk losing the progress we've made in a desperate attempt to slap a patch on the larger problem?

I exhaled and opened my eyes. The beige paint of the hallway wall greeted me with cheerless apathy. Either choice would put people I cared about in danger. And either choice held the potential to change the future of the mortal realm . . . of all the realms. But investigating the disturbances had the added benefit of freeing a lot of unjustly imprisoned fae, including Targe. I'd have to trust that my friends could hold down the fort . . . and accept that I might never be able to return to the simple comforts of a quiet life.

Turning left, I walked briskly to the nearest stairwell and went down two floors. With no idea how long I'd be gone, I had to at least get the ball rolling on the new werewolf pack before I left. I pushed through the door to my office and pulled up short. Sarah was standing near my window, looking down at the protesters.

"I want to talk to you about that shit show in the gym this morning," she said without turning.

"Yeah." I ran a hand over my disheveled ponytail. "Getting you all to work together is going to be—"

"I'm not talking about the werewolves."

I frowned.

She finally turned, meeting my gaze. "You let Weatherly play you like a fiddle today. *You* are the paranatural spokesperson." She stepped forward and jabbed a finger against my chest hard enough to make me wince. "The title the PTF handed you isn't worth jack if you don't hold enough respect to back it up. I get that you had to be diplomatic with those Church assholes, but werewolves respond to action. So either step up and take command or move aside for someone who will."

"I totally agree."

Sarah opened her mouth as though preparing to argue, blinked, then closed it.

"Action number one is that we're going to establish an internal PTF pack," I said.

"When?"

"As soon as possible. I'll call Marc today to sort out the details."

She nodded. "That's good. It will also give you the opportunity to earn the respect of the wolves under your command."

I stiffened, sensing she meant more than just proving that I could take action. "What do you mean?"

She chuckled. "Don't worry. Fights aren't to the death." She patted me on the shoulder and walked past me before I could frame a response. By the time I turned, the door was closing behind her.

She was joking. Had to be. There's no way the werewolves would expect me to fight for my rank. Right? I made a mental note to run the comment by Marc.

I shook my head and circled around the small black desk I'd been given. The surface was covered with stacks of papers and manila files that teetered like foot-tall Jenga towers. My email inbox made the paper mountain on the desk look small. I was pretty sure Weatherly was trying to drown me in paperwork until I snapped and did a swan dive out the window.

Flopping into my chair, I pulled out my cell phone and called Marc, who only came into the office twice a week for our department meetings.

"Is the tour over already?" Marc asked in lieu of hello. "How did it go?"

"Hard to say. I got called out shortly after the tour started, but the part I saw wasn't great."

"What happened?"

"Let's just say I've found reason enough to agree that the PTF werewolves need a more stable hierarchy."

"Was anyone hurt?"

"Just my pride. Sarah tells me I'm losing respect among the wolves."

"That's something we'll need to address then. When do you want to create the new pack?"

"The sooner the better, but I've been called away on business."

"Does this have to do with the fae disruptions reported on the news?"

"Nailed it in one. And if my investigation doesn't go well, we may need the werewolves in fighting form sooner rather than later."

"Establishing the hierarchy will also make it easier to decide who to take with you."

"Actually, I won't be taking any of the werewolves, or any PTF agents at all for that matter."

"I thought you said this was business?"

"It is . . . but not official. The request came directly from Harris. She flew in this morning to talk to me. That's why I was pulled out of the tour. These incidents spread way beyond our current jurisdiction, so no one registered with the PTF can participate in the investigation without endangering everything we've built."

"But you're—"

"Taking a leave of absence, though not entirely by choice. I hope I can rely on you to help David, Garrett, and the new werewolf representative keep a handle on things while I'm away."

There was a beat of silence, then, "They'll have any support I can offer. As do you."

"Thanks. Let's start by arranging this new pack. How exactly does that work?"

"In simplest terms it's an all-out battle for dominance. I'll need to contact the alphas of the packs your agents transferred from before we begin, but we should be ready in a day or two."

"Then I'll leave it in your capable hands."

"You'll need to be there as well."

"David can handle logistics on our side to get all the werewolves where they need to be. I don't want to push this off till I get back, since I have no idea how long my investigation will take."

"As the paranatural director, you need to be seen as at least equal to the new alpha if not above."

My skin grew cool as the blood abandoned my face. *Sarah wasn't joking.*

I sat forward, leaning into the phone. "I'm not jumping into a ring with a bunch of angry werewolves with something to prove. I'd be killed!"

"You don't have to fight per se, but you will need to make a display of strength. If the werewolves view you as weak, any alpha who bows to your orders will also be seen as weak. It would undermine what we're trying to do."

"So you want me to what? Shoot lightning from my fingers?"

"Maybe, though I'd suggest putting a little more thought into it."

I leaned back with a groan. "Fine. I should have a better idea where and when I'll be going after I talk to Kai and Chase."

"The cat's back?" The hint of a growl tinged Marc's words. He and Chase didn't care much for one another—a holdover from the widely held belief among werewolves that a shifter fae had cursed them into being.

"Last night. I'll call you when I know more. Make whatever preparations you can in the meantime." I hung up with Marc and dialed David.

He answered on the second ring.

"Please tell me the rest of the tour is going better than the beginning."

"No one's died yet. If you hurry, you can meet us outside the paranatural apartments."

I sighed and leaned back in my chair. "No point. As of twenty minutes ago, I've been temporarily relieved of duty."

"What? Why?"

"Harris asked me to run an off-the-books errand."

"The fae?"

"Always. Sorry, but it looks like I won't be making movie night tonight."

"Give me an hour to tie up loose ends, and I'll put in a leave of absence."

"No. I need you here. You, Garrett, and Marc are going to have to hold down the fort while I'm gone. If Weatherly and Daniels get free rein, there might not be a paranatural branch of the PTF for me to come back to."

"Then who will you take for backup?"

"Kai and Chase, if they'll come."

"No offense to your friends, but if you're facing the fae, I'd rather you have someone with clearer allegiances at your back. What about James?"

I pursed my lips, recalling our recent argument. Maybe getting James out of town for a few days would give me the chance to convince him testing was his best option. Then again having a vampire by my side when addressing the fae was sure to cause problems, being mortal enemies and all. "I'll think about it."

"What should I tell the Church delegates? They've made it clear they want to speak with you before they make their report."

I pinched the bridge of my nose between my thumb and finger. "For now just tell them I've been called away on a personal matter. I'll let you know when I have more definite plans."

Tucking the phone back in my pocket, I took one last look around the office. The walls were bare. I hadn't yet gotten around to personalizing the space. I wondered now if I ever would. Given the chance, would I be able to make this space, this job, my own? I glared at the pile of unfinished paper-work on my desk—*that* I wouldn't miss, but I did feel bad leaving it for Garrett and Marc. I took a moment to tidy the stacks, trying to put them in some kind of logical order. Hopefully I'd be back in a couple of days, before any major decisions had to be made. But judging by my past experience with the fae and missions of this nature . . . I wasn't going to hold my breath.

When the desk looked slightly less like a war zone, I shrugged into my coat, grabbed my bag, and flicked off the light.

"SHE WANTS YOU to do this without *any* PTF backup?" Emma deflated into the couch cushions beside Kai.

"That's the deal." I took a sip of hot chai tea. My throat had grown raw recounting Harris's request and the background information she'd been able to provide.

Chase bounced one bare foot over the armrest of the chair he was lounging in. He'd changed into dark jeans and a baggy forest-green sweater from the collection of thrift store clothes I'd taken to keeping on hand for strays and drop-ins. His long silver hair was in its usual braid. "What's the point of having paranaturals on their payroll if they aren't willing to use them in situations like this?"

"The partnership between the PTF and paranaturals is still new. We weren't expecting to test it in the field so soon."

"And ye. . . ." He spread his hands.

"They won't go for it," I said. "If these disturbances were here in Colorado, sure, but there are issues all over the world."

"So their solution is to send *one* woman to handle it." He lifted a silvery eyebrow and shifted his gaze to Kai as though silently asking, *How have we not conquered this race yet?*

"If it comes to a fight, I'm sure they'll deploy the paranatural troops." *Eighty percent sure. . . .* "But right now these incidents are more inconveniences than outright attacks, so this is a fact-finding mission. My job is to discover who's behind them and why."

"You know who's behind the spreading desert in Nevada." Kai sat forward and rested his elbows against his knees. "You said Harris showed you a video of a griffin."

I looked at Chase and asked, "Could these be the same griffins I saw when I went to the Shifter Realm?"

Chase scrunched his nose. "I didn't see them when I came through the portal last night, so I suppose it's possible, but the shifters have no desire to go to war with this realm, and the griffins there have more desert than they could need. I don't know what would prompt them to risk this."

"Another clan then?" Kai said. "Not all the griffins chose to align with the shifters."

Chase nodded. "Most didn't. But I have no way of reaching those in the Aerie."

Emma's eyebrows scrunched together. "The Aerie?"

"The realm where most of the flying fae live," I explained, then turned back to Chase. "Could the griffins you know help?"

"Perhaps, though I don't know if they would. They may at least have more information."

"And if not, the Shifter Lord might," I said. "Anika still owes me a favor for shutting down Shedraziel's kidnapping operation."

Chase tensed. "Do not presume too much."

I frowned. "You don't work for her anymore, Chase. She released you from service when she sent you with me."

"That does not lessen my fidelity."

Kai nodded. "Leaving the service of one's lord does not remove one's sense of loyalty."

"Well, I'm not asking either of you to act against your old masters, I'm just trying to get some information." But their words cast a flicker of doubt at the back of my mind as I recalled David's earlier concern—*If you're facing the fae, I'd rather you have someone with clearer allegiances at your back.* If push came to shove, would my friends stand with me against their own people?

"Then we should set off for the Shifter Realm at once." Chase swung his leg off the armrest so both feet were flat on the floor.

"Except the griffins aren't the only problem," I said. "We need to figure out who's dumping trash on the beaches, too. And if the two are related. Considering the circumstances and the scope, I figure it has to be either the undine or the elementals."

Kai frowned. "If it's an elemental, may your gods have mercy, because there's little you can do."

"Elemental involvement seems unlikely," Chase said. "They don't take much notice of life on a small scale."

"I told Harris as much this morning," I said. "So that leaves us with a sea fae."

"Likely someone with influence in the Undine Court considering the area affected. No single fae could've done it, and no army could amass in the ocean without the Court knowing."

"So whether they're behind it or not, our best bet is to make contact with the Undine Court." I glanced between Kai and Chase. "Either of you have friends under the sea?"

Chase shook his head and shivered. "Cats and water don't mix."

"I have an acquaintance who might be able to arrange an audience," Kai said.

"Okay. Chase, you head home and see what you can learn about the griffins squatting in Nevada. Kai and I will meet with his friend and see what we can learn about the Undine Court."

"What about me?" Emma asked.

I blinked and stared at her. "Um . . . you stay here."

A muscle in her neck twitched as she clenched her jaw. She sat up straight and lifted her chin. "I'm not useless, Alex."

"Of course not, but. . . ." I looked to Kai, then Chase. Neither offered support.

"You said it yourself, this is a fact-finding mission. You're just going to talk, and blind or not, I can still listen. I can offer a different perspective. Hell, I can elbow you in the ribs when you start to say something stupid."

"I'm not questioning your usefulness, and I know you're doing well here at the house, but we're talking about traveling to another city, maybe another realm."

"I can't stay in this house forever. This is my life now. I have to find some way to move forward, and a trip to the beach sounds like a great place to start."

"A beach covered in trash."

She pressed her palms together. "Pleeeease."

I scrunched my nose. It was true that there shouldn't be any danger in just meeting with Kai's friend, and the change in environment might do Emma some good. Parking her on a sunny bench by the ocean certainly seemed preferable to leaving her alone in a dark cabin.

I looked at the boys. Kai shook his head. Chase shrugged.

I sighed. "You can come with me and Kai."

Her face lit with excitement.

"But, if there is even the slightest hint of danger, promise me you'll hide."

She nodded.

"And you have to follow my instructions even if you don't like them."

"I will." She was grinning ear to ear.

"If that's settled. . . ." Chase stood up.

"Hang on." I pulled out my phone to check on my deal with Harris. "I'm hoping to send you with a present for Ava."

BY THE TIME I returned to the PTF building, the sun was sinking toward the western horizon, a bloated red orb diffused by the overcast sky. Despite the lengthening days, night fell across the valley by six, and with the sun went the heat. I stamped my feet on the sidewalk at the edge of the parking lot— a good distance from the main entrance and its ever-present mob—and glared at the passing cars, willing one to turn in. I'd been a bundle of nervous energy since my earlier call with Harris, who now stood calmly beside me, seemingly unperturbed by the cold, the waiting, or the noise from the protesters. She'd held up her end of our bargain. The wrongly imprisoned fae were being released. It would take several more hours to clear the paperwork on most of them, but I'd convinced her to rush Targe through the system because he was integral to my mission. He was due to arrive any minute.

I shifted my grip on the pet carrier in my arms. Chase gave a low hiss through the bars.

Harris glanced over. "What's with the cat?"

I blew out a cloudy breath. "He belongs to the fae we're here to meet."

Chase let out another, longer hiss. I had to work to keep my expression neutral. He hadn't been thrilled about being carted around in a cat carrier, but it was the least conspicuous way to transport him. Considering the trouble I was already in over James, the last thing I needed was for Weatherly to discover I was chauffeuring an unregistered fae.

A silvery-gray SUV pulled into the lot, circled toward us, and came to a halt. Two armed guards climbed out. One stood near the back bumper and unholstered his gun. The other approached Harris and held out a clipboard with several sheets of paper attached.

She looked over the documents, signed her name at the bottom, and handed the clipboard back. Glancing at me, she smiled. "Faster and safer than storming the compound."

I gave a noncommittal grunt. Being on the right side of the law definitely had its advantages. Too bad the right side of the law wasn't always on the right side of life.

The guard tossed the clipboard onto the driver's seat and reached for the handle of the rear door.

I squeezed Chase's carrier tighter as Targe stepped out. He was thinner than the last time I'd seen him, his cheeks sunken, but he still stood a head taller than either of his guards and was nearly twice their width, though both looked like high school linebackers. He had to be the biggest damn leprechaun on the planet. He wore bright-orange pants a few shades lighter than his hair and a thin, orange jacket over a white shirt that was stretched so tight across his chest it was nearly see-through. Worn, brown boots without laces settled on the damp asphalt. A set of steel manacles bound his ankles, and thick chains connected them to a wider ring that circled his waist like a belt. A second set of chains was attached to the matching manacles on his wrists.

I pressed my lips tight and locked my jaw. Targe was a respected figure in the fae community. He owned and ran one of the few neutral locations where fae could gather without fear—at least he had before the PTF blew a hole in the building and arrested everyone inside. He'd followed the PTF laws governing fae residents to the letter. He'd maintained a valid visa. He'd paid his taxes. He hadn't been hurting anyone. Yet here he was in a jumpsuit and chains like a common criminal . . . just because he'd sheltered me when I had nowhere else to go.

I stepped forward, but Harris set a hand on my shoulder.

The guard with the gun stood just out of Targe's reach and kept his weapon trained on the large fae's legs, not quite threatening but close enough should he need to shoot. The man who'd carried the clipboard knelt in front of Targe and pulled a key from his belt. He released the manacles on Targe's ankles. Then he straightened and unbound his wrists. Finally, he popped the latch on the belt, and the whole jangling mess clattered to the asphalt.

Targe rubbed one wrist, then the other. He moved slowly and avoided eye contact with his guards.

"He's your responsibility now," said the clipboard guard. He made a "go on" gesture at Targe, who stepped forward. The second guard holstered his gun. The first collected the chains and manacles with a rattle of metal like out-of-tune wind chimes and tossed them in the trunk. Then both men climbed into their SUV and drove away.

Targe looked at me, shifted his gaze to Harris, then Chase in his carrier, then back to me. "What about the others?"

"Those who were legally registered before being arrested are being loaded onto buses as we speak," Harris said. "They'll be taken to the reservation in southern Colorado. From there, they can go where they please, but they'll need to reapply for residency if they want to come back onto human land." She tipped her head. "As will you."

Targe lifted his stony, green gaze skyward. The evening light tinted his coppery curls a bloody red and kissed his pale cheeks pink. The corners of his mouth curved up. He exhaled. A puff of steam streamed from his nose like smoke from a dragon. Then he inhaled and stretched his arms back as his chest swelled. When he looked down at me, there was a watery sheen in his eyes. "How did you accomplish this?"

"Let's just say Harris saw the wisdom in extending an olive branch." I tipped my head toward Harris. "Not all humans are unreasonable."

He met Harris's gaze and lowered his chin in a sort of nod-bow.

"It wasn't entirely altruistic." She turned to me. "I've held up my end."

"And I'll hold up mine. Kai is working to track down a contact who might be able to gain us access to the Undine Court. Assuming he finds her, we'll fly out as soon as we know where we're going."

"I'll have a plane prepped and standing by." She gestured to the helicopter on the roof. "You can use the helo I came in to get to the airport when you're ready to go."

I nodded. "In the meantime, Targe here is going to help us learn more about the griffins squatting in Nevada."

Targe raised an eyebrow, but didn't ask what I was talking about.

"Just remember, his visa's been revoked." She caught Targe's gaze. "If you're found on human land after midnight tonight you'll be back in that internment camp so fast it will make your head spin, and even I won't be able to get you out."

He nodded. "Fair warning."

"Don't worry," I said. "He'll be headed for the reservation as soon as I explain the situation."

"Then I'll leave you to it." She flipped her dangling braids and walked away. The protesters shouted questions as she approached and tried to block her access to the building, but she brushed them aside as easily as she had her hair.

"Come on." I headed in the opposite direction, toward the creek that ran near the southwest side of the complex. The tent and lean-to community in which many of the protesters lived was visible through the winter trees at the far end of the PTF parking lot. The Platte River flowed sluggishly, low in its banks and clogged with ice. Bramble bushes lined its shores, branches bare and dry, awaiting the spring. I set the pet carrier on a patch of hard mud and opened the grill on the front. Chase padded out and sat on a tuft of brown grass. His paws left no marks on the frozen ground.

"I need you to take Chase to the reservation," I said as I straightened. "There's been a development with some griffins in Nevada, and he's going to see what he can learn from the griffins in the Shifter Realm." I glanced at Targe's wrists. My heart ached to see the blisters and lesions peeking from under the cuffs of his jacket. The manacles he'd worn hadn't been pure iron, but a high enough concentration to cause a reaction. That was the only way of preventing a fae as strong as Targe from accessing his magic. "Are you up to it?"

Following my gaze he tugged his cuffs lower. "If that is the cost for my freedom, I will certainly manage."

I cringed. I hated the idea of bartering for his freedom, especially since I was at least partly to blame for his losing it, but both Chase and Kai had assured me that Targe would prefer to view his assistance as payment to keep the scales balanced. I'd rather he helped voluntarily than out of a sense of debt, but maybe I just wasn't fae enough to understand. In any case, citing the trip as payment was the easiest way to get what I wanted.

"I'm sorry I can't give you longer to recover, but we're kind of in a rush."

"Then we shall leave right away."

"How long will it take?"

"I can't cover that distance in one jump, but three should do it. I'll have Chase to the reservation within the hour."

I nodded. "Once you get there, Chase can take you to the Shifter Realm. Ava and Jynx are there."

Targe's expression tightened. A deep frown turned down the corners of his mouth.

"I know you probably aren't thrilled about going into an unfamiliar realm, but you've got three days of protection under the Wayfarer's Clause. Besides, now that Ava and Jynx are married, you're family."

"That's not quite the way fae families work . . . but I take your meaning.

And it will be good to check on Ava."

I clasped my hands together. "Then that's settled." I turned to Chase and knelt down on one knee so he didn't have to strain to meet my gaze. "I'm not sure how the timing will line up, but once you've learned what you can about the griffins, head straight home. We'll join you as soon as we're back from our own fact-finding mission . . . assuming Kai actually gets us an audience."

Kai hadn't had any luck contacting his fae acquaintance so far.

Chase meowed, which I took as agreement.

Targe rubbed his hands together as though trying to warm them, then spread them wide in an arcing motion. The air in front of him shimmered like heat waves over summer asphalt.

Chase gave me one last "meow," swished his tail, and trotted across the muddy ground toward the distortion. He vanished between one step and the next as though erased from existence.

Targe gave me one of his abbreviated nod-bow things and said, "Your assistance will not be forgotten, nor that of your human allies."

"Just keep that in mind when shit hits the fan, because if the situation here in the mortal realm doesn't improve soon, I'm not sure there will be any way to avoid another war."

"Perhaps both sides need to be reminded what the last war cost."

I snorted. "Too bad lives lost isn't exactly something we can show them on a bill."

He tucked his chin. "I wish you luck in preventing the escalation of this conflict, but know that if and when war does come . . . I am not your enemy."

"I wish all the fae felt that way."

He extended his hand, but instead of shaking mine when I reached out, he gripped my wrist. His hand covered my forearm, fingers overlapping. My fingers couldn't even touch around his meaty arm. "Fair winds and safe travels."

I repeated the words, feeling like the whole affair was some kind of ritual whose meaning I didn't quite grasp.

Then Targe released me and stepped through his portal without a backward glance. The nearly invisible ripple in the air vanished. I was alone on the riverbank.

I looked down at the arm Targe had gripped. The trailing end of my tattoo peeked out below my coat.

Not my enemy, huh? That wasn't quite the same thing as a friend, but any fae who wouldn't try to kill me if the species went to war was a win in my book. Still, I'd rather avoid the whole "war" thing altogether.

I took a deep breath, inhaling the scent of damp leaves, frosty mist, and car exhaust. Raised voices drew my attention back toward the PTF building.

Turning away from my moment of peace, I scaled the small slope to the parking lot. David and two other security guards were walking with Daniels and the Church delegates sheltered between them, trying to hold the protesters back as they moved toward a black limo parked at the curb. I trotted over to lend them a hand.

"Ah, there you are, Ms. Blackwood. I was worried you weren't coming back." Ms. Ali had to shout to be heard above the calls of "Freaks belong in cages" and "Keep humanity pure."

The group pushed free of the protesting mob, and the limo driver opened the back door.

"I'm afraid I won't be able to participate in the rest of your visit," I said. "I've been called away on a personal matter."

The delegates exchanged looks ranging from alarm to relief. Ms. Ali closed her hand on my upper arm. "Then I insist you join us for dinner."

I stiffened. "Aren't you meeting the governor for dinner?" I glanced at David and caught his nod.

"You're at the heart of the issues we'll be discussing with him," said Ms. Ali. "You should be present."

I gulped and struggled to convince my racing thoughts that "heart of the issue" didn't necessarily mean "the biggest problem."

Daniels said, "I'm not sure the governor—"

At the same time I said, "I really don't think—"

But Bishop Silva cut us both off. "Surely a PTF official and the governor are on civil enough terms to share a meal?"

Daniels worked her lips like a fish for a second and finally came back with, "Of course."

Pandit Khatun pinned me with his gaze and said, "We won't be able to make a full report until we've interviewed you. Surely your business is not so dire that you cannot spare us a few moments?"

I winced. Refusing to join them at this point would make it seem I was avoiding their company, and these were people I absolutely could not afford to offend. Besides, until I heard from Kai, there was little I could do but wait and worry.

I forced a smile. "I'll join you for as long as I can."

Ali gave a stiff nod, finally released my arm, and climbed into the car. Silva gestured for me to enter next.

I cast one desperate look at David, who shrugged. Then I slid onto the back seat beside Ali and settled against the leather, feeling like a convict on the way to trial. Dinner with Governor Anderson—an admitted Purist whose personal goal seemed to be to drive all paranaturals out of the state, if not the world—and a group of religious leaders whose job was to judge me and poke holes in everything I was trying to create. What could be more fun?

Chapter 5

AFTER DRIVING hardly any distance at all, the car pulled to the curb on Larimer Street in front of the column-framed entrance of the Capital Grille. Daniels and the delegates filed out, and I followed. A light, frosty mist hung in the evening air, a precursor to snow. I smoothed out the fabric of my winter coat, stomped my hiking boots on the sidewalk, and stared up at the old-fashioned lanterns that marked the vaulted entrance to the restaurant. I shifted uneasily from foot to foot as an elderly gentleman in a long tweed coat and a woman whose evening gown peeked out below the hem of her fur jacket strolled into the restaurant ahead of us.

A man in a black suit opened the restaurant's large glass doors and gestured in welcome as we approached. Mrs. Daniels informed the hostess standing behind an oak podium just inside the door that we were joining Governor Anderson. The hostess bobbed in acknowledgment and led us deeper into the building. Triangular lamps of frosted orange glass hung from the ceiling in iron frames, and iron candle holders sat in the middle of every table. This was *not* a fae-friendly establishment. No wonder Mrs. Daniels seemed so at home.

We followed our guide past a curved bar with a shiny black marble counter. Half the thickly padded stools were full, mostly with people in business attire. The air filled with the succulent aroma of tender meats, rich sauces, and the tangy bite of fresh herbs as we wound between the occupied tables of the dining area. I wiped my damp palms on the thighs of my pants as diners glanced at our passing group. Mrs. Daniels was in good company in her dress suit, high-heeled pumps *click-clacking* against the tiled floor. The delegates from the Church each wore the clothing of their respective stations like uniforms at a formal function. Despite my attempt to dress professionally, I couldn't shake the feeling that the eyes of the fancy-dressed patrons fell on me, somehow identifying me as an outsider.

It was almost a relief when I spotted Anderson at a table near the outer wall. His dark, well-tailored suit was a match for any in the restaurant, but clashed with the orange tint of his spray-tan skin. His silver hair was trimmed short around his ears and neck and swept to the side over his wide forehead.

Anderson stood when he saw Daniels. His gaze swept over the delegates. He wore the sparkling smile made famous on his election posters.

Then he spotted me. His smile faltered, but he covered the hiccup with a politician's grace and raised his palms as though offering benediction.

Mrs. Daniels moved past the hostess to position herself between our group and the governor. "Governor Anderson, may I present Ulama Odella Ali, Bishop João Silva, and Pandit Aarav Khatun of the Unified Church." She didn't mention me. Of course Anderson and I already knew each other, but still . . . I recognized the slight.

"Esteemed delegates, I'm so pleased you could join me here tonight. I do apologize for missing the PTF tour earlier. Alas, the duties of a public servant are never done." He turned to me, his smile frozen in place. "And, Ms. Blackwood. So nice to see you again. I trust you've been taking good care of our guests?"

"Actually, we've seen very little of Ms. Blackwood," said Khatun. "That's why we've invited her to join us for this meal."

A small muscle twitched below Anderson's eye. "By all means." He motioned to the hostess. "Another chair, please."

Anderson's annoyance was almost enough to make me forget about the curious glances being cast in our direction. At least I wouldn't be the only uncomfortable person at this meal.

"Then I'll leave you to it." Mrs. Daniels turned to the delegates. "The car will be at your disposal." She shifted her gaze in my direction but left without comment.

Anderson gestured to the four chairs on the sides of the table, inviting the delegates to sit with him. A moment later, the hostess returned with a fifth chair which she placed at the open end, sticking into the aisle. The servers had to swerve around me every time they passed. The hostess handed each of us a menu. I took one look at the prices and nearly choked.

Anderson took a sip from a glass of red wine he must've ordered while waiting for us, then spread a white cloth napkin on his lap and folded his fingers together on the table in front of him. "Mrs. Daniels told me there was a bit of a kerfuffle among the werewolves today." He pinned me with his stare. "And it wasn't the first."

So that's how we're going to play this.

Sarah's chastisement from that morning rang through my head. I was the PTF Paranatural Director. The people who'd been brave enough to join me in this experiment were counting on me to defend them at any cost. I couldn't afford to let my nervousness, pride, or desire to impress the delegates stifle my voice.

I smiled across the table at Anderson, doing my best politician impersonation. "Assistant Director Weatherly chose to break protocol this morning, thus creating an unnecessarily stressful situation."

"Perhaps your 'protocols' were unclear. Weatherly is used to dealing with human employees, after all."

"Which is why he had no business calling the werewolves to muster in the first place."

"No business? He *is* the facility director."

"*Co*-director."

Anderson smirked. "And is your new position everything you'd hoped for when you blackmailed the PTF board?"

I clenched my jaw.

"While I don't entirely disagree with you, Governor Anderson," said Silva, "we're less concerned with how the experiment came to pass than with what it means for the future."

"Well said." Anderson took another sip of wine, draining the glass. "The future is what I've brought you here to discuss."

The delegates lowered their menus and shifted their full focus to Anderson.

"As I'm sure you know, I was elected to the position of governor due in no small part to the stance I took against paranatural inclusion. My constituents don't want paranaturals living or working among them. I'd like your help to end this farce before the conflict escalates."

My stomach clenched. While the election had been close, the sickening truth was that enough people had voted for him that he'd been elected into office. People were afraid of paranaturals, and not without reason . . . but the whole point of this experiment was to prove that that didn't have to remain the case. I pressed my hands flat in my lap, inhaled, and cleared my throat. "I'll admit you ran a convincing campaign, playing on people's fears and ignorance, but people with magic are still people, and most want to live normal, quiet lives. It's you and the Purists who are forcing the conflict here."

"You can't deny paranaturals are dangerous," he said. "Even the non-fae varieties."

"You can't deny guns or alcohol are dangerous either."

"Allowing paranaturals into sensitive positions gives them too much leverage over us. Who's to say, once they have control over a significant portion of our defenses, that they won't stab us in the back?"

I opened my mouth to argue, but Ms. Ali beat me to it. "Can you guarantee that a human in such a position wouldn't pose the same threat?"

"I can," said Anderson with authority. "Because no matter how powerful a human being might be, they can never be as dangerous as someone with magic."

"Which is precisely why the PTF agreed to this experiment in the first place," Khatun said. "Because humans alone could not stand against the magic users seeking to overthrow them. We need magic to fight magic."

"I agree in principle, but these methods. . . ." Anderson waved a hand in my direction. "Giving the magic users *more* autonomy isn't the answer. If the rogue sorcerers taught us anything, it's that they need to be kept on a tighter leash, lest we have more tragedies like the one in Rome."

All three delegates lowered their gazes, their expressions growing dark and distant as they recalled the event. As high-level representatives from their various religions, all three probably had friends among those killed when my father and his rebel sorcerers destroyed the previous seat of the Unified Church of Humanity. Anderson was twisting their emotions to his advantage, but his logic was wrong.

"What happened in Rome was a tragedy," I said. "One that proved, along with countless other examples throughout history, that oppression doesn't work as a stable societal model. You might be able to force subservience for a while, but people will always rise up and fight for their freedom. It's human nature."

"But we're not talking about humans," Anderson said. "And that's the problem. You're trying to grant human rights to beings who aren't. This rampant inclusivity you preach sets a dangerous precedent. Today it's practitioner and werewolf agents, tomorrow you'll be telling me fae should be allowed to serve."

"And why not?" I bunched my fists in my lap. "There are plenty of fae who call this realm their home, who'd fight to protect it even against their own kind if it came to that."

Ali raised a placating hand between Anderson and me like a referee calling a timeout. "I believe we're straying off topic."

"Indeed," said Khatun. "We're not here to talk about the fae, and the issue of whether humans with magic should still be considered human is not a debate we're likely to settle today."

Silva leaned back in his chair. "I agree with Mr. Anderson that we must be mindful of the precedent set by allowing magic users full agent status in the PTF—our main defensive organization against magical threats. Should they turn against us, they'll be in a position to undermine our entire defensive strategy."

"They *are* our defensive strategy," I countered.

A waiter in a black button-up shirt, black tie, black slacks, and shiny black shoes stepped up to take our orders, effectively forestalling the conversation. He smiled nervously, clearly aware he'd interrupted.

Anderson ordered appetizers for the table, crab cakes and shrimp cocktail, followed by lobster bisque, a balsamic ribeye, and a side of parmesan truffle fries. The man had quite an appetite.

The waiter continued around the table, jotting orders on his tiny notepad until he came to me.

"Just water." I handed over my menu.

Anderson gave me another one of those smirk-smiles. "Poor appetite is a sign of a weak constitution."

"And gluttony is a sign of corruption. If I'm not hungry, why eat?"

The corner of Ali's mouth twitched up.

The waiter collected our menus and scurried off.

Khatun cleared his throat. "Whether as tools or allies, I think we can all agree that so long as magic exists in our world, having magic users on our side is necessary to maintain order. Therefore we must find some stable way to implement their use. The question is whether or not Ms. Blackwood's alliance is a viable solution."

"And the answer is clear." Anderson waved a dismissive hand in my direction, keeping his focus on the delegates. "Even as a paranatural herself, she wasn't able to keep the werewolves under control long enough for you to meet them safely. What hope would regular humans have of keeping them in line?"

"That's why we're creating a new pack specific to werewolves serving in the PTF." I cast my gaze around the table. "The problem isn't with the werewolves themselves, it's with the lack of a clear hierarchy between them. Just give us time to get the pack established, and I promise the werewolves will be one hundred percent more settled the next time you see them."

Silva leaned forward. "If the solution is as simple as establishing a hierarchy, why isn't one already in place?" He pursed his lips. "For that matter, as their supervisor, shouldn't you have been able to snap them to attention the moment they started acting up this morning?"

Heat flooded my cheeks. The short answer was yes, I *should* have been able to control the situation if I'd commanded enough respect among either the werewolves or the humans present. No wonder Marc had insisted I present some kind of display of power to back my title, because that's all the authority I had at the moment . . . a title. No, not even that. Harris had temporarily relieved me of duty to send me on her secret mission. I had no authority at all.

"There's nothing 'simple' about the way werewolf packs function." My voice cracked a bit when I spoke. I took a sip of water. "We're not talking about an arbitrary ranking system. Each member has to prove they're strong enough to hold their position in the pack."

"Then how can we ever expect them to take orders from a human superior? Wouldn't they just bite their head off and claim the higher rank?"

"Pack hierarchy only pertains to pack members. The werewolves shouldn't have any problem working alongside humans, just other werewolves who aren't in the same pack. If you want a more detailed explanation, I suggest you talk to our werewolf liaison, Marcus Howard."

Anderson snorted. "Even you, our supposed 'paranatural expert,' aren't sure how these beings will behave." He placed his hands on the table in front of him and leaned in. "This whole ridiculous 'experiment' of paranaturals acting as equals is a disaster waiting to happen, and as the voice of the people here in Colorado it's my duty to protest the PTF's arbitrary declaration that we should be forced to house this ticking time bomb."

Silva raised an eyebrow. "A passionate plea, but we are representatives of the Church, not the PTF."

"The Church may not control the PTF, but its proclamations carry significant weight. If you were to report the divisive nature of this experiment and explain to your superiors that paranaturals are too dangerous to be allowed free rein, the Church could then pressure the PTF board into changing their ruling." The governor glared at me. "We've seen them swayed by such tactics before."

"Your Purist agenda is well known," I said. "But even you must see that a civil war between people with paranatural abilities and those without will only lead to the destruction of both groups and the collapse of our society. It'd be chaos."

"Not if we strike first," Anderson said, turning to Silva on his left. "Cut the paranaturals off before they're able to really establish their coalition."

I shook my head. "If you think the disarray among the handful of werewolves we've got here translates to the wider paranatural world, you're in for a rude awakening. The Colorado experiment may be new, but the established packs are not. They function with a precision any human military unit would envy."

"I for one would like to see if Ms. Blackwood's claims that the werewolves can be integrated safely as functional PTF agents is true." Ali turned to me. "When will this new pack be complete?"

I worried my lower lip between my teeth. "Soon. Hopefully within the next few days."

"What's the delay?" asked Khatun.

"As I said earlier, I have some business to attend to . . . out of town. We'll settle the pack hierarchy as soon as I get back."

Anderson steepled his fingers. "Would this trip have anything to do with the recent fae attacks? Because as I understand it, the affected areas all lie well beyond your current jurisdiction."

Silva leaned toward me. "Do you have some information about this strange behavior from the fae?"

"We don't know with complete certainty that it *is* the fae," Ali pointed out.

"*Pfft.*" Anderson waved the words away. "Who else could it be?"

"And if it is"—Khatun narrowed his gaze at me—"where would your loyalty lie?"

"A fair question," Anderson said. "Humanity, paranaturals, and fae . . . you've got your fingers in a lot of pies."

My gaze jumped from face to face as they all stared at me down the length of the table as if I were some kind of strange specimen in a jar that they were trying to identify.

The phone in my back pocket vibrated, and a strain of my ringtone cut through the noise of the restaurant.

"Excuse me." I dropped my gaze and pulled out the phone, thankful for the excuse to avoid those accusing stares. My own home phone number displayed on the screen. Someone was calling from my landline. I pressed *accept* and raised the phone. "Hello?"

"My contact will meet us on the Santa Monica Pier tomorrow at six a.m.," Kai said without preamble.

I glanced up. Anderson and the delegates were all still looking at me. "I'm headed back now." I ended the call and stuffed the phone in my pocket, then lifted my chin to address my audience. "I'm afraid my time here is up."

"When will you be back?" Silva asked.

"A day or two. I hope you'll all stay to see the difference having a stable pack makes to the werewolves' temperaments." *And I hope it really does make a difference*, I added silently.

Khatun and Ali nodded. Silva frowned. Anderson glared.

"Enjoy your dinner." I pushed back from the table, then wound my way past servers loaded down with trays, tables of well-dressed diners, and savory smells that made my stomach growl. The night had grown several degrees colder in the short time I'd been inside, and the phantom light of the absent sun was barely a blush in the western sky.

I tugged my coat collar tighter around my neck and set off on foot, figuring the car that brought us wouldn't give me the time of day, let alone a ride, now that I was on my own. Besides, the PTF building was only a fifteen-minute walk from Larimer Square, and I could use the fresh air to clear my head.

A block later my hands were shaking, but not from cold. Adrenalin, anxiety, frustration, and self-doubt coursed through me. How was I supposed to represent the paranaturals in the PTF when I was so new to their community? How could I make the delegates listen to me when they saw me as an outsider with split loyalties? And how could I change either of those perceptions when I myself felt like an impostor in both groups? And now I'd been roped into this spy mission when my focus *should* be on securing the delegates' good favor just because Harris thought the little bit of magic in my blood made me an expert on the fae. I sighed. These days I wasn't even an expert on myself.

It's only a matter of time before everything comes crashing down.

I pulled out my phone again, opened my contact list, scrolled down to the one person who always seemed to know just what to say when I was doubting myself, and pressed the button to call James. Even if we weren't exactly seeing eye to eye these days, his simple presence made me feel more solid somehow, more settled in my own skin.

The line rang four times without answer. I hung up when the voice mail kicked in and instead texted, *Need to talk. You free?*

I tugged at the invisible cord that tied our souls together and found my distant anchor to the northwest: Boulder. I was too far to get a sense of his emotions, but the reassuring call of his presence was enough to settle my nerves a bit.

My phone chimed. *Working late at the gallery. Will come over after.*

I scrunched my nose. *After* might be too late. As soon as I picked up Kai and Emma, we'd be on our way to California. I had to drive past the gallery to get home anyway. I'd just pop in.

I had put off telling James about Harris's request because once he knew what was going on, he'd probably insist on coming. I longed to have him with me, but no meeting with a fae, least of all an unfamiliar one, was any place for a vampire, day-walking or not. Somehow I needed to convince him that it was in both our best interests for him to stay and submit to testing while I was away.

THE GARAGE BENEATH Souled Art Gallery was nearly empty. Besides my Jeep, only three parking spots were occupied. James's black Lexus was in the space nearest the elevator. I ran my palm over the hood as I passed and gave a small tug at the invisible connection between us. He was definitely up above . . . but something felt off. Frowning at the ceiling, I stepped into the elevator.

The small steel box carried me up to the lobby. I stepped into the bright lights of the gallery's main floor. Several of my sculptures were on display, waiting to be replaced by the new spring show that I would not be participating in. Joe, the operations manager for the gallery, was typing on a computer at the reception desk. He looked up. His gray-green eyes went wide, and his eyebrows arched toward his slicked-back hair.

"Alex." He tugged at the purple silk tie that seemed to be suddenly strangling him and hustled over to me. "What are you doing here?"

I narrowed my eyes at James's assistant, confidant, and general problem-solver. "I could ask you the same thing. James said *he* was working tonight."

"Ah, yes. He is. He had some contracts to look over and asked me to cover the floor. Let me give him a call. I'm sure he'll be right down."

The uneasy feeling from the garage grew stronger, but now there were other sensations drifting through our bond. Sensations that could not have been further from the boredom of reviewing contracts. My pulse sped up. My palms began to sweat. I felt tipsy.

I turned back to the elevator. "I'll just go up."

"Alex, wait." Joe reached toward me.

I glanced from his outstretched hand to the nervous expression on his usually composed face. I set my jaw. Judging from the emotions I was picking up from James, Joe had every reason to worry about what I'd find in the apartment above.

I stepped into the elevator and pressed the button for the top floor.

Joe lowered his hand, a sad look in his eyes.

When the elevator doors opened again, I was enveloped in a wave of lust. My muscles clenched and went watery all at once. I had to brace against the wall to stay on my feet. Sweet perfume filled the apartment with notes of hyacinth and rose.

Jealousy rose like a beast inside me, but I pushed it aside.

He's just eating, I told myself. *You know how this works.*

Unfortunately for me, James's meals most often took the form of young women with super-model bodies and overactive sex drives.

The muscles in my lower abdomen tightened again in response to James's arousal. I stumbled against the kitchen island.

I gritted my teeth and glanced back at the elevator doors closing behind me. James and I had agreed that he would always try to eat before visiting me so he would never be tempted when we were alone together. I'd had my fill of being a vampire's snack when I was held prisoner by the old master of Denver. I wasn't eager to be anyone's meal ever again. Not even for someone I loved. The trade-off was that I had to accept James would be getting what he needed elsewhere, and that was sometimes a hard pill to swallow. More so when I had to face it head on.

I considered getting back in the elevator. But time was ticking away and I needed to get moving. That's why I'd made this stop in the first place. I couldn't wait for James to finish his meal and get cleaned up.

I made my way slowly through the kitchen, past the floor-to-ceiling windows, toward the back bedroom, trying to prepare with each step for what I would find behind the door.

Remember, I told myself, *no judgment. He has to do this. It's just like eating a hamburger.* I shuddered at that thought and made a mental note to look into vegetarianism.

I set my hand against the door and took a deep breath, which only made me more dizzy, since the perfume scent was stronger here. *Whatever you see, don't freak out.*

I pushed against the smooth wood. The hinges moved without sound . . .

or maybe I wouldn't have heard a squeak regardless over the noises coming from the back room. A giggle, a soft moan, bed springs, heavy breathing. The door swung wide enough to reveal the scene that went with the sounds. I stood in open-mouthed shock.

James had to drink blood to survive. He preferred the taste of blood flavored with lust, but he insisted that didn't translate to actual sex with his meals.

The five naked bodies writhing on his king-sized bed said otherwise.

Taut muscles rippled across James's bare back as he held himself above a cinnamon-skinned woman with long, brown hair. The woman's nails dug into his back deep enough to cut, but James's skin healed as fast as the scratches were made. His face was buried in the curve between the woman's neck and shoulder.

Two other women and a man were tangled together beside him. One of the women arched on her knees and gasped, lifting her face toward the ceiling. A trickle of blood escaped the corner of her mouth. Her stained tongue darted out to catch it. Her glossy black hair cascaded over the kind of alabaster skin you could only get from living without sunlight. She lowered her emerald gaze and found me in the doorway.

"Alex." She drew out the syllables of my name and hissed the end like a snake.

James jerked around, eliciting a whine from the woman beneath him. A wave of guilt slammed into me when his cobalt-blue eyes met mine.

He flipped back the sheet that had covered his lower half and scrambled from the bed.

A tiny voice in my head jumped for joy at the sight of his boxers, still in place, but the shape of them made my sense of betrayal rage all the louder.

"How are my pendants coming along?" Victoria crooned, as though I hadn't just caught her between the sheets with my boyfriend. She twirled a strand of the wheat-blond hair of the man lying next to her. "Not much time left."

The woman James had been feeding from said something in another language and pawed at his side as he grabbed a pair of rumpled slacks off the floor. Blood trickled over her collarbone. When her attempts to drag him back failed to find purchase, she pouted out her lower lip and snuggled closer to Victoria.

"Alex," James said as he stepped into his pants, "I can explain."

"Don't be too harsh with him, dear." Victoria spoke with a sultry purr that made me want to rip her tongue out. "When I found these lovely folks at my club, I remembered how much James used to love French cuisine, and I thought I'd share. You can hardly blame him." She traced one long red fingernail over the naked man's abdomen and leered at me. "You're welcome to join us."

"Victoria." James snapped her name like a whip.

Hot pressure was building behind my eyes. I clamped my jaw shut and spun away from the scene.

"Alex." James's voice followed me, but rather than finding comfort in it I only ran faster.

I choked on the emotions trapped in my throat. Mine. His. I couldn't tell. I couldn't untangle them. I didn't even try. I just had to get out before I drowned in them.

The elevator doors slid open immediately. I pounded the *close door* button, willing the steel to move faster.

James's hand snaked through the three-inch gap between the closing doors. They reversed direction.

"No." I shook my head, struggling to speak past the tightness in my chest. "Get out."

He stepped into the small space. My roiling emotions were amplified by James's proximity. This close it was impossible to ignore his hunger and lust. I was only mildly placated to find the feelings tainted by regret.

I breathed deeply through my nose, trying to steady myself, bracing for a fight. James had brought the floral scent I now recognized as Victoria's perfume with him. The doors slid shut, trapping us together.

"You know how I feed."

"Seriously?" I glared at him. "That's your defense?"

"You know better than anyone what I am. I should not have to 'defend' myself for doing what is necessary to survive."

"Don't you mean doing *whom?*"

A flash of anger danced through his eyes. His fist slammed the side of the elevator hard enough to dent the steel.

I jerked back from the impact, reminded that this new, day-walking James had a much shorter temper than the dignified gallery owner I was used to.

He exhaled and opened his hand. "How many times must I explain before you believe that my method of feeding has no bearing on my feelings toward you?"

"Maybe if 'feeding' didn't involve getting naked in a bed with your ex-girlfriend—"

"If Marcus Howard showed up on your doorstep with a hot, cheesy pizza at the end of a long day, would you turn him away? Or take the pizza and slam the door in his face?"

"Well, I sure as hell wouldn't have sex on top of the pizza box."

He clenched his jaw and pointed at the elevator's ceiling. "I did not have intercourse up there."

"Because I walked in on you." Our voices echoed deafeningly in the small space. Joe could probably hear us as we passed the lobby. I took a deep breath, trying to rein in my temper. "Look, I get that you have to eat, and that means draining humans. I even get that you need to spice up your meals with arousal. I think I've been pretty accepting, all things considered, but finding you in bed with Victoria? That's where I draw the line."

A bell chimed. The elevator doors slid open to reveal the dim concrete of the parking garage and the welcome escape of my blue Jeep.

James followed me out, keeping pace as I crossed the garage. "She's my friend, and has been for longer than you've been alive."

Guilt twisted in my chest. James had lost so much in his long existence. Why shouldn't he cling to someone who'd been with him for over a lifetime? That was more than I could offer. And I didn't want to be one of those significant others who dictated with whom my partner could socialize. James hadn't asked me to cut my ties with Kai or Chase despite the strain of their species' bias toward vampires. But Victoria wasn't just a friend, and every instinct told me she wanted to rekindle what they'd once had.

"She's your *ex-girlfriend*," I shouted, picking up the pace.

He stepped in front of me and grabbed my shoulders, arresting my momentum. His long, strong fingers dug in to the point of pain. "And *you* are my current one."

Frustration, guilt, love, anger, pride, regret . . . they all spilled over me like a waterfall, pouring through our link so I couldn't tell which of us was feeling what. My knees turned to jelly under their pressure. My mind swirled with what was happening here with James, the disastrous dinner with Anderson and the delegates, and Harris's impossible expectations. It was too much.

James stiffened and stepped back so his arms were fully extended. He narrowed his gaze and stared at my face. "You're leaving."

I knocked his hands away, breaking the mental connection, and raised what defenses I could to lessen the link. "That's what I came here to tell you. Harris is sending me on a reconnaissance mission. I'll be gone a couple of days. I suggest you use the time to get your PTF testing done while it's still voluntary."

He shook his head. "I'll go with you."

It wasn't a question or request, just a statement. As though there could be no doubt I'd want his company.

"You'd be in the way."

His nostrils flared as he exhaled. Even without physical contact I could feel his irritation, his insulted pride.

I gritted my teeth, trying to get a handle on my own anger so I could explain the situation. "This is a diplomatic mission involving fae. A vampire would only complicate matters."

"Then I shall keep my distance, but not so far that I cannot help when you call." He lifted his chin. "When do we leave?"

I stared into the cool blue of his gaze and gauged his resolve. I could feel his presence in my mind, poking at my thoughts, trying to tease out the details through our connection.

"I'm picking up Kai and Emma now. You can meet us at PTF headquarters in an hour." I glanced toward the ceiling. "That should be enough time for you to finish your meal."

Pivoting, I marched to my Jeep and yanked open the door. I didn't look back until I reached the exit. When I glanced in the rearview mirror, the garage was empty.

I pulled onto the street and turned toward the canyon that would lead me home. When I was a block away, I tested our bond. Whether due to the increasing distance or because James had closed down his end to prevent me feeling the remainder of his meal, I found nothing but the dull thrum of *I am here* that was our constant connection.

Tugging out my cell phone, I dialed David.

"Change your mind about movie night?" he asked by way of greeting. "I need you to meet me in the lobby of the PTF building with a security team in one hour," I said. "I'm bringing James in for testing."

Chapter 6

EMMA, KAI, AND I each pulled a backpack from my Jeep, small enough to be carry-ons despite our access to the PTF's private plane. The plan was to only be gone for a couple of days, and the lighter we traveled the easier life would be. I closed and locked the Jeep, slung my pack on one shoulder, and turned toward the PTF building.

James was standing two feet away, a living shadow at the edge of the parking lot.

I gasped in surprise and took a step back, bumping into Emma.

"What? What is it?" Emma spun side to side as though searching her surroundings, hands up in a defensive posture.

Kai set a hand against her back to still her, but that only made her jump away and scream.

"It's fine, Em," I said. "It's just James."

She placed one hand against her chest and took several deep breaths. "Don't scare me like that."

Frowning, I studied Emma as she got her breathing under control and the tension eased out of her posture. *How terrifying must it be to walk in total darkness with no idea what's around you?*

My thoughts skipped ahead to our impending trip and all the uncertainties it presented. Even something as simple as getting separated from us in a crowd of regular humans could prove disastrous. I bit my lip as my mind raced through an endless stream of "what if?" scenarios. *I could still leave her behind. . . .* But did I have the right to limit her experiences out of fear for her safety? Recalling the way she'd pleaded not to be treated as an invalid, I clamped my mouth shut. *Kai and I will just have to protect her if shit goes sideways.*

"I apologize for startling you," James said.

Emma shook her head. "Not your fault."

"Come on, Emma." I took her hand and placed it against my elbow so she could hold on as I led her inside. "Let's get this over with."

Kai took up position on the other side of me, putting himself between me and James. I'd given Kai and Emma a heads-up about my plan to trick James into submitting for testing, but I hadn't mentioned the scene I'd walked in on or the argument we'd had lest they think I was just being petty. Still, a few feet was hardly enough to guarantee he wouldn't sense my betrayal before we made it through the front door.

I glanced in his direction.

He met my gaze and frowned, a small crease between his eyebrows.

I snapped my attention to the front of the PTF building and focused on my worry about Emma. Hopefully, my guilt and concern for her was strong enough to mask those same feelings over what I was about to do to James.

The area in front of the main entrance was clear, the protesters having called it a day. The trees near the bank of the Platte were silhouetted by dancing firelight from the ramshackle community where many of them would spend their night before taking up positions on the sidewalk again tomorrow. I spotted David and two uniformed security guards waiting behind the large glass doors in the lobby. There was also a security guard stationed at the reception desk for the night shift.

I pulled open the door and tipped my head to indicate James should enter first. Kai took Emma's hand and led her through, taking her to one side. I brought up the rear. The four of us stopped in the waiting room in front of the guards.

"Thanks for coming," I said.

"Of course." David shifted his attention to James and nodded. "Evening, James."

James frowned but returned the nod. "David." His gaze skipped to the flanking security guards. "What's going on?"

David glanced at me. That was all it took.

James spun, eyes narrowed.

No amount of concentration could keep my emotions secret from him at this point. I saw the exact moment my betrayal registered.

He clenched his fists at his sides. Anger rolled off him like waves crashing against my guilt. "Really? This is your response to Victoria? That's childish, even for you."

Heat rose to my cheeks. "This has nothing to do with Victoria."

His hand flashed out, fingers wrapping around my wrist. The walls between us crumbled completely. He raised an eyebrow.

I looked away. "It's *mostly* not about Victoria."

Peeling his hand off my wrist I sandwiched it between both of mine, pushing as much assurance and sincerity through the connection as I could. Yes, I was angry about finding him in bed with Victoria. Yes, that was something we would need to deal with. But all of that aside, I believed leaving him behind was the best option.

"For you, maybe."

"For both of us," I corrected. "Weatherly's been on my ass since Arlington about the fact that you're still not registered. If we don't take care of this now, he's prepared to drag you in by force, and he'll take great pleasure in doing so."

He bared his teeth. "I'd like to see him try."

"*I* wouldn't." I set one hand against his cheek. "This way we have some control over the situation. David will oversee your testing, make sure all the fair treatment protocols are followed. Just let him write down that you're fast and strong, and you can be out of here by tomorrow night, registration in hand."

A small muscle in the side of James's jaw twitched. *It's not only me that I'm worried about.* His gaze pierced my soul, teasing out all the underlying emotions I was wrestling with. *A lot can happen in a few days. If I'm here, I won't be able to help you if you get into trouble.*

"Staying here and taking away some of Weatherly's and Anderson's ammunition is the best way you can help me right now." I squeezed his hand. "I need to prove to them, the Church delegates, and the whole world that paranaturals can be trusted. That means following the rules whenever possible." I stared deep into his eyes. *One way or another, you're going to set an example. Help me send the right message.*

James stared back at me for several seconds as our audience watched in silence, then he blew out a long, slow sigh. "If you truly believe this is the best way for me to help you . . . I'll stay." He kissed the back of my hand. *And perhaps this will earn me some mercy from your wrath?*

"Don't push your luck," I muttered, but the corners of my lips pulled up. The skin on the back of my hand tingled under his warm breath. An electric charge sang through my body, tightening my muscles in a most distracting way.

I freed my hand. The currents of lust coursing through me eased but didn't dissipate entirely. Even my anger over his horrific lack of judgment regarding Victoria couldn't dampen the physical reaction I had to James. "I'll see you in a few days."

He smiled, a mischievous twinkle in his eye. "I look forward to making up with you when you get back."

I STEPPED OUT of the cab that had picked up Emma, Kai, and me from the Ocean Park Hotel, where we'd caught a few hours of sleep after touching down in the Santa Monica airport last night. Moving to one side, I yawned and rubbed grit from my dry eyes as Emma slid out behind me. A warm, salty breeze blew into my face, tugging and tangling my hair. I inhaled deeply, then coughed. Salt wasn't the only scent on the wind. The musky odor made me want to cover my nose.

Kai followed Emma out of the back seat and closed the door. I handed the cab's fare through the passenger window. "Keep the change."

The tattooed woman in the driver's seat counted the bills, nodded her thanks, and pulled back into the traffic flowing along Ocean Avenue like the currents of its namesake. Sunrise stained the eastern horizon pink. Silhouetted palms danced in the wind and cast long shadows over wide walkways that were already bustling with pedestrians despite the early hour and the stench blowing off the beach.

Kai took point, leading us under a blue-white-and-yellow arch that spanned the entryway of the Santa Monica Pier. He scanned the area as he walked and kept his hands against his belt, where his sword was hidden by glamour. He'd cast a similar spell on my sword, allowing me to wear it without raising suspicion. I tightened my grip on the invisible hilt. Despite my fae heritage and the smattering of magical training I'd managed between crises, my repertoire of spells was woefully lacking. Even the basic glamours fae children learned to hide their true natures were beyond me.

"Remember," Kai said as he walked, "you'll need to convince Vale that you're acting with the full support of the PTF, but if you're caught in an outright lie, you'll lose all credibility, and likely any chance of gaining the information you want."

"That's the third time you've said that," Emma said. She clung to my sleeve just above the elbow, trailing me like a shadow. Her other hand was raised in front of her chest to give warning in case she was about to bump anything. Our progress was slow as she slid her feet over the pavement.

"I want to make sure Alex remembers."

"I'll remember," I said.

"If we *do* get an audience at court, you'll have to be even more careful." He sighed and shook his head. "I hope Vale knows enough about what's going on that we can avoid an actual trip to the Undine Realm."

I smirked. "You've said that, too."

I was also hoping to avoid a trip to another realm. I glanced at Emma. The plan was for her to hang out on the boardwalk while Kai and I talked to his contact. If we needed to go to the Undine Court to sort this mess out, she'd go back to the hotel and wait for us to return. Despite her assurances that she'd be fine, I didn't like the idea of leaving her alone.

We crested a narrow overpass, and I got my first look at the ocean proper. The pier stretched out over shimmering blue waves. A wooden staircase dropped to a small parking lot, packed to capacity, nestled to one side. A wide buffer of white sand lay between the pavement and the water, but almost every inch of it was covered with trash. Twisted chunks of rusted metal, Styrofoam cups, glass shards, mangled flip-flops, and a plethora of multi-colored plastics littered the beach. Another gust tugged my hair and made me want to gag as the musk and mildew of the pile washed over me. I shaded my eyes and squinted, but the line of debris stretched out of sight in either direction.

Emma wrinkled her nose. "So much for getting some fresh air."

I chuckled. "Still happy you came?"

Either the trash tsunami hadn't been tall enough to reach the pier proper or workers had cleared the area, because the pathway leading into the commercial section was open. We passed a huge, indoor merry-go-round, a string of restaurants, and several souvenir shops. Closed signs hung in a few of the windows, but the shops that were open seemed to be doing a brisk trade despite the stink and sad state of the beach. Vendors sold hot dogs and cotton candy to people in cut-off shorts and tight T-shirts. Men and women strolled, jogged, and occasionally Rollerbladed around us as we made our way past the roller coaster and Ferris wheel toward the distant end of the pier.

I scanned the crowd on the viewing platform beyond the Harbor Office building, shifting my focus to detect magic, and spotted the tell-tale shimmer of a glamour around one woman leaning against the painted rail. Her raven-black hair streamed in the wind as she stared out over the sun-kissed waves. If not for the shimmer of glamour, I would have taken her for an average teenage human in a white tank top, a pair of pastel-pink sweatpants, and cork sandals.

I nudged Kai. "Is that your friend?"

Kai narrowed his eyes at the woman. "No, but I think that's who we're supposed to talk to. That's Annabrae. She holds a similar rank in the Undine Court as Rhoana does in Bael's."

I stiffened. Rhoana was the captain of Bael's personal guard. If a person of that rank had come. . . .

"Maybe this means you'll get your wish and have your questions answered without having to travel," Emma said. "Why else would they send someone so important?"

A little of the tension eased from my chest. "That's a good point."

"I don't like them changing the terms of this meeting without telling us," Kai said.

"Maybe it was a last-minute decision," I said. "Either way, Emma's right. This is the perfect opportunity to get our questions answered here and now, and that's what we want."

His lips compressed to a thin line. His knuckles turned white on his invisible hilt.

I frowned. "Maybe you should stay here with Emma."

He shook his head. "I can't protect you from back here."

"This is a diplomatic mission. Remember? We're beyond the point where swords can protect us."

"And I would remind *you* that fae diplomacy and swords are not mutually exclusive."

A wash of anxiety swept over me. I'd fumbled more than once when mincing words with the fae, so swords were not an altogether unlikely outcome. Still, we didn't want to start there. Especially on a pier crowded with human bystanders. "Point taken. Just hang back while I make contact, okay? I'm hoping words will be enough here."

Kai huffed.

"If she draws a sword, you can rush in and save me."

"Fine, but now it's even more important that you don't slip up. Remember, bluff if you can, but don't lie."

"Bluff, don't lie. Got it." I transferred Emma's grip to the flaking blue paint of the rail. "I'll be back in a minute."

"Be careful," she said.

I took a deep breath. Now that we were out beyond the tide line, the salty air that slapped my face was free of the stench of decaying garbage. I straightened my shoulders and approached the glamoured woman. "Annabrae?"

She continued to stare at the water as sparks of sunlight flashed upon the crests of the waves.

Squinting to sharpen the focus of my magical vision, I gazed through the shimmer of glamour surrounding her. Her skin, a deep brown, took on a slightly green complexion, and the black of her hair shone with indigo highlights. The ridge of her nose was nearly flush with her high cheekbones, and her nostrils turned to slits like a fish's gills. The red blush drained from her lips, leaving them nearly the same color as her hair.

I copied her pose, resting my elbows against the railing and leaning out over the water. We stood side by side in silence for several minutes. People continued to bustle around us, though most stayed in the theme park area. Kai and Emma remained where they were. I could feel Kai's stare boring a hole in my back.

"This mess was not our doing." Annabrae's voice was deep and calm.

"Do you know who it was?"

"The mess belongs to humans. Many among my people would argue that it has simply come home."

I glanced at her from the corner of my eye. Her gaze remained on the water.

"Are the undine responsible for washing the trash ashore?"

"What is your goal here, Alex Blackwood?"

"To find out who's stirring up trouble between the humans and fae."

"Should you not have begun such an investigation in your own court?"

"I don't belong to a court."

Now she did shift her gaze to me. Her eyes were such a clear blue as to seem almost white. Her focus flickered to Kai behind me. "You deny your kinship to Enchantment?"

I pursed my lips, then shook my head. "I don't deny the connection . . . but I'm not a part of their court. Not really. Besides, I'm sure they aren't to blame for the current situation."

She raised an eyebrow. "Are you?"

I watched the dawn light dance across the surface of the water. I had Bael's word that Enchantment would make no move against the mortal realm for at least a year, and the word of a fae was binding—though come to think of it, I wasn't sure what would happen if one tried to lie. I filed that question away for a later date. One mystery at a time. "I am."

"Interesting." Annabrae returned her gaze to the ocean and once more lapsed into silence.

"The PTF is worried the fae are starting a war," I said. "Are you?"

She frowned, straightened, and said, "We shall see what kind of greeting the ocean gives you." Then she pushed me over the rail.

I flailed, trying to grab the railing as I tumbled over it, but the smooth metal slipped through my grasp. I hit the water from two stories up. Tingles sparked through my body at the impact, and the air was knocked from my lungs as I plunged beneath the surface a scant few feet from a support pillar. Spots danced in my vision as I sank, too stunned to move. Then my chest began to burn. I twitched my arms and legs, but the movements were sluggish, my limbs weighed down by the saturated fabric of my T-shirt and jeans. My boots were anchors tied to my feet. I kicked them off and struggled to follow my bubbling breath toward the light.

My fingers brushed the surface, then something wrapped around my torso. I was yanked backward with the force of a speedboat. The shimmering lights of the surface and the promise of air faded above me as I was dragged farther out and deeper down. I struggled and strained, but there was nothing to attack, nothing to grab. It was as though the water itself was propelling me.

The pressure grew heavier. The fire in my lungs increased until I was sure I would pass out. Was this the "ocean greeting" Annabrae had mentioned? Did she intend to drown me?

The last precious bubbles left my lips. I stopped looking for the lost light. I stopped trying to swim, or even move. My limbs dragged like ribbons through the water as I continued my descent. I focused all my remaining strength on suppressing the urge to inhale, but it was a losing battle. The strain in my chest felt like a creature trying to tear its way out of my throat.

Then the last of my strength was gone, and the water came rushing in.

Chapter 7

ICY WATER SURGED down my throat and filled my lungs, dowsing the fire. Numbing cold spread through my chest. I waited to die.

Rather than growing darker, the water around me began to lighten. I exhaled. Liquid flowed from my lungs. Curious, I inhaled again. More water flowed in, smooth as air.

Tiny green lights appeared around me, murky at first, then growing clearer as the distance between us shrank. I squinted and found that the lights were attached to organic spires coiling up through the water on either side. One such spire glided past on my right, closer than the others. A curious face looked out at me, silhouetted in a green-lit window, as I was dragged past.

I tried to twist so I could see where I was going, but the constant pressure on my chest and abdomen didn't allow me to do more than turn my head as I continued my backward descent. More spires filled the area around me, joined by lacy fans of bright pinks, oranges, and blues. Coral tubes like empty ice cream cones stood in haphazard clusters. Bone-white arches roughly marked the shape of a city, and all around me the lights grew brighter. Iridescent green and yellow shone from holes and crevices or hung in strings that undulated like flags in a breeze. The shadowy shapes moving between the structures became more distinct as I dropped down among them.

Two such shapes, one on either side of me, came into focus and matched my pace. They were similar in form, with long equine faces, streaming seaweed manes, and scaled tails that flashed in the green lights as they swished. Dredging through my fae species studies, I came up with the name kelpie. Each of my escorts bore a long wooden spear tipped with silver in their webbed hands. A moment later, they started to hum.

The sound was eerily clear despite the muffling effects of the water, and a moment later a second hum sounded from somewhere behind me. My course shifted suddenly from a diagonal descent to a horizontal line. My heels scraped inlets into a patch of soft, black sand. I passed under another of those bone-like archways and between two more kelpies who stood guard to either side, spears at the ready. These two held their positions. The two that had accompanied me split off to the sides and out of my peripheral vision. All at once, the pressure that had been steadily propelling me vanished.

I floated, disoriented, for a moment. Then I got my arms and legs working. I paddled myself into what I thought was a vertical position and twisted to get a better look at my final destination. My heart was pounding. Water continued to fill and empty from my lungs as though I was breathing air. The organic arch I'd passed through was one of dozens that enclosed an oval space that could only loosely be called a room. The floor was made of fine black sand that bore the ever-shifting ripples of the current. Clumps of bioluminescent plants draped the coral arches, bathing the area in light. Coral sculptures in every shape, texture, and color decorated the edges of the room. There was no ceiling. Spires rose beyond and above the walls of the room, giving the impression that I was standing at the center of a budding flower with its petals curved slightly in above me.

Or on the palm of a closing hand.

I pushed the thought away.

All four of the kelpie guards took up that eerie hum again and raised their faces to the open roof. At the far end of the oval, three new shapes were descending. The two on either side were small, sleek creatures, with stout bodies, short snouts, and whiskers. One was such a pale gray it would have looked white if not compared to the bleached arches. The second was darker and sported brown spots on its back. Together they swam in playful rings around the third figure.

The central fae was larger than the other two but not as large as the kelpies. What she lacked in size, however, she more than made up for in presence. From below, she resembled a cloud of tentacles—some as wide as my thigh, others as delicate as string. Each was laced with thin, translucent flesh that billowed like the finest fabric as the tentacles undulated. From the waist up, the fae woman had pale, purplish-gray skin with webbing between her fingers and gill slits on either side of her neck. Flexible spines connected by gossamer webbing traced her forearms and the sides of her face, while a larger fin stood along the central ridge of her skull. On either side of that ridge drifted hair as fine as spider silk in a cascade of deep indigo. Her nose was nearly flush with her face, and her lips blended with the rest of her skin. Her eyes were wide, seeming almost too large for her face, and jet black from edge to edge.

I couldn't tell where her gaze was focused, but I felt her attention on me as she settled even with me in the water. Her torso was bare, but the coiling tentacles beneath her gave the impression she wore an intricate gown of swirling fabric. While I flailed my arms and legs to keep my orientation like a clumsy toddler, she clasped her hands together over her abdomen, seeming to hover perfectly in place without effort.

"My lord." Annabrae seemed to form out of the water itself, and I jerked sideways at suddenly finding her so close. Ignoring me, she lowered her chin to her chest and brought both hands to her forehead in a triangle shape.

"Well met, Anna." The Undine Lord, for she could be nothing less, gestured to me. "This is the daughter of Enchantment you spoke of?"

"Yes, my lord. She begs audience with you." Annabrae spoke with her head still down, hands to her forehead.

I opened my mouth and moved my lips, but all that came out was a muffled burble.

One corner of the lord's mouth inched up. "You do not possess the appropriate vocal chords for speaking underwater." The partial smile dropped. "Considering the circumstances, you should be grateful we have allowed you to breathe."

Panic swelled within me as I glanced back and forth between Annabrae, who must surely have been the force that dragged me here, and the Undine Lord. If the lord chose not to grant me an audience at this point, what could I do? How could I convince her if I couldn't make a sound? And if she turned me away, would Annabrae return me to the surface? Without being able to speak the phrase that granted diplomatic protection to visitors, was there anything to prevent Annabrae from revoking whatever spell she'd cast and letting me drown? Would my body wash up on the shores of Santa Monica, or would I just decompose here and become part of the black sand?

"I understand you've come to make an accusation." The lord's resonant voice jarred me out of the dark spiral my thoughts had taken. "On whose authority do you come?"

She made a casual gesture in my direction.

We drifted in silence for a moment until she said, "Well?"

"Answer," hissed Annabrae, her head still bowed.

I opened my mouth and said, "Um." The word drifted across the water. My voice was slightly distorted but recognizably mine. Some of the panic left me as I savored the sound. Then my focus snapped back to the task at hand, and all the stress returned.

"I haven't come to accuse," I said. "I'm only seeking information."

"Only," she gave a delicate snort, and a stream of bubbles trickled from the slits of her nostrils. "As if knowledge wasn't a powerful commodity."

"I only meant—"

"I grow tired of repeating myself. On whose authority do you presume to request this meeting?"

"Um. . . ." *Bluff, don't lie.* I glanced sideways at Annabrae, wishing Kai were with me. "I've come on behalf of the PTF."

"Then why make arrangements through a fae knight? And why come on your own? My experience with the PTF is that they prefer to work through official channels with all the pomp and circumstance."

I shifted. The motion made me spin slightly and have to paddle to regain my alignment. "I was asked to contact you unofficially, to see if this matter could be resolved quickly."

She frowned. "If you have no official PTF jurisdiction in this matter, you have no power to negotiate, and therefore no right to claim protection as their envoy."

If my mouth could have gone dry in that moment, it would have. As it was, a knot seemed to lodge in my throat. Without the protection granted to a visiting envoy, they could do anything they wanted to me.

"Tell me then, what reason do I have not to feed you to my guards?"

The kelpies hovering near the edge of the room both adjusted their stances, tightening their grips on their spears.

Again I glanced at Annabrae, but she remained perfectly still and silent. I'd find no help there.

Mind blank, I blurted, "I also carry the protection of the Lord of Enchantment." Pulling my gaze from the kelpie guards, I refocused on the Undine Lord. "I'm—"

"We know well who you are, Alex Blackwood, kin to Bael the Destroyer." The lord's tentacles rippled in agitation as though a strong wind had kicked up to ruffle the layers of her skirt. "That honor will earn you few friends here."

Movement drew my attention to the shadowy area just beyond the white arches with their glowing plants. The ground seemed to rise, a hill pushing out of the black sand. Then it sank, and the area beside it rose in a smooth undulation that ran around the outer perimeter of the area I was in. Light glinted occasionally off the crests of the rolling hill, highlighting the edges of purple scales. A deep keen sounded through the water, seeming to come from everywhere at once. It was a sound like the plates of the Earth shifting. The scaly ripple continued around the room until a fan of dark fins like the ribbed canvas of junk boat sails lifted into view amid a cloud of black sand. Each fin was roughly the size of a city bus.

"Peace." The Undine Lord lifted both hands and closed her eyes, then began to hum a higher, more melodic tone that wove into the deeper sound like thread through a braid, joining and binding it. The dark shape beyond the arches settled down, its tail kicking up a cloud of silt.

"My father," the Undine Lord said, the black pools of her eyes once more turned in my direction. "One of the few survivors of Bael's massacre."

Father? My gaze flicked between the massive serpent and the petite woman. *I guess that's where she gets her frilly fins.* I licked my lips and tried not to imagine the size of the sea dragon wrapped around the room . . . and how easily he could crush me.

"Your lord was clever to send you, a mortal representative, to track his wayward general, but you were a fool to come without the full backing of the PTF."

"He's not my lo—wait, what? General? Are you talking about Shedraziel?" My brain scrambled to switch tracks from the knee-jerk response of denying Bael was my boss to the word "general" and its terrifying implications. If Shedraziel was somehow involved. . . . I shook my head. "That's not possible. Bael gave me his—" I snapped my mouth shut. Even while at peace, the fae realms were political adversaries, and information was a precious commodity. If the undine didn't already know that I was behind Bael's decision to postpone his invasion of the mortal realm, I wasn't going to tell them. Such an admission would only solidify the misconception that I was somehow bound to him, whether through debt or loyalty.

The Undine Lord remained silent through my moment of mental gymnastics, but the dark focus of her gaze was a constant prickle against my skin.

"Bael didn't send me," I said at last. "He doesn't even know I'm here." I didn't want to be associated with Bael's crimes at the best of times, but especially not when my life was in the hands of one of his victims. I bunched my fists and forced myself to take a deep breath, but the water that flooded my lungs didn't soothe my nerves nearly so well as the air it had replaced. "I came here on behalf of the mortal realm to find out if the sea fae were responsible for the trash that washed up on our shores. A simple yes or no, and I can get out of your hair."

"*Your* shores. A *simple* answer." A deep sound like distant thunder flitted at the edge of my hearing. The vibration shook my bones. "Your arrogance rivals that of Bael himself."

"I'm only trying to prevent future conflict between our people."

"And what would you do if you learned we were responsible for your current situation?"

I double-checked her words in my mind. Phrased as a question, there was no actual admission of guilt.

"I'd report my findings to the PTF and recommend we open negotiations immediately, before the situation devolves any further."

"Do you have the authority to negotiate for humanity?"

I frowned. "No. The PTF would send someone more qualified."

She drifted side to side. I got the impression she was pacing. "You claim to act on behalf of the PTF, but you do not carry their support. You claim kinship to the Lord of Enchantment, but deny fealty to him." She tapped one long, webbed finger against her chin. "It would seem the truth is that you have no authority . . . and therefore no protection."

She abruptly came closer with one strong pulse of her limbs.

I back-paddled, but there was nowhere to go. I was literally out of my element.

"I invoke the Wayfarer's Clause." The words were out of my mouth before I even registered them.

The Undine Lord's eyes were pools of oil, staring at me from inches away. A rainbow sheen rippled across the darkness. Her lips parted, stretching into a smile that showed the jagged tips of barbed teeth. Tilting her head to the side, she addressed Annabrae. "Put her in a cell."

The lord's tentacles brushed against me as she propelled herself backward in a gush of bubbles.

Annabrae's hand wrapped around my upper arm like a shackle.

"Wait! Under the Wayfarer's Clause you have to host me for three nights as your guest, safe from harm."

My words passed into the darkness above as the Undine Lord vanished beyond the edge of the light provided by the glowing plants.

"My lord knows well the bindings of such a claim." Annabrae's grip tightened. "You will survive until the clause has lapsed."

And after that? I was too afraid to voice the question.

Annabrae glided back the way we'd come, dragging me behind her. I kicked my legs and moved my free arm to keep from feeling totally out of control. The two kelpies who'd accompanied us into the room followed as far as their companions, then split off at a steeper angle, perhaps returning to the place where they'd first encountered us. The two by the door didn't even twitch as we passed.

We swam a foot or so above the black sand that stretched away like a wide, undersea street. Coral structures created the illusion of walls bordering our path, broken in places by organic arches through which I glimpsed open areas like the audience chamber. A number of kelpies, selkies, grindylows, naiads, and merfolk swam along the corridors. Many glanced up at our passing. A few bent their heads together to whisper. I got the uncomfortable feeling that I was being paraded through the city. Beyond the coral, just at the edge of my vision, larger shapes moved. None so massive as the tail of the dragon that encircled the audience chamber, but with fins and tentacles that had probably fueled many sailor's stories about sea monsters.

Annabrae led me into the open end of a coral tube that was large enough to drive a car through. The tube was coated on the inside with a sort of moss that made the whole structure glow a faint pink. Beyond the tube there seemed to be less traffic, or at least fewer spectators. The coral walls fell away, and we crossed a large, unmarked expanse. Bioluminescent seaweed grew up through the dark sand below, first in patches, then as a lush carpet of green, and finally like a forest around us that filled the area with a faint green glow. A narrow ribbon of black continued to the opening of a spiral structure like a huge, coiled shell set on its side. The exterior of the shell was brown and crusted, with several holes punched through its surface. The inner walls were a brilliant opalescent white. A table and chairs that looked to be carved from stone occupied one side of the room, while a hammock woven from green fibers hung along the other. The ceiling spiraled up into a vault with the holes I'd seen from the outside acting as windows through which I could see the seaweed forest.

Annabrae released my arm. Before I had time to even consider my freedom, the water around me vanished.

I dropped to the slick, polished surface below and began coughing up great burning lungfuls of seawater. When I inhaled, the air was cold and dry. My sinuses were on fire. My eyes streamed. My hair and clothes wrapped me in a clammy embrace as the weight of the water they'd absorbed pulled me down. The bubble of air continued to expand around me, pressing back the ocean until the interior of the shell was an island of breathable air.

Annabrae strolled to the wide opening through which we'd entered, walking on human legs. "Enjoy your stay."

She stepped through the shimmering wall of water and melted away.

I stayed on my knees for a few more moments, gasping in the cold air and coughing up the last of the seawater in my lungs. Once I was breathing normally, I rose. My bare feet skidded on the slick floor that shone with a faint rainbow sheen. My clothes dripped, leaving puddles on the polished white surface. I made my way carefully to the room's entrance and pressed my hand to the wall of water. My fingers passed through without resistance.

Whatever spell Annabrae had cast that allowed me to breathe on my way here was clearly gone, but perhaps I could recreate it. I worried my lower lip between my teeth and stared at the wall of water as if it was a puzzle to be solved.

My fae magic ranged from minor enchantments, which I mostly sucked at, to imbuing, which I sucked slightly less at. I could try to imbue myself with the ability to breathe underwater, but that magic wasn't particularly good at altering living beings from their natural state. The magic practiced by human practitioners on the other hand—the magic I'd inherited from my father—could do just about anything so long as there was enough ambient energy to channel and the caster could picture the desired outcome clearly enough.

I stretched my fingers, trying to get some warmth into the stiff joints. Then I opened my left hand and began drawing energy. I pictured myself in the water, breathing naturally. I imagined the way the water had flowed in and out of my lungs while I was with Annabrae. I held that thought firmly in my mind and channeled the magic through my body.

I can breathe underwater.

I stepped up to the rippling wall.

I can breathe underwater.

I pushed my face through the surface.

I can breathe underwater.

I opened my mouth.

I can brea—

Liquid fire filled my lungs. I staggered back, coughing and spluttering. I gasped and heaved.

It took even longer for the racking coughs to subside this time, and when they did I was left shaking on the damp floor.

I guess my magic isn't quite up to the task.

When my racing heart calmed and the searing pain in my chest subsided to a raw ache, I stood up and once again faced the wall of water. I ran my fingertips over the surface, creating a series of ripples. It was a brilliant prison. *No bars, no guards. Nothing keeping me in . . .* I stared at the darkness beyond the glowing kelp forest . . . *except an ocean and the need to breathe.*

Chapter 8

LOOSE HAIRS BRUSHED against my cheeks as I swung in the hammock, creating an artificial breeze in the otherwise perfectly still bubble of my prison. Nothing else moved. The contents of my pockets were laid out on the stone table. My keys were none the worse for wear. My wallet was ruined— leather and saltwater were a bad mix—but the credit cards and IDs in it would be fine. If I was lucky, the cash inside would still be usable when this ordeal was over. If I was very, very lucky, I might still be in a position to spend it. My cell phone was toast.

My fingers touched the smooth wall at the height of my arc, and I pushed off, swinging back toward the center of the room. I hadn't seen Annabrae in many hours, maybe even days. I'd been given three meals since my arrival, delivered by grindylows—creatures about the size of a rottweiler with leathery, dark-brown skin, deep-set eyes the color of dying embers, wide mouths that never quite closed over their needle-like teeth, and a lower body composed entirely of tentacles. The ambient light provided by the glowing plants outside never wavered, so there was no way to gauge the passage of time other than the meals.

The food itself was always some sort of seaweed salad adorned with chunks of salty pink meat and crunchy bits that might as easily have been crushed barnacles as nuts or seeds. When my meals were delivered, the grindylows always stayed on the far side of the water wall, only reaching in far enough to set my tray on the floor. Each meal also came with a sealed silver container of sweet red wine. Not my first choice as the effects of dehydration set in, but better than saltwater. All in all, the accommodations left quite a bit to be desired.

A small noise like a snippet of a kitten's purr came from the entrance. The sound ricocheted around the smooth interior of the shell like a bullet, piercing the stale air and shattering the muffled silence that had been pressing in around me as I lay in the hammock. Twisting, I lost my balance and tumbled to the floor as the hammock flipped mid-swing.

When I looked up from my hands and knees, the empty dishes I'd stacked by the entrance had been replaced by full ones. Dark-red eyes watched me from the far side of the water barrier. I rose to my feet and took a step. The grindylow's gaze flicked down to the sword on my hip, its visibility a harsh reminder that Kai's magic could not reach me here. I opened my mouth to assure it I meant no harm—anything to get it to stay, to break the monotony of my isolation—but my voice cracked from disuse and a parched throat. The grindylow spun away, my empty tray and thermos clutched to its chest. By the time I reached the entrance, the dark tentacles of my waiter were all I could see as the creature retreated along the black sand path and vanished into the seaweed forest.

There was a *splash* behind me.

I spun.

Flying at me through one of the "windows" punched in the shell was a small, furry, gray figure with black eyes, a flat snout, and a face full of whiskers. I barely had time to register the glint of green light on the blade in its hand before it cannoned into me and carried me through the wall of water.

I twisted on impact, but a sharp pain told me I hadn't been fast enough to avoid the blade altogether. Still, a knife wound wasn't my primary concern as I found myself separated from my bubble of breathable air with barely a gasp left in my lungs.

Kicking away from my attacker, I struggled to get back to my prison, but human limbs were no match for a creature designed for water. The selkie, for that's what it was, darted between me and the air I so desperately needed. I managed to draw my sword in time to deflect the thrust of its knife, but without any purchase I was pushed even farther from the doorway. Changing tactics, I went on the offensive, but the drag of the water made my swing slow.

The selkie easily darted under the blow and closed the distance between us once more. Its short, slender blade sliced through the water with ease. Time seemed to pause as my brain catalogued all the variables of the situation and screamed the result to my frozen body.

At this distance, in this element, there's no way I can avoid that knife!

My mouth opened involuntarily, and the last of my oxygen escaped in a silent scream that was carried into the darkness above on a stream of bubbles.

The world jolted sideways, wrenching my limbs like a corner taken too fast on a poorly-made roller coaster.

Stale air slapped me in the face.

I skidded across the polished opal of my prison floor, leaving a trail of water streaked with blood. My sword was no longer in my hand. I curled on my side, wincing as the gash puckered and a fresh stream of blood oozed out. Cringing, I forced myself to turn, to look back toward the entrance and the death that was surely coming for me.

But the selkie hadn't followed me through, and it wasn't alone in the seaweed forest. Two shapes exchanged blows, darting through the water like

I never could.

I eased myself up onto one elbow to get a better view of the battle. I couldn't tell which shape was which, or even what species I was seeing, blurred as the combatants were by distance, obstructions, speed, and my own dizziness. The seaweed trees swayed where the fighters passed. In some places whole segments were sheered and floated away toward the surface. The selkie's gray belly flashed for a moment through a window on my right, followed closely by a darker shape that seemed more shadow than form.

The tell-tale sounds of clashing weapons, grunts, and heavy footfalls I'd come to associate with such battles were disturbingly absent as I sat in my stale, silent bubble and tried to track the fight through sight alone. I twisted, grimacing every time I shifted my injury, trying to catch a glimpse of the shapes again, but they could have been anywhere in the wide ocean around me. I couldn't fight. I couldn't run. With the limited supplies available to me, I couldn't even clean or dress my wound. All I could do was wait and hope whoever came for me didn't want me dead.

Movement drew my focus to the main entrance. The selkie's sleek gray fur emerged from between the seaweed fronds. My breath caught. I shifted my weight, pushing back from the door, but blood loss coupled with my quickened breath made my vision swim when I tried to move.

The selkie continued forward, but it moved strangely, not at all like the graceful glide I'd seen before. Its fins dragged along the sandy ocean floor, and its head sagged at an awkward angle. Its front flippers hung limp. Then a flash of light brought my attention to the ground. My lost silver sword lifted as though raised on invisible strings. Squinting, I could just imagine the faint outline of a figure standing between the two visible objects.

The selkie, the sword, and the shifting shadow connecting them all moved toward the entrance to my prison-slash-sanctuary. The tip of the sword came through first, then the slack face of the selkie. Then a bare foot with greenish-brown skin settled on the opalescent floor.

Annabrae seemed to emerge from the water itself as she passed through the wall, solidifying as she entered the open air. A gossamer gown of translucent blue materialized with her, as though the sea itself draped her in place of clothes. She carried my sword loosely in one hand. In the other, she gripped my selkie attacker by the back of its neck.

"Finally." Annabrae released the selkie, who dropped to the floor with a wet *slap*. "I was beginning to fear we'd reach the end of your three days without incident."

I pulled my gaze away from the limp selkie to stare at Annabrae. "Heaven forbid."

She waved my sarcasm away. "Though I do apologize for my tardiness. I was monitoring your server's departure when this one attacked, which was no doubt his plan."

I glanced again at the selkie. Like the kelpies and grindylows I'd met, I'd been unable to distinguish his gender. "Is he dead?"

"Just unconscious. Though, as a traitor, his remaining life will be short. You need not fear him."

I shook my head. "That's not . . . never mind. I take it you were expecting him to attack me?"

"Not him per say, but someone, yes. Though I thought you'd acquit yourself better."

She tossed my sword onto the floor beside me. It clattered against the polished shell, making me wince. It seemed all my time straining to hear in the silence had made my ears more sensitive.

She gestured to the blade. "Beautiful craftsmanship, but not a very practical weapon for underwater combat."

"Next time, I'll be sure to bring a knife," I said dryly. *Though I doubt any weapon would matter when my limbs are pushing through water.* I eyed the sword but didn't pick it up. I was in no condition to fight, and even the small movement of sheathing the blade would require me to take pressure off my wound, which was still bleeding freely despite my best efforts. "If you knew they were coming, why would you—" I snapped my mouth closed so fast I nearly bit my tongue. I glared first at the selkie, then at Annabrae. "You were using me as bait."

"Let me see that." Annabrae knelt beside me and plucked at my fingers, trying to get at my side.

I winced as the air reached my wound and a fresh gush of blood welled out. The metallic scent of blood mixed with damp and salt reminded me of a Mayan sinkhole I'd once explored in the Yucatan.

My eyelids fluttered. Mixed with the water, it was impossible to tell how much blood I'd lost, but I was getting lightheaded. That was never a good sign.

Annabrae clucked her tongue, then set her hand against my side. The blood stopped flowing immediately, and the sting of salt in the wound eased. A numbing coldness seeped into my skin.

"You need to drink." She rose and crossed to the entrance.

I poked at the wound. It wasn't closed. It just wasn't bleeding anymore. "How did you—"

"Blood is mostly water." Annabrae dumped the contents of my freshly delivered canteen on the floor and reached a hand toward the water wall.

"I can't drink salt water."

Ignoring me, she made a strange, coaxing motion with her hand. A stream of water no thicker than my finger flowed sideways out of the wall and trickled into the thermos. When the container was full, she came back to me. "Drink this."

"I told you, I can't—"

"You will find no salt in this water. Now drink."

Suspicious, I took the offered canteen and sniffed the contents, which was pointless since the entire room smelled like salt. I tipped the liquid to my lips and took a sip. The water was cold and pure. It tasted like the most delicious nothing I'd ever swallowed. I gulped down the rest of the mug without pausing for air. Then I gasped. "Finally. I've been so thirsty."

Annabrae filled the canteen twice more before I stopped chugging the contents.

Once I'd caught my breath, I prodded the wound again. It wasn't as bad as it had first looked with the water amplifying the amount of blood. It was a clean cut that sliced along my ribs, deep enough to need stitches. Nothing my fae healing abilities couldn't handle, assuming I lived long enough, but my shirt was ruined.

I looked at the prone selkie. "Who is he?"

"A traitor."

"So you said. Why'd he try to kill me?" I narrowed my eyes at her. "And how did you know he would?"

She sighed and motioned toward my hammock, indicating that I should get comfortable.

I eyed the temperamental furniture ruefully, considering just how many times I'd tumbled out of it during my captivity so far. "I'll stay on the floor."

"Suit yourself." She knelt beside the selkie and pulled out a knife.

"Wait." I lifted a hand, but before I could do more, she'd made a small slit along the front of the selkie's throat. My outstretched hand flew to my mouth. I wasn't happy about being attacked, but that was no reason to kill a helpless person!

I blinked and studied the wound. There didn't seem to be any blood.

Annabrae gripped the selkie by the flesh on the back of its head and tugged. The seal face pulled back like a hood, revealing a pale-skinned boy of about twelve with brown freckles along his nose and cheeks. His shaggy, dirty-blond hair was dry.

My gaze traveled down the length of the boy's body. A seam had appeared just below where Annabrae had made her cut, splitting the boy's belly—or what I'd thought was his belly—down the center like a long coat. Human fingers peeked from the ends of wide, gray sleeves. A pair of leathery flippers were draped over the boy's feet like tuxedo tails.

Annabrae stared down at the boy and shook her head. "Oh, Tamin. What have you gotten yourself into?"

She dragged the limp boy over to the sloping wall of the room and peeled off the seal skin he wore like a coat.

I looked away, embarrassed by the unconscious boy's nakedness but aware that my human social conditioning was not shared by many among the fae, most of whom saw nothing wrong with walking around in the buff. "Can't you leave his clothes on?"

"I could." She tossed the skin, which now looked disturbingly like a deflated seal balloon, onto the hammock. "But this is safer."

I tipped my head toward the boy. "He's unconscious."

"For now." She crouched in front of me. "You've come to our court at a difficult time. While I'm loath to admit it, especially to someone connected with another court, there is a certain amount of unrest among my people. Some are unhappy with the current leadership." She motioned toward the boy. "Your arrival provided a means of weeding them out."

From what I'd seen, civil unrest and political backstabbing were hardly rare occurrences in any fae court. Bael seemed as concerned with plots against him being perpetrated by his own people as threats from other realms, and from what I'd seen during my time with the PTF, human governments weren't much better.

"Maybe that's just the curse of being in power," I said. "You can never make everyone happy."

She snorted.

"You still haven't explained how you knew he'd attack me."

"As a political envoy, you would have had the protection of my lord, and such protection would make you an easy target for those wishing to undermine her." She shook her head. "You were foolish to seek us with only the illusion of authority. Had I known, I would not have brought you." She straightened with a sigh. "At least you had enough intelligence to claim the Wayfarer's Clause, else the entire plan might have been ruined."

"What would have happened if I hadn't claimed it?"

She looked down at me, her expression cool and unwavering. "You would have had no protection in our court. At that point, the lord would have had to kill you herself to prevent losing face."

I swallowed the sudden lump in my throat. Fae politics were murky at times, but their results were often very clear cut. Most mistakes ended in death.

I glanced at the selkie boy. "What are you going to do with him?"

Annabrae followed my gaze. "We will learn what we can about his conspirators. Then he will be put to death for treason against the lord."

I licked my salt-crusted lips. "And me?"

She studied me in silence for a moment. "First, I must ask you a question."

"Shoot."

She shifted her weight. "Did you truly not know of the escape of the mad general?"

I looked away and took a deep breath. I needed to gain as much goodwill here as I could, but I didn't want to give away any information they didn't already have—like the fact that I was the reason Shedraziel wasn't in prison anymore. "I know she got out of the prison realm Bael trapped her in after the war, if that's what you mean."

"It's not."

Frowning, I met her gaze. "Shedraziel is in Enchantment."

She continued to watch me, then gave a slow nod. "If you truly do not know, perhaps you are not Bael's creature after all."

I bunched my fists and inhaled, preparing for a tirade on exactly what I thought about that, but Annabrae stilled me with a raised hand. "You came here to discover who deposited the garbage on your shores."

I pressed my lips together and nodded.

"You assumed, not unjustly so, that the sea fae were responsible. But you do not have the whole picture." Giving a stiff nod, she marched to the hammock and lifted the selkie skin in one hand. Then she headed for the entrance. "Come."

"What about him?" I gestured to the unconscious boy.

"Without his skin, he is as human as you. Your prison will become his." With that she stepped through the shimmering wall. She didn't dissolve into the water this time. She turned and extended her free hand. Her dark hair fanned out around her.

I double checked to make sure my injury was still sealed before retrieving my sword and rising to my feet. I was a little lightheaded, but nothing a good nap and a few more canteens of water wouldn't fix. I slid my sword back into its scabbard, which, unlike my wallet, didn't seem to mind being soaked in seawater. *Go, go magic.* Then I collected the contents of my pockets from the stone table, cast one last glance at the adolescent face of the selkie who'd come to kill me, and approached Annabrae. Taking a deep breath, I reached through the liquid wall, closed my fingers around hers, and stepped into the water. Trusting she wouldn't let me drown after saving my life, I inhaled. The cool liquid of the Undine Realm filled my lungs once more.

Annabrae did not lead me through the streets of the underwater city this time. Instead, we kept to the seaweed forest as we circled the green, blue, and purple lights that illuminated the more populated areas. After skirting the edge of the city for about five minutes, I noticed a larger structure set a little apart from the other lights. Like the city, it was composed of a multitude of corals and shells in a variety of shapes and colors, but it had a sense of cohesion about it that made it read as all one structure. It was toward that structure that Annabrae pulled me.

I didn't see a single other soul, save some of the larger shadowy shapes in the distance beyond the city. From the seemingly erratic path Annabrae took through the kelp, I wondered if she had some way of sensing other people and was avoiding them. Or maybe the kelp forest was off limits to regular folk. Or maybe it was actually the middle of what passed for night and everyone else was asleep. I had no way of knowing, but the contrast to my previous tour through town seemed too much not to be deliberate.

As we approached the large structure, the pinpricks of light that had marked it from a distance resolved into a variety of clinging plants that cast a faint glow over what could only be described as a palace. Fronds of purple and green spiraled up towering shell turrets and lined the tops of layered sea fan walls. Shelves of coral jutted into the water beneath delicate archways to create rail-less balconies. Thick fingers of multi-colored stone, coral trees dotted with leathery leaves in bright colors, and tufts of delicate grasses that danced in the current filled a stretch of black sand that separated the palace from the rest of the city like a sprawling European garden. A thick path of pearly-white crushed shells brightened by thin, iridescent-yellow fronds snaked through the garden to an archway that must have been at least twenty feet across and twice that high. Smaller arches pierced the outer shells of the palace at irregular intervals.

Rather than using any of the many arched entryways, Annabrae dragged me straight up the side of a coiling corkscrew tower of dark-brown shell and in through a window near the top.

How can they protect against intruders when people can just swim in through the windows? But then I'd often approached Bael's keep from the air; maybe this wasn't so different. Anything was possible when magic was involved.

The window led to a well-lit room that seemed much larger than its outer shell suggested. Maybe it was just a trick of the light, or maybe the space didn't follow the rules of human physics . . . wouldn't be the first time.

Like my prison, most of the furniture was carved from stone. Unlike my prison, there were many different items, including a wardrobe, coffee table, and bench, all carved in exquisite detail with a delicate sea motif. A coat of living carpet covered the floor in gently swaying white strands that tickled my ankles when I brushed against them. Plants that cast a fiery glow from the long yellow stamen and wide red petals of their flowers were placed in bouquets around the room like lit sconces.

The Undine Lord lounged in a hammock not unlike the one I'd struggled with in my prison, though hers was wider and filled with pillows and a blanket woven from colorful fibers. She sat up abruptly when we came in. "They've come then?"

Annabrae nodded, releasing my arm.

The lord sighed, sadness slackening her expression for a moment. She looked up and met my gaze. "Then it seems I am decided."

She nodded to Annabrae, who bowed low, gave me one sharp look, then melted away into the water as she had when she first left me stranded in my bubble. This time, however, she hadn't left me alone. Swallowing past the tightness in my throat, I turned back to face the Undine Lord.

She was watching me.

"I don't trust you," she said.

"Odd then that you'd let me keep my sword when we're alone and you're unarmed."

"I am never unarmed in the ocean. You breathe by my grace. Should I so choose, you would die before your sword left its sheath."

I swallowed, hating the way the salt-saturated water reinforced her threat.

"But I trust Annabrae's opinion. She would not have brought you here if she believed your intentions were malevolent." Her tentacles coiled restlessly along the edges of the hammock, twisting into the fabric. "Therefore I'm going to offer you a deal."

The seemingly constant knot in my stomach, which had eased briefly, now tightened again, constricting around my organs like a python. Deals with fae were not generally a good idea. Especially with fae who clearly didn't like you and would just as soon send your severed head as a gift to your genocidal grandfather.

"What kind of deal?"

"The kind where we both get something we want. But first there is something you must know." She shifted on the hammock and gestured to the stone bench near the coffee table.

This time I took the offered seat, swimming clumsily to the bench and sort of pulling myself down to it. I slid my fingers over a beautiful relief of sailing ships and leaping dolphins carved along the edge.

"My court is in disarray."

I jerked my gaze away from the artwork on the bench and stared at the Undine Lord. I'd never known a fae to be so blunt, especially about anything that could make them look weak.

"I would not normally share such information with an outsider," she continued as though reading my thoughts. "Especially one related to Bael, but these are not normal times. It seems I have little choice if I wish to preserve both my authority and my family."

"What's going on?"

"I'm sure you are aware that many among the fae believe we should not have compromised with the humans to end the last war between our races . . . that a clear victory one way or the other would have been a preferable out-come."

I nodded.

"More so among those of us who live close to nature—those who see themselves as caretakers. Humans disrupt the natural balance of their world with little regard for the beings who share it. You pollute the water, the air, the land. . . . There are many among the nature courts who would see the war finished if only to prevent further damage to the ecological balance of your world."

"I'll admit humans haven't been historically responsible in the way we advanced our industries, but we're trying now. We have new policies to reduce deforestation and pollution, and—"

"Bandages on an infection when what's needed is amputation."

I stiffened.

She waved a placating hand. "I am not suggesting the human race be eradicated." Her dark gaze skewered me. "That is not *our* way. But there are some, as there are in any society, who believe a positive outcome justifies any means."

My thoughts jumped to Purity, not officially condoned by the Church or PTF but a manifestation of people's wishes to return to a simpler time— a time when magic was reserved for bedtime stories, and fairy tales weren't real. "So we're looking for a group of zealous outliers."

"Several groups, in fact, but coaxed to action by a single voice. Bael's mad general has been set loose upon the world, and I fear we shall all pay a hefty price for her revenge."

I shook my head. "It can't be Shedraziel."

She continued to stare at me with those fathomless black eyes.

I shifted in my seat. I needed to know what was really going on, and one truth deserved another. "Bael gave me his word that Enchantment wouldn't move against the mortal realm for at least a year."

The gills flared on the sides of her neck. "Even Bael could not break such an oath, which means Shedraziel has severed ties with him." She shook her head. "That is not good, but I can't say I am surprised. Shedraziel has never been one for playing second fiddle."

"That sounds like you know her pretty well."

One corner of the lord's mouth quirked up. "Many centuries ago . . . Shedraziel was my sister."

Chapter 9

I STIFFENED IN MY seat and spluttered in surprise. "How can Shedraziel be your sister?" My voice cracked on the question. I coughed—or gargled—to clear my throat. "She works for Enchantment."

The lord pursed her lips and stared at me for a moment. Her expression was pinched, as though she was considering something that made her feel ill. She exhaled a stream of agitated bubbles, then jerked her head in one curt nod. "You should understand who, and what, you face." She looked out the window through which I'd entered, her gaze growing soft and distant, and said so quietly that I almost didn't hear, "Perhaps I need the reminder as well."

When she turned back to me, her calm mask would have made any poker player proud. "Shedraziel's ability to manipulate others goes well beyond military command and court intrigue. She is a siren."

I shuddered, remembering the way her voice pulled me, forcing muscles to move against my will. If not for the true name I carried and James's command to do what I must and return to him, I would have been helpless to resist her. As it was, it had been a struggle.

"I see you are familiar with the pull of her call." She rubbed one hand absently along the opposite arm, as though brushing away her own unpleasant memories. "There are few true sirens left. They were hunted by the other races, much like dragons, out of fear. That is how Shedraziel came into my life—an orphan babe whose parents had been slain because they'd crossed a line. I was only a child myself at the time. I didn't understand then the political advantages of having a siren in my service. I only knew that I was no longer alone in the nursery. I had a companion. And so we grew up together, inseparable, powerful, and destined to rule over the Undine Court side by side. At least, that was the plan."

She sighed and shifted in the hammock, her tentacles coiling in agitation. "Shedraziel came into her power young, and she was strong. Strong enough to be a lord in her own right. I didn't give that much thought at the time. Being a powerful fae myself, it seemed only natural that the sister of my heart would be extraordinary as well. But the power to bend others to one's will is quite . . . intoxicating.

"Nearly from the moment of my birth, it was known that I would be the next Undine Lord. I was given the best tutors and the best protection. My would-be subjects scraped and catered to my every wish in deference to the title I would one day hold. Shedraziel was given the same consideration, but as we grew older, I began to see a difference in the way we were treated. While all bowed and smiled where I passed, they cowered from her. Stories reached my ears of Shedraziel forcing servants to dance for her until they collapsed from exhaustion, or sing until they ran out of breath."

Her words stirred my own memories of the mock court Shedraziel had built within her prison—where kidnapped children, both fae and mortal, performed for her entertainment until their skin split and their bones broke. She'd used them till they were spent, then dined on their corpses, the cannibal queen of a nightmare world. I'd saved those I could, including Emma's younger sister, but the images . . . and the smells . . . would never leave me.

"I didn't believe those stories at first." The Undine Lord didn't seem to have noticed my reaction, absorbed as she was in her own thoughts. "Having come to me secondhand I thought them mere exaggerations—the complaints of those who resented having to serve." Her tentacles went slack, limply draping the sides of the hammock as though all the life had drained out of them. "I should have listened."

She lapsed into silence for so long that I grew antsy on the hard bench, but I didn't know what to say. The story clearly wasn't over. I chewed at the inside corner of my lip and waited for her to find words for her memories.

"One day, after a particularly harsh talking to about duty and respect from my mother, the then-lord, I locked myself in my rooms and told the servants I didn't want to be disturbed. I wasn't surprised when Shedraziel found her way to my bedside, but I was annoyed. I told her to go away. She replied only that she wanted to go for a run on the beach and wished for me to join her." The lord frowned and narrowed her eyes. "I don't particularly enjoy leaving the water. I find holding the illusion of legs to be quite uncomfortable. Still she insisted. When I rolled over with the intent to ignore her, she grew irritated. She demanded that I join her for a run on the beach. I was barely sixty years old at the time, far too young to have earned my true name. To my horror, my body rose at her command and I found myself swimming with her out my bedroom window."

The grown woman on the hammock before me seemed to shrink in on herself as she told her story.

"We swam to the shore of an island not far from the palace and climbed onto land. I tried again to say that I didn't want to play, but Shedraziel only told me to get on my mark. My body complied without consent. She told me to beat her if I could, then she gave the command to run. I was the faster in water, but Shedraziel had less trouble on legs than I and she quickly pulled ahead. But my body would not let me fall behind. She had told me to win. So

I ran faster. My muscles strained past their ability. My lungs burned, and I grew lightheaded. My vision shrank to the piece of driftwood she'd marked as our finish line, far down the beach. I ran faster than I ever had before. Faster than I'd thought myself physically capable of going. I lost all track of Shedraziel in my need to go faster, to reach that mark first.

"When I passed the driftwood plank I dropped to my hands and knees and vomited onto the sand. Then I collapsed to my side and gasped, fighting back the darkness that tugged at my consciousness as my body twisted with agonizing cramps. Shedraziel dropped to the sand beside me, laughing. She slapped my shoulder and congratulated me on a race well run, my first victory on land."

The lord's expression wrinkled into a scowl. "There on that beach I saw for the first time what Shedraziel was capable of, and it scared me. I was angry and humiliated. I was supposed to be the next Lord of the Undine Realm and I could not even hold my ground against my own playmate. I demanded that if she truly loved me she would promise never to use her ability on me again. She seemed genuinely surprised by my upset and frightened that I should think she did not love me. She swore that she would never again use her siren powers to control me. With her oath in place we returned to the palace and put that night's troubles behind us, but when I passed my first century and gained the power and protection of a true name, I was secretly relieved.

"Two more centuries passed before I ascended to the lordship, and during that time Shedraziel was my shadow, her voice in my ear, her hand at my back. When my mother returned to the water and I became lord, Shedraziel was by my side, my confidant and advisor, just as we'd dreamed as children. But as time passed, it became clear that we had different visions for the future. She was always eager for change, desperate to cast aside anything that spoke of tradition, concocting and abandoning projects faster than anyone could keep track of."

I nodded. I'd discovered that much about Shedraziel's personality when I visited the prison Bael had created to punish as well as contain her. It was a realm of stone trees that never grew with stone leaves that never fell. Eternal twilight cast a flat, even light over the unchanging landscape from no discernible source. A person could walk the circumference of that frozen world in a matter of hours and never spy a movement or hear a sound that was not their own. And because of the time settings imposed on that world, Shedraziel had been the sole inhabitant for years—a lifetime by human standards—until a few deluded fools who couldn't leave well enough alone broke her seal and whetted her appetite for entertainment. That's when kids started disappearing—stolen toys to alleviate her boredom.

"When I would not follow through on her half-baked schemes, she stopped asking for permission. Using her position as my aide, coupled with her ability to sway lesser fae, she enacted several plans without my knowledge or consent before they were either brought to my attention and shut down or abandoned due to her own waning interest. I reprimanded her when appropriate, but never more than a slap on the wrist. She always claimed her intentions were to benefit me in some way, to strengthen the Undine Realm, and I believed her. I loved her despite her many flaws and did not think for a moment that she would intentionally betray me.

"She continued to abuse her position and her power in minor ways until, inevitably, she went too far. This was at a time before human beings became widely aware of the fae, when they still imagined us to be no more than wild stories brought on by too much drink through long dark nights. Shedraziel was smitten with the mortal realm, with its ever-changing smorgasbord of sensations. Knowing that secrecy was our greatest protection, and aware of the difficulty we had adapting to the quick shifts in mortal societies, I declared that my people would not interact with humans except in dire emergency. But even the command of her lord could not stop Shedraziel from pushing boundaries. Such was her spirit.

"She would venture to known shipping routes and observe the passing vessels. Occasionally, she would lure men to the water, for I had set no rules in regard to humans who fell into the sea. From them she would hear stories of distant cities and impossible inventions, and when she had her fill she would let them drown. Sometimes others would join her on these exploits, young fae who were more curious than clever, or those too frightened to deny her when she wanted company. But the humans had advanced more quickly than we realized, and it was not long before stories of the shoals where the siren sang spread. The sailors became hunters. Her careless defiance cost three fae their lives. That was not something I could overlook."

The lord's dark gaze seemed to focus on something beyond my sight.

"After a public punishment and demotion, Shedraziel seemed to fall in line. I should have known her contrition was an act. Two years passed without incident, then she led a coup. I still don't know how many of my people turned against me willingly versus how many were swayed by Shedraziel's silver tongue, but the result was the same. The carnage was devastating."

I realized my mouth was hanging open and closed it with a soft *click*. Apparently Shedraziel had been unhinged long before the destabilizing effects of her isolation in Bael's prison.

"Even then, with the blood of my subjects on her hands, I could not kill my dearest friend, the sister of my heart. In a moment of sentimental weakness . . . I banished her instead. She fled to the Realm of Enchantment, to a lord whose tastes better suited her own, and rose to the rank of general."

She turned to face me once more, her inky stare seeming to hold me in place.

"That was not so very long ago, and there are those here at court who are not well pleased with the way things have played out under my rule."

"So the disarray you spoke of . . . you think Shedraziel is trying to overthrow you again? To take over the Undine Realm?"

"It is more complicated than that, I'm afraid. And more personal. I don't believe Shedraziel any longer holds designs on ruling a realm. Judging by her behavior, I'd say her time in Bael's prison has pushed her nature, which was far from stable at the best of times, into the realm of chaos."

"So what does she want?"

"If I had to guess, I'd say she wants to set the universe ablaze just to watch it all burn. But there are a few of us, myself included, to whom she's dedicated personal pyres. To that end, she has taken my daughter."

I stiffened, trying not to picture the faces of children in cages, starved, drugged, and half mad. I'd saved dozens. Many more had been too far gone, and who knew how many she'd devoured by the time I arrived.

"So she's taken your daughter hostage to force your hand."

"She has taken my daughter, my named heir, in order to supplant me." The webbed fingers of her hands closed into fists. "My official position has always been to keep the undine to ourselves and avoid conflict with the mortal realm, but not all share my conservative views. My daughter is young and headstrong. She does not yet understand the value of stability, and many see her as a chance for reform. Should Shedraziel manage to incite a rebellion in my daughter's name while the girl is under her control, many will flock to that banner."

She shifted her weight, sliding gracefully off the hammock. Her tentacles undulated beneath her, carrying her to the window. She rested one hand against the delicate arch and stared out. "You came here to discover who had emptied your oceans of refuse and deposited it on your beaches." She glanced back at me. "It was my father."

Rising, I moved cautiously to the window, taking a position beside her. In the distance, in the dark space between the palace and the city, shadowy hills moved. The tail I'd seen earlier was only one small part of the creature that waited in those shadows.

"True dragons are much like elementals, especially as they get older. Day-to-day concerns become too small for them to bother with most of the time. They're aware of what happens around them, but in the way a human is aware of their heart beating—it only comes into focus when something calls attention to it. Many elementals lose the power of conscious thought entirely, becoming instead a part of the natural world. Those who've chosen the path of a guardian react only when their territory is threatened, but their reactions are swift and severe. Others, like my father, choose to commit their abilities to a trusted intermediary."

She raised a hand to her throat. The curved black nails at the ends of her fingers stroked the bare skin over her collarbone. "He gave my mother a jewel, so that if she had need she could call upon him without explanation."

I looked at the lord. "You're saying there's a gem that controls that?" I pointed to the scaled curves in the distance.

"He can still be reasoned with, but the gem ensures his immediate cooperation when time is of the essence."

"Shedraziel stole it?" I guessed.

"She would not dare do so herself. Besides, not just anyone can use it. My father created the stone to protect his family and ensure our line remained lords of this realm. The stone passed from my mother to me and would have one day gone to my daughter."

A picture formed in my head as the pieces of this puzzle began to click together. "You think Shedraziel got to your daughter and persuaded her to take her inheritance early."

"And with it she instructed my father to purge your oceans of that which did not belong as a rallying call to those displeased with the status quo. By the time I reached him and was able to make him see reason, he'd finished with most of the Pacific."

"He would have kept going if you hadn't intervened?"

She nodded.

I thought of the mounds of rotting trash washed up on the Santa Monica Beach. Similar scenes had been reported along the coasts from Alaska to Chile and across the water from Russia to New Zealand. That was just the litter from *one* of the world's oceans.

"What will you tell the PTF when you return?" She didn't look at me when she asked the question, but I got the impression she was studying me closely as I considered my response.

I had come to find out who was responsible and report back. *But who is responsible?* I turned the question over in my head. The dragon had physically dumped the waste, but the lord's daughter had given the command, and Shedraziel may have been controlling the girl. I shook my head. "You mentioned a deal. I assume you didn't tell me your story just to send me on my way."

"Indeed." Turning away from the window, she clasped her hands behind her back and paced the room, if such a smooth motion could be called pacing. "Shedraziel is keeping my daughter, and I presume my father's necklace, beyond my reach. I want you to retrieve them for me."

"Where are they?"

She shook her head. "Somewhere without water. Otherwise, I would have found her by now."

Like maybe an artificially expanded desert guarded by griffins? I nearly bobbed onto my toes as the idea took root. "And in exchange you'll clear the beaches?"

She pulled up short. "The mess humans have made is their own. I will not help return that pollution to the sea."

"Then what do—"

"If you return both my daughter and my necklace, I will aid you in quelling Shedraziel." She leveled her black stare at me. "Believe me when I tell you that you will need my help."

"If you can take her out, why do you need me?"

She turned away. "As I said, she is somewhere without water. That makes finding her difficult, and the outcome a less than sure thing. Every moment my daughter and the necklace remain missing, the turmoil in my realm grows stronger. As your attempted assassination proves, there are dissidents seeking to undermine me, to draw support to the banner of reform. I cannot allow such opposition to spread, and a prolonged search for a target as elusive as Shedraziel would spread my attention too thin."

"So I find your daughter and, by extension, Shedraziel, who you presume is holding her, then you deliver the final blow."

"We both get what we want."

I chewed my lower lip, studying all the angles. "What actual proof do you have that Shedraziel is behind this? That your daughter isn't just trying to usurp your throne on her own?"

"None but rumors and intuition, but this unrest is not limited to my realm. I do not believe the forest folk are responsible for the human disappearances in Europe any more than I am for the tsunami of litter on your shores. Someone is stirring up trouble for trouble's sake, and Shedraziel is the only fae I know who would take joy in doing so."

I would have paced the length of the room if not for the awkwardness of my underwater movements. So I drifted instead, twitching my arms to keep in place as I bobbed in the gentle currents constantly swirling around me. "Okay." I swam over to the lord. "You've got a tentative deal. I'll report what I've learned to the PTF and see if I can confirm Shedraziel's involvement. If what you've told me checks out, I'll look for your daughter."

She glided to a vanity table hewn from dark stone, the mirror draped with glowing pink strands, and opened an ivory jewelry box. The box was open for only a moment, just long enough for her to pluck something out. When she returned to me she extended her hand. Pinched between her thumb and forefinger was a large yellow-white pearl. "When you find my daughter, smash this pearl at her feet. I will take care of the rest."

I plucked the pearl from her grip and brought it close enough to examine. It seemed like a perfectly ordinary pearl to me. I tucked it into my pocket.

"Annabrae will return shortly to lead you back to the surface. Until then, make yourself comfortable." The Undine Lord rose with a powerful surge of her tentacles and a cloud of bubbles that carried her through a hole in the ceiling. When the froth of her passing dissipated and she didn't reappear, I glanced around the room.

Make myself comfortable, huh?

No guards, no doors, and seemingly unrestricted access to snoop to my heart's content.

Yeah, right.

I didn't believe for a minute that the lord wasn't aware of everything I was doing in that room. Hell, maybe she could track me across the whole ocean. The thought made my skin itch, as though invisible watchers stared at me from the shadows. Regardless, she'd given me her trust. I wasn't going to break that by snooping. Turning back to the window I looked out over the undersea city and waited for my ride.

THE TRIP BACK from the Undine Realm was similar to the trip there. Annabrae arrived through the hole in the ceiling through which the lord had ascended, startling me near out of my skin as I scanned the horizon for her approach. Instructing me to relax, she pressed herself against my back and wrapped her arms around my ribs. I looked down and saw nothing but water squeezing me tight. Then I was swept off my feet.

Again I was dragged backward, which this time meant I could see the city shrinking away from me. The black sand streets vanished first, followed by the colorful coral and smaller buildings. The glow of the bioluminescent plants winked out in waves. The white spirals of the palace towers were last to vanish into the murk. Then there was nothing but the dark water rushing past and the constant pull toward the surface.

There was an instant of bone-jarring shock when I passed between realms. The sensation of being momentarily turned inside out then snapping back into place that accompanied portal travel must have been masked on my last trip by the panic of drowning. Then the darkness gave way, gradually at first, so I didn't even notice the change until ripples of light danced around me.

The pressure around my chest suddenly vanished. I exhaled. My next breath seared my sinuses and seized my lungs. I kicked for the surface.

My face broke through to a slap of warm air. My flailing arms splashed droplets into my face as I gasped, choked, and tried to keep my head above water. When my racking coughs subsided to something more manageable, I paddled in a circle. The Santa Monica Pier jutted into the water slightly to my right. The beach ahead was a hundred yards off. There was no sign of

Annabrae. Facing the open water one last time, I shouted over the gentle waves, "You could have warned me!" Then I turned my back on the horizon and swam to shore.

My arms were noodles by the time my bare toes scraped the ground. I was still coughing with every other breath. My lungs ached. My throat and sinuses were raw. I crawled onto dry sand on my hands and knees, but inches from my fingertips the high tide line was marked by rubbish—not something I wanted to wade through.

I sat for a moment to catch my breath and scanned the pier. Crowds of people walked its length. The Ferris wheel turned a lazy circle, colored lights flashing along its spokes. Several shapes stood looking over the rail at the far end, but I couldn't make out Kai or Emma. Shading my eyes with one hand, I squinted at the eastern horizon. The sun wasn't much higher than when we'd arrived at the pier. Since time flowed differently in each realm, I guessed I'd only been gone for less than an hour despite my days of captivity in the Undine Court.

Heaving to my feet, I prodded the wound on my side. It was sore, but I was pleased to see whatever magic Annabrae had used to stop my blood from seeping out was still working. My shirt had been sheared through on the right side, leaving water-logged, blood-stained rags to sway and slap around the injury. Between that and my missing shoes I looked like a shark attack survivor—not great for avoiding notice on a crowded boardwalk. Checking my pockets I found my keys and wallet still in place. The pearl the Undine Lord had given me was also present. I pulled my cell phone out of my back pocket and pressed the power button.

Nothing happened.

There goes another one, I thought ruefully as I tucked the useless brick away. *Probably best I give my report in person anyway.*

"Alex!"

I spun toward the sound of Kai's voice. He and Emma were descending a set of steps that led from the pier down to the beach. I trotted toward them, keeping to the surf.

Kai paused at the base of the pier. Any farther and he'd have to pick his way over garbage. Not a problem for him, but Emma was clinging to his elbow.

"Wait there," I called.

I stepped delicately into the litter, cautious of any glass or metal that could cut my bare feet. Travel over the garbage was slow, made slower because my footing would suddenly give way when a clump of half-rotted sludge slid under my weight. The smell that rose off the trash made me gag. After what felt much longer than the few minutes I actually spent traversing the expanse of ocean litter, I reached the warm sand at the base of the pier steps.

"You're injured." Kai took a step toward me.

I lifted a hand to stop him. "I'm fine. How long have I been gone?"

"About twenty minutes," he said. "As soon as you fell, Annabrae melted off the end of the pier. I would have jumped after, but. . . ." He cast a side-long glance at Emma.

"You did the right thing. At the speed I was whisked away, you never would have caught up."

He bunched his fists. "I should have been with you."

"Done is done. No point overthinking it now."

"What happened down there?" Emma asked. "Kai said you never came up after you fell."

"Annabrae took me to the Undine Realm."

"Did they take responsibility for the garbage?"

I glanced at the trash I'd just climbed over. "Not exactly."

"How did you get injured?" Kai's voice was tight with barely checked anger.

"That's a long story, one I'll tell you on the way back to the hotel, but first I need a new shirt."

Emma's eyebrows rose. "What happened to your shirt?"

"Wait here." Kai took Emma's hand off his arm then skipped up the steps two at a time and ducked into the nearest souvenir shop.

Emma traced her hand up my arm, groping over my wet face and hair, then down to my tattered shirt. Her frown grew when she found the torn edges of fabric. "This is so frustrating. I didn't even know you'd fallen until Kai told me. I couldn't help look for you. Then when Kai said he spotted you out in the water, he couldn't get to you very quickly because he had me slowing him down." She shook her head. "You were right, Alex. I should have stayed home."

I chewed my bottom lip, struggling to find words. I'd agreed to let her come so she didn't have to sit around the house feeling useless, but how was this any better? Thinking it over I said, "I can't imagine how this situation would have played out any differently if you could see. Can you?"

Her crestfallen expression smoothed a little as she considered my words.

"Kai had full use of his faculties and couldn't prevent me getting shoved over the rail. Hell, for that matter, you might as well blame me for being caught off guard. And once I came up, there was nothing to do but wait for me to swim ashore. You moving faster wouldn't have made any difference." I squeezed her hand in mine. "There's no sense in pointing fingers when we're all in this together."

Her lips were pressed in a tight line, but at least she no longer looked as if she was going to cry.

Kai came down the pier steps and thrust a shopping bag into my arms.

Inside was a loose, tie-dyed T-shirt advertising my love for the Santa Monica Pier, a pair of olive-green Bermuda shorts, and pink flip-flops. I looked up from his purchase and smiled. "Not exactly my style, but I'll take it."

"It's what was available, though considering the price, you'd think they were spun from pure gold."

"Pretty standard for a tourist trap." I ducked under the pier to change out of my stained, wet clothes. At least the stomach-turning condition of the beach meant there weren't many prying eyes. The items Kai had bought were baggy but comfortable and much better than the alternative. After carefully transferring the contents of my pockets, I stuffed my old clothes into the bag, tied it closed, and tucked it under my arm. "Let's grab a cab back to the hotel. We've got plans to make."

I SHIFTED IN THE wide seat of the private jet Director Harris had put at my disposal and stared out the clear, rounded rectangle set in the curved wall. The fields of eastern Colorado were a patchwork quilt in shades of brown below. Colored dots moved along black ribbons, growing denser near towns then petering out again as we crossed the countryside. The plane banked left, and the fasten seat belt sign flashed on with a *ding*. The pilot's voice sounded over the intercom. "We're on final approach, Ms. Blackwood. A chopper is prepped and waiting to take you to the PTF building."

I glanced across the aisle at Emma. She sat with her face tipped up, staring at the ceiling, looking at nothing. The rest of the seats were empty.

Kai should be arriving at the Sequoia Reservation right about now.

As though reading my thoughts, Emma asked, "Do you think Kai will be all right?"

I shifted my gaze back to the window. "He'll be fine."

"He didn't seem too happy about going back to Enchantment so soon after renouncing his position as a knight."

A tight pang hitched in my chest. Kai had given up his position in Bael's court to stay in the mortal realm. Sending him back, even as a messenger, had to be rubbing salt in that wound. "There was no other choice. We need to verify whether Shedraziel has really broken ties with Bael, and I need to tell Harris about the Undine Lord's proposal, check in with Chase, and start planning the mission to Nevada. There wasn't time for me to make the trip to Enchantment myself."

"Do you really think Bael will see him?"

"If not Bael, he should at least be able to reach Rhoana. If he can convince Bael's captain, she'll see that he gets an audience."

"What if Bael doesn't agree to help?"

I sighed. The three of us had gone over every argument we could think of to convince Bael it was his responsibility to deal with Shedraziel if she was wreaking havoc in the mortal realm. Even if she'd broken ties with him, the fact that she'd been in his charge when we made our deal meant that I could still hold him accountable for her actions. If he didn't want to risk breaking his word, he'd have to help me stop her. Or so I hoped.

"We'll cross that bridge when we get there."

The wheels of our plane touched down with a light bump, and we taxied to the waiting helicopter. A short walk across the tarmac saw Emma and me strapped into a second, less comfortable pair of seats and fitted with headsets. Moments later, we were back in the air, soaring over an I-70 traffic jam baking under the noonday sun.

I could get used to this.

I turned to Emma and said into my microphone, "Do you think—" I gasped as a wave of shock, frustration, worry, elation, confusion, and anger slammed into me.

"What's the matter?" My headphones gave Emma's voice a staticky echo. Her face was turned toward me. Wrinkles of concern scrunched her forehead.

I took a shaky breath. "I . . . I don't know." James was still miles away. For his emotions to slam through our link like that. . . . "Something's happening at the PTF facility. Something bad."

I tried to call back along our connection, to get a clearer picture, but all I found were the ripples of that first burst of emotion.

I whipped out the replacement phone I'd spent a small fortune on at the airport kiosk in Santa Monica and called Harris. There was no answer. Neither did I manage to reach David, Marc, Garrett, or anyone else whose number I could remember. My chest grew tighter with each unanswered call until I could barely breathe. The muddle of James's emotions continued to bombard me. I got the sense he was too busy to even notice my attempts to connect with him. I gripped Emma's arm. "I don't know what we're flying into. You should stay in the helicopter till we know it's safe."

Emma's mouth twisted into a grimace. She gave one stiff, downward nod.

As the helicopter soared over the sunlit city of Denver, the feelings I was getting from James grew stronger. I started getting flashes of images. People. Guns. Blood.

What's happening? I screamed the question over and over in my head as forcefully as I could.

Attack. The word popped into my mind carrying the flavor of James's voice and a sense of exhaustion.

I'm coming. Moving awkwardly in the cramped compartment, I pulled my sword belt out of our luggage and strapped it on. James had the speed, strength, and stamina of a vampire. Anything that could wear him out was not something I wanted to face unarmed. I swallowed the bile snaking up the back of my throat.

The helicopter banked around the northern edge of the city, and the PTF building came into view. The four-story structure stood at the center of a scene of chaos. Bodies tumbled together on the surrounding grounds and parking lot like ants boiling out of a kicked hill, too numerous and frantic to make out clearly from this height. It looked as though dozens, if not hundreds, of people were engaged in an all-out war on the PTF lawn. Cars had been overturned in the parking lot. A few unmoving bodies lay around the perimeter. The densest fighting seemed to be centered on the area just in front of the main entrance. Sunlight glinted off the upper windows of the atrium, momentarily blinding me as we came in for our landing.

The helicopter touched down. I ripped off my headset and was out the door before the rotor even slowed. The wind from the spinning blades flattened my hair and clothes. Goose bumps sprang out over my skin. I gave silent thanks that I'd taken the time to change out of my California beachwear at the hotel before hopping on the plane home. Unfortunately, I hadn't packed a spare pair of shoes, so it was in my new pink flip-flops that I raced across the roof.

I leaned out over the edge. The shapes on the lawn were clearer now, though still too piled together to make out distinctly. Some of the combatants wore the uniforms of security guards. Some were clearly city police. Some wore normal clothes. Most disturbing were the figures with fur who moved on four legs. The werewolves had shifted. Many were setting upon the humans around them like beasts gone mad, but I also saw wolves fighting wolves.

"What the hell is going on?"

Tracing the thread of my connection to James, I shifted my focus to the edge of the parking lot where a black SUV had been tipped onto its side. Several wolves seemed to be targeting the vehicle, but they were being held back by a blur that solidified only long enough to send one reeling before moving to the next. James. He was defending the car, but the wolves were stronger and there were more of them. He couldn't hold them back forever.

I'm here. I sent the message across our link.

James's relief was mixed with worry, and his focus quickly shifted away from me again. Protecting the people in that car was taking everything he had.

As the last hum of the helicopter engine died, the sounds of the battle below took its place—gunshots, shouts, screams. Another sound floated on the wind, just at the edge of hearing. I cocked my head to listen. The scene below me slipped out of focus. The sounds became muffled, as if I'd stuffed cotton in my ears.

The new noise was like the memory of a song from somewhere in my past. I could almost recognize the rhythm but couldn't recall the words. Something about it made me afraid. Then a burning hatred flooded me, chasing back the biting cold of the wind. A face appeared in my mind—tanned skin, silver hair, and a wide, white smile. Anderson.

I need to kill Governor Anderson. Everything will be better once he's dead. Everyone will be safe.

My fingers cramped around the hilt of my sword. The skin on my right arm tingled.

This isn't right.

There was a scream behind me.

I looked back. Emma was on her knees, crawling across the roof with one hand pressed to her temple. She seemed to be sobbing, or choking. Her shoulders jerked in time with her ragged breaths, but she kept inching forward.

The blind hatred, the drive to find and kill Anderson, faded slightly when I saw her—enough to let me register that something was very, very wrong.

Then I realized why the noise sounded so familiar. It *was* a song I'd heard before. A song that coursed through my blood and my bones. A song that drove away thought and logic and left only blind obedience. The wind was carrying the song of a siren.

I guess that answers the question of whether or not Shedraziel has left Enchantment.

Chapter 10

TAKING A DEEP breath, I closed my eyes and focused on the core of my being, the true name I'd gained in the fae naming trial that protected me from the type of subconscious manipulation Shedraziel was trying to exert. My head cleared. The voice was still there, whispering, but now that I knew what was happening it was easier to resist. And the pull wasn't even a fraction as strong as it had been last time. I opened my eyes and looked over the battlefield. Shedraziel wasn't calling to me specifically. Her attention was spread over all the fighting bodies.

I returned to Emma, who'd stopped moving about halfway between me and the helicopter, and dropped to one knee beside her. She was gasping and shaking. Sweat stood out on her brow, glinting in the afternoon sun.

I grabbed her shoulders. "Emma!" I gave her a shake. "Snap out of it."

Emma blinked, then blinked again. Her eyes widened. She tilted her head and looked around as though she were searching for something. "What . . . ?"

I exhaled, both relieved and surprised that I'd been able to wake her. "Shedraziel." The name came out as a growl through my clenched teeth. "She's enchanting everyone in this whole area, making them fight each other."

Emma's gaze swung in my direction, lifting to my face almost as if she could see me, but her eyes remained unfocused. Her mouth was open in a startled "oh."

I squeezed her shoulders. I didn't want to leave her alone and confused, but I had to get down to the chaos below. Shedraziel would most likely be right in the middle of it, enjoying her handiwork. If she was casting over the whole area rather than targeting specific people, the enchantment might shatter if I took her out.

"I have to go. Stay here until I get back." I started to rise, but her hand darted out and grabbed my forearm, halting me.

I looked at the point of contact.

So did she.

"Emma . . . can you . . . ?"

"Something happened." She looked into my face. Again I got the impression she was seeing me, but her eyes were still unfocused. "When she took control of me, just for a second, she tried to access my magic."

My mouth went dry. I searched her milky gaze. "Did you use magic?"

She cocked her head, as though about to shake it, but stopped. "I'm not sure. There's something. Not like before, but. . . ." Again she looked around. "The voice in my head told me to channel my magic, and I couldn't *not* do it. Even knowing it wouldn't work, I tried." She released me and rubbed her hands over her arms. "It hurt, like my whole body was being torn apart, but I kept pulling, trying to reach the energy I knew was there. Then the voice went away. Or faded, I guess. It's not gone entirely, but I got the impression it moved on when it didn't get what it wanted from me. When I opened my eyes just now . . . I could see."

I sat back on my heels. Sounds from the battle raging below drifted up to us. I needed to get down there, but I was too stunned to move.

"That's not right." She frowned. "I'm not seeing. I'm—" She flapped one hand as though she could pull the word from the air. "I don't know. Feeling, maybe? But I know where you are." She turned her cataract stare to the east. "And I know where Shedraziel is."

"You. . . ." I followed the direction of her gaze, squinting. "How?"

"That's where the threads lead."

I looked from Emma to the battle and back. "What threads?"

She shook her head again. "A bunch of the people below have them. Not all. They shine like glowing ribbons in the fog, and they all lead back to the same spot." She looked at me, then set a hand against my chest. "You have one, too, but yours goes somewhere else."

I looked down, half expecting to see a gossamer ribbon trailing out of my chest. "Where?"

She turned her head as though following a cord, then pointed to the place where James was fighting.

I licked my lips and swallowed past the lump in my throat. If Emma could "see" the connection between James and me, maybe she really was seeing the bindings Shedraziel was using to control people. I looked to the east. "Shedraziel's over there?"

Emma's mouth drew into a stiff line. "She's moving." She pointed to the southeast. Her finger moved as though tracking.

I shifted my focus, softening my gaze to the point where I could sometimes see the Rift energy that swirled beneath the surface of the world—the energy practitioners like Emma and myself tapped into to cast magic. Gray clouds rolled across the battlefield. The indistinct hint of faces peered out of the darkest folds—demons watching the carnage, looking for an opening. But I could find no trace of the ribbons Emma claimed to see.

I looked again at the fighting figures that spanned the ground between the PTF building and where Emma's finger was pointing. It would be hard to pass through that chaos even alone. Protecting Emma as well. . . . I exhaled a frustrated sigh. But the sooner I got to Shedraziel, the sooner the fighting would stop. I wrapped my left hand around Emma's right. "It'll be dangerous, but I need you to guide me to her."

What little color there was in Emma's cheeks drained away. She took several deep breaths then gave a stiff nod.

I stood up, pulled her to her feet, then drew my sword and headed for the roof-access door.

The upper floors of the PTF building were deserted. With the thick walls dampening the sounds of the battle outside, walking down the hallways was like walking through a ghost town. We moved as fast as I dared, but every sound made me jump, and my skin itched with nervous anticipation every time I rounded a corner. When we reached ground level, everything changed. The hallway just beyond the stairwell was smeared with blood. Gouges had been taken out of the walls. Some in the shape of bullet holes, others made from claws. Two security officers were dead on the ground. The door at the far end had been ripped off its hinges.

My mouth went dry, but I forced myself to move, to take first one step and then another down that hall. I stepped over the limp arm of one of the dead guards sprawled on the floor. I kept my gaze forward, trying not to see the young woman's face, and thought, *I have to put an end to this. Deals and prisons don't work on Shedraziel. Nothing short of death is going to stop her.*

Half a year ago, I would never even have considered killing someone, no matter the circumstances. At this point I'd been responsible for more deaths, either directly or indirectly, than I cared to think about. The faces of those whose lives I'd ended with my own hands haunted my dreams nearly every night. And yet I wouldn't change what I'd done. I didn't think I'd lose much sleep adding Shedraziel to that list.

Emma tripped and stumbled into my side.

When we both regained our balance, I turned to her. "Exactly how much can you see?"

"Not whatever that was."

I glanced down at the corpse and decided Emma didn't need to know what she'd stepped on. "Can you see the hallway we're in?"

She wobbled her hand back and forth. "You know how when practitioners channel energy we can sort of see into the Rift?"

I nodded. "It's like a swirling fog overlays everything, draining the color and making the world hazy around me."

"This is kind of like that, like I'm walking through the fog of the Rift, but certain spots are brighter or darker. The space around us right now is pretty dark, but you . . . glow. Oh!" Her face lit, and she tapped my arm excitedly. "It's like those splotchy baby pictures you get with an ultrasound, where you can see the image but you're not a hundred percent sure what you're looking at."

"And Shedraziel's threads? Those glow?"

She nodded. "Almost as bright as you."

I frowned. I'd only ever peeked into the Rift, as all practitioners did when drawing on the energy to cast magic. I couldn't imagine walking through a whole world like that. And if she really was seeing into the Rift, what about the demons who lived there? Could she see them as well? Could they see her? I shivered; we didn't have time to unravel this mystery right now. "Let's keep moving."

The main lobby was in shambles. The lower window frames of the atrium stood empty, their glass spread in shattered shards across the ground. The back wall was pockmarked with dozens of large-caliber bullet holes. Fabric and stuffing were scattered around the plush chairs that used to decorate one side of the lobby. The reception desk ended in splintered wood and granite gravel.

"Be careful of your footing. There's a lot of debris." I led Emma slowly across the decimated lobby.

Beyond the blown-out walls, I could finally make out the details of the fight in front of the building. PTF security guards like the two I'd seen in the hall lay all over. Interspersed among them were men and women in everyday clothes. Broken signs and posters smeared with blood littered the ground. I recognized the faces of some of the protesters I'd had to walk past every day since I took the co-director position. Some of the injured lay unmoving. Others groaned and writhed. A few were trying to drag themselves to safety. Everyone was covered in blood, and in some places dismembered limbs or unidentifiable chunks of flesh littered the ground.

Upright combatants trampled those underfoot as they continued to fight. A group of ten or so people circled a werewolf with dappled-gray fur. The werewolf was limping slightly, favoring its back leg, but the injury wasn't enough to drop him. It spun and snapped at the nearest humans, who seemed to have run out of bullets and were now doing their best with belt knives and bare hands. Similar pockets of conflict were playing out all over the front lawn. The scents of blood, sweat, and discharged guns filled the air. Grunts, growls, shouts, and screams overlaid each other into a confusion of noise that blanketed the area and made individual sounds difficult to pinpoint. Under it all, the notes of Shedraziel's spell drifted across the battlefield. Bullets rained from the nearby street where police officers had formed a perimeter, but the close combat made the projectiles as likely to hit friends as foes, if anyone even knew which was which.

Squeezing my hilt so tight that my fingers began to tingle, I crouched low and dragged Emma toward the river, aiming for the cover of the trees.

After half a dozen steps, Emma gasped and pulled me to an abrupt stop.

A man with crazed eyes that showed white all the way around jumped out of the bush I'd been heading for. He charged straight toward me, teeth bared like a wild animal.

I reacted on instinct, slashing a backhand arc across the man's chest. I hadn't put much force behind the blow, but the man's momentum carried him into my blade and the sword sliced deep through fabric and flesh. He toppled backward with a howl, both hands flying to his chest as though he could hold the wound closed.

I stumbled back a step, bumping into Emma. The last time I'd been in a fight like this, I'd known who my enemy was. It had been scary and exhausting, but whether with magic or metal, my attacks had been justified. The man I'd just dropped wore the uniform of a PTF security guard. He wasn't an enemy. The people fighting on both sides of this conflict were victims of Shedraziel's song.

Grabbing Emma's wrist I dragged her away from the wounded man. Unfortunately, that took us closer to the heart of the battle. We skirted a cluster of people, humans by the look of them, all fighting tooth and nail like gladiators vying for their freedom. I stumbled several times as I picked my way over fallen bodies. I didn't dare slow to determine whether or not any of them were still alive. Emma kept pace surprisingly well.

"I think I'm getting the hang of this," she said as she avoided the grasping hand of a man with a gash across his face.

The densest fighting seemed to be centered around James and the overturned SUV he guarded. I wanted to go to his side, but I wouldn't be much help against the six or so werewolves he was keeping at bay. Better to take out the source of this chaos and hope the werewolves came to their senses before James or whoever he was guarding was seriously hurt.

I scanned the faces of the nearest humans. I recognized many from the halls and offices of the PTF, but I didn't see David, Garrett, Harris, or Weatherly. David would be out there somewhere, leading the security force. I sent a silent prayer that he would survive and hoped the rest had gotten to safety, even Weatherly. I didn't want to consider the fallout if an out-of-control paranatural killed a PTF officer.

"This way." Emma tugged my arm and pointed slightly to the south. "I think she's just past those trees."

I looked at the trees she was pointing to and swallowed my surprise that she could see them . . . or sense them, or whatever she was doing.

Nodding, I tightened my grip on her hand and changed direction.

We'd only taken a handful of steps when a werewolf slammed into my side.

Emma yelped as my hand was pulled from hers. All three of us fell, but we rolled in different directions when we hit the ground. I barely made it up to one knee before the werewolf was on me again.

My back hit the ground with enough force to knock the air from my lungs, but as I was falling I thrust with my sword, putting my full strength behind the blow. There was no point holding back against a werewolf, even if they were a friend. My blade sank into the wolf's side, but the impact barely slowed it down. Curved teeth the length of my fingers sank toward my neck.

Memories of another werewolf standing over me—another set of fangs ripping into me—swarmed my vision, threatening to plunge me into panic.

I'm not the same person I was then.

Drawing on the energy around me, I released my sword and pressed my open palm against the werewolf's chest. Its fur was thick and coarse. Its ribs heaved beneath my hand. The points of its teeth made contact with my shoulder, sinking into the flesh above and below my collarbone.

Closing my eyes to keep the panic at bay, I focused the gathered energy, filtering it through my body, refining it into what I needed. I exhaled.

The werewolf's teeth dragged across my skin as its weight lifted off me. Luckily, it hadn't had time to fully close its jaws.

I opened my eyes in time to see the wolf hit the ground a few feet away. The fur on the underside of its chest was blackened. Tendrils of smoke curled off it. The acrid smell of burnt hair filled the air. But the werewolf was already climbing to its feet. Even a point-blank fireball wasn't enough to keep it down for long.

I managed to sit up and clamped a hand over the seeping cuts on my collarbone. *There goes another shirt.*

My sword protruded from the wolf's side, buried nearly to the hilt. With a groan and a crack like the snapping of bones, the fur on the werewolf's front paw peeled back, its claws shrank, and the pads of its foot grew into human fingers. The transformation lasted only long enough for him to grab the sword and pull it free, then the shape of the wolf rolled back into place. In that moment, one side of the wolf's face had reverted enough for me to recognize the man beneath. *Faolan.*

My blade clattered to the ground.

Faolan took a deep breath, perhaps testing the damage done to his side. Then his cloudy-blue gaze settled on me. His muscles bunched, preparing to spring.

I shifted my weight, cradling my injured arm. Blood seeped down my chest, staining my shirt and cooling my skin. I started drawing power again. I didn't want to hurt Faolan, but I couldn't afford to be stopped here.

Faolan launched toward me with one powerful thrust of his legs.

I focused the energy building inside me into my right hand.

A blur of tawny-brown fur slammed into Faolan from the side, knocking him off course. My static bolt arced harmlessly past. Two werewolves hit the ground a few feet to my left. The newcomer was about the same size as Faolan but more lean. Sarah was one of the few werewolves I could easily recognize in her wolf form.

Faolan twisted to snap at Sarah. His jaw closed around her foreleg, but her teeth were already locked on his neck. They rolled and snapped, grunting and whining as they tumbled across the ground.

So maybe some *of the werewolves managed to keep their heads. But why Sarah and not Faolan? He's the most even-tempered wolf I've ever met.* I shook my head.

I was tempted to stay and help Sarah—the fight seemed too evenly matched to call—but my goal lay ahead.

"Emma," I hissed.

Her attention jerked from the fighting werewolves to me. She started crawling in my direction, feeling her way over the uneven ground and sprawled bodies.

I stood up and noticed I'd lost one of my flip-flops. Rather than look for it, I kicked the other off, then went to retrieve my sword. The blade was smeared with blood.

A shadow passed overhead, too fast to be a cloud. I glanced at the clear blue sky, shielding my eyes against the sun. A shimmer of light like heat waves over a summer street rippled across the air.

"Oh my god." Emma was crouched by my leg, staring up at the sky. Her milky gaze traveled in circles, following the shimmer above. "What is . . . tha . . .?" Her eyes rolled back, and her eyelids fluttered closed. She toppled backward and lay still.

Combatants dropped like stones around me. PTF security guards, police officers, civilians caught in the crossfire—they all dropped. Sarah and Faolan continued to struggle, but they shook their heads as though fighting off sleep, and their movements were sluggish. The werewolf I'd seen surrounded by humans near the entrance took two unsteady steps, swayed, and toppled over.

I glanced toward the overturned SUV. James was still fighting, but he was moving slow enough now for me to see him clearly. His chest was bare and smeared with blood from already-sealed gashes. He wore the loose, blue cotton pants given to all potentials during testing. He must have been in the middle of his test when the fight broke out. He slammed his fist into the jaw of a black wolf hard enough to make me wince. The wolf staggered back but didn't fall. Whatever was affecting the humans wasn't quite enough to stop the werewolves in their tracks.

A series of gunshots rang out. I dropped low and looked around. The shots had come from the trees Emma had been leading me toward. Shapes moved among the bare branches. A dozen or so people were still on their feet. From the angle of their guns, they weren't shooting at me. They were aiming up.

I checked Emma's pulse—slow and steady. She seemed to be asleep.

Sheathing my sword and keeping low, I scurried toward the line of trees. The shooters continued to fire round after round into the sky, never so much as glancing in my direction.

I slipped into the trees and circled behind the gun-happy humans. Nestled near the Fifteenth Street underpass were the semi-permanent shanties and colored tents of the refugee community. The slaughter here was every bit as bad as what I'd seen on the PTF lawn, made all the worse by the fact that none of these people wore uniforms. The bodies of adults and children alike littered the ground. Blood-matted hair and shredded winter coats draped limp forms that stared with vacant eyes. The light of the afternoon sun shining on their corpses brought no warmth.

Standing in the middle of the massacred residents was Shedraziel. She looked almost exactly as she had the last time I'd seen her. Swaths of purple silk draped her cerulean skin. A thin sword hung in a jeweled scabbard at her waist. Her long hair, which faded from indigo to teal, was twisted and pinned into intricate plaits. Her sea-green eyes were focused on the sky.

Crouching low in the winter-bare bushes, I began channeling energy. Even without the ability to control me from a distance, Shedraziel was not an opponent to take lightly. She had centuries of experience with war. Ideally, I needed to take her out in a single shot. I considered and discarded several spells as I continued to gather energy. Practitioner magic could theoretically do anything the caster could imagine, but the more complex a spell was, the harder it was to picture clearly and the greater chance it would backfire or fall apart. That's why most practitioners stuck to the basics, especially in combat—elemental manipulation, projectiles, shields.

Shaping the magic into projectile spikes seemed like my best bet. They'd be fast, hard to see, and could do a lot of damage. I twisted and compressed the magic within me. As I drew more energy, the gray clouds of the Rift crept into my vision like tendrils of fog, but the demons I knew lurked there remained hidden. They hadn't bothered me much since I'd learned to filter the energy I drew, making it nearly impossible for them to taint the stream enough to possess me. That and the natural resilience provided by my fae nature seemed to be enough to keep the residents of the Rift at bay.

When I had three magic javelins, each two feet long and tapered to a needle point, hovering in the space between my hands, I focused my gaze like a targeting laser on the center of Shedraziel's chest. With luck, one would pierce her heart and this fight would be over.

A shriek unlike any I'd ever heard filled the air, seeming to come from all directions at once. My muscles tensed. My teeth clenched. My nerves were set on edge.

"Yes!" Shedraziel raised her arms in triumph.

The steady gunshots of the nearby humans cut off.

The muffled *thump* of a large impact sounded not far away, but I refused to look. My attention was tunneled on Shedraziel. I took a steadying breath and exhaled, just as David had taught me to do when aiming a gun. Then I pictured the result I wanted as clearly as I could and let my invisible weapons fly.

The first javelin found its mark. Shedraziel's eyes went wide and she staggered back, but she was fast to recover. The second and third were swept aside by strips of fabric from her dress that seemed to flow around her in defiance of gravity.

Shedraziel glared at the bushes behind which I crouched.

"*Tsk, tsk,* Alex. That wasn't very sporting." She wrapped one hand around the magically condensed air impaling her and gave a stiff tug. My javelin pulled free. The tip was coated red. She let the weapon fall.

I released the spell. The bloodied javelin and its two companions dissipated back into the ether before it hit the ground.

Shedraziel straightened and took a deep breath, puffing her chest. The bleeding seemed to have stopped already, though a long streak of crimson stained her abdomen.

So much for ending this quickly.

"Why don't you come out so we can speak face to face?"

I wrapped my hand around my sword hilt. I was a mediocre swordsman at best. Shedraziel was a seasoned soldier with hundreds if not thousands of kills under her belt.

"Don't make me ask again." Shedraziel waved a lazy hand toward the humans who were no longer firing into the sky. I expected them to turn their guns on my hiding place, but to my horror, each placed a hot barrel against their own head.

"All right," I shouted. I stood and faced Shedraziel with as much dignity as I could muster. Part of me still expected to be riddled with bullets at any second.

Shedraziel smirked. "Closer." Then her gaze shifted to the sword on my hip. "Leave that there."

I gritted my teeth, but pulled the sword free and dropped it to the ground as I stepped forward out of the bushes. Every fiber of my being screamed that I shouldn't obey her. I didn't have to obey her. She couldn't control me.

But she can control them. My gaze flickered to the figures in the trees. Men and women in PTF security guard uniforms. My breath caught as I recognized David among them, his expression blank, the tip of his Glock pressed to his temple.

"Did you have a nice chat with Nadeera?"

I swung my attention back to Shedraziel. "Who?"

She smiled, a cold smile full of spite. "The Undine Lord."

The pearl!

Hope surged as I recalled the lord's token nestled in my pocket. She'd instructed me to break it at her daughter's feet, and she'd take care of the rest, but what would happen if I broke it at Shedraziel's? Surely, if we could stop Shedraziel here and now it would be no problem to rescue her daughter afterward. Hell, without Shedraziel controlling her, the lord's daughter might make her way back to the Undine Realm on her own.

I took another step forward and slipped my left hand into my pocket. "She told me why you were banished, why you went to work for Bael."

She snorted.

"Does he know you're here?"

"Are you surprised?"

I took another step forward. My fingers closed around the pearl. How much force would it take to break it?

"Your plan to force a conflict between the humans and undine has failed."

"You think you are so clever, but you understand nothing." She tipped her head slightly, as though listening to the wind. "Can't you hear it?"

"I have a true name. Your spell won't work on me."

She shook her head. "Not that."

I frowned.

"The song of chaos." Her gaze grew distant, as though she was seeing something beyond me—beyond the dead on the ground, the suicidal soldiers, and the battlefield. Then she closed her eyes and tipped her face toward the sky. "Soon the dams will break, and chaos will drown this pathetic world. It will spill and spread until we are brought full circle."

I pulled the pearl free of my pocket, lifted my arm, and prepared to throw it down with all my might.

A single gunshot rang out.

Searing pain tore through my calf. My leg folded under a weight it could no longer support. I hit the ground hard, slamming first my hip, then my side. My hand sprang open with the impact. The pearl rolled away, undamaged.

David stepped into my vision. His uniform was torn and smeared with blood. A ragged gash bled along one cheek, and his lower lip was split. He stopped near my feet. His gun was pointed straight at my head. His expression remained neutral.

"Goodbye, Alex." The words came from both Shedraziel and David, two voices speaking in unison.

Kicking out with my injured leg, I slammed my foot into the side of David's knee as hard as I could.

I screamed.

David's leg buckled.

The gun went off.

A chunk of dirt puffed three inches from my head.

My ears were ringing, muting the world. The wound in my leg was an angry wasp nest radiating pain. I kicked out again, catching David under the chin. A wave of nausea hit me as the shock of impact jangled my screaming nerves.

David fell backward, but he still had his gun.

I scrambled over and flattened myself on top of him, pinning him like a wrestler.

He lifted the gun, and I grabbed his wrist with both hands.

Another wild shot rang out, loud even through the ringing in my ears.

I flinched, and David rolled, pulling me down as he gained the upper hand. He straddled my waist. His weight on my diaphragm made it hard to breathe.

There was a series of distant pops.

David jerked twice. A plume of earth erupted near my hip. Then another near my head.

I tipped my face toward the remaining humans. Their guns were lowered and firing in my direction. David had inadvertently saved me by reversing our positions, but the soldiers didn't care. So long as they were under Shedraziel's control, they wouldn't hesitate to kill us both.

Drawing energy faster than I could safely filter, I raised a wall of rock between myself and the incoming bullets, making sure it was high enough to protect David, too.

As I cast my spell, the clouds of the Rift closed in again, faster than before. This time the hazy faces of the demons were present, but their attention wasn't on me. I tipped my head further, trying to see the area directly above me.

Shedraziel stood inverted from my perspective, hanging off the world like a bat. The fog was thickest around her, and the faces in that fog seemed to be speaking. She glanced once in my direction, then turned and walked away. She was leaving.

If I lose this chance. . . .

I turned my focus back to David. His weight still pinned me to the ground. A crimson stain was soaking through his sleeve near his shoulder. "I'm really sorry about this." Taking one hand off his wrist, I punched him as hard as I could in the gunshot wound. My fist came away bloody.

He grunted and recoiled. I used that moment to reverse our positions again.

I glanced up. Shedraziel was nearly beyond view at the far edge of the camp.

I am here. James's voice in my head was like taking a full breath after too long underwater, infusing me with life and hope.

The *pings* of bullets hitting my earthen shield cut off as James took the rest of Shedraziel's pawns out of commission.

Go after Shedraziel! I tried to send a picture of where I'd last seen her, a sense of direction. I wrapped the message with urgency. *We can't let her get away.*

He hesitated, torn between following my wishes and ending my struggle with David. But short of delivering a quick death, any assistance would delay James longer than we could afford. Shedraziel already had a head start.

"I can handle this," I shouted. "Go!"

James turned away from me with an effort. His irritation was like a swarm of bees in my head as he raced after Shedraziel. I glanced at his back as he skirted the tents and passed into the shadow of the overpass.

David's fist connected with my jaw, snapping my head to the side. Blood filled my mouth.

Focus!

David was stronger and more experienced at fighting than I was. It was taking everything I had just to keep my position on top. Luckily, I wasn't limited to physical attacks.

Drawing in energy like a sponge, I softened the ground between my knees until the dirt shifted like quicksand beneath me—a trick I'd seen a demon-possessed sorcerer pull at the battle of Wilmington.

David flailed and writhed as he sank into the earth. When his torso was covered, I stiffened the ground. He stopped sinking.

Now for the tricky part.

Left as he was, David would just dig himself out as soon as I got off him, so I turned my attention inward, focusing on the part of my magic that came from my fae heritage—the ability to imbue.

When I touched my fae magic, it was like grabbing a live wire; my own thoughts and emotions surged through me, unfettered. Worry, guilt, confusion, anger. . . . Shutting them out, which was my first instinct, would only block me from my magic. Dwelling on them would distract me to the point of making my magic ineffective. I took a deep breath and let them all wash over me. Thoughts plucked at my attention—Emma and her surprising new ability; the fact that James had fought to protect the PTF in my absence despite the argument we'd had when I left; curiosity about the invisible whatever-it-was shot down above the battlefield; the unshakable feeling that every person Shedraziel hurt was on my head for the deal I'd made that let her out of prison in the first place; irritation with Bael for failing to control her, and at myself for believing he would. I let the thoughts slide through my mind like a river, careful not to linger too long on any one lest it snag and create a dam.

Beyond my thoughts and emotions lay my magic. I pushed it into the dirt encasing David and sought the core of the material, the atoms and molecules that made it what it was. Then I focused on the elements that held the traits I wanted—iron, copper, lead. I used my magic to coax those to the surface, sharing their properties with the softer minerals around them until a bar of solid metal spanned David's chest, pinning him in place.

Drawing my focus back to the physical world, I slipped to the side and twisted the gun out of David's hand. He groped and grabbed but couldn't reach me.

"Sorry." I checked the clip to make sure his gun still had bullets then struggled to my feet. Putting weight on the leg with the bullet hole sent pain lancing through my nerves that nearly toppled me. I gritted my teeth and adjusted my stance. "This should all be over soon."

Gripping the gun with both hands, I hobbled after James and Shedraziel as fast as I could.

The far side of the underpass took only a few moments to reach, even lurching from tree to tree for support, but it felt like an eternity. Not only was every step agony, but every second was another chance for Shedraziel to slip away. I could feel James fighting. He'd reached her in time, but he was barehanded and exhausted against a master swordsman. Worse, I could feel the sluggish pull of Shedraziel's magic taking hold in James. Maybe she couldn't control him completely yet, but she was slowing him down enough to negate the advantage of his vampire reflexes.

Even as she and James came into view on the bank of the river, Shedraziel's sword sliced through James's chest in a silver arc. Crimson droplets flew. James staggered back.

Bracing my shoulder against a bare-branched ash tree I leveled David's gun, exhaled, and fired. The kickback was stronger than I was used to. I jerked too much to risk a second shot with James so close.

There was a *ting* of metal on metal. A bright spark flared on Shedraziel's blade, there and gone in an instant.

I stared in open-mouthed horror. *Was that just the worst luck ever that I hit her blade, or did she actually deflect the bullet?*

I took a breath and reset my aim.

Shedraziel smiled and stepped into the river.

James lunged toward her, hand outstretched.

She narrowed her eyes. "No."

James stumbled as Shedraziel spoke.

I squeezed the trigger.

This time my bullet didn't hit anything. Between one breath and the next, Shedraziel sank into the icy flow of the Platte River.

James crashed to his chest on the ice-crusted rocks. He rose to his knees and looked at me, one hand pressed to his temple as though his head ached. Blood seeped from a long, thin line that stretched from his hip to his heaving chest. The wound shrank as I watched, closing faster than any mortal could hope for but slower than James was used to. He was out of energy. My gaze ran over the smears of blood covering his body, the tears and stains on his pants. Even James couldn't face a pack of rabid werewolves and a seasoned fae general and come out unscathed.

I limped toward him, but I'd barely taken two hobbling steps before he was at my side. He slipped one arm around my waist, taking my weight. Together we stared at the sluggish current of the river where it split, the larger portion continuing south while the Cherry Creek tributary wound east toward the center of the city.

I opened my mouth to speak.

An explosion sounded in the distance, rattling the windows of the nearby buildings. I flinched. James curled around me reflexively, but there was nothing for him to shield me from. A thick plume of smoke rose above the buildings to the southeast like a dark hand reaching for the sun.

I uncurled and stared at the darkening sky. "Where do you think that was?"

"Judging by the direction and distance . . . it was probably around the capitol building."

An image of Governor Anderson popped into my head. "When I first heard Shedraziel's song, I had an overwhelming urge to find Governor Anderson." I looked at James, a sour twist cramping my stomach. "Where are the practitioners?"

He shook his head. "I never saw any. By the time I reached the main floor, the lobby was in chaos. The Church delegates were under attack from the werewolves. David's guards and the few agents who'd been on the premises were struggling to hold them back."

My mouth went dry. "The delegates were here?"

"Harris, Weatherly, and David managed to get them to an SUV, but the wolves overturned it before they could drive away."

"That's why you were guarding it." I pressed my palm to his chest. "Thank you."

He nodded. "Though I'm not sure saving their lives will mean much in the grand scheme of things once news of what happened here gets out."

"We can use all the goodwill we can get." I looked one more time at the rising smoke, then sighed and turned back the way we'd come. "Let's go assess the damage."

Chapter 11

DAVID WAS RIGHT where I'd left him, but he wasn't flailing anymore. He was scratching at the edges of the metal pinning him down. I stopped well back, out of sight behind him. James matched my movements like an extension of my own body.

"David?" I called.

He swiveled his neck, trying to find at me. "Alex, is that you?"

James and I stepped to the side so David could see us. "More to the point," I said, "are you *you?*"

David's gaze dropped. Deep lines creased his forehead. "I *think* so, but . . ." He stared at his hands, opening and closing them as though grasping for something that spilled through his fingers. "I could see everything that was happening. I . . . I. . . ." He looked up. "I shot you."

I forced a smile. "You weren't yourself."

"Yeah, but—"

"I know better than anyone what it's like not to be in control of your own actions." My mind flashed back to a few months ago—it felt like a lifetime—when the then Master Vampire of Denver had held me enthralled. I'd also felt the pull of Shedraziel's call before, though neither experience could compare to the compulsion I'd felt from James when he used my true name. I cast a sidelong glance at him. Despite his oath never to use that power against me, the utter surrender I'd felt when following his order still made me shudder.

"There's no point in dwelling on that which you cannot change," James said. I wasn't sure if he was addressing David's comment or my unspoken thoughts. He gestured toward the battlefield hidden behind the trees. "You were hardly the only one so affected."

Using James as a crutch, I hobbled closer to David, then I handed the gun to James and knelt. "The important thing is that you're back to your old self. Let's get you out and go find Emma."

I looked up at James. "While I get him loose, I need you to look around for a small, white pearl. It rolled away in the struggle."

He lifted one eyebrow but began inspecting the ground around us.

I placed my hands over the rough metal strap I'd made to trap David. Tapping into my power should have been easier now that I wasn't fighting for my life, but that actually made all the thoughts and emotions harder to ignore. The insistent worry about where Shedraziel had gone, the mysterious explosion, and what would happen next were like wasps stinging me over and over as I tried to focus.

I collected my power and dove into the core of the metal, finding the links I'd strengthened, the minerals I'd coaxed, and shifted them back to the way they'd been until the dirt on David's torso was just dirt. I sat back with a sigh, injured leg out to one side.

David wriggled out of the shallow hole. Wincing, he unzipped his jacket and fingered a deformed slug embedded in the vest beneath. He tore off the fabric of his stained sleeve and used it to wrap the ragged gash across his bicep.

"You okay?" I asked.

"A few bruised ribs and a flesh wound," he said. "Nothing I won't survive." He glanced at my bloody calf. Guilt twisted his expression.

"I'll be fine," I said.

My stomach growled. Casting magic, especially fae magic which was drawn from within, used a lot of energy. My body was reminding me I hadn't had more than seaweed salad in the past few days.

"You should rest," James said. "And we should patch your wounds."

I looked over my shoulder at him. "Did you find the pearl?"

He frowned but showed me the white sphere pinched between his thumb and finger.

"What is it?" David asked, kneeling to tie his second torn sleeve around my calf.

"Hopefully a way out of this mess." I winced as he cinched the bandage tight. I opened my hand, and James dropped the pearl onto my palm. *If only I'd managed to break it.* I tucked it in the pocket of my pants and struggled to rise.

James stooped to balance me.

"We need to check for survivors, identify the dead, and find out what got shot down."

David held his hand out to James, palm up.

James looked at me, a question in his expression.

I nodded.

He returned the gun to David and said, "Lead the way."

David checked his clip, just as I had done, then moved in the direction of the PTF building with his gun pointed at the ground. When he reached the trees, he knelt by each of the guards who'd been shooting at us to check for a pulse. Again and again, he shook his head and moved on.

I looked at James. *Did you kill them all?*

This close, with my arm across his shoulders and his around my waist, there was no barrier between us . . . and no remorse in James's heart.

You were in danger.

You didn't have to kill them.

There was no time for delicacy.

They were being controlled.

Exactly. I've seen vampire thralls walk on broken legs and fight even as they bled out. These people would have continued to be a threat so long as Shedraziel held them. It's unfortunate that they lost their lives, but I will not apologize for my actions. You were in danger. Given the choice again, I would do the same every time.

I looked from corpse to corpse as we picked our way between the bodies. Most had their necks snapped. A fast death, at least.

"I just wish there'd been another way," I whispered. *You could at least feel bad about it.* I couldn't stop the thought from forming, but if James was bothered by my judgment, he gave no indication.

People were moving on the parking lot and lawns in front of the PTF building, but it was no longer the frenetic motion of battle. Men and women sat in a daze, looking around as though they'd just woken up but thought they might still be dreaming. Many people cried out as injuries they'd sustained while in their trance-like state suddenly flared into their awareness. Police officers watched warily from the perimeter, holding back reporters and camera crews who'd come to claim a story. Two ambulances had arrived, and sirens in the distance promised more, though depending on the fallout from that last explosion they might be redirected. There was no sign of whatever had fallen from the sky.

Emma was where I'd left her. She was on her hands and knees, looking side to side with wide eyes. Now that Shedraziel and the effects of her song were gone, I wondered if Emma still retained her sonar-like sight.

"Emma," I called as we approached.

She jumped and turned toward my voice. "Alex? What happened? Where are you?" Emma raised one of her hands, groping in my direction.

I took her hand, giving her an anchor to balance as she stood. "Emma, did you lose . . . what you were doing before?"

She frowned. "I'm not sure. I was wide open to my magic before . . . or what would have been my magic if it had been working properly. When I woke up, everything was dark again. I might be able to recreate it, but—"

"Now's not the time." I patted her hand. "Don't worry Emma, we'll figure it out. I promise."

She nodded and squeezed my fingers.

"Alex!" David had his gun leveled at a werewolf who was loping toward us.

James covered the gun with his free hand, pushing it toward the ground. "That's Marc. He was helping me defend the delegates."

"So he wasn't affected by Shedraziel's spell?" I tapped a finger against my chin. Marc was an alpha, which might explain his resistance . . . but Sarah wasn't.

Marc shifted as he approached, going from four paws to hands and feet and finally straightening to walk on two legs. His clothing hadn't survived the change.

David stripped off what remained of his coat and tossed it at Marc's chest, nodding toward the nearby camera crews. "Unless you want your junk on TV."

"We have a problem." Marc tied the borrowed coat around his waist like a sarong. "We cannot allow the emergency workers to take any of the injured to the hospital."

I glanced at the ambulances. EMTs were pulling out stretchers. I ran my gaze over the field of injured. Some had been shot or beaten, but some. . . . A knot lodged in my chest. "Anyone attacked by a werewolf will turn."

The color drained from David's cheeks. "All of them?"

"Not all," Marc said. "But those infected who don't turn will die."

"How long until we know if a person will turn?" I asked.

"The disease takes a few hours to fully convert a human to a werewolf. During that time, the victim will be feverish and wracked with spasms. If the disease converts enough tissue before the infection kills the person, they'll shift."

"If Luke were here, he could identify which people were infected and ease the transitions," Emma said.

I looked at David.

"On it." He pulled out his cell phone.

As a non-combatant practitioner, Emma's mentor Luke had been allowed to continue living in his house in Boulder rather than getting lumped with the sorcerer-practitioners and werewolves in our "paranatural hotel." That would have kept him safe from Shedraziel, but also meant it would take him at least half an hour to reach us. I turned to Emma. "Did he teach you how to identify werewolf infections?"

She nodded. "But as I am now I—"

"You can walk me through it. I don't have much experience with healing, other than on the receiving end, but with your knowledge and my magic we'll make do until he gets here." I turned to Marc. "First things first. With everyone on edge, anything that seems threatening will be a target. Collect all the werewolves and take them into the gym for now. Have them shift back and get dressed. There should be plenty of clothes in the locker room."

"Wouldn't it be better to get them out of this area entirely?" David asked.

Marc shook his head. "If we take off now, it will look like we attacked the PTF of our own accord. Better to remain and answer questions so the human authorities know we were victims here, too."

"Assuming they're willing to listen." I met Marc's gaze. "I can't guarantee the cops, or even the PTF at this point, will believe you. If you'd rather take your people out of the line of fire, I'll understand."

He shook his head. "You'll need us here once the victims start changing. New wolves aren't safe to be around." He met my gaze, and I knew we were both thinking about the night my friend Sophie and I had met a brand new, out-of-control werewolf.

I looked around the battlefield again. This many new werewolves would be. . . . I rubbed my hand over the scars that covered my left arm from wrist to elbow.

Marc turned away. "We'll be in the gym."

"See if you can find me some shoes," I called as he ran over to a nearby, gray-pelted wolf. He relayed his orders then moved on. Furry figures were scattered all over the area. None had risen. Were they injured, dead, or just trying not to make obvious targets for the nervous police officers with their guns still pointed toward the field?

"We need to find Director Harris and convince her to make a triage area to sort the werewolf victims from other injuries."

David pulled a walkie off his belt, but the bottom was a mess of cracked plastic and loose wires. He put the useless device back with a sigh and pointed toward the edge of the parking lot. "Last I saw her was over there. We were trying to clear a path for the delegates' SUV . . . until it got flipped. That's about when I lost control. The last time I saw Director Harris, she was fighting two of my security officers."

"What about Weatherly?"

James snorted. "He climbed in the car with the delegates."

I wasn't surprised Weatherly had tried to save his own skin, but at least his cowardice made him easy to find. "Let's head for the SUV."

David offered the elbow of his uninjured arm to Emma, while James continued to support me around the waist. Together we picked our way to the parking lot. People were becoming more alert. Some asked us what was going on. A few members of David's security team joined us. From the other side of the property, a group of police officers started a similar journey, moving toward us in a cluster with their guns pointed out. The EMTs moved with them, checking bodies and giving instructions to those still conscious.

More people were getting up all over the field.

We have to get control of this situation quickly.

Twenty paces from the advancing police group, David stopped and lifted a hand, bringing us to a halt. A woman in her mid-thirties with brown skin and dark hair pulled back in a high ponytail stepped to the front of the other group. Like her companions, she wore a dark-blue uniform with a gold badge on her breast. She held her gun with both hands, pointed just low enough not to be threatening.

"Who are you?" she asked.

"David Nolan, Chief of Security at this installation." The woman glanced around, clearly not impressed with our security. "You need to quarantine this area." He pointed to the medics. "Don't let them take anyone to the hospital until they've been cleared."

The woman reached up and pressed a button on the radio strapped to her shoulder. "This is Officer Ramirez. Initiate quarantine procedure. No one crosses the perimeter."

One of the medics, a young man with long blond hair tied back by a scrunchy, wire-frame glasses, and dozens of freckles across his pale cheeks asked, "What kind of outbreak are we looking at here?"

"And is that what caused everyone to go berserk?" the policewoman added.

I shook my head. "The chaos was—"

"Is it safe to come out?"

I, along with everyone else, turned toward the new voice. Bishop João Silva's salt-and-pepper hair, narrow brown eyes, and double chin stuck up from the skyward side of the SUV. He held the door open above him with one hand.

"Yes, you can come out now," I said.

Officer Ramirez glared at me. "And who exactly are you?"

"PTF Assistant Director Alex Blackwood."

"So you're in charge here?"

"No, she most certainly is not." Weatherly's face had popped up beside Silva's.

"Director Harris should be around here somewhere," I said. "She's in charge."

"But until she is found, *I* am the senior PTF official. Now kindly come and help us out of here."

Ramirez motioned with her hand, and two officers moved to the SUV. The blond medic went with them. When Weatherly was halfway out, she turned back to me. "You were saying about the cause of all this?"

I nodded. "A powerful fae, not aligned with any given realm. She has the ability to manipulate people like puppets. She was affecting this whole area."

"Nonsense," Weatherly said as he stepped closer. "I didn't feel anything of the sort."

"Not everyone was affected."

He raised his chin. "More likely the werewolves simply saw an opportunity and took it."

"But not all of the paranaturals were attacking." Silva had exited the

SUV and stood adjusting his bishop robes. "A few seemed to be protecting us."

David cleared his throat. "I can tell you from personal experience that the woman Alex is talking about can control people." He indicated my leg. "I shot Alex while under her influence. And my own people shot me. As soon as she was gone, my head cleared, but I had no control while she was there."

The other two Church delegates joined us. The groups stared at one another, anxious expressions on every face.

"She's the one behind the chaos in the world right now," I said. "She wants the humans and fae to go to war."

Weatherly straightened, lifting his chin. "If the fae want—"

"Not the fae," I corrected. "Just this one very unstable, very powerful woman."

Weatherly opened his mouth again, but David cut him off. "Regardless, we need to deal with the situation at hand before we can worry about catching the person responsible." He turned to Ramirez. "What can you tell me about that explosion we heard?"

Officer Ramirez studied the ground. "It was the capitol building. Thirty-seven injured. Four fatalities so far."

We all looked toward the smoke billowing over the treetops.

"Governor Anderson?" I asked, remembering the image Shedraziel had placed in my head . . . the overwhelming need to find and kill the governor.

Ramirez shrugged. "I don't know the specifics."

"So the attack here may have been a diversion," David said. "A way to split the response teams."

I glanced at the Church delegates. "I think it was more than that. Shedraziel is trying to sow chaos, to keep every faction of human, fae, and paranatural at each other's throats. If three official representatives of the Church were killed by paranaturals, I don't imagine the Church would look very favorably on our alliance."

Emma cleared her throat. "I realize this is all very important, but we still need to sort the injured."

"Right." I turned to the delegates. "Were any of you injured by a were-wolf? Even a scratch?"

Silva, Ali, and Khatun each checked themselves and shook their heads.

I exhaled. "Anyone injured by a werewolf is in danger of turning into one; that's how the change is spread."

The blond medic frowned. "So werewolfism is a disease?"

"More like a magical mutation," James said.

Weatherly and the delegates looked at him with expressions ranging from suspicion to awe. After his display protecting their SUV, there could be no doubt that James was a powerful paranatural, but they still didn't know exactly what he was.

I waved my hand. "Whatever it is, we need to contain it as much as possible. We've called Luke. He's the best healer in the state. In the meantime, Emma and I will do what we can."

Weatherly snorted. "She's blind. What can she do?"

Emma stiffened.

"More than cower in an SUV while other people fight her battles," I snapped.

Weatherly took a step back as though struck.

Ignoring him, I pressed on. "I've asked the remaining werewolves to wait in the PTF gym for now. We're going to need their help containing anyone who changes. New werewolves are unstable." I caught Ramirez's gaze. "You'll need to keep your people well back once they start turning."

"I'll organize any remaining security officers and PTF agents," David said. "We'll help you guard the perimeter." He looked at me. "We should shoot any wolf who tries to leave the area."

I met his gaze. I hated that order. New werewolves were innocent victims, scared and out of control, but they were dangerous. I looked around the field. Who knew how many of the injured were infected. The werewolves we currently had might not be able to subdue them all. I nodded. "They can't be allowed to leave."

Weatherly sneered. "Finally, something we can agree on."

I turned to the lead medic. "Do what you can to treat the injured, but bring anyone with an open wound"—I looked around and pointed to the cordoned-off area of leveled earth west of the building that would one day be the site of my sculpture—"there."

The medic looked at Ramirez, who looked at Weatherly.

Weatherly waved his hand. "Do as she says. The last thing we need is any more of those creatures getting loose."

Ramirez gave orders over her radio, then headed back to the perimeter with Weatherly and the delegates in tow. David and the handful of officers we'd collected on our walk joined them. They'd help form the perimeter, escort the medics, and move the injured.

I tugged James in the direction of the clearing I'd indicated, and he brought Emma. We'd made it barely ten feet when a streak of motion near the ground caught my attention. I pulled up short. A gray cat was slinking between bodies. When he caught me looking, he met my gaze with bright-green eyes.

"Chase?"

He gave a single *meow*, turned, and headed back the way he'd come. He paused after a few steps and looked over his shoulder as if to say, "What are you waiting for?"

I glanced at James, who nodded and changed direction.

Chase led us into the trees that separated the PTF lawns from the green-belt path along the river. The tops of the trees nearest the river had been snapped off. Limbs littered the ground. Lying on the path among them was a young girl. She looked to be about eight years old with pale-purple hair that hung in long straight strands over her snow-white skin and obscured her face. Blood streaked her side and one arm.

"Is that . . . ?" I took a step forward. "Zeraldi?"

"Zeraldi?" Emma asked. "Isn't that the name of the dragon you saved from Shedraziel's prison along with my sister and the other kidnapped kids?"

"Yeah." I continued to stare at the girl in dumbstruck surprise.

The air around the gray tabby shimmered. He seemed to melt and stretch until Chase was standing in human form, buck naked, on the path beside the equally naked girl. With me barefoot and bloodstained and James in nothing but a pair of tattered pants, Emma was the only one of us properly dressed for the February weather, though neither of the men seemed affected by the cold.

"We got here as fast as we could," Chase said.

I looked from him to the girl, then back to him. "How did you even . . .? Where did you . . .?"

"While I'm sure you have many pressing questions," James interjected, "perhaps this is not the best time and place for this particular reunion."

I glanced behind me. A number of medical teams were moving through the battlefield now. Those who could walk were being led toward the space I'd indicated. Emma and I had work to do. I studied Zeraldi's side. She had several puncture wounds. Probably bullet holes from the shots that had brought her down. "Will she heal all right on her own?"

"She should," Chase said. "Given time and space to rest."

I chewed my lower lip. Zeraldi and Chase were both in the mortal realm illegally. They couldn't afford to get caught. Chase was strong, but he couldn't carry Zeraldi at speed all the way back to my house, which was the only safe place I could think of for them, and he didn't know how to drive a car.

I lowered my arm from James's shoulder and stepped away from him. "I need you to take her and Chase back to my house."

His gaze moved to the troops behind us.

"We'll be fine now that the fighting's over," I said.

"You're about to be overrun with new werewolves."

"Once we've identified the ones who are going to change, we'll lock them in the PTF's holding cells and have Marc and the others stand guard." I bit my lip. *Hopefully that's enough to hold them.*

As if voicing my thoughts James said, "This facility is designed to hold fae, and only in the short term. I had no trouble breaking out of my cell, and

I'm nowhere near as strong as a werewolf."

"Then come back once they're safe," I said. "We're wasting time arguing."

A muscle jumped in the side of his jaw. He lifted Emma's hand free from his elbow and stooped down beside the unconscious girl. He looked up at me. "If she wakes up and finds herself in the arms of a vampire—"

"Chase will be there to explain." I narrowed my eyes at Chase, who was wearing an expression that made it seem he might very much like to see what would happen if a dragon woke up in the arms of a vampire. "Just hurry."

He lifted the girl easily in his arms, cradling her to his chest. Then he straightened and looked at Chase. "Ready for another run?"

The corner of Chase's mouth rose. When the three of us had previously needed to evade the authorities, James had managed to outpace Chase even carrying me in his arms. I got the impression Chase was eager for a rematch.

Chase-the-man shrank back to Chase-the-cat in a shimmer of magic.

"I'll be back soon," James said. Then he was gone in a blur with a gray streak keeping pace near his ankle.

"Come on, Emma." I set her hand on my arm. "Let's get to work."

My designated sculpture area had been at the border of the conflict, so there weren't many people nearby, although one man had been impaled by a piece of rebar sticking out of the ground near the edge. The medical teams had already brought over stretchers with the most severely wounded, and were doing their best to treat the injuries when Emma and I arrived.

"Where'd you get off to?" David asked. He and five others in PTF or Denver PD uniforms had formed a circle around our work area.

I shook my head.

David glanced behind me, clearly wondering where James had gone, but kept his mouth shut.

I helped Emma get settled on the ground, then knelt beside the first victim. She was a PTF secretary, not someone who should ever have seen combat. From the pulped flesh on her abdomen I guessed she'd been shot from behind several times—probably while trying to flee.

"She needs surgery and a transfusion," the blond medic from earlier said as he pressed wads of gauze against the wound. "I need to know if she can be moved outside the quarantine."

I nodded. "Emma, what do I do?"

She pulled her jacket collar tighter as a cold wind tore past us. "It's similar to the shift in focus when you're creating a filter to channel through. Once you're there, you should be able to see a sort of aura around the person. A full human or a full werewolf should look more or less uniform, but early on, the infection should look like something separate, something that doesn't belong."

Pursing my lips, I shifted my focus as I did when drawing magical energy. The gray clouds of the Rift coiled at the edges of my vision, but I wasn't actually channeling, just looking. The woman lying in front of me still looked like a woman . . . a woman dying a painful death. I shifted my focus again, searching deeper—sort of like trying to make out the picture in one of those hidden-image puzzles. I continued to search until I reached the very core of her being, the knots and strings that made her who and what she was.

"I don't see anything out of place."

"Then I can take her to the hospital?" The medic's question snapped my focus back to my physical reality.

I glanced at Emma, then at the woman. She would die if she didn't get proper medical help soon, but. . . . *What if I missed something?*

I imagined the damage a newly transformed werewolf could do if it got loose in a hospital.

"Let me check another." I glanced at the handful of people the medics had carried over so far. One man had a set of four parallel lacerations across his chest deep enough to show bone—definitely made by claws. I pointed. "Him."

"I need to get this woman—"

"I have to be sure." I scrambled to the man's side and, as fast as I could, dropped into the trance-like state that allowed me to see beyond the physical world. I didn't have to try hard to identify the infection Emma had described. Dark tendrils fanned out from the slash marks, twisting together with the man's base structure, choking off healthy tissue.

"Yes, you can take her," I said. "She's clean."

I ignored the scuffle of feet and the woman's pained grunt as the medics carried her toward the perimeter and one of the waiting ambulances. The way the infection moved through the man's body, twisting itself through the building blocks of his genetic makeup, looked remarkably similar to the way the demon taint had moved in James when it tried to take over.

I chewed my lower lip. I'd never had occasion to study the core of a werewolf, to see how the magic was bound to the person. If it worked the same as it did with vampires—

"What about this one?"

My attention snapped up to the blond medic. He was standing over my current patient, waiting for a diagnosis.

I shook my head. "He's infected."

The medic pointed to the man on the stretcher and then to the side. Two cops carried the litter to the indicated spot. Three more victims had arrived while I was distracted, taking the vacated spaces and then some. I wanted to take a closer look at what the infection was doing. Maybe if it wasn't too anchored yet. . . . I licked my lips, barely willing to even *think* the possibility, let alone voice it. *Maybe there's still a chance to avoid the transformation.*

But the people around me were dying of physical wounds, waiting to hear if they could receive proper treatment. They didn't have time for me to experiment.

I moved to the next injured person—a woman who'd lost an eye along with a significant chunk of her face. My stomach churned. Bile surged in the back of my throat. I took shallow breaths to avoid being overwhelmed by the smells of blood, sweat, and fear. The woman was infected. She was moved beside the first man. The next man was clean, having suffered a gunshot wound, broken leg, and shattered jaw.

Everly Harris was among the second group brought over. She was unconscious. Blood seeped through a bandage above her left eye and stained her blue business suit, but I didn't see any other obvious injuries. I looked at the medic who'd brought her. "I thought we were checking the most severely injured first?"

"Aside from being unresponsive, she has several broken ribs, a punctured lung, a shattered wrist, and internal bleeding. She may not be as mangled looking as some, but her injuries are severe."

I looked down at my boss in horror. My mouth had gone dry as the medic listed her injuries. Whether or not she became a werewolf, it didn't look like she'd be taking the reins back from Weatherly any time soon.

I shifted my focus and began my search for any sign of infection, starting with the gash on her head and working down to her toes.

I shook my head. "You can take her to the hospital."

As the medic and his escorts carried Harris away, I considered the list of her injuries and wondered if she wouldn't have had a better chance of survival if she'd been infected. Werewolves didn't heal as fast as vampires, but they could recover from just about anything given a little time.

"Good luck," I whispered. Then I turned my attention to the next injured person.

The people who were brought to me for judgment blurred together after that. As the battlefield emptied, the number of those I couldn't send to the hospital grew. Some bodies were taken away without my consultation, piled at the far end of the lawn—corpses could wait. The injuries of the people brought for assessment became less severe as the most critically wounded were either taken away for treatment or given up on, but the condition of the people left with me began to deteriorate. Every infected person was soaked in sweat despite the chilly afternoon. I was shivering in the replacement clothes and sneakers Marc had brought me from the locker room. Once the most severely injured had been sorted, one of the medics took the time to bandage my leg and shoulder properly.

Luke showed up about forty minutes after I'd made my first prognosis.

I looked up from a young man, barely more than a child, who must have been among the protesters caught in the first assault. I'd just pronounced the boy infected. I nearly fainted with relief to see Luke striding toward the triage area. His thick black hair was twisted into quarter-inch tufts that curled over the tips of his ears and the frame of his glasses. He wore a red sweatshirt, blue jeans, and sneakers, and he carried a backpack that was almost certainly stuffed with medical supplies. Less comforting were the two armed police officers who accompanied him with their guns leveled at his back.

He didn't smile or wave in greeting when he met my gaze, though I caught a twinge of worry when his eyes passed over Emma. He stopped at the edge of the assessment zone and said, "Status?"

Emma jumped at the sound of Luke's voice and turned her face as though searching for him.

I waved an arm to indicate all the people behind me. "These ones were infected by the werewolves." I pointed to the most recent arrivals. "These I haven't looked at yet."

"You're doing them one at a time?"

I frowned. "There's another way?" I glanced at Emma.

"Perhaps not at your level." He set his pack down and took a step back. Then he spread his hands parallel to the ground and closed his eyes. He didn't move after that except to breathe.

I shifted my focus to the magical spectrum, hoping to see what he was doing, but he looked exactly the same.

After a moment, he pointed to two of the people I hadn't yet checked. "These two are clean. The other is infected." He turned to look over the lawn and parking lot. We'd managed to clear about two-thirds of the casualties, and the people who were left had only minor injuries. They were waiting under guard to be brought to me in groups. "Those ones haven't been checked yet?"

I nodded.

"Wait here." He crossed the lawn, his two shadows keeping pace, and repeated his arms-up ritual near the remaining combatants. He took considerably longer before lowering his arms. When he did, he pointed out a handful of people and said something to the guards. The cops who'd been watching the group split up. Half led the people Luke had pointed out toward me. The other half took the remaining people toward the perimeter. Other than the dead waiting to be identified, the battlefield had finally been cleared. A total of twenty-three people had been infected—more than Marc's entire pack.

When Luke returned, he wasted no time in directing the remaining medics. "I'll do what I can to stabilize those with the worst injuries." He glanced at Emma, then away. He spotted David among the guards, a white bandage around his head and his arm in a sling. At least he'd been clear of infection. "You can start moving those who don't need medical attention someplace where they can be locked up and guarded. We've still got some time before people start changing, but we might as well—"

"There's something I want to check first," I said. Standing unsteadily on my injured leg, I hobbled over to him and pulled him slightly away from the group. "I think the werewolf infection may work the same as what happens when a vampire is changed. The foreign entity fuses with the person's existing core structure until the two are inseparable. At that point, the person becomes a werewolf . . . or a vampire."

"As much as I'd love to discuss the various theories of magical mutations with you, Alex, we don't have time right now."

I pointed to the group of infected. "These people aren't fused yet."

He nodded. "It takes a few hours for the infection to run its course. At that point, they'll either—"

I waved his explanation away. "When I was looking for the infection I could see the tendrils working their way into the person's body, converting them from human to werewolf. I saw the same thing in James when he was struggling with his demon, and I was able to help his human side regain control."

Luke narrowed his eyes at me. "What are you saying, exactly?"

"If I can reverse the conversion process before it gets too strong a hold, while their body still remembers what it's supposed to be, maybe I can stop them from turning."

He shook his head. "There's no cure for this infection, Alex. The magic changes people at a cellular level."

"So can I."

He stared at me for a moment, then looked over my shoulder at the people spread around the area. He sighed. "If you think you can help them, try. But if you find you can't—which will more than likely be the case—don't take too long to quit. I can use your help making sure as many of these people survive the transformation as possible."

I nodded and turned to David. "Change of plans. We're going to keep everyone together a little while longer."

Luke and I both got to work. He would do his best to keep everyone alive. I needed to find out if I could keep them human.

Chapter 12

I LOOKED OVER the injured people. All were showing signs of fever now. Some complained of nausea, headaches, and cramping muscles. The medics worked busily around those in the worst condition, doing what they could with the limited supplies they had. Luke had settled himself between the first infected man I'd identified and the woman with the missing eye. He had one hand pressed to the man's chest and the other on the woman's forehead. When I shifted my focus, I could see a faint green glow around his hands.

I continued my inspection down the row toward the most recently identified victims. What I was going to attempt would be taxing. I needed someone with some strength left, someone who wouldn't drop dead as soon as I started working.

I spotted a middle-aged woman sitting near the edge of the triage area. The right sleeve of her previously cream-colored sweater was in tatters, revealing thick bandages that wrapped her arm from shoulder to wrist. She stared at her lap, cradling her limp hand.

I rubbed the scars along my left arm in sympathy and knelt beside the woman. "Hi. I'm Alex."

"Sachi." Her voice was flat and distant, dulled by shock. She continued to stare at her hand.

"I'd like to try to help you," I said.

"I'm going to turn into one of those things." She had an Asian accent that matched her straight black hair.

"Not if I can help it."

Her gaze finally lifted. Her brown eyes sparkled with unshed tears. "You can fix me?"

"That's what I want to find out, but I need a volunteer to test my theory. Can you help me?"

Her jaw set. The fear in her eyes shifted to resolve. "What do you need me to do?"

I smiled. "We need to fight the infection inside you."

Confusion flickered across her expression. "You have medicine?"

I set my hand on her shoulder. "I'm going to use magic to remind your body what it's supposed to be."

She stiffened. "You're a practitioner?"

I pressed on, unwilling to get sidetracked by the details of my mixed heritage or her potential prejudices. "In order to do that, I'm going to need your cooperation. It won't be comfortable, but I need you not to fight me."

She frowned. "Why would I fight you if you're curing the infection?"

My smile became strained. Frightening the woman wouldn't help, but I needed her to be prepared. The first time I attempted something like this with James, he'd almost died. Granted I wouldn't be going quite so deep this time—hopefully—but the risk was still there if the woman reacted poorly to my poking around.

"As I said, this is going to be uncomfortable. Just stay strong, and remember who you are." I gripped both her shoulders. "Are you ready?"

She gave a short, jerky nod.

I took a deep breath and let my awareness slip beyond the physical world, past the woman's skin, past muscle and bone. The threads at the core of her being were pale pink laced with white ribbons. I shifted my attention to the area near her wound. Purple-black sludge with a silvery sheen coated the pink like viscous oil. The wound itself was almost entirely converted. Tendrils of the dark material reached deeper, seeking the woman's core. I couldn't be certain, but I suspected that once the contamination reached her core, the woman would transform.

I fell back slightly, settling into a space between the advancing sludge and the woman's core.

Now for the hard part.

My practitioner magic could get me this far, but it was my imbuing, my fae magic, that I'd need to make the necessary changes. I just hoped I would have enough.

I called up the reservoir of rosy energy nestled inside me. With my magic came the familiar wash of emotions that accompanied it. Fear was a tight knot in my chest. Doubt slipped like a cold wind through the cracks in my confidence.

My dream for a paranatural alliance might die here. I should have ended Shedraziel the first time we met. Instead I made the deal that let her out of her prison, and this is the result. I let the guilt and frustration wash over me and fall to the periphery. Arguing with my subconscious would only anchor the thoughts and distract me from my work.

As my thoughts and emotions settled around me like river silt, I sank into my magic, or maybe it swelled to fill me. Wrapped in that magic, I reached out to the woman. If I wanted to chase out the infection, I needed to know what she was supposed to be.

Images flitted through my mind—*two young children, a boy and girl, running on a soccer field; a man with a scratchy beard and soft brown eyes that crinkled when he laughed; a farmhouse, cows, sheep, pigs; flashes in the sky; fire and lightning; the vibration of too-close explosions; a line of white moving across the cornfield, bleaching everything in its path; running; screaming; a tent by the river.* The woman's body jerked. I tightened my grip, holding her steady.

She was a refugee from the Faerie Wars, displaced by a waste.

Armed with the woman's sense of self, I dove toward the infection. The questing tendrils were easy enough to snap, unanchored as they were. Where the contamination was thicker, I kneaded my magic into the tissue, fusing and reforming it as though forging a piece of steel. The soft pink and white of the woman's natural state absorbed the darkness, overwhelming it as I funneled magic into her to give her the advantage she needed. She knew who she was. So long as she remembered that, we could convince the infection that's what it should be, too.

But the deeper into the infection I waded, the harder it was to remember the woman. Images of racing on four legs over moonlit rocks and stalking rabbits through tall grass flashed through my mind. The infection knew what *it* was, too—what it would become once its magic had run its course. The mutation and I were essentially trying to do the same thing. If I wanted to win this tug-of-war, I needed stronger anchors on which to draw.

The man with the laughing eyes stayed to defend the farm. The woman went back after, but he was gone. The house was standing, the land intact; the insurance company wouldn't pay. But who could live in a waste? Years in the refugee camp, working odd jobs to buy groceries and school supplies. Scraping. Saving. A fresh start. Now she served soup and sandwiches in the camp to those who hadn't made it out.

The woman squirmed beneath my hands, trying to pull away from me, from the memories, but I continued my onslaught. If even one molecule of contamination remained, the whole process would just start over the second I pulled back. I used the woman's pain and loss to direct my magic, but also her fortitude, her determination, her love for her kids—every moment, past and present, that made her who she was. Unlike what I'd done to James, I didn't need to change this woman into something new; I just had to strengthen who she was so the infection couldn't take hold.

She will not become a werewolf.

I twisted my magic with Sachi's memories and poured them into the infection, chasing it back to its source. Oily darkness clung to the edges of the deep gashes in her arm, the infection's last stand. I bombarded it with Sachi's memories, her hopes, her fears. The pink tissue slowly swallowed the black. I checked her over once more from head to toe, paying close attention to the wounds, but not a speck remained.

I sighed and slumped, letting my hands fall away from Sachi's shoulders. I took several deep breaths, centering myself in my own body, before looking up.

Tears streaked Sachi's cheeks. She was so pale her skin seemed almost translucent, and she was shaking like a leaf in a gale. She couldn't seem to catch her breath.

"Are you all right?" I winced as soon as the words left my lips. Of course she wasn't all right. She'd just had a stranger rummaging through her memories and secrets.

She held my gaze. "Is it gone?"

"I think so."

She lunged forward, wrapped her arms around me, and sobbed into my shoulder. "Thank you. Thank you. Thank you."

Reaching up as far as I could with my arms pinned to my sides, I patted her back awkwardly.

"We should have Luke double check, just to make sure I didn't miss anything." I smiled. My heart was racing. If Sachi really was cured. . . . I looked around the group of injured men and women who'd been detained.

I struggled to untangle myself from her hug. Then I climbed gingerly to my feet. My vision swam. I swayed. My stomach clenched and grumbled. I looked again at the group around me, and my euphoria turned to dread. Twenty-three potential patients, and just one had nearly wiped me out. If each one took at least that much energy—and there was no reason to think they'd get any easier—how was I going to help them all? And if not all . . . how could I possibly choose?

Sachi rose beside me, worry wrinkling her brow. "Are *you* okay?"

I nodded and started toward Luke at a slow shuffle.

The man Luke had been treating was breathing shallowly. Sweat slicked his bare skin, and bandages strained around his chest with each inhale. Luke now had both his hands over the woman with the missing eye. He stared at her with an expression of deep concentration. Sweat ran down his forehead.

I chewed my lower lip. The longer the infection had to set in, the harder it would be for me to chase it out, but I dared not interrupt Luke's work.

Shifting my focus, I watched him stitch the woman's cheek back together with magic, growing new skin and sealing seams before my very eyes. He couldn't put her back together entirely—even a healer as skilled as Luke couldn't regrow an eyeball—but with his help she just might live.

The light around Luke's hands faded. He sagged back on his heels and let out a noisy exhale.

"How is she?" I asked.

He twitched as though startling awake and looked at me. "Aside from the obvious, she has massive intracranial swelling. I don't know if I can save her." His gaze shifted to Sachi, who stood a pace behind me. "How'd your experiment go?"

"I think it was a success."

His eyes widened. Clearly that wasn't the response he'd been expecting.

I tugged Sachi forward. "This is Sachi. See if you can find any trace of the infection."

Luke stood up and took one of Sachi's hands between both of his. Then he closed his eyes.

Sachi looked nervously at me.

"Just hold still a sec," I said.

When Luke opened his eyes a moment later, they were filled with wonder. "You're sure she was infected?"

"She was in the last group you brought over when you arrived, and I saw it inside her clear enough." I wrung my hands together. "Is it gone?"

He looked Sachi up and down as though he couldn't believe she was real, then he nodded. "Not a trace."

"So I'm not going to change?" Sachi's voice cracked on the question.

He patted her hand. "I don't believe you will."

She turned to me. "Can I go? My children must be so worried."

I wanted to tell her to go hug her kids, but what I'd done was too new to trust just yet. "You'll need to stay a bit longer, just to be on the safe side."

Her smile collapsed. "But—"

"Your family would be in danger if we're wrong," I said. "Are you willing to take that chance?"

Her eyes widened. She shook her head.

I waved over one of the cops standing guard around our group. He was short and plump, with dark hair and an insane number of freckles. "Please take this woman to Conference Room B, then find Sarah Nazari in the gym and ask her to stay with her."

The man frowned. "I don't know who that is."

"Wouldn't Marc be the better choice anyway?" Luke asked.

"We need him on hand for the ones we *know* are going to change."

"I'll take her," Emma piped up from behind the cop. Luke, Sachi, the cop, and I all turned to look at her. She was sitting pretty much where I'd left her. "I'm not much use out here, but I know my way around the PTF building well enough to find Sarah in the gym. And I can stay with Sachi and whomever else you send there to help keep them calm." Her gaze met mine, and I was reminded of the way she'd looked at me on the rooftop when her strange "sight" kicked in.

I stepped away from Sachi and knelt next to Emma, whispering in her ear. "Did it come back?"

Emma smiled. "I wasn't just sitting here doing nothing while you and Luke were working."

I glanced at Sachi. "If we're wrong and she still changes. . . ."

"That's why Sarah will be there."

Luke shook his head. "You're in no condition to—"

"Emma knows what she's capable of," I cut him off. "Better than either of us. If she says she can do this, she can." I helped her to her feet and placed her hand in Sachi's. "Find Sarah and wait in Conference Room B. And take Officer—" I waved at the cop.

"Ramos," he supplied.

"—Officer Ramos with you so he knows the way. Hopefully, I'll have more people for him to escort soon."

Emma, Sachi, and Officer Ramos headed for the shattered lobby of the PTF building.

"You shouldn't cater to her like that," Luke said.

"And you shouldn't coddle her," I shot back. "She's more capable than you think."

He grumbled and shook his head but let the matter drop.

I gestured to the two patients he'd been working on. "Should I try decontaminating one of these?"

"Honestly, the woman's more likely to survive if she *does* change, assuming I can keep her stable that long. Without a werewolf's ability to heal, I don't think she'll make it."

My mouth went dry. *Die as a human or live as a werewolf. What a choice.* Unfortunately, she wasn't conscious to make it.

Luke pointed to the man. "I think I've got this one out of the woods. See what you can do."

I nodded and moved to the man's side. Luke went back to working on the woman.

My magic was easier to access than it had been with the woman because I'd already faced the fears and concerns blocking my path. Not that they'd gone away, but they were no longer acting as a barrier to my magic.

Does Bael have to face the truth of himself every time he wants to imbue something?

I couldn't even imagine the kind of emotional baggage a centuries-old fae with at least one attempted genocide and the destruction of a planet to his name would be carrying around.

I exhaled and let that thought spiral away with the others, focusing on the task at hand.

The infection was stronger in this man. His wounds were deeper and closer to his heart. Most of his torso was already converted, overgrown with the same sludge-like substance I'd found in the woman, but his core was a deep burgundy.

I tugged at the threads of who he was, looking for a foothold. Images flashed past my awareness. *Andrew Martin. His friends called him Drew. He was an off-duty PTF field agent who'd stopped by to use the gym. He'd been in the lobby when all hell broke loose.*

I dug deeper and found an ex-wife, a recent crush on a downtown barista, a golden retriever named Milo, memories of basic training and time served in Afghanistan, lost friends, saved friends, a lonely Christmas in a minimalist apartment.

I wrapped invisible fingers into those memories at his core and pulled them toward the infection, just as I had with the woman, reminding his body who he was—*what* he was.

The contamination fought back. It knew what the man could become. The mutation had memories, too. The freedom of running through the night. The speed. The strength. The power.

I pushed harder against the spread, but I could feel Drew wavering, enticed by the possibilities the mutation was offering.

"Come on, Drew," I growled between clenched teeth. "Work with me here."

The man hovered at the edge of consciousness. His eyes rolled back and forth beneath their lids. Sweat beaded on his upper lip. He groaned softly. His breath was coming faster, straining his bandages.

I coaxed one strand of his being back to burgundy only to find another had turned black. It was like playing a game of "Whack-a-Mole," and my energy was flagging. My own breath quickened as though I was running a race. My concentration began to splinter. My stomach cramped painfully, nearly doubling me over.

Drew began to twitch as though having a seizure. I pressed his shoulders down as hard as I could.

Luke was at my side in an instant. The green glow of his magic seeped into Drew, easing tense muscles and slowing his heart.

I took my hands away and sat back on my heels, staring at the dark mass in his chest. I'd made barely a dent. Even as I watched, the infection surged and spread, reaching into Drew's core.

"I can't save him," I whispered.

Luke patted me on the shoulder. "That you can save any will be a miracle. Move on to the next one."

I nodded and waved David over. Now that we knew I couldn't stop this man's transformation, we might as well prepare for the inevitable. "Take this guy to one of the holding cells on the lower level, and get Marc in there with him."

He nodded and called for a stretcher on his radio.

I tried to stand, but dizziness overwhelmed me.

David grabbed my arm, steadying me as I sat back down. Luke frowned. I waved them both away. "I just need to catch my breath."

Luke's frown remained in place, but he returned to the patient he'd been working on when Drew had started to convulse. There were too many people who needed his help for him to spend time worrying about me.

"Don't push yourself too hard." David gave my arm a squeeze before leaving with the medics and the man I'd failed to save.

I come. James's touch on my mind was like a life preserver buoying me up from my exhaustion as his inner strength bolstered my own.

I smiled and sent back, *Bring food.* James's presence might increase my mental fortitude, but my physical body was running on empty. I needed fuel.

Worry filtered through our connection. He wanted to protect me, and I loved him for it, but there was no one else who could do what I could do. No matter the strain, succeed or fail, I couldn't stop until the job was done.

I didn't try to stand again. I crawled to the next injured person—a man with a bandage around his neck and shoulder. His black cargo pants and utility belt marked him as one of David's security officers. His eyes were closed, and he was breathing evenly, though a medic held an oxygen mask over his mouth and nose.

"How is he?" I asked.

The EMT, a woman with a high ponytail and blue-framed glasses, looked over the patient at me. "Two gunshot wounds. One barely missed his heart. We removed the bullets and patched him up, but that's all we can do here."

I frowned. *If those were his only injuries, how did he get infected?*

I checked the wounds. Sure enough, dark strands of mutation traced the hole made by one of the bullets, but only one.

The shot must have passed through a werewolf before hitting him, transferring some blood. I shook my head. *What shitty luck.*

I set to work one more time, calling up my magic, getting to know my patient, pushing back the infection. This time, I was able to return the man's infected tissue to cherry red without much trouble. Maybe it was because of the way the mutation had been transferred, or maybe this man just had a stronger sense of self than my previous patient. Whatever the reason, Jason Donovan would not be turning into a werewolf tonight.

I sat back from Mr. Donovan. A warm, wrapped package was pushed into my hands. I opened my eyes, looking first into the cornflower blue of James's gaze then down at the burger he'd placed in my lap.

I smiled. "Thank you."

He lifted two large brown sacks in one hand and gave them a shake. "Not the most nutritious of meals, but it was fast and there's plenty of it." He searched my face. I could feel his presence probing my mind as well. "How are you doing?"

I lifted one shoulder in a half shrug and unwrapped my burger. "I think I've prevented the change in two so far."

His eyebrows lifted. "That's incredible."

"There was another that I couldn't help." I took two quick bites, stuffing my mouth.

He shook his head and knelt beside me. "You give yourself too little credit, Alex. You are, unequivocally, the most remarkable person I've ever met in all my long existence." He tucked a stray hair behind my ear. His eyes grew distant. A soft smile curved his lips as he stroked my cheek. "I am so lucky to have found you."

I paused in my chewing and leaned into his touch. *We're both lucky.*

The burger he'd handed me, along with a second, vanished in a matter of seconds. Then it was on to the next injured person. Hours passed in the rhythm of assess, imbue, eat, repeat. James kept to the periphery of the triage area, out of the way of the medics who scurried from person to person, but he was always at my side when I sat back from an attempt, success or failure. His constant presence at the back of my mind was a rock in the storm of emotions dredged up by my magic and the crashing waves of memories that washed over me as I sought the core of each infected individual.

I was halfway through working on a woman with a mangled leg when the screams began. I'd sent six more people to Conference Room B and three to the holding cells. The remaining injured had been growing more restless with every passing minute—clothes and hair soaked in sweat, anguished moans, twisting and curling in on themselves as they sought to escape the pain of being in their own bodies. The medics distributed what painkillers they could and tried to hold the people down when they thrashed. The guards around us grew more tense. Sidearms left their holsters. Then a man with shoulder-length sandy-blond hair let out a blood-curdling shriek. The bones beneath his skin started to shift, bulging and boiling beneath the surface. He screamed again. The sound twisted and choked as his neck and face changed shape. His back arched. His limbs went rigid.

"Move aside," Luke shouted. Every gun barrel was centered on the writhing man. The medics trying to hold him down made a space for Luke to reach his side. Luke set one hand on the man's forehead and the other on his chest. The tension eased in the man's body. Though he was far from relaxed, at least he didn't look as though he were about to snap himself in two. Luke shook his head. "We're out of time."

David stepped forward. He looked at the man under Luke's hands, then around at the remaining infected. "Can we keep them sedated?"

Luke shook his head but didn't look up. His attention was all for the man under his hands. "The transformation will burn any sedatives out of their system."

"Then we need to get the rest of these people locked down."

"I'm not done yet," I said.

David shook his head. "We can't risk waiting any longer. If they change out here in the open, we won't be able to contain them all, and we may end up with more casualties." He turned to address the guards. "Three to a team. Lead them, carry them, drag them if you have to, but I want a gun on them at all times until they're in a cell. Move!"

The guards split into teams as David instructed, each cluster taking one of the soon-to-be-werewolves. Most of the injured allowed themselves to be led away, moving like sleepwalkers. I wasn't sure if their placid attitudes were due to fever, drugs, or despair, but at least they didn't cause any trouble. A few were unconscious and had to be carried. One woman started screaming and thrashing. It took four men to hold her down long enough for a medic to get a needle in her arm. One man tried to talk his way out of going, arguing about his rights and threatening to sue, but he was in no condition to put up a fight.

David approached the woman I'd been working on, flanked by two police officers.

I placed a protective hand on my patient. "At least let me finish this one."

David pursed his lips.

"I'll stay with her." James was suddenly standing between David and me. "The woman will not be allowed to harm anyone, least of all Alex. You have my word."

David looked James up and down. He gave a stiff nod, then gestured for his group to collect the next doomed soul.

I looked at James. "Thank you."

He met my gaze. "If she begins to turn, I will do what I must."

A vision of the dead bodies scattered beneath the trees around the refugee camp flashed in my mind. I swallowed, my mouth dry, and turned back to my patient.

Her name was Gwen. She was a new PTF agent just out of orientation. She had a four-year-old daughter waiting at home, watched by her mother while Gwen was at work. There was no father, just some faceless high school mistake. I could feel the woman's determination to get back to her little girl. She was fighting the infection with everything she had. I couldn't let her lose.

Funneling my magic into Gwen's body, I bolstered her defenses. Her leg was almost entirely converted, but her core was still strong. She knew who she was and who she wanted to be. A mother. A daughter. A protector. A fighter. Together we pushed the infection back.

Sweat poured down my face, dripping off the tip of my nose and making my lips salty. When the last trace of infection had been eradicated from Gwen's leg, I sat back on my heels with a heavy sigh and wiped my forehead.

James placed his hand against my back, warm and solid, supporting me. "Is it done?"

I nodded, too tired to respond with words.

Gwen's eyelids fluttered opened. Her mouth moved, but she had even less strength left than I did, plus the lingering effects of the fever. She licked her lips, held my gaze, and nodded.

I smiled and nodded back, then turned to James. "Can you take her to the conference room with the other people we don't think will change?"

He set the brown sack with the remainder of the burgers he'd been doling out in my lap, lifted Gwen easily into his arms, and was gone in a flash.

I hope I was right about the nature of the werewolf infection. I hope Gwen and the others won't turn. I hope this wasn't all for nothing.

I looked up at the late-afternoon sky. The bottoms of the clouds were blushed with pink and orange. The sun shone on my face from low in the west, but there didn't seem to be any warmth in it.

I fumbled at the bag on my lap with numb fingers, finally managing to unwrap a burger that had long since lost its heat. I bit off a chunk and chewed. I could have been chewing cardboard for all that the flavor registered. I was tired enough to sleep for a year, but I forced my jaw to keep working. I swallowed and took another bite, over and over until the food was gone. I still felt wrung out, like my body might shake to pieces at any moment.

I stared after the group of guards who'd taken the last of the infected inside. The world swam and swayed. Silver sparks burst like fireworks around the edges of my vision. Then James was at my back. His strength bolstered me, his calm confidence was an anchor in the storm.

"Let's get you home." He scooped me up.

"Take me inside," I said. "There might still be time for one or two more."

He frowned. "You've given all you can."

I shook my head. "So long as there's a chance, I have to try."

"The cells are closed," he said softly. "All we can do now is wait and see how many make it through."

I buried my face against his chest and tried to hold on to the fact that I'd managed to save at least some.

Chapter 13

ICE CRUNCHED beneath my Jeep's tires as James navigated the last bend in my driveway, bringing us in view of the house. The snow that had been relegated to shadowy patches in the city covered my property in a crusted layer of white. Frozen footprints dotted the landscape, marking the paths I most often tread like pockmarks. Daylight had faded as we wound our way up Boulder Canyon, but the faint light of the crescent moon reflected off the snow to create a bluish glow over the land.

James pulled the Jeep into its usual spot and cut the engine. Silence fell over us, as muffling as the blanket of snow muting the forest. Emma had stayed behind. Once Luke was done with the werewolves, she wanted to talk to him about the strange new vision Shedraziel had awoken in her and the possibility of her magic returning. The idea that someone who'd suffered a burnout could get their magic back. . . . I shook my head and looked at my house. The front window was aglow, but the curtains were drawn, so I couldn't see in. Chase and Zeraldi would be inside—another issue to deal with before reaching my bed. I sighed and pushed the button to release my seat belt.

"We can talk to Chase in the morning." James's words were startlingly loud in the quiet.

I shook my head. "We don't know how much time we have."

James circled the Jeep before I got my door open. He helped me down, taking the weight off my injured leg, and led me to the house.

When he opened the door, warm air rushed into the night, stirring my hair. I paused on the threshold. It had been almost exactly a day in the mortal realm since I'd left, but so much had happened. I closed my eyes, thinking about my time in California and the Undine Realm, marveling at the impossibilities magic made possible. James closed the door behind us, sealing out the cold.

"'Bout time."

I opened my eyes.

Chase peeked over the back of the couch. One bare foot was visible on the armrest. "Guess you had quite the mess to clean up."

I looked around. "Where's Zeraldi?"

He tipped his head toward the hallway that led to the back rooms. "Put her to bed. She should be right as rain when she wakes up."

I pictured the gaping holes I'd seen when she was lying on the sidewalk and looked down at my bandaged leg. My fae healing would have me walking normally soon enough if I managed to get some proper food and rest. I looked at the first door in the hallway. My bedroom. I could almost hear the call of my mattress as though it, too, were a siren luring me in.

It was an effort to drag my gaze away and settle it back on Chase. "How'd your mission go?"

James half carried me to an armchair. Once I was settled, he moved to the kitchen and opened the fridge.

I kicked off my shoes and rubbed my frozen toes, knocking loose a few clumps of snow that had followed me in.

"The griffins in the shifter desert are all still there. They have nothing to do with the group in Nevada, but they had heard some grumblings from the Aerie Realm. That's pretty much all I learned before—"

Someone cleared their throat.

We all looked toward the hallway.

Zeraldi was standing in the opening in her human form—not glamoured but physically shifted. Her pale skin shimmered slightly under the light as though she were covered in glitter, and no mortal ever had eyes like hers—molten-gold with vertical pupils. Glossy strands of lavender hair hung to her waist. She wore one of the sundresses Chase's sister, Jynx, had left behind when she ran off to get married. Red strawberries with curling green vines dotted the pale-pink fabric that swished around her knees, adding to her youthful appearance. Her feet remained bare.

Chase jerked a thumb at Zeraldi. "—she showed up."

"Yeah, not that I'm not thrilled with your help—I assume that was you who made everyone fall asleep—but what were you doing there in the first place?"

James closed the refrigerator door.

Zeraldi's gaze shifted to the kitchen. Her eyes narrowed.

"He's not so bad once you get to know him," Chase said.

"He is tainted." She frowned. "But he is different."

"He's the one who brought you here to heal," I said. "Otherwise the human authorities would have found you."

She nodded to James and walked across the living room to the remaining armchair, but she didn't turn her back on the kitchen where James was making a sandwich out of the contents of my fridge. Once Zeraldi was settled on the faded cushion, she smiled at me. "The last time we met, we didn't have much occasion to speak."

"Yeah, that was . . . hectic."

James came out of the kitchen carrying a plate with two slices of multigrain bread stacked high with sliced ham, crisp lettuce, provolone, and avocado in one hand and a glass of milk in the other.

My stomach grumbled, and my mouth started to water. Despite already eating four times as much as I normally would in a day in just the past hour, I was starving.

He walked the long way around the living room so as not to cross behind Zeraldi's chair, which I appreciated. He set the plate on the coffee table, pulled it within easy reach with a screech of wood against wood as the legs scraped across the floor, and set the glass beside it. I moved the plate to my lap and dug in.

James glanced at the couch, but perched on the arm of my chair.

Zeraldi and Chase watched the whole production in silence—her frowning, him smirking.

When I'd swallowed my third bite and downed half the milk, Zeraldi continued. "You freed me from Shedraziel's prison, for which I am exceedingly grateful. I've come to repay that debt, both to you and to her."

I choked down the half-chewed bite in my mouth and took another swig of milk so I could speak. "You're going to help us stop her?"

"I'm going to help you *end* her." She didn't even blink when she said it. The fae had a very different mentality about killing than humans, and this one had plenty of motivation to want Shedraziel dead.

I nodded. "Glad to have you on board, Zeraldi."

"You may call me Zee." Her gaze shifted to Chase. A slight blush rose on her pale cheeks. "I am told it is the custom in this realm to shorten one's name among acquaintances."

"You haven't been in the mortal realm before?" James asked.

The color abruptly left Zee's cheeks. "No."

Shedraziel only stole children. I pictured Zee as I'd first seen her, in her dragon form, chained in a stable with Shedraziel's other captives. *By fae standards, Zee might not be much older than the eight-year-old she appears as in her human form.*

"Zee found me in the shifter desert with Targe and the griffins." Chase leaned back and crossed his legs, drawing everyone's attention and redirecting the conversation. "She just showed up and started barking orders."

Zee gave him a tight smile. "Swiftness was required if we were to reach Alex in time to be useful."

"How did you know I was in trouble?"

Her gaze settled on me, assessing. "How much do you know about dragons?"

I swallowed. Kai had once asked me exactly the same question . . . right before he told me my grandfather was responsible for decimating their species and destroying their home world. "Not a lot except that they were the progenitors of some of the other fae races"—I nodded to Chase—"like the shifters, and there aren't many left."

"We were also the origin of the elementals. Like other fae, we were born with certain affinities, making some forms of magic easier to master than others. The color of our scales indicates with which elements we are most in tune."

I nodded and took another bite of my half-eaten sandwich. Hortense had told me something similar during my seemingly endless fae history lessons.

"Opal dragons," she said as she placed a hand against her chest, "are exceedingly rare. Our affinity is to the spirit."

I frowned. "What does that mean?"

"Rather than manipulating water or air, we can see beyond the veil of reality and affect the incorporeal."

I continued to stare.

"They're also oracles and dream walkers," Chase said.

My mouth dropped open. "You can see the future?"

"Sometimes," she said. "Though my visions do not show *the* future. I see images from many possible futures, all open to interpretation. The more likely the future, the clearer the image. Shedraziel's attack, your need of my presence, and your companions' arrival in the Shifter Realm were all quite clear. Other images were not."

"So you met up with Chase and came to help because you saw the attack in your vision, and you put everyone to sleep to prevent Shedraziel from controlling them."

"She also gave Targe a mission," Chase said, "before we left the Shifter Realm."

"What mission?" James asked.

"To gather allies." Zee looked at James, then away. She shifted in her seat, gave herself a little shake, then met his gaze again. "The fight here was not the one I've come to warn you about. Shedraziel is planning something much worse."

I leaned forward, my sandwich forgotten. "What else did you see?"

Her gaze flicked back and forth, focused on nothing. "A silver necklace with a blue jewel half buried in desert sand. The necklace turned into a snake, the jewel its eye, and slipped beneath the dunes."

I chewed my lower lip. Could Zee have seen the gem the Undine Lord had asked me to retrieve? And if so, what did it mean that the necklace was lost in the sand?

"I saw humans and fae lined up like wooden soldiers in two even rows, but all mixed together. Then all at once they lifted their hands, pointed to the figure across from them, and fell down as one. They lay in two neat rows where they'd stood, and a shadow walked the path between them."

I set my sandwich on its plate and rubbed my hands together, trying to work feeling into my cold fingers. "It doesn't take an oracle to see where the world is heading if things keep on the way they are. Shedraziel's plan isn't just to reignite the war between humans and fae, she's sowing chaos between all the factions so there will be infighting as well."

"Like what happened at the PTF building," James said. "No one could tell who was on which side."

My stomach clenched. My half-eaten meal felt like a lead ball. "Framing the undine for polluting the coasts, making people disappear in the Black Forest. . . . She's doing everything she can to make people paranoid and scared so they'll turn on each other."

James nodded. "Panic is the fastest way to destabilize peace."

"And because Shedraziel is known as Enchantment's general, the other lords will read this as a unilateral play for power on Bael's part," Chase said. "They'll want to either grab their own piece of the pie or use the excuse to slip a knife in an enemy's back. Either way, they'll be drawn into the chaos."

I braced my elbows against my knees and rubbed my temples, picturing the horrors I'd seen at the battle of Arlington multiplied a hundred-fold and played out all over the world. "We have to stop her."

"My vision included several difficult-to-interpret images, including tearing fabric, a gong, a drowned city, and a mountain shaped like a sleeping giant. I saw you, Alex, walking through a city of light crowded with people. You held a pool of water in your cupped hands. The sun and moon shared the sky in the water's reflection. Then you opened your hands, and the water poured out. When the drops splashed against the ground at your feet, all the people in the city of light vanished. Sand blew through the streets and buried the buildings. Then the lights went out, and you were alone in the dark."

I shivered.

"I do not know what all of the images mean, but I believe that if you face what is to come alone, you will fail."

James wrapped an arm protectively around my shoulders, squeezing me to his side. Our invisible tether thickened to a heavy cable as he closed the space between us. "Alex will never be alone so long as I'm alive."

"Then I hope you are alive when these events come to pass." Zee said. "But just in case, I have set other arrangements into motion."

"Targe," I guessed. "That's why you told him to gather allies."

She nodded. "You must gather all those you can to your banner. If you fail, Shedraziel wins. We must not let that happen."

"But even if we gather an army," James said, "we have no idea when or where Shedraziel will attack." He quirked an eyebrow. "Unless you can be more specific about this 'city of light' you saw?"

She shook her head. "As to the when, the moon reflected in the water was two days past its current phase. I've instructed Targe to gather all those he can on the mortal side of the Colorado Reservation before that time."

"So we have a time frame," Chase said. "Now we just need to figure out where to send our soon-to-be-army."

"And how to get them there," James added.

"Assuming Targe can actually convince anyone to help," Chase finished.

I leaned into James, taking comfort from his nearness. "In the refugee camp, Shedraziel talked about breaking dams to drown the world. I assumed she was talking about the chaos she was spreading, but if you saw a submerged city in your vision . . . could she have meant that literally?"

"Destroying a dam would certainly cause problems," James said. "Not just flooding, but a disruption to power, irrigation . . . who knows what else. It could certainly make the lights go out."

"But even if she is going after a dam, which one?" I shook my head. "And it's still just a guess based on one random phrase and a vague vision of a flooded city." I smiled at Zee. "No offense."

"None taken," she said. "You're right to be cautious. Prophecies can be dangerous and fickle things. The images I see can be figurative or literal, and there is no way to tell which until they come to pass. Many people have attempted to prevent a certain future only to bring about the very fate they hoped to avoid."

I stared at the plate on my lap, no longer interested in the remainder of my sandwich. *If changing the future were as simple as seeing what to avoid, the dragon home world would never have been destroyed.*

MUSIC BLARED. I jerked awake, groping for my phone on the bedside table.

"Leave it," James murmured. One of his arms was draped across my chest.

The weight reminded me uncomfortably of the dream from which I'd just awoken. A constricting serpent had squeezed the air from my lungs and pulled me beneath sand dunes that were spreading across Denver like a tidal wave.

I pushed arm, blanket, and sheet off in one motion and twisted to perch on the edge of my bed. My skin was sweat-slicked and clammy. I shivered. I finally managed to locate my phone. David's lopsided grin lit the screen. I pressed the talk button and lifted it to my ear.

"Alex, you need to get over here, now."

I rubbed a hand over my face, trying to get my thoughts in order. "What? Where? What's happened?"

"Weatherly called me in this morning for an emergency meeting at the legislative services building, behind what's left of the capitol, to discuss the future of the PTF paranaturals. Anderson and the Church delegates are here, too."

I straightened, suddenly wide awake. "Why wasn't I called? I'm in charge of paranatural relations, for fuck's sake."

"Marc and Garret were excluded, too. My guess is Weatherly's hoping to get through this meeting without any awkward arguments on the paranaturals' behalf. I doubt he would have included me either except he needs me to coordinate security for the werewolves."

I dragged my hand through my hair but got caught in the tangles. "Stall as long as you can. I'm on my way."

I set the phone back on the table and turned to face James. His blue gaze was fixed on me.

"I have to go."

"I heard." He frowned. "Be careful, Alex. Politics is a very different sort of battle, and you're still learning the rules of engagement."

"I'll be fine." I stood up and started digging clothes out of my dresser. "Besides, I need to tell them what we learned from Zeraldi. We may not know where Shedraziel will attack, but we've got a time frame."

His frown deepened. He sat up, bracing his back against the headboard. The blanket and sheets dropped to his waist.

I paused in my rummaging to admire the contours of his arms and chest, the tight, toned curves of his muscles.

One corner of his mouth twitched. An invitation drifted across our connection.

I shook my head. "I have to go."

The twinkle in his eyes dimmed. "And what exactly are you going to say? Telling them about Zeraldi's prophecy will only cause trouble."

"Then I won't mention the prophecy, or Zeraldi, but they need to know what we're up against. I can at least tell them the undine aren't responsible for the beach trash. Maybe that will ease the fae-human tension a little bit and give us some breathing room to get this mess sorted out."

"You think they'll take your word for it?"

I tugged on a clean sweater and slammed the dresser drawer closed. "Whose side are you on?"

"Yours. Always. That's why I feel it necessary to point out the potential holes in your strategy, of which there are many."

"Well if you've got a better suggestion, I'm all ears."

"Zeraldi claims you need as many allies as you can muster. That includes those sworn to the PTF. Just remember that those with whom you share a title do not necessarily share your goals."

I laughed. "As if I could forget that I'm not playing on the same team as Weatherly and Anderson. I just hope Harris is still in my corner after yesterday's carnage, assuming she's even awake, and that the Church delegation remembers who fought to protect them." I sat on the bed to pull on my socks, then leaned over and planted a firm kiss against James's lips.

He caught me in his arms, pulling me closer. Warmth and desire flooded our connection, laced through with pride.

As much as he grumbles and pokes holes, he supports what I'm doing. I smiled against his mouth and pulled back. "Wish me luck."

He held on a moment longer, then relaxed his arms. "Call if you need me."

Chase was a curled ball of gray fur on the back of my couch when I reached the living room. He lifted his head, yawned, and blinked his luminous green eyes as I darted into the kitchen, popped a slice of bread in the toaster, and grabbed the half-full carafe of liquid heaven. I was in and out in under two minutes, running to the car with a travel mug of coffee in one hand and a piece of jellied toast in my mouth.

The drive down the canyon seemed endless, every curve slowing me down. When I reached the outer edge of Boulder and the turnoff to Luke's neighborhood, my thoughts turned to Emma. Had she and Luke been able to figure out what Shedraziel's impossible compulsion had done to her?

My phone buzzed against my thigh, and the first few chords of the wicked witch theme song from *The Wizard of Oz* filled the cab. I peeked to verify the ring belonged to Victoria, then dismissed the call.

I so don't have time for that drama right now.

But Victoria's call brought back the image of her in James's bed, and all my insecurities bubbled to the surface. So much had happened since I got back that I'd completely forgotten to be mad at him.

Am I still mad?

The phone rang again. This time I just ignored it. After a moment the ring cut off, but a second later it was back.

I gritted my teeth, punched the button to answer, and growled, "What is it, Victoria? I'm busy."

"Yes, I can imagine." Her voice was smooth as warm honey with just the hint of a southern drawl. "The recent excitement at your PTF facility is why I'm calling."

I held my breath and concentrated on navigating the traffic in front of me as I sped through the city.

"I saw you on the news. Not a very flattering portrait, I'm afraid. Not like James, fighting off those werewolves in all his bare-chested glory."

My heart dropped through the Jeep's floor and got flattened by the back wheels.

"You lied to me, Alex."

"I'm not sure what—"

"Don't insult me." The honey was still there but laced with a heavy dose of arsenic.

I swerved to avoid rear-ending a silver Taurus that had stopped short for a yellow light. "I really don't have time to discuss this right now."

"A vampire who can walk in daylight unaided goes far beyond some simple trinket."

I scoffed. "A day-walking amulet is hardly simple."

"This will change . . . everything."

"Not if Shedraziel plunges the world into chaos and war. I don't know if you've noticed, but I've got bigger concerns right now."

"More important to you maybe, but I assure you, nothing is more important to me. How did you do it?"

I pressed the button to disconnect the call and tossed the phone on the passenger seat. It rang four more times before I reached Denver. Then Victoria either got sidetracked or finally took the hint that I wasn't going to answer her calls.

She is definitely going to be trouble.

I sighed and took the off-ramp downtown. Snowflakes drifted through the air, pinpricks of ice barely big enough to see against the pale sky, but they speckled my windshield as I drove to the address David had given me.

The roads around the capitol building were cordoned off, though the police tape was barely visible through the crowds of people gathered around the perimeter. Some were reporters with camera crews; some were just curious gawkers. There were also more protesters than I'd ever seen in front of the PTF building waving signs and banners. Shouts of "No more magic!" rang out, audible even with my windows up.

Behind the line, the white stones of the capitol building were charred black. The golden dome was gone, and the entrance columns were piles of rubble on the steep stairs leading to the main entrance. The north side seemed largely untouched, but the south wing of the building had collapsed, ending in jagged walls halfway up. Emergency workers moved around the grounds, securing the site.

I shuddered. *Even if we stop Shedraziel, will regular humans ever trust magic users after something like this?*

I shook my head. *Can't think that way. Just deal with the next step. Leave tomorrow's problems for tomorrow.*

I found a parking space along Sherman Street and raced down the wet sidewalk toward the legislation building. The air was so cold it burned my lungs. Puffs of frozen breath trailed behind me like the exhaust of a steam engine. I rounded the corner on Fourteenth Avenue. A set of stairs led up to a series of Ionic columns supporting a carved entablature. Nestled at the center was a pair of ornate wooden doors. I burst through the doors and stumbled to a stop on the slick tiles of the entryway.

A young man in a dark-blue suit jumped up behind an oak desk, his eyes wide and skittish. "What's wrong?"

I flashed him my PTF credentials and said, "I'm late for the meeting. Where's Governor Anderson?"

Relaxing slightly, he pointed down the hall to his left. "Room D."

I took off before he could frame another question.

Room D turned out to be a modest-sized conference room just off the main corridor. I pushed the door open and stepped inside without bothering to knock.

"—agree on that." Governor Anderson was sitting at the head of a long oval table. His suit was rumpled. His silver hair was combed but oily. Dark circles sagged beneath blue eyes shot with red.

A twinge of guilt sparked in my chest. This man had been the target of an assassination attempt yesterday, and he'd likely spent a good deal of the night sorting out the aftermath. The fact that he was alive at all was a minor miracle according to the update Officer Ramirez had relayed while Luke and I were working on the werewolf victims. Cynthia Daniels hadn't been so lucky. Much as I hated the woman, I was sorry she was dead.

Bishop Silva, Ulama Ali, and Pandit Khatun sat along the near side of the table, their backs to me. David and Weatherly were on the far side.

David's shoulders relaxed slightly when his gaze met mine.

Weatherly glared. "What are you doing here?"

The Church delegates twisted to see me.

I closed the door, circled around to the end of the table opposite Anderson, and sat down. "As Deputy Director in charge of Paranatural Relations, I should have been included in this meeting, as should Marc and Garrett."

Weatherly sniffed. "Consider yourself relieved of duty."

"That's not your call."

David shook his head almost imperceptibly.

"Actually, it is," Weatherly said.

My heart skipped a beat, and my palms grew sweaty.

Anderson leaned forward, resting his forearms on the polished black table. "Unfortunately, Director Harris was incapacitated in yesterday's attack on the PTF building. She has yet to regain consciousness. As her senior-most assistant, Mr. Weatherly is now acting director not only of Colorado, but all of the Western US."

"And as such," Weatherly continued, "I hereby inform you that your position with the agency has been suspended indefinitely."

My mouth opened and closed a few times before I managed to say, "This experiment was sanctioned by the entire PTF board. You don't have the authority to override their ruling."

"Face it," Anderson said. "Your *experiment*"—he drew the word out—"has already failed."

I glanced at the delegates. Khatun shifted in his seat and looked away. Ali and Silva met my gaze, the first with apparent sympathy, the second as though curious what I might do next.

Weatherly leaned back in his seat and steepled his fingers. "I've already petitioned the board to reopen the matter. I'm confident that, given yesterday's events, they'll discontinue this farce. Until then, I suggest you leave with what dignity you can."

I clenched my fists. "Until the board votes, I'm still an assistant director with the PTF."

"An honorary title at best. Without Harris to back you up, you have no authority here."

"You need magic on your side now more than ever."

Anderson scowled at me down the length of the table. "How far will you go to protect your precious paranaturals? Practitioners destroyed the state capitol. Werewolves tried to rip apart these esteemed delegates." He gestured to Silva, Ali, and Khatun. "And still you claim we should trust them?"

"What happened yesterday wasn't their fault, any more than it was David's fault for shooting me."

David shifted in his chair.

"All of the attacks yesterday were caused by the same person. A fae named Shedraziel."

Ali adjusted her glasses and pinned me with her intense gaze. "So you admit the fae were behind the attack?"

I shook my head and lifted a single finger. "*One* fae. One seriously deranged and dangerous person that you are going to need a massive amount of help to stop."

"And let me guess," Weatherly said. "You alone can provide that help."

"Not alone, but I have the connections you need." I splayed my fingers on the cold surface of the table. "Humans don't stand a chance against Shedraziel. What happened yesterday was only a taste of what she's capable of. Only people with strong magic will have any hope of stopping her."

Khatun raised an eyebrow. "Yet you claim the practitioners who attacked yesterday were also her victims?"

"Practitioners are still human. They stand no better chance than the rest of you."

"And the werewolves?" Weatherly asked. "Or do you claim they're human as well?"

"Some of the werewolves were affected by Shedraziel's spell, but some managed to resist. I haven't had a chance to speak with Marc about it yet, but if we can figure out why some of the werewolves were immune to her magic, maybe we can protect the rest of them. In any case, the werewolves alone won't be enough. The only beings with magic strong enough to face Shedraziel on even terms are the fae."

Anderson's abrupt laughter echoed through the conference room. "Last month we were faced with a paranatural threat that you convinced the PTF only other paranaturals could handle." He spread his hands. "So here we are with freaks galore standing at our backs. Now we've got a rogue fae, and you insist that the only solution is more fae. I'm beginning to see a pattern."

"Whatever you may think of me or my motivations, that doesn't change the facts."

"Yes, and the fact is that the peace treaty with the fae is over. Like it or not, we're at war. Whether with all paranaturals, or just the fae, or even just one fae doesn't matter. You claim that the only way for us to survive is to broker more deals with more magical beings. But I say that rather than complying with your manipulative efforts to subvert the PTF with a greater dependence on magic, we'd be better served eliminating the magic that's already here, as we should have done years ago."

Weatherly thumped his palm on the table. "Here, here!"

I gaped at them. "That's like amputating your arm so you don't have to deal with the splinter in your finger."

Anderson leaned forward. "If you're to be believed, and this is all the work of a single mastermind, that *splinter* is already responsible for killing dozens of people in Europe, polluting all the beaches bordering the Pacific Ocean, and turning northern Nevada into a desolate wasteland."

From what I'd seen of Nevada, that last didn't seem like much of a change, but I kept that observation to myself. "I'm not saying she doesn't need to be stopped. I'm saying you don't have the right tools to do it."

"The battery of missiles pointed at the Black Forest right now would beg to differ," Anderson shot back.

I worked my mouth for a moment, unable to form words as my mind struggled to process what I'd just heard.

David recovered first. "You're going to launch an attack on the German Reservation?"

"The PTF board approved the strike this morning," Weatherly confirmed. "The missiles will launch in"—he looked at the crystal face of his gold watch—"about an hour."

I jumped to my feet. "Are you out of your mind?"

Khatun sat forward, both palms pressed to the table. "Was the Church included in this decision?"

"They were informed," Weatherly said. "Most of your leaders were behind this course of action."

"But not all." Ali pursed her lips and leaned back in her chair. Her gaze grew distant as though she was lost in thought.

It was nice to know at least *some* members of the Church council weren't willing to condone sneak attacks and wholesale slaughter. The recent decimation of the old Church headquarters had left a lot of council seats open, and Purity had been quick to snatch them up. But they hadn't been able to make a clean sweep in the elections since their plan for using drug-enhanced humans to put down the sorcerer rebellion had failed so miserably.

"What is the expected human impact?" Bishop Silva asked.

"The area around the forest is being evacuated, though many had already left due to the disappearances."

I shook my head. "Reservations are protected by elemental guardians. They won't let you destroy the portals."

"By the time the fae know what hit them, the forest and all of their precious portals will be gone." Weatherly met my gaze. "We're about to free central Europe from fae influence."

Anderson clasped his hands on the table and smiled at me over his laced fingers. "Assuming all goes well, I intend to fully endorse a similar strike against the reservation here in Colorado, and I predict other areas forced into close proximity with fae strongholds will do likewise."

My throat constricted, and my mouth went dry as Anderson's words mingled with Zee's in my head. *I've instructed Targe to gather those he can on the mortal side of the Colorado Reservation.* If Anderson bombed the reservation, he'd take out all my waiting allies in a single strike.

"You can't." The words were a bare whisper between my parched lips.

"Excuse me?" Anderson cupped a hand to his ear. "What was that? A protest from a half-breed freak-lover whose only claim to authority is lying unconscious in a hospital bed?" He settled back in his seat. "I'll be sure to give your opinion due consideration. In the meantime, I suggest you take Director Weatherly's advice and return home. As of noon today, I'm enacting a house-arrest policy on all paranaturals in the state, whatever their current status. I've already mustered local National Guard personnel to state active duty to enforce the mandate. Any paranatural caught on the streets for *any* reason will be arrested." He smiled. "And thanks to you making Colorado a mecca for paranaturals, we've got an extensive registration list to identify them from."

"What about the werewolves and practitioners employed by the PTF?" I gritted out between clenched teeth.

"The handful of sorcerers you had on staff were arrested and fitted with control collars for their involvement in yesterday's bombing, as were their paladin guards.”

Silva shook his head. “I still can’t believe paladins participated in that attack.”

That was the first I’d heard of paladin involvement, but it made sense. If Shedraziel’s song targeted practitioners, her spell wouldn’t have differentiated between paladins and sorcerers.

“The werewolves,” Anderson continued, “both existing and those unfortunate enough to be cursed last night, are still under guard in the basement of the PTF building.” He fixed his gaze on David. “As head of security you will be responsible for transporting them all to a more secure holding facility as soon as possible.”

“All of them?” David stiffened in his chair. “What about the ones who helped defend the delegates and civilians?”

“All of them,” Anderson said.

“But—”

Weatherly turned on David. “Do your job or find another.”

David glanced at me.

I shook my head. At least with David still on the payroll, *someone* would be looking out for the werewolves.

“I’ll make the arrangements.” His words were clipped. A muscle twitched in the side of his neck.

“As for the fae,” Weatherly said, “all visas are hereby revoked in the Western US. I anticipate my counterpart will make the decision nationwide by the end of the day.”

I turned to the Church delegates. “How can you just sit there and let this happen? If not for the intervention of magical beings, you all would have died yesterday.”

Ali sighed and closed her eyes. “If not for the presence of magical beings, our lives would not have been in danger in the first place.”

“We’re grateful to your friend for protecting us,” Khatun said. “But Ms. Ali is right. While magic may have saved us, it’s also the root of the problem.”

“Speaking of your *friend*,” Weatherly coated the word in scorn, “Mr. Abernathy’s tests were incomplete. Once accommodations have been prepared for the werewolves, he will join them.”

“If there’s nothing else.” Anderson made a shooing motion.

I stared in mute horror for a moment, unable to come up with any argument that might divert this train wreck of a meeting. Everyone in the room stared back at me as the silence stretched and grew awkward. Most wore hard expressions. David winced and studied his lap when I caught his gaze.

My mind was blank. My body was numb. I walked slowly to the door, my arms and legs stiff with a cold deeper than the winter air outside.

They're going to blow up a reservation. Maybe all the reservations. They're going to arrest everyone with magic. They're going to start a witch hunt worse than history's ever seen. I glanced over my shoulder at the people gathered around the table. Only Weatherly was still watching me, the light of satisfaction bright in his eyes. *They're going to give Shedraziel exactly what she wants.*

I stepped into the hall, closed the door, and walked out of the building in a trance of despair and disbelief. The snow had grown heavier, the flakes larger, but I didn't even feel the cold as I walked back to my Jeep and slid behind the wheel. I didn't start the engine. Didn't even pull the keys from my pocket. I just gripped the steering wheel with both hands until my knuckles turned white and rested my head on the hard curve between them.

Six months since I found out I wasn't human. Six months of fear and pain. I'm tired of fighting. Tired of having to prove myself. Tired of watching friends suffer and die. And all for what? My voice is no louder now than when I was just a mid-level artist peddling sculptures in James's gallery.

I exhaled. My breath hung in a frozen cloud around my face.

So you're just going to roll over? asked the voice inside my head. *To hell with everyone who supported you and everything you sacrificed?*

I rolled my head from side to side. *What else can I do?*

I leaned back against my seat and thought of all the impossible obstacles that hadn't turned out to be impossible after all. The one common factor? I had help.

If you face what is to come alone, you will fail.

I pulled out my phone and scrolled through my contacts until I found Uncle Sol. Despite not being a blood relative, and as messed up as our relationship had become after I learned he'd been lying to me my whole life, he was still the closest thing I had to a parent. Aside from that, he had more authority in his little finger than I did in my whole being. If *I* couldn't convince the PTF they were making a mistake, maybe *he* could.

Chapter 14

"TO WHAT DO I owe the pleasure?" Uncle Sol's voice drifted through the line.

"Have you been paying attention to the news?"

"I'm retired. The only news I'm interested in these days is whether or not the fish are biting and what's for lunch."

"There's trouble brewing."

"There's always trouble."

"Major trouble. World-ending trouble. I need you to come back."

He sighed. "I'm an old man, Alex. I've done my duty, cashed in my markers, and burned my bridges. It took all of what influence I had left to avoid getting buried in some dark hole after my actions at Arlington. I intend to enjoy what's left of my life on a nice beach with a drink in one hand and a book in the other."

I watched the snow accumulate on my windshield. "Sounds nice."

"It is. So unless you're calling because you want to visit for a weekend of staring at the sea, there's nothing I can do for you."

"I get it, I do, but I need your help to convince the PTF they're making a mistake."

"No you don't."

"I do. I've tried on my own, but Weatherly revoked my position. I no longer have any authority."

After a long pause he said, "There are two kinds of authority. That which is given and that which is earned. The first comes in the form of titles and affiliations, and because it's given it can also be taken away. The second is the respect you earn just by being who you are and living your life accordingly. When I left the PTF I lost the titles I'd carried with that organization, but many of the people I'd worked with chose to follow me into exile because they respected me as a man and a leader. In the end, the authority you claim for yourself will always be stronger."

"You built that respect and authority over a lifetime. I don't have that kind of clout."

"Did that roommate of yours give up his position with the fae court on a whim? Did the werewolves follow you into battle because they don't value their lives? Did the PTF board agree to cooperate with paranaturals because it would be easy? You have more clout than you give yourself credit for. You just need to find a way to use it effectively."

"That last example's not working out so well."

"Whatever hardships you're facing, you'll handle. My time is over; it ended with your father. That's why I stepped down. It's time to hand the reins over to the next generation."

"But I'm not ready."

"No one ever is. Life is a sink-or-swim game. All you can do is the best you can and hope to hell that's enough."

I bit my lower lip. "What if it's not?"

"Then you'll join me on the beach, and we'll play chess and drink our worries away till the world ends."

I recalled the peace of sitting on a fire escape, sipping root beer and playing game after losing game of chess with Uncle Sol when I was young.

"But don't you dare show up until you've given everything you've got," he said.

I nodded to the empty air. "Thanks, Uncle Sol."

"Anytime, kiddo."

The line went dead. I cradled the phone in my lap, rested my head against my seat, and pictured Sol on a lounge chair at the beach.

The snow had built up on my windows so only a slim strip of clear glass near the top showed the world outside. Sight and sound were muffled. I took a deep breath and enjoyed the sensation of being cocooned, cut off from all the troubles outside my car. Then I exhaled and placed the key in the ignition. One flick of the wipers knocked loose my isolating shell.

MY FIRST STOP after the disastrous meeting was the PTF building. Like the capitol building, the area was cordoned off and ringed with protesters undeterred by the weather. Workers were busy clearing debris from the lobby. Since the rest of the building had been largely untouched, it would probably be open for services within a week. I pictured the men and women taken to the holding cells last night. How many had survived their change? Had they managed to change back? Then I thought of Marc and the other stable wolves who'd stayed to help . . . and were now prisoners.

I jerked the keys from the ignition and climbed out. *I might not be able to free them, but I can at least check in and let them know what's happening in my own words. I owe them that much.*

I pressed through the crowd of protesters and reporters, keeping my head down so as not to be noticed until I ducked under the caution tape and headed for the entrance. A few workers glanced in my direction, but their job was cleanup, not security. I made it as far as the lobby, but when I turned toward the hall leading to the nearest stairwell, a young man in full PTF riot gear jumped in my path.

He had a slightly pudgy face spotted with dark freckles. His blue eyes were wide with surprise, and his hand hovered near the tools on his belt as though thinking he might have to use one.

Coleson? Carlson? I couldn't quite remember the guy's name. He was fairly new to the PTF. What I did remember was that he'd volunteered to be partnered with a paranatural, not been forced into it. As I recalled, I'd teamed him up with one of the sorcerers we'd finally gotten cleared for duty. I frowned. *One of the people Shedraziel used to blow up the capitol building.*

"Ms. Blackwood," he stammered. "What are you doing here?"

"I've come to speak with the werewolves." I moved to step around him, but he shifted, blocking my path.

"Sorry, ma'am. I can't let you in."

I blinked and stared at him for a moment. "I'm the assistant director."

He shifted his weight and wouldn't meet my gaze. "Director Weatherly's orders, ma'am. He specifically told us you weren't to be allowed in."

I focused on my breathing for a moment, edging my blood back from a full boil to a slow simmer. "When did he give this order?"

"Last night, ma'am. Just after you left."

He didn't even wait for Harris's prognosis.

I finally managed to pin down the man's flitting focus. He winced when our eyes met. "I just want to talk to them."

"I understand, ma'am, but I can't let you through. The director was very clear."

"*Acting* director." I balled my fists, blew out a noisy sigh, and forced my hands open again. I tipped my chin to indicate the hallway behind him. "Can you at least tell me how they're doing?"

He relaxed visibly. His shoulders dropped from around his ears, and his posture shifted back onto his heels. "Everyone you sent to Conference Room B was released to the hospital about an hour after you left. One person died from complications during surgery. Far as I know, the rest are alive and well . . . and still human." He glanced behind him. "The others . . . they took a long time to change. Three didn't survive. Those who did are under the care of the werewolves we already had on hand." He shook his head, his gaze unfocused. "I've never heard screams like that before."

I patted him on the arm.

He jerked, jolted back to the present by my touch.

"Thanks for telling me."

He nodded. "Sorry I couldn't . . . you know." He twitched his head toward the hall.

"Yeah." I turned to go.

"Ms. Blackwood?"

I glanced back.

"My partner. . . ." He stared intently at the ground. "She gonna be all right?"

"I don't know. But thank you for caring enough to ask." I crossed the debris field of the lobby and ducked back under the caution tape. Much as I wanted to tear the building down to free my friends at that moment, I couldn't. All else aside, letting a bunch of newly changed, out-of-control werewolves loose wouldn't help anyone, except maybe Shedraziel.

The protesters jostled me on my way back through the crowd, having realized I was somehow connected to the PTF even if they didn't know exactly who I was. At least one reporter recognized me, calling out my name. He dragged a cameraman in my direction.

I trotted to my Jeep as fast as I could and slammed the door before the reporter with the toothy smile could shove his microphone in my face. Then I swung out of the parking lot with a death grip on my steering wheel.

My next stop was Saint Joseph Hospital, where Everly Harris had been admitted. She had a room in the intensive care unit so the nurses could keep a close eye on her. Her physical injuries didn't seem to be life threatening, but she had yet to wake up. The nurse I spoke to said she had severe intracranial swelling.

I stood by her bed and looked down at the woman who'd supported my idea for a human-paranatural partnership.

"Weatherly took your job," I said. "He's having fun lording it over me, which sucks, but the real problem is that he doesn't understand what he's doing." I looked up at the ceiling and sighed. "The PTF is going to attack a reservation." I shook my head. "No chance the violence will end there."

I pursed my lips and looked back down at her. Her eyes moved back and forth beneath their lids. Was she dreaming? Could she hear me?

"I'm not giving up," I said. "I don't know what I can do yet . . . but I'm going to do *something*." I reached out and gripped the hand not wrapped in bandages. "You'd better not give up either." I squeezed her fingers. We weren't friends, exactly, but we were allies. I respected her. Unlike a lot of PTF officers I'd met, she actually listened and assessed before making decisions. I leaned forward and whispered, "My life would be a whole lot easier if you'd just wake up."

Five minutes passed with no change. The machines around her bed continued to beep and whir. Eventually, a nurse came in and chased me out. I left the hospital with a heavy heart and cold determination.

I'm going to prove her trust in me was not misplaced.

By the time I pulled to a stop in front of Luke's house in Boulder, the sun was almost directly overhead. The emergency broadcast announcing

Anderson's paranatural arrest order had cut into my music three times as I sped along Highway 36. I did not want to test the effectiveness of his house-arrest policy, and I wouldn't put it past him to have a cop tailing me to slap on a pair of cuffs at the stroke of noon. I cut the engine and jogged to the front door.

I raised my hand to knock, but the door opened before my knuckles made contact. Emma stood on the other side, hand on the doorknob, smiling. "Hello, Alex."

I raised an eyebrow. "I take it you've sorted out this whole magical vision thing then?"

"Not exactly." She took my hand, drawing me inside.

Luke was standing in front of a brown leather recliner in his living room. He was smiling, too, but deep creases furrowed his brow. "It really is remarkable," he said. "Her magical conduits were completely destroyed by the backlash, but her body seems to have found a way around that. I've never seen anything like it."

She closed the door. "Our best guess is that when Shedraziel's spell tried to force me to draw magic, my body formed new pathways to try to accommodate the command."

Giddy joy bubbled up in my chest. I'd been the one to demand too much magic from Emma when we fought my father. I'd caused her backlash. I'd broken her. I didn't even care that it was Shedraziel I had to thank for this miracle if it meant my friend was healed. I threw my arms around her. "That's amazing, Emma. I'm so happy for you."

"It's not as simple as that," Luke said.

Emma pulled my arms loose and stepped out of my hug. "I can't channel magic the way I did before. I can't store it in my body." She took another step away. "Luke says I'm interacting with the energy directly now."

I scrunched my nose. "What does that mean?"

"It means she's found an entirely new way of casting magic." Luke stuffed his hands in his pockets and shrugged. "At least, it's a kind I've never come across in my research."

"In simplest terms, I can see, and sometimes touch, the Rift energy practitioners convert to cast magic, and because that magic exists to a certain extent within everything—"

"You can perceive what's around you."

She nodded. "But it's kind of like looking at a monochromatic painting through a piece of fogged glass. The lines are all blurry and indistinct, but the energy is denser in certain places, and that gives things shape." She pointed to Luke. "People and other living things seem to have a lot of energy in them. Even non-magic users." She waved her hand in a vague gesture around the room. "Inanimate stuff has energy, too, but not very much. I have trouble telling apart the chair or table from the floor."

"She was up half the night running obstacle courses," Luke said.

Emma pointed at me. "You glow really brightly, and there's even a bit of color. I'm not sure what that's about."

I frowned. "What color?"

She squinted at me. "Sort of a purplish-red."

My fae magic looked red to me, while the practitioner magic I channeled was blue. "This is . . . incredible, Emma. When we get back to the house I'll be curious to know if Chase and Zeraldi are different colors, too. Speaking of which, we need to go. Anderson's put a noon curfew on all paranaturals, and we're no exception."

Luke nodded. "We heard the announcement."

I looked from him to Emma and shifted my weight. "You could stay here if you'd rather. It might be better for you to keep working on your new"—I waved at her—"thing. I'd certainly understand."

She worried her lower lip between her teeth. "You're still going after Shedraziel, aren't you?"

"The details are a little hazy at the moment . . . but yeah. I am."

She nodded. "Then I'm going with you."

I shifted my weight again and looked at Luke.

"It's not his decision," she said. "Or yours."

"Blurry shapes, my ass," I muttered. "You can tell which way I'm looking."

She smiled. "You're easy to read."

"Right." I crossed my arms and studied her. "Even if you're not exactly blind anymore, you're still human. There's no way to protect you from Shedraziel's magic."

"Then maybe I won't be there when you actually fight her. That doesn't mean I can't be useful in some other way. I can at least help you plan." She crossed her arms, mimicking my stance. "Besides all my stuff is at your house."

I chuckled. "Fair enough."

She turned to Luke. "Thanks for helping me get a handle on this."

"Just take it slow. We have no idea what your limits are, or what might happen if you pass them."

She nodded. "I promise."

Luke looked at me, his expression serious. "You, too. I'm tired of patching you up."

I smiled, waved, and ushered Emma out the door. Knowing whom I faced, I couldn't make that promise.

Emma and I climbed aboard my Jeep, and I pulled out of Luke's neighborhood. I cut my gaze across to her. She sat with her eyes closed, hands folded loosely on her lap. "So does this new style of magic mean you don't have to worry about demon possession anymore?"

She frowned. "I'm not sure. I still see them when I touch the energy. In fact, they're quite a bit clearer than they were before."

I shivered, picturing the demons I'd seen in the energy that fueled my practitioner powers. Clawed hands and burning eyes; serrated teeth and leathery wings; scales, spikes, tusks, and quills. No two demons were alike, and I'd rarely gotten a clean look at one, but I'd seen enough to give me nightmares. I certainly didn't want to see them any clearer.

"Since I'm not pulling the energy into my body I don't think they can possess me." She shrugged. "At least not any more easily than a non-magic human."

"So how does this whole casting-without-channeling thing work?" I asked as I turned the Jeep up the canyon. *Twenty minutes to noon. We'll just make it.*

"I'm not sure yet. It's nothing like the magic I was doing before. So far all I've managed to do is move a couple small objects and short out a lightbulb."

"And see."

She smiled and nodded.

"Can you do it constantly? Or does it eat energy like casting magic?"

"It takes a little energy, but more than that, it takes concentration. Right now the images I see sort of flicker in and out whenever my mind wanders. That's pretty tiring."

So she can't just leave it on all the time.

She suddenly jerked in her seat, her body rigid, her hands pressed to the center console and her door.

"What is it?" I scanned the road, the sidewalks, the yards we were passing. An elderly man was walking a shaggy white dog by the side of the road. A couple kids on bikes sped past us in the opposite direction.

She sighed and relaxed, but her hands stayed clenched. "It's confusing when I'm moving this fast. Stuff suddenly appears, and then it's gone before I can even register what it was."

"How far do you see?"

She wobbled her head side to side. "I think it depends on how much I'm *trying* to see. When we were on the PTF building I had no problem seeing the whole battlefield, but at Luke's I didn't see anything beyond the walls of his house."

"So maybe try to see just the inside of the car?"

"Actually, I already turned it off. I'm pretty tired from all those obstacle courses. I could use a break. Just don't crash."

"I'll do my best," I said dryly.

The rest of the drive was quiet. I switched to a Green Day CD when the steep canyon walls cut off the radio reception. Emma seemed almost asleep next to me with her eyes closed and her head lolling against the backrest. The snow that had been melting on the streets in Denver was sticking up near Nederland. By the time I pulled onto my driveway, there was a decent coating of fresh powder over the ice.

As I rounded the final bend and came into view of my house, I slammed the brakes.

Emma jerked in her seat, groping the dashboard. "What happened?"

"Kai's back."

I eased the Jeep in beside the champagne-colored Toyota Corolla Kai had driven the first time I'd met him. The car had since been returned to the way station lot just outside the fae reservation. The only reason I could think of for its presence was that Kai had once again borrowed it after completing his mission to Enchantment.

I hope he's brought us good news.

Emma stepped out of the Jeep and started for the porch before my feet touched the snow, so I supposed she'd turned her magical "sight" back on.

When I stepped through the front door, Emma was standing to one side tugging off her shoes. James was in the farthest chair, facing me. He was wearing a light-blue, button-up shirt and black slacks from the collection of clothes he'd recently moved into my closet. Chase wore a pair of faded jeans and a loose white T-shirt and straddled one of the dining chairs with his arms folded over the top. Zee was sitting on the couch in her borrowed sundress. Kai was in the recliner at the near end, still wearing his clothes from yesterday. I blinked, stunned for a moment by the absurdity of the scene—of my life. A day-walking vampire, a dragon, a shifter, an ex-knight, a backlash survivor who could somehow still use magic, and me—a one-of-a-kind practitioner-fae hybrid—just sitting around my living room. All I needed was a werewolf or two to round out the menagerie.

I chuckled to myself and pushed the door closed behind me, stepping out of my sneakers. It was mind-boggling to think that just half a year ago I'd wanted nothing to do with the fae or magic. I hadn't even known werewolves and vampires were real. Yet the scene in my living room was oddly comforting.

Not long ago I would have been uncomfortable to walk in and find so many people in my space, but circumstances had changed. Not just in the wider world, but with me personally. While I still enjoyed my quiet time, I no longer craved solitude. I was no longer so worried about being abandoned that I pushed people away to avoid the pain of losing them. Somewhere in the past few months, without my even noticing, my goals had shifted from protecting myself and living my life in peace to protecting the friends I'd let into my heart at all costs. If only Maggie and David were there, the scene would be complete.

Kai twisted in his seat. "Alex. Emma. James and Chase were just filling me in on what I missed. Sounds like you've had quite the time of it. I'm glad you're both safe."

The word "safe" rang in my head like a bell as Anderson's threat against the fae reservation replayed in my memory. Not only that, but the visa revocation and paranatural house arrest. If Kai had been any later leaving the reservation he could have been stopped at the gate and turned back, or arrested on the drive here, or if he'd been really slow in returning he might have come out of Enchantment just as Anderson launched his attack.

I pressed my lips together. *It might not happen.* I balled my fists. *But it could, and Kai could easily have become one of the casualties.*

I crossed the space between us in three steps and wrapped my arms around his neck. "I'm so glad you made it."

Kai hugged me back, though the angle was awkward with me bending over him. "I've only been gone a day."

James cleared his throat.

Kai and I pulled apart.

Emma took my place and gave Kai a quick hug. "Welcome back." Then she moved to the far end of the couch and sat down.

Kai watched her progress with a frown. His eyebrows puckered together.

"How did your meeting go?" James asked.

I winced and shook my head. "Just a sec." I snagged the remote off the coffee table and brought the TV to life. After a quick scan of the news channels showed nothing relevant, I pressed the mute button, dropped into the last free seat on the couch, and said, "Really bad."

I looked at Kai. "Please tell me Bael is doing something to stop Shedraziel."

He nodded. "According to Lord Bael, plans were already in motion to bring her to heel."

I perked up. "That's great."

He flinched.

"You don't believe him?" James asked.

Kai shook his head. "I would never question Lord Bael's truthfulness."

The way he kept including Bael's title made me wonder if he was regretting his decision to leave his service as a knight of the realm.

"But?" Chase prompted.

"But his timing seemed a bit suspicious," he said.

I tilted my head to one side. "How so?"

"Well, Shedraziel has been at work in the mortal realm for several days at least. Assuming she has also visited other realms to muster troops to her cause, she must have been gone from Enchantment for a significant amount of time."

"Certainly long enough for Bael to notice," James agreed.

I frowned. "You think Bael knew but chose not to do anything?"

Kai looked away from me. "I think his sense of urgency may not match the needs of the mortal realm."

"Did you tell him I'm holding Shedraziel's actions against his oath?"

He nodded. "At which point he was very quick to point out that he was already taking measures to stop her. He says he's assigned a special team of well-trained, combat-hardened fae, all with true names and led by Rhoana, captain of his personal guard, to go after her, but he has been reluctant to send his troops into the mortal realm for fear it would be seen as an act of war."

Zee snorted. "He probably doesn't want to risk the lives of his own people while he believes someone else might clean up his mess."

I studied the young dragon. Her expression was neutral, but there had definitely been some strain in her voice when she talked about Bael. Again, I wondered what had motivated him to wipe out an entire world—not that there could be any justification for such an act. Would he let the mortal realm fall to chaos with as little remorse?

"Rhoana gave me this." Kai pulled a small glass sphere from his pocket—a communication device I'd seen the fae use before. "She'll contact me if Bael's spies get actionable information on where to find Shedraziel, and we can do likewise if we find her first."

"Assuming they've gotten off their collective asses and come to the mortal realm," James amended.

"So backup may be coming," I said, "but we don't know when." I sighed and slumped against the couch cushions. "We don't have time to wait on Bael and his questionable priorities."

Kai nodded, his expression solemn. "Zee told me she predicts a major event will happen tomorrow."

"Not just that," I said. "The PTF is launching a missile strike on the Black Forest Reservation today." I glanced at the clock. "They may have already, and Governor Anderson wants to do the same thing here in Colorado."

The room fell silent as my words sank in. Then everyone started talking at once.

"He's going to bomb the reservation?" Emma shrieked.

Kai and Chase both jumped to their feet with cries of, "I have to warn them."

James just shook his head and mumbled something that was drowned out by the others' cries, but ripples of unease filtered through our bond.

Zeraldi was ashen faced.

"It gets worse," I said. Kai sat back down, but Chase remained standing.

"Everly Harris is in a coma, which makes Weatherly the acting PTF director for the western US. He's revoked all fae visas, and Anderson's placed all paranaturals under house arrest. Members of the National Guard are patrolling the streets to enforce the policy. Considering our status, I'm sure they're watching this place. If we leave, we'll be arrested."

Chase scoffed. "Hardly a concern when I've been right under their noses all this time."

I nodded. "Since they don't know about you and Zeraldi, you might be able to slip back undetected, but Emma, James, and I don't have that luxury. Weatherly's already threatened to ship James to a holding facility along with the werewolves, and since Kai checked out of the reservation this morning I'm sure Weatherly will jump on the chance to toss him in with that group once he realizes he's here."

"So your experiment has failed," Chase said. He didn't sound surprised.

"Not necessarily. The point was to prove that humans and paranaturals could benefit from cooperation. We can still prove that."

"And when paranaturals accomplish something to the benefit of the humans not only without their cooperation but despite their interference?" he asked. "What does that prove?"

"Our first priority should still be to warn the reservation about the impending attack," Kai said.

I bit my lower lip. "We don't know for sure it's going to happen. What if we warn them and they decide to launch a preemptive strike? We could end up causing the very conflict we're trying to avoid."

Zee nodded. "Such is the danger of foreknowledge."

I studied her. "Can you tell what will happen? Get another vision?"

"I do not have the power to fully control my visions; I cannot navigate the currents of time on a whim. And as you pointed out, even if I saw an attack, it may be caused by your actions in trying to prevent it. Do you still want me to try?"

I looked around the room. Chase shrugged. Kai was so tense the tendons were standing out along the sides of his neck. Emma stared at her lap.

James met my gaze. "It seems you already have as much knowledge as we could reasonably expect to gain from a prediction."

"I could perhaps offer aid in another way," Zee said. "I could deliver your warning without the need to send someone to the reservation."

I frowned. "How?"

"Dream walking."

I raised an eyebrow. "You can talk to people in their dreams?"

"Wouldn't the person need to be asleep?" Emma asked.

"Not just in their dreams, though that does make it easier." Zee tapped one delicate finger against her chin and looked up as though trying to find an explanation that would make sense. "I guess you could say that I can communicate with a person's subconscious."

I wrinkled my nose, thinking of the stray thoughts and images produced by my subconscious. "And they can understand you?"

"Let me show you." She set her hand over mine where it rested on my thigh.

I was suddenly standing in a cloud of swirling mist, similar to the Rift energy I saw when casting magic. I looked down. I didn't seem to have a body.

"Consider this a staging ground for your subconscious." Zee was suddenly beside me, though more as an impression than a physical presence. Gone was her little girl body. Here she was a beacon of shining white in the vague shape of a dragon. "If you were sleeping, we would have entered your active dream, and the dream would have dictated the form I took."

Her words were not a sound, more like a sudden understanding of the feeling behind them that sprang fully formed into my mind, not unlike the way James and I communicated when our connection was at its strongest.

"And you can do this over a distance?"

"To varying degrees of success, but yes. The more distance, the weaker the connection. I could not, for example, put someone to sleep as I did the combatants on the battlefield yesterday if I were not in close proximity. I cannot reach across realms, and the greater the distance the more difficult it is to pinpoint a single person accurately."

"So we can't specify who your warning would go to?"

"In this case I believe we can. Knowing that we would need to convey more information once it became available, I imprinted on your companion, Targe, before we parted ways. Once I have touched a person's subconscious, as I now have with you, it leaves a residual trace that I can use to identify them in the future. So long as Targe is within the mortal realm, I will be able to reach him."

I suddenly found myself back in my physical body, sitting on my couch. Everyone was exactly as I'd left them, and Zee was once more in the unassuming body of a little girl. She removed her hand from mine.

I took a shaky breath. "How long were we . . . um, in there?"

James's eyebrows drew together. "In where?"

Zee smiled. "As in a dream, time has no meaning in that place."

"So we could have talked forever and no time would have passed in the physical world?"

She nodded. "Or at the very least, so little as to be imperceptible to you."

"Then I guess it should be safe to wait on the warning. Even if the PTF decides missile strikes are effective, it will take Anderson a while to arrange one. We can decide whether or not a local attack is likely once we know what happened at the Black Forest. Speaking of which"—I flicked through the stations on the muted TV again—"I feel like there should have been a report by now."

"Maybe the governments are keeping it quiet so as not to alert the other reservations," James said. "Most elementals could deflect a missile if they knew it was coming."

"Maybe." I drummed my fingers. "If we haven't seen anything about it in the next hour, we'll send the warning to Targe regardless. We can tell them to evacuate to another realm, just in case."

"But if they go through a portal we'll lose the only sure backup we have in facing Shedraziel," Kai said.

"And I won't be able to reach them anymore," Zee added.

"Which is why we're going to wait a little longer, but I won't risk getting them blown up."

"If only we knew exactly where Shedraziel was going to appear next," Emma said. "Then we could just tell Targe to take everyone there."

"Even if we had a destination, we can't have a bunch of fae marching off a reservation until we're ready for the fight, and according to Zee's vision of the moon, that's not till tomorrow. If we move too soon we could either provoke a response from the local PTF and cause the conflict we want to avoid, or tip off Shedraziel that we're on to her and lose the element of surprise." I balanced the remote on my knee and rubbed my temples. *If only I still had enough sway with the PTF to get them to cooperate, all this would be so much easier. Wake up, Everly!*

I shifted, and the remote slipped off my knee. Emma grabbed it before it hit the floor.

"How did you . . .?" Kai gaped at Emma.

Chase and James were staring with similar expressions.

She set the remote on the coffee table and gave Kai a mischievous smile. "There were a few other things that happened while you were gone."

It took a few minutes to explain how Shedraziel's attempt to commandeer Emma and activate her damaged practitioner abilities had resulted in her current condition, but once everyone understood they were full of congratulations.

"A whole new style of magic." Kai shook his head in seeming disbelief. "Hortense is going to be furious she missed this."

I chuckled. "I doubt Emma wants to become a guinea pig to satisfy Hortense's curiosity."

"Actually," Emma said, "I'd be willing if she could provide more insight into how this works. I think Luke has helped about as much as he can with his tests." She twisted to look at me. "And for the record, all fae look different. It's not just you."

"Different how?" Zee asked. She was the only one who'd taken Emma's revelation in stride.

Emma's expression pinched as she considered her response. "What I see is hazy, like shapes in smoke, and the density of the smoke seems to relate to how much energy or magical potential the object has. People have the sharpest definition, but everything is the same sort of blue-gray color. Except you guys." She pointed at Chase, Kai, me, and Zee. "Your shapes are varying shades of red."

"Not mine?" James asked.

She shook her head. "But your shape is very dense," she added as though offering a consolation prize.

"What you see with this 'sight' of yours seems similar to my experience when dream walking," Zee said. "Perhaps I could be of some assistance in understanding your new ability."

I recalled the gray mist in our dream-walking conversation and how it had reminded me of Rift energy. "That's a good idea, Em. Couldn't hurt to pick her brain at least."

Zee stiffened. "Pick my brain?"

"It's a human phrase," Chase said. "No harm will come to you."

"Ah." She settled back.

I swapped places with Emma so she and Zee wouldn't have to talk past me and picked up the remote again. "I guess that puts the rest of us on news duty."

James pulled out his phone. "I'll check online to see if something has been leaked."

Half an hour later, I was still flipping channels and wondering if I should tell Targe to evacuate after all. My skin felt itchy with anticipation. I shifted constantly and bounced my leg like a caffeine addict. As much as I was dreading news of the disaster, the waiting was almost worse.

"I'm going to make us all some lunch." James stood and headed for the kitchen without waiting for a response.

I watched his retreating back. There was one more development I hadn't shared yet. I glanced at the others. Kai was watching the TV with a glazed expression. Emma and Zee were deep in a conversation about the perception of energy. Chase had reverted to his cat form and was snoozing on the back of the couch.

"I'll give you a hand." I passed the remote to Kai.

"If there's any of that fudge-ripple ice cream left, I'll take that," he said as he took over the job of flipping through the channels.

James already had the ingredients for sandwiches out on the counter. His arm moved rhythmically as he sliced a tomato on my cutting board.

I smiled, remembering the first time I'd seen him cook in my kitchen. He'd seemed so out of place. Looking back on that moment I realized that the awkwardness hadn't come from James at all but entirely from my own perception. I'd known him for two years at that point . . . but I hadn't known him at all.

I stepped up behind him, wrapped my arms around his waist, and pressed myself against his back. The smell of blackberries and cloves wafted off him. He paused his rhythmic chop and dropped one hand to cover mine. His touch was warm. Perhaps it was because of our soul-deep connection, but sharing my space with James now seemed like the most natural thing in the world.

I tightened my grip, snuggling closer. I wanted to stay frozen in that moment forever, but the memory of Victoria's call was a flea eating away at my contentment.

"There's something on your mind," he whispered.

I could feel him prodding at the edges of my thoughts.

I sighed and let the moment go. Stepping around him, I grabbed the lettuce and started stripping off leaves. "Victoria called me this morning." I spoke quietly so those in the living room wouldn't hear. "She saw you on TV . . . without your shirt."

His hand froze halfway through lifting the knife to resume his cutting. He exhaled and set the knife down on the edge of the cutting board. He stared at the partially cut tomato. "What did she say?"

I gathered the lettuce leaves, dropped them in the sink, and ran some cold water. "She knows we lied." I turned off the faucet and braced my hands against the sink, staring into the basin of crisping lettuce. "What will she do?"

"That depends on what she thinks she has to gain. Did you tell her how it was done?"

I shook my head. "I hung up on her."

He chuckled. "I suppose that's one way to deal with her."

"Ignoring her was an impulse, not a solution."

He sighed. "If Victoria believes there's a chance she can gain the ability to walk in daylight permanently, she might not share the news of my condition with the council." He wobbled his head side to side. "Unless she thinks they're likely to find out on their own. Then she will want to use the news as currency before it loses its value."

"And if she tells the council?"

He shrugged. "The balance of power on the council is quite delicate. They may choose to assassinate me simply to prevent the possibility of one of them becoming stronger than the others."

My chest grew tight, making it difficult to breathe. *How can he talk about his possible death in such a cavalier way?*

"It's more likely the council will wish to assess the situation in more detail first. They'll probably summon me to a meeting, at which point they will attempt to determine if they can take my day-walking ability for themselves. When they determine they cannot, they will probably execute me."

I felt lightheaded. "So either way, they'll try to kill you?"

"Most likely."

"And Victoria would turn you over to them knowing that, even though she"—I choked on the words—"cares for you?"

"If she has something to gain? In a heartbeat."

I squeezed the sink tighter, grinding my nails against the steel.

James stepped up behind me, pressing close, and slipped his arms around my waist in an echo of my earlier embrace. He kissed me behind the ear and rested his cheek against the top of my head. "Do not borrow troubles from tomorrow when we have more than enough already. Even if the council were to learn of my situation today, they are governed by mistrust and self-interest. They will not be quick to act."

I exhaled, letting myself relax against him as his calm carried through our link and soothed my jangled nerves. "You're right. One impossible task at a time. The vampires can wait." I laid my arms over his, hugging him back. *I love you.*

He nuzzled the side of my neck, squeezing me tighter. "Whatever comes, we will face it together."

"Hey, guys," Kai called from the other room.

I sighed and called back, "Your ice cream is coming."

"You might wanna come see this." He unmuted the television, and a deep baritone voice cut in mid-sentence. "—the widespread devastation caused by this unprecedented earthquake."

James and I rushed back to the living room, all thoughts of lunch and vampires forgotten.

Chapter 15

A MIDDLE-AGED anchorman with silver streaks in his slicked-back, black hair sat behind a news desk on the television screen. A box in the upper right corner scrolled through pictures of broken buildings, uprooted trees, and crumbled roads. "While minor earthquakes are not uncommon in the region, this is the largest ever recorded in that area, measuring 7.4 on the Richter scale and blowing away the previous record of 5.3 from 1978. The epicenter was near Freiburg im Breisgau, Germany, but tremors were felt in Nuremberg, two hundred miles away. Many human communities, as well as the Black Forest Fae Reservation are thought to have been completely destroyed, but relief workers have not yet gained access to the most impacted areas."

"So they really did it." Chase had shifted back to human form and was sitting naked on the couch beside Emma, staring at the TV.

"That's it then." I gripped the back of the couch as a wave of dizziness washed over me. "The fae and humans are at war."

"But not openly," James said.

I frowned and gestured to the TV. "That seems pretty out in the open to me."

"He's right," Kai said. "They didn't mention anything about an attack. Just an earthquake. The only reason we know better is because Weatherly told you the PTF's plan."

I shook my head. "Even if the general human population is kept in the dark, the fae will know they were attacked."

"Will they?" James asked. "If there were no survivors and the evidence is buried in an earthquake?"

We all fell silent. Images of the towns where reporters had gained access continued to scroll past as the anchorman droned on about casualty reports, relief plans, building costs, damage to infrastructure, and so on.

Kai suddenly twisted in his chair to stare at the front door. "Someone just crossed my security ward."

I glanced out the front window, wishing not for the first time that Kai had been able to set the ward around my house so more than just he could feel it. A black SUV pulled to a stop behind my Jeep, blocking it in. I didn't recognize the car, but it had the sort of nondescript-yet-threatening look of a government-issued vehicle.

Did Weatherly find out Kai was here? Or has he come for James?

I looked around the room. "Kai, Chase, Zee, you all need to hide in the back. If you see an opening, slip out the window into the forest." I turned to James. "You should probably go with them."

"No more playing by their rules?"

I shook my head. "Weatherly made it clear our truce is over. I'm afraid you'll have to go back to being a fugitive."

He stepped close, set his hands on my shoulders, and kissed my forehead. "Then let us run together."

I gave him a quick hug, then stepped back before I could change my mind. "Emma and I aren't breaking any laws as long as we're here in the house. I can get more information talking to them than on the run with you."

He brushed his knuckles over my cheek. "We'll be back when the coast is clear."

I nodded.

"I'll stay," Chase said, "in case you're wrong and end up needing backup." He shrank back to a gray tabby.

I rolled my eyes but didn't argue. No one had any reason to think Chase was anything more than a normal house cat. "Fine." I pushed against James's chest. "Now go."

Zee and Kai had already gone down the hall. After one more moment of hesitation, James followed. A knock came at the front door a second later.

"There's only one," Emma said. Her face was scrunched in concentration, fists bunched in her lap. "Not a magic user."

"Can you tell if there are others farther away? Hiding in the forest maybe?"

She shook her head. "Just the one as far as I can tell . . . but I could be wrong."

If Weatherly were coming to arrest my friends, he would have brought backup.

The knock sounded a second time. I grabbed the remote and muted the TV, then headed for the door. When I pulled it open, my jaw dropped. Bishop João Silva was standing on my porch.

"What are *you* doing here?" I was so over being diplomatic.

Bishop Silva stiffened and adjusted the little cape that was part of his official outfit. Snow was still falling. Several white flakes dotted his black-clad shoulders. He wore no coat, and his polished black shoes didn't seem like they'd have much traction.

"I thought you should know the attack on the Black Forest is over."

I frowned. "You came all the way out here to tell me that?"

"Among other things."

I hugged myself in a vain effort to hold back the leaching cold, both inside and out. My chest was so tight I felt as if my lungs might collapse.

"Did Anderson get the results he was hoping for?"

Silva licked his lips and shifted his weight. "Might we continue this conversation inside?"

I blinked. It hadn't even occurred to me that a delegate of the Unified Church would want to come inside my house . . . but then I hadn't expected to find one on my doorstep either. I moved to the side and gestured for him to enter.

He stepped inside only far enough for me to close the door. He didn't make any move toward the furniture.

Emma was still on the couch. She stared blankly ahead as though watching the silent television. Chase was a ball of gray fur on the armrest.

I gestured to the TV. "We've been watching the news about the 'earthquake' in Europe." I made quotation marks around the word with my fingers.

"The earthquake was real," he said. "Though the PTF and participating governments have done their best to cover up its cause."

I nodded. "They don't want the fae to learn about the attack until they decide if they're going to do it again."

He shifted his weight. "You were right about the elemental guarding the reservation. Even with no warning of the impending attack, it was able to deflect many of the missiles. Enough got through to create several craters and set the forest ablaze, but then the earthquake happened. We knew there might be some collateral damage, but this. . . ." He gestured to the report playing out silently on my TV and shook his head. "Dozens of towns have been completely destroyed, including Strasbourg and Stuttgart, which were well outside our evacuation zone."

Relief mixed with guilt and remorse in a sickening combination that made me want to puke, but if the casualties were bad enough, they might act as a deterrent to future attacks. "Does that mean Governor Anderson has changed his mind about attacking the reservation here in Colorado?"

Silva pursed his lips. "No. Despite the collateral damage, Governor Anderson still wishes to employ a similar tactic here, and Director Weatherly seems inclined to support him."

I was glad I hadn't eaten lunch yet as my stomach did a somersault, twisted into a knot, and plummeted to the floor.

How can they not see that violence will only cause more violence?

I studied the hard lines of Silva's face, looking for answers in his brown eyes. "Why come all the way here to tell me personally?"

"You don't seem like the type of person who'd sit back and watch the world burn just because someone told you to."

I kept my mouth shut, wondering where this was going.

"Then again, maybe I'm wrong." He walked over to the mantle and squinted at a picture of David and me with our friend Aiden on a beach in

Mexico. "I only just met you."

"So what, you thought you'd come babysit me? Make sure I don't cause any trouble by alerting the fae?" I kept my tone light, but the thought twisted barbs into my gut. If Silva stuck around, it would severely complicate my ability to act.

"Quite the contrary," he said. "I'm here to dangle a carrot, in case I overestimated your conviction."

I blinked and stood there with my mouth hanging open. Of the three delegates, I would have named Bishop Silva as the least likely to take my side.

"Don't misinterpret my actions. I have no love of the fae, but another such act would undoubtedly lead to a retaliatory attack on a massive scale. My objective here is to preserve human lives." He stared at me for a moment before continuing. "All things considered, do you believe the fae want a war?"

I crossed my arms and considered all the fae I'd met. The majority had seemed, if not entirely happy, at least content with the status quo before the events of the past few months. It was increasing intolerance from the Purists that had brought things to a boil. "Some, but not most."

He nodded. "Then perhaps there's still hope." He clasped his hands behind his back and lifted his chin, addressing me like a professor giving a lecture. "As much as I believe the fae are a threat that needs to be mitigated, I also believe they are too strong for us to control by force. The last war decimated both sides, and we were barely able to force a draw. With the recent loss of our most experienced sorcerers, another conflict would likely have a devastating outcome for the human race." He shook his head. "Peace between the species is our best option. But to achieve that we need to remove the 'splinter' in both our sides."

"You're seriously suggesting an alliance?" I felt as if I'd just stepped off the Tilt-A-Whirl.

"You want to prove that magical and non-magical beings can coexist. Consider this an investment in that future."

"Where was your concern for the future when Anderson was ripping into me this morning?"

"The governor and director are in no way obligated to listen to my opinions, but the council of the Unified Church *will* listen to what I have to say." He puffed out his chest. "If you stop the fae you claim is responsible for the current conflict before irreparable damage is done, and assuming the fae are willing to deal, I'll recommend the Church council use all its sway to force the PTF to the negotiating table to discuss a new treaty. Whether or not peace can be achieved at that point. . . ." He shrugged.

I narrowed my eyes. "So that's the carrot?"

"As an added bonus, you can once again prove the usefulness of your paranatural brethren. Let's not forget that my fellow delegates and I came here in the first place to determine whether the Church would support or decry the inclusion of paranaturals in society. That directive hasn't changed."

Emma, fists clenched in her lap, piped up from the couch, "How many times will we have to prove ourselves before we're treated as equals?"

Silva glanced at her and shrugged. "People are slow to change. The world even more so."

"You're asking me to openly defy the law," I said. "I'll be branded a fugitive . . . *again*."

"Succeed and I will claim your actions were sanctioned by the Church."

I chuckled, finally seeing his angle. "Thereby taking credit for the win without ever lifting a finger."

"And pressuring Anderson to pardon you lest he alienate the Church, which up till now has been one of his biggest supporters. Face it, Church support is the only chance you and your friends have for a happily-ever-after."

I sighed, weighing his words. *If I fail, he can claim this conversation never happened. If I succeed, he takes the credit for stopping a war. Win-win for him. But he's not wrong about our need for pardons when all this is over, and Anderson isn't likely to grant those without leverage, so maybe I can win, too.* Of course, there was nothing to stop Silva from going back on his word once the work was done. Unlike the fae, humans could, and often did, lie to get what they wanted. Not that it mattered. I was going after Shedraziel regardless. Silva was right about my personality; I couldn't sit by and watch the world burn.

"All right." I stuck out my hand. "You've got a deal."

Bishop Silva's palm was cold and dry. His grip was tight. He gave our joined hands one stiff downward tug, then released me. "I don't expect we will see each other again until this matter is resolved." He stepped around me and opened the door, then paused and looked me up and down. "Good luck."

I flipped the lock on the door once it was closed behind him and waited until I heard the rumble of his engine and the crunch of ice as he backed out. I shifted the curtains over the front window and peeked out in time to see a pair of taillights vanish around the first bend in my driveway.

"All clear," I called.

Zee, Kai, and James emerged from the hallway. We all headed toward Emma and resumed our places around the coffee table. I clicked off the TV.

"That was unexpected," Chase said, shifting back to two legs.

Since everyone in the house but Emma had superhuman hearing, and she'd been present, there was no need to repeat my conversation with Bishop Silva.

"I'm not sure how much faith we want to put in his promise." I tossed the blanket from the back of the couch at Chase, who wrapped it around his waist before sitting down.

"I think he was sincere," Emma said.

We all looked at her.

She shrugged. "I can't be certain, of course, but his heart rate and breathing didn't change at all. He seemed calm."

"You could tell that?" I asked.

She shrugged again.

"Regardless," James said, "the bishop's cooperation doesn't change much for us. We were already planning to go after Shedraziel."

"True," I said, "but it's nice to know there might be more waiting for us afterward than a jail cell or a lethal injection."

"And he did confirm that Anderson is still planning to attack," Kai added.

"Yeah." I rubbed the back of my neck. "I guess it's time to warn Targe so he can get everyone to safety."

"If only we knew where to send them," Chase said. "Or how."

"We may not know where Shedraziel will strike next, but we do have a lead." I shifted on my cushion. "The Undine Lord promised reinforcements to fight Shedraziel if I returned her daughter, and if that daughter has been with Shedraziel for any length of time, she may know something about her plans."

"So you want to go after the daughter," Kai said.

I nodded. "I think Shedraziel is keeping her prisoner in the Nevada desert, guarded by griffins."

"That would make sense," Chase said. "If you want to trap an undine, you'd need to keep them away from water."

"Maybe the kidnapped daughter can tell us Shedraziel's plan. There's even a chance Shedraziel will be there. She must have a base of operations *some-where*." I sat up a little straighter as the idea took root. "We should have Targe and his troops meet us at the edge of the desert. That will give us backup *and* get them out of the line of fire."

James frowned. "I doubt even Targe can open a portal over such a distance."

Zee shook her head. "But a series of portals, perhaps."

"Like how he got Chase to the reservation," I said.

"Nevada's a lot farther than the reservation," Chase pointed out.

"What if they went through a fae realm to the reservation Kai used in California first?" I asked. "That should put them closer to Nevada."

"No way Bael lets an army take a shortcut through Enchantment," Kai said. "Even a friendly one."

"They could use the Shifter Realm," Zee said. "I don't think Lord Anika would have a problem so long as they don't remain."

I glanced at Chase, who nodded. "Then we'll tell them to use the Shifter Realm as a shortcut and portal the rest of the way. We'll gather what forces we can here and meet them at Quinn River Crossing tomorrow. That was reported as the northern edge of the expanding desert." I looked at Zee. "Make sure to tell them not to enter the desert until we get there. If Shedraziel *is* there, we can't waste the chance to take her down."

Zee nodded and closed her eyes, then opened them again so quickly it was barely more than a long blink. "He says they will be there by dawn tomorrow."

The response caught me off guard since it didn't seem as if enough time had passed for Zee to have made a connection, let alone had an entire conversation. Then I remembered that the strange space through which she dream walked had no time.

"All right, that's one problem solved. Let's see what other troops we can muster up before we skip town."

KAI'S COMMUNICATION orb remained resolutely blank.

"That's four tries," James said. "They didn't come."

Kai sighed, nodded, and tucked the oversized marble back in his pocket. "I'm sorry, Alex."

"It's not your fault Bael is a self-centered asshole."

He cringed. Despite having given up his position as a Knight of the Realm, it was probably difficult for him to hear people insult the lord he'd served loyally for years.

"Forget what we don't have," I said. "Let's focus on what we do have. Zee, Shedraziel seems to control people on a subconscious level. Can you protect our folks against that with your dream walking?"

A small pucker appeared between her eyebrows. "Perhaps one or two. But I would be unable to do anything else, leaving me vulnerable." She frowned. "I would rather not."

"What about how you stopped the people fighting at the PTF building?" I asked. "There were lots of people there."

"I merely rendered them unconscious so she could no longer control them. That would not help in this case since we need them to fight."

"Could you knock out Shedraziel and the people she controls?" Emma asked. "That would solve a lot of problems."

Zee shook her head. "Fae minds are more protected that human minds, and Shedraziel is very strong."

I sighed and leaned back against the couch cushions. I'd suspected as much since Zee hadn't been able to stop Shedraziel at the refugee camp, or even prevent the controlled humans from shooting her down, but it still sucked. "Then Emma, Kai, and James . . . you'll need to stay behind when we move in to face Shedraziel."

Kai's expression was grim, but he nodded. As much as I knew he wanted to fight, without a true name he'd only be a liability against someone who could turn him against his own friends with a whisper. Emma and James, however, were not convinced.

"I broke free of her spell last time," Emma said.

"She cast a blanket spell that targeted practitioners." I shuddered at the memory of the momentary bloodlust I'd felt to hunt down Governor Anderson. "I felt it too. It wasn't anything like having her target you directly. And for all we know, the only reason you were able to snap out of it was because your magic didn't respond the way she expected it too. You said yourself she tried to make you draw energy through your burned-out conduits. Now that you've got another way of casting, that may not protect you."

She opened her mouth, most likely to argue, but James cut in. "You expect me to sit on the sidelines while you ride into battle with just these two"—he pointed at Chase and Zee—"and whatever ragtag team Targe has managed to scrounge together?"

"Better than having you turn against us at a crucial moment," I countered.

"Have you forgotten that I was unaffected during the attack on the PTF building? If not for me—"

"I know." I raised a hand to forestall him. "Believe me, I know. And I'm grateful. But I saw you stumble at the river. She might not have been able to pull your strings right away, but she was wearing you down. We don't know how long you can resist her."

Kai raised his hand to draw our attention like a kid in a kindergarten class. "And with Targe bringing unfamiliar fae into the picture, you'll have more than just Shedraziel to worry about."

I cocked my head in confusion. "Zee specified Targe only bring allies with true names."

"But not necessarily people we know personally, and with all the chaos of a battle, who's to say one or more of them might not use the confusion to rid the world of a vampire who happens to be distracted beside them?"

I swallowed hard. "You think they'd target James even if they're fighting on the same side?"

"Are you willing to risk it?"

"Would they even know what he is if we're fighting in daylight?"

"They'll know," Zee said quietly. She cut her gaze across to James, watching him through her lashes.

"Do *you* have a problem with him?" I asked, suddenly concerned that the few allies I'd managed to hang on to were about to break apart.

"Not against him personally," Zee said, "but I can feel what he is . . . what's inside him." She shifted and rubbed her hands together. "His presence makes me uncomfortable."

"If we toss him in with a bunch of fae without warning, they're not going to wait for an explanation," Kai said.

James rubbed a hand over his mouth and stubble-lined jaw. Frustration pulsed through our bond. "So even if I were to prove immune to Shedraziel's control, my presence might still be a liability to our efforts."

"I'm sorry, James." I leaned forward and squeezed his thigh. "You can travel with us as far as the rendezvous but not into the desert."

He set his hand over mine.

Emma slumped in her seat, deflated by James's defeat.

I sat back and clasped my hands, resting my elbows on my knees. "That just leaves the werewolves."

James frowned. "If you're worried about Emma and me, surely you can't be suggesting—"

"Not all the werewolves were affected by Shedraziel's spell. We need to find out why." I gave him a half smile. "Who knows, maybe we can even find a way to guard you, Emma, and Kai. Then you'd just have the bigoted fae to worry about."

"How do you know their resistance was any more reliable than Emma's or mine?"

"I don't. And I won't until I get a chance to talk to Marc in more detail. It may be they were just lucky and there's nothing we can do to guard against Shedraziel's control. But we still need to find out." I pressed my palms together. "At the very least we need to get them away from Weatherly. I thought playing by the PTF's rules would keep them safe, but if Weatherly's going to keep them locked up without cause or recourse. . . ." I shook my head. "I can't let that happen."

"So what?" Kai asked. "Another raid on the holding facility?"

James smiled. "At least we know the layout."

"And there may still be some fae on the inside who would help us fight in exchange for opening the door," Chase said.

"Not this time." I met Chase's gaze. "Even if the fae in holding were willing to help, we don't know anything about them. There might not even be any with true names among them. Besides, it'll take a while to arrange transport for twenty-some-odd werewolves. I'm hoping we can get to them before they ever reach that facility." I pulled out my cell phone.

Chapter 16

DAVID ANSWERED on the second ring. "Hey."

"Hey yourself. Did you hear about the earthquake?"

"Yeah." He sounded tired. "It hasn't derailed Anderson's warmongering, if that's what you're wondering."

"Can't say I'm surprised." I tightened my grip on the phone. David would never betray me, but I wouldn't put it past Anderson to tap his phone . . . or mine. Somehow I had to get the information I needed without compromising either of us. "I'm actually calling to see how the werewolves are holding up and maybe offer some advice on how to move them safely."

"You're offering to help imprison your friends?"

"I'm trying to ensure no more innocents get hurt. The transfer would happen regardless."

"Fair enough. We've got three vans and two National Guard escort vehicles scheduled to take them to Genoa this evening. Weatherly wants them out from underfoot as soon as possible."

"Cramming that many werewolves together could be dangerous. You saw what happened in the gym, and the newest ones will be even worse."

David hesitated then said, "They'll all be sedated for transport."

I pursed my lips. Having the freshly changed werewolves sedated might be a blessing, but I'd been hoping the others would be awake to help when we sprang our ambush.

"This is awkward as ass, Alex. I don't like playing on opposite sides. If you want me to step down, just say so. You'd be doing me a favor. This whole damn situation is giving me an ulcer."

"No. If someone like Weatherly takes over, you can bet a trigger-happy guard will see one of the werewolves twitch in their sleep and decide tranquilizers aren't enough. I need you to keep them safe for me." I paused for emphasis. "It's a long stretch from Denver to Genoa."

For a moment all that came over the line was David's breathing, then, "Especially at eight o'clock at night. Not much out there to keep a driver awake on I-70."

I smiled, grateful that he'd understood what I needed without my having to spell it out. "Keep your head down, David. I'll see you soon." I hung up.

Emma leaned forward. "Did you get what you needed?"

I nodded. "The transport is happening tonight at eight via I-70. We need to be in place by then." I pictured the region east of Denver. "We should wait to hit them outside the city proper but not too far."

"Bennett," James said. "The town is set back from the highway, the area around it is open farmland, and there are several access roads nearby."

"Okay." I braced my hands on my knees and looked around at my friends. "We hit them just before Bennett."

Kai shifted his weight. "Are you sure this is worth the risk? We don't even know if the werewolves will prove effective against Shedraziel."

"We need all the help we can get, and other than named fae, Marc and Sarah"—I glanced at James—"and maybe James, are the only people who've proven resistant to her control."

"There were three," James said. "Three werewolves fighting the others at the PTF building."

I frowned. "Who was the other one?"

He shrugged. "But there were definitely three."

I pinched my lower lip between my thumb and forefinger, thinking. "There's one more member of Marc's pack who joined the PTF. If it was him—"

"Maybe Marc's pack has some sort of immunity!" Emma blurted.

"If that's the case," James said, "perhaps we should encourage the rest of his pack to join us."

"My thoughts exactly." I pulled up the number for Auntie Yu, second-in-command of Marc's pack. With him out of the picture for the moment, she'd be calling the shots. She picked up on the fifth ring. I wondered if the delay had been innocent or if she was reluctant to take my call.

"What do you want, Alex?" Her voice, thick with an Asian accent, snapped like a whip.

Reluctant. Not that I can blame her after the way things turned out.

"I wanted to check on you, what with the lockdown and all." I chose my words carefully. "How's everyone doing?"

"Anxious. No one has heard from Marc since yesterday." There was a long pause. "He told us there'd been an incident at the PTF and instructed us to gather and wait at his home until he made contact."

I nodded to myself. Marc's first priority was always to keep his people safe. By sending them to his property he not only kept them from being picked off one by one, but since his land backed to open forest, his pack could disappear into the wilderness at the first sign of trouble. And lucky for me, his house was only a little more than a mile away through that forest. I smiled and sent a silent "thank you" to the universe for finally giving me a piece of good news.

"That's smart," I said. "You should stay put."

"Do you know what's happening?" Again her voice slashed like a whip, demanding answers. "Are we in danger?"

That's why she picked up. She wants to know if it's time to take the rest of the pack and run. I bit my lip, wondering how to say what needed saying without giving myself away in case the line was tapped. "Marc is probably concerned about communicating over the phone. I'm sure he wants you to stay where you are so that if he sent someone to get word to you they could."

A long silence stretched across the line. Eventually, she said, "I hope you have more to say the next time we speak."

The connection went dead, cut off from her end.

I tucked my phone away and headed for the coat rack. "James, I need you to get me over to Marc's house without being seen. Assume both properties are under surveillance."

James, Kai, and Chase all stood up.

"Just James," I said as I pulled on my shoes.

"I know the forest better," Chase said.

"But the werewolves don't like you," I reminded him, then shifted my gaze to Kai. "Any of you. And it sounds like most of the pack is present. Without Marc there to rein them in. . . ." I shrugged. "You're the one who pointed out what could happen if James showed up in a group of fae. The same is true for you and werewolves."

Kai raised his hands in surrender and sat back down. "Point taken."

"They still blame us for their existence?" Zee asked.

"Not all, but enough that I don't want to risk bumping into someone who does. Not when I need their help." I tied my shoes, zipped my coat, and put on a black-and-purple knit cap. "Ready to go?"

James tied his own shoes, which were somehow still shiny black despite all the mud around my house. He slipped his arms into his knee-length wool coat and started on the buttons. "Do you think people are watching the house itself or just the road?"

"I'll check." Chase dropped to all fours and shrank before anyone could argue. The blanket around his waist fell to the floor as he walked over to me on gray paws.

I wonder if changing shape hurts? Not that any self-respecting fae or werewolf would admit it if it did. I pushed the errant thought away as Chase poked the front door with a paw. I opened it a crack. He slipped out.

He was gone barely a minute when a soft *meow* came from the porch.

I opened the door again, and he slipped back inside. He shifted right beside me, close enough that his magic tickled my skin. His nose nearly touched mine.

I took an involuntary step back, which only served to bring the rest of him into view. My cheeks warmed.

He smiled. "Two poorly disguised agents are camped out near the main road."

James's chest bumped against my back. His hands settled on my shoulders. He spoke from right beside my ear. "I'll take it from here."

Chase's smile grew wider. He opened the door himself. Not a crack, as I had done, but wide open, letting the snow-laced air blow across his bare skin. Then he stepped to the side and bowed with a flourish. "She's all yours."

James's fingers tightened. A ripple of annoyance trickled through our bond. Then he scooped me into his arms and the house was rushing away behind us.

James flowed smoothly between bare-branched trees and snow-laden pines that became blurs of smeared color on either side of us. His legs pumped as we raced over the ground toward Marc's house, but his arms held me securely to his chest.

I tightened my grip around his neck, pulling myself closer to his ear. "What's going on with you and Chase?"

He shook his head. "Forget it."

I prodded at the fluttery feelings clogging our connection. "You're mad at me."

"Now's not the time, Alex."

I curled my knuckles into his collar. "Tell me."

He sighed. "I just don't see how you can get so upset about me feeding with Victoria when you've got naked men walking around your house on a daily basis."

"I usually make him wear clothes," I mumbled. "And it's not sexual with Chase. That's just how shifters are."

He raised an eyebrow. "You think he doesn't want to sleep with you?"

"I wouldn't put it past Chase to sleep with *anyone*, but it's a moot point because *I'm* not going to sleep with *him*."

"Yet you can't believe the same about my relationship with Victoria?"

"I caught you in bed together!"

"Feeding. And I've found Chase in your bed plenty of times."

"As a cat."

He slowed. "You think that makes a difference?"

I opened my mouth, dumbstruck. Did James see snuggling with Chase when he was a cat in the same light as sleeping with another man? Did Chase? Was I cheating on James without even realizing it?

He stepped into a clearing, stopped, and set me on my feet a dozen yards from Marc's back porch. My hand trailed down his arm as he moved away, but I snagged his fingers before we lost the connection completely.

"That hadn't occurred to me." I shifted my weight, unsure where to take the conversation. "Do you want—"

"I don't need you to change, Alex. And I know that Chase won't." The corner of his mouth lifted, then fell. "I just wish you could extend me the same courtesy."

He headed for the French doors at the back of Marc's house. I let myself be pulled along by our connected hands, but I couldn't stop thinking about how I'd let my insecurities turn me into a hypocrite.

James rapped his knuckles against the glass-and-metal storm door.

The door opened. Yumeko, more commonly referred to as Auntie Yu, stood framed in the doorway. The top of her head barely reached my shoulder. A long braid of black streaked with silver hung down her back. She wore a cream-colored sweater, a pair of clingy, dark-blue yoga pants, and pink socks. Deep lines traced the edges of her mouth and eyes. I had no idea how old she actually was, but she'd reached old age before she'd been turned into a werewolf. The fact that she'd survived despite her advanced years was a testament to how tough she was. She narrowed her eyes at me, and her steely, dark gaze was full of power and focus.

"That was fast." She stepped to one side.

I slipped past James and Auntie Yu, entering Marc's mudroom. It was just as I remembered from my first visit to his house—a top-of-the-line washer and dryer, baskets of laundry, a huge chest freezer. I glanced at the reinforced door that led to his cellar and the dungeon where I'd woken up on that first visit. At the time, I'd thought it was some kind of medieval torture chamber. I now knew the cages were a security precaution to contain out-of-control werewolves. If Weatherly hadn't stripped me of my influence with the PTF, I probably would have suggested the new werewolves be transferred into Marc's custody until they got a handle on their new lives. Now . . . ? I pictured the victims of yesterday's attack locked in cells at the Genoa facility. The accommodations might be similar, but here they would have been supported, their new lives explained. Isolated among humans, they'd have to face the terrifying changes forced upon them alone.

"We'll chat in the living room." Yumiko's voice snapped me out of my rumination as she closed and latched the French doors behind James.

I pulled my gaze away from the door to the basement and went instead to the simple wooden door that let into the house proper. The large living room was crowded. The couch and three armchairs all had occupants. One man was sprawled on the worn carpet in front of the fireplace reading a novel with a bare-chested man on the cover.

I walked over to a woman who was perched on the wooden sill of a bay window with a sketchbook propped in her lap. "Hey, Sophie."

She looked up from her drawing. I was relieved to see she'd put on a little weight since the last time I'd seen her, so she no longer looked like a skin-covered skeleton. She nodded and the cropped bangs of her short blond hair dropped in front of one eye. She swept it back with the hand holding her pencil. "Alex."

Auntie Yu set a hand against my back, directing me toward one of the occupied chairs. She cleared her throat, and the young man who'd been sitting with one jean-clad leg over the armrest sprang to his feet and scrambled over to the corner. His name was Tim, and he was the first werewolf I'd ever met—the one who'd given me the scars on my left arm and turned Sophie. He offered me a gap-toothed grin from his new position at the edge of the room and settled cross-legged on the floor.

I sat down in the vacated chair.

Auntie Yu moved toward the seat directly across from me. She didn't make a sound, but the occupant, a man I'd never met before with ochre skin and short black hair, stood and squeezed onto the couch between an equally unknown woman and Sarah's husband Gilbert—a scrawny, unassuming college professor with a mop of untidy reddish-brown hair and glasses that magnified his blue eyes. The final chair was claimed by Jedd, a Hispanic man who, if I wasn't mistaken, was third in the pack hierarchy. No one offered James a seat, so he stood behind my chair.

Auntie Yu looked around the room. Her gaze settled on the man reading by the fire. "Dillon."

"Hm?" The man, Dillon, didn't look up.

"Put down the book and pay attention."

He sighed, closed his book, and rolled over, propping his head on one elbow. He had shoulder-length brown hair, light-brown eyes, and a hard expression. "Why are we even listening to her?"

"Because she knows what's going on at the PTF. She may be able to help."

"The last time Alex *helped* us, we lost Oz."

My chest tightened as though Dillon's words were a hand that had reached through my ribs to squeeze my heart.

"That wasn't her fault," Yumiko said. "And she took down the man responsible."

"But she lost the video of Sophie's transformation," Dillon pressed. "If not for that, the werewolves would never have been outed, and we wouldn't have had people at the PTF facility to begin with."

"You can't blame Alex for that," Sophie said. She stared at her sketch-book while she spoke. "I'm the one who lost control."

"Any of us would have in that situation," Auntie Yu said, her voice gentle. Then she turned her gaze back to Dillon, and the steel returned. "Casting blame will solve nothing. We need to decide how to move forward."

"Marc said to stay put." Gilbert pushed his rectangular glasses further up his nose and leaned forward, resting the plaid-patched elbows of his tweed jacket against his knees. "Sarah said the same. We don't want to make matters worse."

"How much did they tell you about what happened in Denver?" I asked.

"They said some fae bewitched a bunch of werewolves into attacking humans," said Yumiko. "That everyone was returned to their right minds but they were staying to smooth things over and deal with those who'd been infected during the fight. Marc ordered us to lay low here until we heard from him."

"That was before the governor's lockdown order," Jedd said. "For all we know, Marc and the rest are prisoners now."

They all looked at me.

I swallowed hard, nearly choking on the boulder in my throat. "Everly Harris is in a coma. Weatherly has stepped in as acting regional director, and I've been relieved of my position with the PTF."

Gilbert dropped his head into his hands.

I suppose Sarah's told him about Weatherly.

"Marc and the other werewolves at the PTF building have been detained," I continued.

Inhales mixed with the sounds of rustling fabric and creaking furniture as several people adjusted position, either out of shock or in preparation to speak.

I took a deep breath and hurried on. "But they aren't the only ones in danger. We all are. There's a fae named Shedraziel who's been stirring up trouble. She's the one behind the chaos at the PTF building yesterday, the capitol bombing, the trash on the Pacific beaches, the disappearances in Europe . . . all of it."

"So the fae have gone to war." Jedd whispered the words, but they rang out like an explosion.

"No." I shook my head. "Shedraziel is working on her own. She's pitting the fae realms against each other, too."

"To what end?" Yumiko asked.

"As far as I can tell? Chaos. Complete and utter chaos. And she's succeeding. She's already gotten the PTF to break ties with the local paranaturals and launch a missile attack against a fae reservation. If things continue as they are, no one will be safe."

"All the more reason for us to spring our people before the situation grows worse," Dillon said.

I nodded. "I agree."

Every gaze zeroed in on me with laser-point focus. The silence grew so dense, the only sound was the deafening pound of my own heartbeat.

Dillon sat up and slapped his thigh. "Well damn, and here I thought I wasn't going to like what you had to say."

Yumiko frowned. "You're advising us to break our people out of the PTF facility and go into hiding?"

"Not exactly." I quickly outlined my plan to lead a group of fae to Nevada in the hopes of finding and stopping Shedraziel. "If we can figure out why some of the werewolves weren't affected by Shedraziel's magic—"

"Figures." Dillon shook his head. "Now that she's not bosom buddies with the PTF, she needs soldiers to save her faerie friends. She doesn't care about us."

"Dillon's right," Jedd said. "Sounds to me like you're looking for cannon fodder."

I jerked back as though slapped. "I'm only—"

"They *were* affected," Yumiko cut in.

I swung my focus back to Marc's second-in-command. "What?"

"Marc, Sarah, Xander . . . they were all affected."

I shook my head. "No, they fought against the other werewolves."

Auntie Yu's gaze drifted around the room, meeting each pair of eyes. "You all felt it, didn't you?"

"Felt what?" James asked.

"Werewolf packs are more than just people who share a common affliction," she said. "We're connected by deep bonds set in place through ritualistic magic. Marc, Sarah, and Xander all pulled heavily on those bonds yesterday."

I sat up straighter. "You think that's why they were able to resist Shedraziel's control?"

"Pack members can draw on the strength of their brothers and sisters to aid in all manner of things, including breaking free of enchantments."

I glanced over my shoulder at James. "The bonds must anchor them, sort of like true names do for the fae." I frowned. "But the other wolves all came from established packs, too. Why couldn't they do the same?"

"Pack magic isn't as strong over a long distance," Gilbert pointed out.

Auntie Yu shook her head. "It's not just that."

I raised an eyebrow.

"You were planning to forge a new pack among the PTF wolves."

I nodded.

"Marc had already started making preparations on your behalf, including calling the existing pack leaders of those who'd joined the PTF to have their bonds severed."

My mouth went dry. "So the ones who got possessed didn't have pack bonds to draw strength from."

She shrugged. "It's a theory."

"Then all of you should be safe from Shedraziel's control."

Dillon scoffed. "And we're back to cannon fodder."

I glared at him. "Look, I won't deny what I'm asking is dangerous, and maybe you don't feel like this is your fight, but the sooner Shedraziel is put down the better for all of us, werewolves included." I shifted my focus back to Auntie Yu. "I can't force anyone to fight, but whether or not you choose to join me, I still think breaking the werewolves loose before they get transferred is our best course of action."

She pursed her lips, studied me for a moment, then gave one sharp nod. "We'll work together to free Marc and the others. *Then* we'll decide whether or not to join your crusade."

"Fair enough. David is in charge of transporting the werewolves. They're moving out at eight tonight. The plan right now is to hit the caravan on the long stretch of highway before they reach Genoa. A few well-placed illusions and an ambush should make short work of the guards." I pressed my palms together. "The big question is how to get everyone out of the state before Anderson and Weatherly catch on. Especially since the werewolves will be sedated for transport."

"I could fly a few," Dillon said, "but nowhere near all of us would fit in my plane."

Gilbert raised his hand. "I have an idea."

I looked at Sarah's husband. Even knowing what he was, knowing that *anyone* could be turned into a werewolf, I had trouble reconciling the mild-mannered man with the vicious beast I knew he could become. "What did you have in mind?"

He lowered his hand and looked around the group. "As some of you know, I've joined the local One Earth chapter."

"They know you're a werewolf?" I asked.

He nodded. "Not at first. I thought it best to let them get to know me as a person before springing that particular tidbit, but even after I came clean they were quite welcoming."

"That's great and all," Jedd said, "but how does it help us?"

"The goal is to get out of the state without being arrested. The nearest border would be to the east, but that's the wrong direction if your goal is Nevada. That means doubling back through Denver and making a run for Utah, which takes about five hours on the highway."

Dillon rolled his eyes. "Get to the point, Professor."

Gil scowled at the interruption. "What better way to evade the authorities than to give them another target to focus on?"

"You're suggesting a diversion?" Jedd asked.

Gil leaned forward, gesturing with his hands as he spoke. "If we can convince enough One Earth members to flood the streets tonight in protest of the lockdown order—"

"Anderson's goons will be too busy with crowd control to notice us slip by." I grinned, then frowned. "But that would take a lot of people. Do you really have enough One Earth contacts who'd help us?"

"One Earth has over a thousand members in the metro area alone, and from what I've observed, they seem genuinely enthusiastic about interspecies cooperation."

The man next to Gil moved his hands in a series of quick gestures. I noticed a hearing aid hooked over his ear.

Yumiko responded with a similar flash of hand signals.

I raised an eyebrow.

Yumiko cleared her throat. "Kieran says that if we trust the wrong person, it could be *us* who ends up in an ambush."

"We don't have to tell them *why* we need the protest to happen tonight," Gil said.

I straightened as an idea took root in my mind. "Maybe we should."

The werewolves exchanged confused glances.

"Not about the ambush . . . but if we gave the One Earthers a good enough reason to join the protest, it wouldn't matter that they were also acting as a diversion for us."

"What reason?" Yumiko asked.

"That earthquake in Europe was actually a PTF attack on the Black Forest Reservation," I said. "Anderson wants to do the same thing here in Colorado."

Gil nodded. "That's certainly something One Earth would want to protest."

"So we leak the information that Anderson is planning a military strike against the reservation and arrange a protest rally in Denver for eight thirty tonight. At the very least we'll get our diversion, and if we're really lucky and enough people speak out against it, maybe we can derail Anderson's plan."

James set his hand on my shoulder and squeezed. Pride and hope mingled in our bond. The plan was coming together. I reached up to cover his fingers with my own.

"Now all we need is enough cars to transport all those unconscious werewolves," said Auntie Yu. And just like that, my moment of contentment shattered. "How many people were turned in the attack?"

"Nine, I think."

"Plus the ten we already had," said James. "And this lot."

Dillon let out a soft whistle. "That's a lot of bodies to move."

The woman to whom I hadn't yet been introduced straightened with a smile that shone in stark contrast to her dark skin and made her brown eyes twinkle. "I may be able to help with that." She waited for a nod from Auntie Yu before continuing. "The woman I'm dating is a big rig trucker."

Jedd nodded. "A semi-trailer would have enough space for all of us."

"And one more semi headed west on I-70 shouldn't raise any eyebrows," I agreed.

Yumiko pointed at the woman, then at Gil. "Make your calls."

They both pulled out cell phones. Gil moved into the attached kitchen while the woman headed deeper into the house for more privacy. Dillon flopped onto his back and opened his book. Jedd settled lower in his seat, folded his hands across his stomach, tipped his head back, and closed his eyes. Yumiko lifted a pair of needles and a forest-green ball of yarn attached to about six inches of knitted fabric out of a basket beside her chair.

I looked up and back, catching James's gaze. He shrugged.

I guess there isn't much else to say until we know if our plan has a chance.

Patting James's hand, I slipped out of his grasp and sauntered over to the bay window. Sophie didn't look up at my approach. I paused near her shoulder and peeked at her drawing. It was a sketch of the room and its occupants as they had been when I walked in.

I pointed at Gilbert. "That's a really good likeness."

She nodded.

I shifted from foot to foot. "Thanks for speaking up earlier. It's nice to know you don't blame me for what happened."

"Yeah, well, there's plenty of blame to go around."

"Right." I started to turn away.

Sophie lowered her pencil and said, "Wait."

I froze, then turned back to face her fully.

She tapped the tip of her pencil against the corner of her sketch pad, making a collection of random stipple marks at the edge of her drawing. "During the last full moon, I found a little valley tucked back in the high country. It's way off the beaten path, totally undisturbed. I'd like to go back there to do some sketching." She ran one finger of her free hand down the spiral binding of her sketchbook. "You could join me . . . if you wanted."

Her invitation was clearly an olive branch, an offer to wipe the slate clean and try to salvage our friendship. Still I hesitated. The last time she'd invited me somewhere I'd ended up as a vampire's plaything.

"If you're nervous about being alone with me, we can invite Marc and James to chaperone; call it a double date."

"Are you two dating?"

She shifted her weight and looked out the window. "I'm not sure what we are. Being part of a pack is . . . complicated."

I nodded and cast a sidelong glance at James. I might not be part of a werewolf pack, but I could commiserate with being in a complicated relationship.

Sophie cleared her throat and set her pencil against her page, darkening the shadow beneath Jedd's jaw. "Anyway, it was just an idea. You—"

"Sure." The word popped out of my mouth without a thought, but once it was out, my nervousness eased. I exhaled and continued, "I'd love to do a sketch hike with you."

The pencil stilled, shaking slightly in her grip. She didn't speak or look at me. She just gave one brisk nod.

"We're all set." The woman with the trucker contact trotted into the living room with her phone held high in triumph. "Claire will meet us in Bennett."

Auntie Yu lowered her knitting. "Good work, Tamara." She looked toward the kitchen. We all followed her gaze. Gil was pacing back and forth on the far side of the arch that marked the border between the two rooms. "Now if we can just finalize our diversion."

We continued to watch Gil as he made another two circuits of the kitchen island. Then he hung up.

I moved next to James and took his hand, holding my breath.

Gil looked around the room. He smiled. "We're on."

My exhale was joined and amplified by several others. Murmurs broke out around the room as the werewolves started speculating on everything from how many people would join the protest to what the newest werewolves might be like.

Gil cleared his throat. "I've also arranged a ride that should be able to get us to the ambush site undetected."

I blinked. I'd been planning to subdue the agents guarding my driveway and steal their car for the first leg of the journey since Anderson's goons wouldn't likely pull over one of their own, but I'd assumed the werewolves would circle around the city on four paws to reach the ambush.

"Enough for everyone?" I asked.

"So long as you don't mind getting cozy. We'll swing by your place at six o'clock tonight. Wear shoes you can run in."

Yumiko set her knitting on top of its basket and stood to show us out. "It looks to be a long night. I suggest we all get what rest we can."

Chapter 17

I TOSSED AND TURNED on my bed, tangling in my sheets. Every time I closed my eyes, my mind filled with worries and what-ifs. I opened my eyes and glared at the water stain on my ceiling. I rolled onto my side, punching down the lumps in my pillow. Light leaked around the edges of my curtains. I blew out a sigh. The breath hit my arm and curled back into my face, hot and stale. I grumbled and rolled to the other side. I closed my eyes, opened them again, threw back the covers, and sat up.

"This is pointless." The words came out as a growl through my clenched teeth.

I grabbed a sweatshirt out of my closet and pulled it on over my T-shirt. I slipped into a pair of black jeans, ran a brush roughly through the tangles in my hair, and stalked out in search of distraction.

"I thought you were going to get some rest before tonight." James was sitting in my favorite spot—an overstuffed armchair I'd brought home from a thrift store. He held a glass of red wine in one hand and a mystery novel from my "to-be-read" pile in the other. There was no sign of my other housemates, so I assumed they'd all found beds.

I gestured to the book in his hand. "You aren't."

His expression turned patronizing. "I require much less, as you well know."

I sighed and flopped down on the couch only to stand up again right away and start pacing. "I just can't seem to relax."

"Perhaps you should spend some time in the studio. That often settles you."

I nodded. "That's a good idea." I grabbed my shoes and sat down again to tie them. "If I'm not back by—"

"I will not only ensure you aren't left behind but that you have a proper meal before we go." A smile softened his lips and twinkled in his eyes.

I smiled back, grateful not only for his promise but for the sense of security his presence gave me. Whatever else was going on between us, he had my back and he always would. I could feel that truth like a pulse through our bond.

"Thanks." I walked to his chair, leaned over, and planted a lingering kiss against his lips.

When I pulled back, he caught me around the waist. The mystery novel fell to the floor. "On second thought . . . perhaps we can find a better way to relax you."

I laughed and finished retreating, trailing my hand down his arm. "Too late. I've got my shoes on."

He raised an eyebrow. "I can deal with that."

He caught my fingers, holding me in place. He reached around me to set his wine glass on the coffee table and traced my thigh and side with his emptied hand as he straightened. There was barely an inch between us. His lips brushed my neck, my jaw, and found my mouth once more.

An involuntary, *"Mmmm,"* snuck past my lips.

He stepped into me, one hand cupping my butt, lifting my weight. I wrapped my legs around his waist, crossing my ankles at the small of his back. All thoughts of the studio and the coming night vanished as he carried me back to my bedroom.

I PULLED THE quilt up to cover my bare shoulder and pressed closer to James's side, drawn to his heat like a moth to flame. My body was warm, my muscles liquid, but the weight of contentment pulling my eyelids closed couldn't stop my mind from racing ahead, doling out images of possible futures as though I were an oracle. I ran my hand over the familiar planes of James's abdomen and up to his chest, trying to anchor myself in the moment. He twitched when my fingers found his ribs. The rapid pulse of his heart beat against my palm in testament to our recent exertions. Our legs were tangled together. Cold air tickled my toes where the covers had ridden up. The sweat on my scalp cooled and made me shiver.

His arm tightened around my back. "You still can't sleep?"

I tipped my face to look at him.

He cupped my jaw with his free hand. "After all that?"

I compressed my lips in resignation. "Apparently not." I rolled onto my back, trapping James's arm beneath me, and dug my fingers into my hair.

"Should I be insulted that you found my distraction inadequate?"

I glanced at his face. There was laughter in his eyes, but also sorrow. He really had hoped I'd relax enough to fall asleep.

"Your *distraction* was more than adequate." I propped myself up on my elbow and leaned over, pressing a long, deep kiss to his mouth. I snagged his lower lip between my teeth when I pulled back, giving it a playful tug. "But we can't just have sex forever. The real world is still out there . . . waiting."

He cradled my hips with both hands. "We could try."

I chuckled. "We've already beaten our previous record. You really think you can go again?"

"For you, my dear?" He kissed me. "Anything."

I patted his cheek. "Well I can't. Not if I want to be able to walk tonight."

He settled back with a sigh and let his hands fall away from my waist. "As you wish. But let the record show that I was willing."

"And able." I rolled to my side of the bed and stood up. "I think I'll head to the studio after all. Do you want me to bring you your book?"

He shrugged. "I'm pretty sure I know how it's going to end."

I glanced over my shoulder. "Maybe there will be a twist."

"When you've lived as long as I have, there are very few surprises."

"I could do with a few less surprises in my life." I collected my clothes off the floor, dressed, laid one last kiss on James's forehead, and opened the bedroom door.

"Alex."

I glanced back. James had both hands tucked behind his head. He was staring at the stain on the ceiling.

"Surprises are what make life worth living."

I pulled the door closed and headed to my studio.

Frost had turned the dead grass around my house to icy shards that crunched beneath the snow. My breath came out in visible puffs. Snowflakes drifted lazily through the air on the tail end of the storm, some falling from the sky, some blown off the branches of trees. The snow wouldn't be a problem at the lower elevations where our ambush was going to take place, but the mountain roads would turn to ice when the sun set. I just hoped it wasn't enough to close the pass and trap us on this side of the divide.

The inside of my studio wasn't much warmer than the open land separating it from my house. The forge was cold, and the cinder block walls and cement floor seemed to sap the warmth I carried with me as I moved to the back where my materials for the PTF sculpture were stored.

I pulled out a six-by-six sheet of brass that needed to be textured, laid it on three stumps I'd arranged in a triangle for that purpose, and wheeled over my oxy-acetylene torch. The piece was too large to work all at once, so I started in one corner, annealing the metal to make it more malleable. Then I grabbed a ball-peen hammer off the pegboard wall. My fingers were stiff with cold, which weakened my grip. Setting the hammer down, I turned on my stereo, cranked up the volume, and put in my ear plugs. I breathed on my hands and rubbed them together before picking up my hammer again. Then I started to swing.

I matched the rhythmic *clang* of metal striking metal with the downbeats in my music, falling into a trance that let my mind wander while my body moved on autopilot. This section of brass was going to be patinaed to create a high contrast between the darkened indents and polished surface, then attached to one side of the "fae path" of my spiral walkway.

I thought about the bridge I was trying to build between the species—

had been trying to build ever since I learned I walked the line between worlds. But my mind spiraled to Shedraziel and how close she was to tearing it all down around me. My magic stirred as I continued to pound away at the metal. I didn't call it up intentionally as I did to cast a spell, but it responded to my focused concentration. I opened myself when I created art in the same way I opened myself to imbue objects. My magic couldn't tell the difference.

Every strike of the hammer carried a little of my frustration with it, forging the emotion into the metal.

I sat back and blew out a sigh. Frustration was *not* the feeling I was going for with this piece.

I set down my hammer, shook out my arms, annealed a new section, and started again. The hammer fell, the metal moved, the music blared, and my thoughts circled back to Shedraziel.

Even if we find her in time, she's a centuries-old general. She has minions and magic, and more skill with a sword than I can manage even with a gun. My hammer clanged to punctuate the thought. *I need more than luck and loyalty.*

Clang. Clang. Clang.

I need an advantage. Something she won't expect. I bit my lip. *A surprise to throw her off balance.*

My hammer impacted the metal but didn't rise.

I need iron.

I looked down at my handiwork. The surface of the brass was covered with erratic dents. I set my hammer aside and rested both palms against the metal. All the heat from the annealing had vanished. I took a deep breath and opened myself to the echo imprinted in the metal. My own frustrations bounced back at me, but intermingled was a thread of hope.

It's a start.

I glanced at my material pile. Iron and steel rods were propped in the corner. Any one of them would give Shedraziel pause if I managed to hit her with it, but they were clumsy weapons and I didn't have time to refine them.

I rubbed both hands over my face. *Maybe Anderson will lend me one of his bombs.* I chuckled to myself.

I'll take my gun, but in the end it'll probably come down to magic and swords, and she can kick my ass with either.

I considered the beautifully crafted sword I'd received from Bael, made from a silver alloy and strengthened with magic. Silver swords were the norm at court, since duels were common, and no fae could carry a steel blade without suffering from the iron in it. I tapped my chin and looked again at the iron rods.

Unlike most fae, I could use a steel blade, but it would be dangerous for my companions and the chances of getting close to Shedraziel with such a weapon. . . . I shook my head, then froze.

"What if she didn't know it was steel?" I whispered as I pulled out my earplugs and turned off my music. "If she thought my sword was silver, she'd believe she had the upper hand." I snorted. "Who am I kidding? She definitely has the upper hand." I pinched my lower lip. "But if she underestimates me, I've got a better chance of catching her off guard."

I thought about the first time we'd crossed paths. The only reason I'd been able to get close to her was because she thought I was under her control, and the only blade I'd been able to use was a needle forged purely of magic. I'd nearly had her that time, and I'd been kicking myself every day for failing to follow through.

"She's powerful and clever, but she's not invincible."

Abandoning my brass, I left the studio and tromped back across the yard to the house. I kicked the snow off my boots and stepped inside. Warm air hit my face, rushing toward the open door, while the cold outside breeze pushed against the backs of my legs, seeking a way inside. The house was filled with the smells of seared meat and seasonings.

"Mmm. . . ." My mouth began to water. My stomach grumbled. "What is that amazing smell?"

James raised a wooden spoon in greeting. "Dinner."

I crossed to the kitchen bar that separated the two rooms and peeked over the counter. Cubes of beef bubbled in a brown liquid in my deepest pan. Potatoes, carrots, and an onion stood in a line along one edge of the cutting board like prisoners awaiting execution. My chef's knife glinted on the board. There was also a collection of jars beside the stove that I was pretty sure represented every spice I owned, plus an empty bottle of wine.

I nodded toward the bottle. "Binging are we?"

"It's in the sauce." He covered the pan with a lid, set his spoon aside, and picked up the knife. "I wasn't expecting you back so soon. The stew will be ready in an hour."

I took one more deep whiff then pulled back. "Just enough time to try my idea."

He raised an eyebrow.

I smiled and turned away. "I'll tell you about it at dinner . . . if it works."

I grabbed the sword off my dresser and slipped back outside, wishing I could take the savory smells with me.

I RAN A HUNK of sourdough around my bowl to sop up any remaining dregs of my second serving of stew and popped it into my mouth. Then I sat back with a sated sigh and patted my abdomen. "That was amazing."

"What's for dessert?" Kai asked, wiping his mouth on a paper napkin. He leaned toward Zee, who sat beside him at the dinner table. "The sweets in this realm are spectacular."

"More importantly," James said, turning to me, "did your idea work?"

"What idea?" Emma was pushing vegetables around her plate, looking groggy. She'd slept right up to the call to eat.

I smiled and pushed back my chair. "Let's find out."

I'd propped my sword by the coat rack when I came in from the studio to shower and eat. Now I retrieved it and handed it to Kai. "What do you think?"

He frowned. "It's the sword Bael gave you."

My smile grew as the butterflies fluttering in my chest flapped faster. *So far so good.*

"With one small change."

He looked at the sheathed blade, bounced it on his palm, gripped the hilt, and drew the sword. He held it easily, giving a test swish over the dinner dishes. He shrugged, looked back at me, and said, "It seems the same to me."

I clapped my hands together and grinned. "I was really hoping you'd say that." I glanced at Zee. "Do you notice anything odd about the blade?"

She turned her golden gaze on the sword, studying its length, then shook her head. "It is beautiful and well balanced, but not extraordinary in any way that I can see."

I circled the table so I was standing between their two chairs and held out my hand. Kai placed the hilt in my palm. I closed one eye and peered down the tapered length of the blade. "This sword was enchanted to stay razor sharp. It's just one molecule thick along the cutting edge."

Zee cocked her head. "This is extraordinary by human standards?"

"Yes, but that's not why this blade is special."

"How do you know there's just one molecule?" Emma asked. "Or were you just being poetic?"

"I know because those molecules along the edge are the only ones I changed," I said, recalling how meticulously I'd worked to find the very smallest elements to imbue. The work had been delicate and grueling—nudging one tiny speck at a time with my magic—and I still wasn't sure I'd succeeded. "At least I think I did." I glanced at Kai. "Are you willing to be my guinea pig?"

"That depends on what you're testing."

"I used my magic to change just the very edge of this blade to iron."

He and Zee both jerked away from me.

"You can't tell it's there, right?" I looked back and forth between them, settling on Kai. "You didn't feel anything when you held it?"

He shook his head.

"Then I at least didn't change too much. The question now is whether I changed enough to have any useful effect. But for that"—I shrugged—"I need to test it."

"You want me to let you stab me?"

"Not *stab*. A little nick should do. Just enough to tell if the iron affects you."

He sighed. "Fine." He held out his hand. "I'd rather do it myself if you don't mind."

I passed back the sword. He set the scabbard on the table between our dinner dishes, pulled up his right pant leg, and slid the sword against his calf. Kai hissed. A short, thin line of blood appeared.

He held the sword out to me. I took it, wiped the blade with a napkin, and sheathed it. James got up and circled around the table so he could see. We all leaned closer, staring at Kai's leg, except Emma, who asked, "What's happening?"

Kai winced. He dabbed a napkin against the cut to wipe away the blood, but as soon as he pulled the napkin back, more blood seeped out.

Zee knelt beside Kai, leaning so close it looked as if she might lick his leg. "It's not healing."

"And it burns," Kai said. "More than the initial sting."

James wrapped an arm around my shoulders and said in an awed voice, "You poisoned the blade."

"Let's just hope I can hit her with it."

AUNTIE YU KNOCKED on my door at six o'clock sharp. She stood buck naked on my porch, her long black and silver hair blowing around her face and shoulders in the frigid breeze. I shivered just looking at her.

I hooked a thumb behind me to indicate the living room. "Do you want—"

"Are you ready to go?"

Guess that's a no on talking inside. "We're all set."

"Our ride is meeting us in the parking lot of the Blue Owl Bookstore on the south edge of town. We need to hurry."

"You're sure this 'ride' can get us to the ambush site undetected?"

She nodded. "I've no doubt James can keep up. What about the rest of you?"

I stifled a laugh. The bookstore was a few miles away since we'd have to circle around to the far side of town. Not an easy trek over uneven terrain. "Chase would be all right, and Zee can fly, but the rest of us. . . ." I shook my head.

"Can this Zee person carry you?"

I called over my shoulder. "Zee, how many can you carry?"

She looked up from the conversation she was having with Chase on the couch. "Two. Perhaps three."

So James carries one, Chase runs, and the rest go on Zee. I glanced at Emma sitting patiently in her chair. A stuffed canvas backpack rested by her leg. Magical vision aside, I wasn't comfortable with her clinging blindly to a flying dragon. "Emma, you're with James. Kai and I will ride with Zee." I nodded to the dragon. "If that's all right with you?"

She nodded and stood. The rest of my companions followed suit, each lifting a pack of one kind or another. Some held medical supplies, others bore food. Each of us was also equipped with whatever weapons we were comfortable using. In my case, that was the modified sword on my belt, the light-imbued knife on my leg, and the Ruger in my holster. Kai wore his sword openly, which looked ridiculous juxtaposed with his faded jeans, Green Day concert T-shirt, and yellow hoodie. James was dressed in dark jeans and a gray long-sleeved shirt. Despite his skill with a blade, he didn't have any weapons besides his bare hands, but I'd seen those do plenty of damage. Chase and Zee were similarly barehanded, and Emma carried only the hunting knife I'd given her in case of emergency. Hopefully she wouldn't be near any actual fighting.

Once everyone filed into the yard, I turned out the lights, pulled the door closed, and locked it. The last time I'd gone on the run from my home, I hadn't even been able to do that. I looked toward my sleeping studio. I'd left the sheet of partially textured brass on the stumps. How long would it be before I got back to it? I straightened and took a deep breath. *I'm not being chased off this time. This is my choice.*

I turned away from my studio and my home and stepped onto the trampled snow. Wolf eyes glinted in the shadows of the trees at the edge of my driveway.

"See you in Nederland," said Auntie Yu. Then she shifted, her shape twisting and reforming, bones popping. I winced. Werewolf changes weren't nearly as fluid or easy to watch as fae transformations. The shapes hidden beneath the trees slipped away when Yumiko reached them.

James wrapped me in a quick hug, kissed my cheek, then scooped Emma into his arms and raced after the departing werewolves. I looked at Chase. "You'd better get a move on."

He set one hand on his hip, cocked his head to the side, and said in a condescending tone, "Let's think about this, shall we? I can either try to keep up with a bunch of muscle heads or snuggle in a warm lap and let someone else do the work." He tapped a finger to his chin as though giving serious consideration to both options. "That's a tough one."

I rolled my eyes. "Fine, I get it. You can ride on my lap."

He tugged his sweatshirt over his head and threw it at me. By the time I looked up from catching it, Chase was sitting on his empty pants as a gray tabby. I grabbed his pants, knocking him into the snow. He hissed and shook his damp paws.

"Oh please, you walk around barefoot all the time. Just a second ago you were standing there without shoes. Don't pretend it bothers you now." I stuffed his clothes into my bag along with the bottled water and snacks I was carrying. "It'd serve you right if I left these here and made you walk around naked." *Except that would bother me more than him.*

"Are you ready to go?" Zee had been observing our banter from the edge of the porch.

"Sorry." I zipped my bag. "I get talkative when I'm nervous."

"You must be nervous quite a lot."

Kai choked, and Chase made a chuffing sound—the cat equivalent to laughter.

I scowled. "Let's go."

Zee slipped out of Jynx's sundress and handed it to Kai. Then she walked into the middle of the open area in front of my house. The rest of us stood back. The air around Zee shimmered as she began to change shape. She didn't seem to melt the way Chase did or break and reform like the were-wolves. Zee's transformation was more like someone's chest inflating when they took a deep breath, everything shifting smoothly as though it were the most natural thing in the world. Her arms, legs, and neck stretched. A tail grew from her back, flicking snow and ice when it twitched. Her shoulder blades bulged until two elongated forms protruded from her back. Her pale skin became almost transparent. Then it turned an opaque, opalescent white that shimmered like moonbeams on water. The extra appendages on her back opened with a *snap* that strained the gossamer membrane of her ribbed wings.

I'd seen the transformation once before in the other direction, when she shrank from what I'd originally taken for a giant boulder to a little girl in Shedraziel's prison. This way was much more impressive.

Zee dropped to all fours and turned one luminous, golden orb on me. The vertical slit of her pupil swelled to bring me into focus in the failing light.

I will need an area at least this large to land in. The words filled my mind though Zee's lizard-like mouth hadn't moved.

An offshoot of dream walking? Or can all dragons project their thoughts? I shrugged off my curiosity. It was unlikely there were enough dragons left for the answer to matter. "There are some wide shoulders along the Peak to Peak Highway just south of our meeting spot. You can land in one of those, and we'll backtrack on foot to the rendezvous."

She hunched her shoulders and ducked her head so her long muzzle was resting on the snow. Kai took this as an invitation and climbed deftly up Zee's foreleg. He settled between and just in front of her wings, straddling her neck.

I hefted my bag higher onto my shoulder and approached. Zee's skin was smooth, almost slippery beneath my hand. Squinting, I could make out thousands of tiny, glittering scales. I set one foot in the crook of her elbow. There was no give. Her muscles were solid as stone.

Kai offered his hand, and I used it to step fully onto Zee's arm. Then I had to jump to get my stomach onto her neck and swing my leg over. The ridge of her spine scraped my chest. I settled my weight and braced as best I could with my thighs splayed. It reminded me of riding a barrel-chested old mare at summer camp when I was nine.

"Lean forward," Kai said from behind me.

I did as instructed, shifting my center forward. Kai scooted until his legs were pressed against me, my backpack sandwiched between us. He reached around and set his hands to either side of mine, locking me in place. Chase bounded up and curled himself in the small cavern created by my arms, legs, and torso.

I frowned. *James is right. I'm a hypocrite. I need to cut him more slack with Victoria.*

Zee lifted her head. Her wings snapped out to the sides. Her weight settled back on her haunches and shifted side to side like a cat about to pounce.

"You're going to make us invisible, right?" I called. "Like above the PTF building."

Zee sprang into the air with the force of a catapult. I slid back two inches, pressing closer to Kai than I thought possible. Then the massive wings to either side swept down and pushed us even harder. The air, which had been cold down below, turned bitter. I tucked my chin into the collar of my coat and took shallow breaths to keep my lungs from freezing. I hunched my shoulders to guard my ears from the rushing wind that was all I could hear. *No wonder dragons learned to talk without sound.*

Through eyelids squinted against the onslaught of the wind, I found an orange ribbon of sunlight lacing the high peaks to the west, though night had already fallen across the valley. Zee pumped her wings and pushed us higher, then banked south toward the matchstick model of Nederland. Pinpricks of light shone out of the darkness—cabins scattered through the forest, then a denser cluster where streetlights and businesses crowded together like bodies seeking warmth and comfort from the encroaching dark. The reservoir sat to the east like an abyss, devoid of light or texture.

The forest pressed against the south edge of town, dense and dark except where roads cut through the trees. A few scattered headlights wound along the Peak to Peak Highway. Zee circled twice above a stretch of road with a wide gravel shoulder—a turnout for slower traffic and wildlife watching. The trees bowed and bent under the pressure of her downdraft as she slowed our descent, shedding their snow like a dog shaking off water.

Her feet hit the ground like an earthquake, toppling me forward. Chase yowled as my chest squashed him against Zee's neck. He darted out of the shrinking space and jumped to the ground. Kai was a weight on my back for half a second, then he slipped away, landing lightly beside Zee's massive, taloned hand. I swung my leg over and slid down her neck like a kid on a slide, falling to my knees when I hit the ground. Zee was an eight-year-old girl again before I climbed free of the drift I'd landed in.

Kai handed her the sundress, which she put on without fuss—not that a coatless, bare-legged child wandering through the woods in a sundress would draw all that much less attention than a naked one.

We cut northeast through the trees, scrambling and stumbling over the steeply sloped, rocky ground. The moon, having shared the sky for most of the day, wouldn't be making another appearance for quite a while, and the stars weren't strong enough to break past the lingering cloud cover left by the passing storm.

By the time we came out of the forest catty-corner to Blue Owl Books, we'd spent more travel time on the ground than we had in the sky. I was breathing heavily, the cold forgotten. Skylights looked out from the bookstore's barn-style roof, casting a halo over the building and effectively hiding the outside world from those within. A staircase wrapped around the side of the weathered wood to the closed door of the upper entrance. Crouching low, we trotted across the intersection, past a sign advertising coffee and ice cream, and around the corner. Gil and another man were leaning against a white-and-purple FedEx van parked in the dirt lot around back.

"What took you so long?" Gil asked.

I braced my hands on my hips, still trying to catch my breath from our jog through the woods. "We can't all see perfectly in the dark."

He smiled and pushed away from the truck, nodding to his companion. "This is Trevor. He just finished making deliveries and is heading back to the lot."

Trevor was a short, wiry man well into middle age with a weak chin and a beak of a nose. He wore a thick red flannel that looked like a tent on him, denim jeans, steel-toed boots, and an ear cuff in the shape of a dragon. He raised a hand in greeting, then squinted at me and adjusted the gesture to point instead. "Hey, don't I know you?"

I shook my head.

"Yeah, yeah, you're that lady who ripped the PTF board a new one on TV last month. The paranatural spokesperson."

"Um . . . yeah." I shifted my weight uncomfortably.

Gil hooked his thumb toward the truck. "Everyone else is packed in if you're ready to join them."

I nodded and waved for Zee, Kai, and Chase to follow me.

"Um." Gil held up both hands. "It's tight."

I stopped short, panic drumming in my head. "We won't all fit?"

"We might be able to . . . but it would be better if we didn't." He chose his words carefully and didn't meet my gaze.

"Because they're fae?" I asked through clenched teeth.

Trevor shifted his attention to my companions, studying them.

Gil lifted one shoulder. "Some of our members are less tolerant than others. Not that they intend to cause trouble," he added quickly. "Just . . . tight space and all."

"I can track you from above." Zee offered.

Shoving my irritation aside, I turned to her. "Can you take off from here?"

She looked around. "I will need to do so from the road, but yes."

"And you'll be invisible?"

"I will ensure that I am unobserved," she said.

So not exactly invisible. I tucked that piece of information away for later. "Fine. You and the boys can follow from above."

Gil opened the back of the truck for me. It was packed wall to wall with werewolves, plus one put-upon looking vampire, and Emma. Metal shelves were bolted to the walls, each with two furry-form werewolves tucked underneath. The rest of the pack had changed to take up less space. There wasn't a single inch of unoccupied floor. Even though the vehicle had seemed large from the outside, I couldn't imagine how I was going to fit. And to top it off, only Emma, James, and Gil were wearing clothes.

"You weren't kidding about the crowding issue," I muttered. Now I was happy my fae friends had been forced to fly despite the sour taste it left in my mouth.

James offered me his hand, and I used it to steady myself as I stepped onto the bumper. The overwhelming smell of wet fur and hot breath assailed me. I wedged myself between James, whom I didn't at all mind being pressed up against, and Auntie Yu.

"See you on the other side," Gil said. Then he closed the door, sealing me in the claustrophobic darkness.

"He's not coming?" I whispered to the dark.

"He's riding up front to give us warning if there's trouble." Auntie Yu pitched her voice so low I could barely hear her. "And to keep an eye on the driver."

The floor and walls vibrated to life with the engine. There was a jerk that threw me into the closed door, and we were off. Everyone swayed together, bumping shoulders, hips, knees, elbows . . . and other body parts, as the truck turned out of the parking lot and onto the main road. I stumbled twice, overcompensating each time I collided with another body in the dark, before finding some semblance of balance. James didn't seem to have any trouble staying upright, so I clung to him like an anchor.

Half an hour to Boulder. Double to clear Denver. Anxiety twisted in my chest as we bumped along in the dark.

James's thumb stroked my arm where he gripped my shoulder.

Each time the truck stopped, everyone tensed, but a few seconds later we would rock forward again—just the usual flow of traffic. There were no sirens, no gunshots, just the rumble of road noises echoing through the dark container. My legs began to cramp with the constant effort of staying upright on the unsteady floor, but there was no room to stretch. My shoulder ached where I'd collided with one of the metal shelves navigating an early turn. The temperature crept up as the many occupants sucked the oxygen from the space. I began to feel disconnected, as though my consciousness was somehow floating free in a shifting abyss. I wasn't even sure if my eyes were open or closed. Time and distance vanished. Then the constant vibration I'd grown accustomed to suddenly cut off.

James's hand tensed on my arm. Yumiko bumped me as she sank into a deeper stance, ready to spring. Steel hinges squeaked. A strip of less impenetrable darkness appeared, then widened into a square of night. A gust of blessedly cold air wafted over me, clearing my head and settling me back into my body.

"Gil reckons this is where y'all want off." Trevor waved a hand at the field behind him. Despite the lack of moonlight, the fresh snow gathered around the stalks of wild grass lit the night with an eerie glow. The road was wet but clear, cutting through the white like an asphalt river. "We're on a frontage road 'bout five minutes outside Bennett."

Gil stepped around the side of the truck. The werewolves relaxed with a collective exhale. "Nothing for miles around but open farmland and the airfield just to the north. With any luck that's where the PTF will assume we've made our escape. That should keep their eyes off the roads even when they do realize what's happened."

Trevor gestured again to the open space behind him. "If y'all want to hop out, I need to get back to Denver pronto if I want to switch rides in time to join the protest."

I stepped out first, walking off the stiffness in my legs as the others filed out behind me. There was a squat farmhouse and what looked like a cell phone tower on the horizon to the north. To the south a short fence of weathered wooden stakes draped with thin wire separated the snow and grass along the road from the snow and grass in the field. Otherwise, the landscape ran uninterrupted to the horizon. Somewhere in that direction was the highway . . . and the place where we would set our ambush.

Chapter 18

THEY'RE COMING. Zee's warning came as a flash in that gray nothingness that was my subconscious.

"They're coming." I echoed the words to those around me and sent them through my link to James, who was standing farther away and might not hear. The werewolves all dropped to their furry bellies in the dead grass, blending as best they could with the land. Kai and I also dropped to the ground. The snapped-off stalks of wild grass dried out from the long winter months jabbed through my clothes, making me itch. The fresh snow quickly melted beneath me, soaking into my shirt and jeans. I set my hands on the marker in front of me—a sigil Kai helped me craft. Eight such markers ran around the edge of the area we'd chosen for our ambush. Kai mimicked my position about twenty feet in front of me, marking the far boundary of our spell.

I licked my lips and looked to the southwest.

James was a silhouette against the slate sky, a single pillar on the flat landscape that marked the edge of the highway. He spread his arms low to his sides until he resembled a handled corkscrew ready to pop.

Five blocky shapes appeared out of the west, speeding toward James.

I could almost feel the strain of James's spell as his fatigue leaked through our bond. He didn't make a habit of casting large-scale illusions and was out of practice.

I tensed my fingers over my sigil in commiseration. My magical education had been mostly a sink-or-swim practical affair. This type of ritual enchantment was still a mystery to me. I could only hope I'd followed Kai's instructions well enough.

One hundred yards from James, the approaching vehicles changed course. Not a full turn, but a slight shift to send them our way while the real road curved gently in the opposite direction.

James's triumph swelled inside me.

The drivers of the caravan believed they were still following the highway, but their new path would take them far enough from the real road so as not to draw attention from cars that might pass later. With any luck, no one would report trouble until we were long gone.

The caravan bumped through the field, flattening grass to carve a path at sixty miles an hour. We'd chosen the smoothest stretch we could, but the occupants were probably starting to wonder about the quality of their shocks.

The first truck in the train passed the small sage bush we'd designated as our cue.

I focused on the sigil under my hands, opened myself to the energy around me, and poured my magic into the spell. The sigil turned as white as the snow we'd cleared to place it and shone between my fingers like a beacon. The light shot to the right and left, leaving a shining trail. When the spell reached the second set of markers, it arced to the next, till finally it slammed into the light racing from Kai's side of the field and sealed the spell.

I'd seen an area effect like this once before, shortly after Kai and I first met. I fervently hoped this encounter would go more smoothly than that one had.

The lead vehicle hit a bump and swerved slightly, a sure sign that Zee had done her sleep trick. Kai and I continued pumping energy into our sigils. The ground turned soft. The wheels of the vehicles sank into the mud, slowed, and finally stopped. The front of the convoy was nearly to the shimmering boundary of our spell. The second in line bumped into the first, and one by one the trucks jolted to a stop with their bumpers touching and their wheels stuck four inches deep in the mud. When the last vehicle rocked to a stop, the light cut off from Kai's side of the field.

I lifted my hands off the sigil. My fingers tingled with residual energy. The afterimage of the glowing barrier flickered in my vision every time I blinked.

The werewolves were moving before I'd gotten to my knees. They shifted to a chorus of popping bones and muffled moans. Eight shapes closed in on the convoy. Doors were pulled open on each of the vans to reveal human bodies piled together on a padded floor. No seats. Each werewolf was bound hand and foot with zip ties—for all the use those would have been if the wolves had truly intended to put up a fight. It looked as though they'd been tossed in without regard for safety or comfort.

Marc's pack grabbed the unconscious passengers and draped them, one on each shoulder, like bags of grain. Then they sprinted north toward the frontage road and our waiting ride.

A gust of wind blew a strand of hair across my face. When I tucked it back, James was standing beside me. "Any injuries?"

I shook my head. "So far it all seems to be going to plan."

"How novel." He patted me on the back, then trotted to the last van to pick up his cargo.

Vehicles approach. A silver sedan and a red truck.

I rocked on my feet as I came back to my senses. Zee's dream walking was aptly named. I felt as if I were just waking up every time it happened.

"Company," I yelled. "Everybody down."

My companions dropped to the ground or darted for cover. I sank to my hands and knees, curling into a ball. One set of headlights swept past. Then another. We all remained still until the second pair of taillights vanished in the distance, then everyone was moving again.

"Alex." Kai waved from the passenger side of the lead vehicle.

A small overhead light came on when he opened the door, highlighting David's slack features. He didn't seem to have any visible injuries. His chest rose and fell in shallow, even breaths. I set my fingers against his neck just to be sure. His pulse was strong.

"Should we take him with us?" Kai asked.

My first reaction was, *of course*, but as I stared down at my sleeping friend, I realized that was just a selfish impulse. I wanted to keep my friends with me, where I could protect them, but David was safer where he was than where I would lead him, and the last thing I wanted was another death on my conscience.

"We'll leave him here, a victim, just like the driver."

"Weatherly might assume he helped us anyway."

"If we take him with us, they'll have proof." I shook my head. "This way he might be able to stay out of the crosshairs, and he can't help against Shedraziel anyway. He did his part keeping the werewolves safe this long." I brushed the dark curls away from David's forehead, kissed his temple, and closed the door. "Let's catch up to the others."

I raced over the snowy field, sucking in frigid air and puffing out billows of steam. The wind cut through my damp clothes and made me shiver. Kai kept pace by my side. Despite their loads, the werewolves quickly outdistanced us. James made two trips, tidying up the ambush site and masking our trails as only a vampire could, and still managed to beat us back to the frontage road.

I stumbled to a stop as soon as my soles touched pavement, bending at the waist and bracing my hands against my thighs. Even though the bullet hole had already healed to a puckered scar, thanks to my fae blood, my calf felt like it was on fire. The muscle was still reknitting.

Tamara's girlfriend—the owner of the silver-and-black big rig parked on the shoulder—was standing to one side of the open back of a shipping container. She was barely more than five feet tall with wide hips, a narrow waist, and a flat chest. Her skin reflected light like the snow on the ground and her orangey-red hair clung to her scalp in frizzy curls. She watched the procession of werewolves—some awake and naked, others sedated and bound—as they filed past her into the back of her truck.

Emma was already inside, helping direct the new arrivals, cutting bindings, and making everyone comfortable. Tamara's girlfriend had been thoughtful enough to toss as many pillows and blankets as she could round up into the back for us. Once all the rescued werewolves were laid out, the rest of the wolves filled in around them, shifting back to their furry forms and claiming what space they could. It was tight, but not as shoulder-to-shoulder tight as the last truck had been. Kai, Chase, and Zee settled near the opening—a man, a child, and a cat separated from the others by a foot of no-man's-land. Wolf eyes watched them from deeper inside, wary and waiting, and again I was struck by the daunting magnitude of my task. If the lingering animosity between species couldn't be forgotten even after working together to pull off this rescue, would the wider world ever be able to move forward in peace?

James looked at his watch. "The protest should have started five minutes ago. If we're going to use its cover, we should leave now."

Our chauffeur thumped the side of her truck. "All aboard."

James and I climbed inside and sank to the cold metal floor in the space between the wolves and the fae. The heavy doors of the shipping container clanged shut with a solid *thud* that echoed through the space as the locks were set. Two small battery-powered lanterns had been set out on the floor. Their lights were barely enough to reach the corners of the container, but at least we wouldn't have to spend the next six hours in total darkness.

James rested his back against the wall and opened his arms.

I smiled at his invitation and scooted into his embrace, relaxing against the curve of his torso with his legs on either side of mine. Folding his arms around me, he rested his cheek on the top of my head and whispered, "Try to get some sleep."

MY LIMBS JERKED as I jolted awake, blinking gummy crust from my eyelashes and trying to recall my surroundings. Bodies moved around me. Lots of bodies. The air was heavy, warm, and stale. A weight rested across my chest. I looked down and found James's arm draped over me. He inhaled, and his chest swelled against my back, lifting me. I blinked a few more times to clear my hazy vision. People were walking past. Low voices conversed in murmurs. I turned my head to the left. A rectangle of night sky was framed by the edges of the cargo container. The clouds were gone, leaving a clear view of the sparkling ribbon of the Milky Way shining in the multihued darkness of space.

James shifted beneath me. "Shall we disembark?"

I sat forward, stretched, and climbed to my feet. Most of the werewolves had already exited. My fae friends were nowhere to be seen. Emma was gone. I followed the stragglers out of the container.

When I hopped off the back bumper, my feet came down on red dirt.

There was no snow. The air was cool, but not the lung-freezing cold of home. Scrub brush and sage dotted the land, and sandstone plateaus broke the horizon, all cast in the silvery glow of the stars. There wasn't a man-made structure or artificial light source to be seen.

"Welcome to Green River, Utah, or thereabouts." Our driver raised her arms over her head and turned a slow circle, encompassing the barren landscape. "I hope the ride wasn't too uncomfortable."

"You didn't have any trouble?" I asked to cover my guilt at having slept through the whole trip.

She shook her head. "I got stopped at one checkpoint in Denver, but the officers got a call to help with a riot at the capitol building. They waved me through without searching the back." She grinned. "You should have seen how many people marched on the capitol when they heard what Anderson was planning."

I matched her smile. "I would have liked to see that."

"There was another checkpoint just before the Eisenhower tunnel, but they took my word that I was on a deadhead run. It was after ten and four below by then. I think they just wanted to get back inside. Once I was over the divide, it was smooth sailing."

I rubbed the last vestiges of sleep from my eyes and looked around again. The truck's occupants were standing in clusters, the fae slightly apart from everyone else. Marc raised a hand and came toward me.

"Alex." He squared off and gripped my shoulders. "Yumiko told me what you've done." He squeezed. "Thank you."

"It was the least I could do, but I'm afraid I've got a favor to ask."

He let his hands fall away. "She told me about that, too." He looked over his shoulder at the gathered werewolves, old and new. "I'm afraid I can't help you this time."

I stiffened. "But Shedraziel—"

"Is dangerous. She needs to be stopped." He turned back to focus on me. "And I hope you accomplish that, but my duty is to my pack and the new wolves who were turned."

"I need fighters who can withstand Shedraziel's spell, and Auntie Yu seemed to think it was your link to the pack that let you do that."

He nodded. "Shedraziel took me, same as the others." He studied his feet. His jaw tightened. He clenched his fists. "I've never felt so helpless."

I reached out to comfort him, but he stepped away. "Then I felt the pack. Those who weren't affected. I drew on their strength and found myself. That's how I was able to shake loose from Shedraziel's control. And once I was in my right mind, I was able to help Sarah and Xander do the same." He shook his head. "But it wasn't soon enough. Some of these new converts"—he glanced again at the group behind him—"were our victims."

"It wasn't your fault," I said.

"But it is my responsibility." He sighed. "I'll take them north, to Montana. We'll shelter with the pack there until . . . well, for a while at least."

I bit my lip. "What about the PTF werewolves? Are you taking them as well?"

Freeing the wolves had been the right thing to do, but if I came out of all this without even one more fighter to help defeat Shedraziel. . . .

"They don't fall under my jurisdiction any longer. It will be up to them where they wish to go."

"But they need a pack, an alpha, if they're going to be any use against Shedraziel."

"I'd already had most of your recruits severed from their existing packs. If they choose to remain and fight by your side, I'll help them complete the ritual to form their pack. Remember that at least one will need to remain separate from the battle to anchor the others."

I nodded. "Let's see if I've got any volunteers."

I stepped around Marc and clapped my hands, drawing everyone's attention. "As most of you know, I'm heading west to fight a fae who's threatening the stability of our world. Marc has decided that his pack will go north to seek sanctuary in Montana. He'll be taking all the new werewolves with him." There were a few mutterings among the wolves. I hurried on. "Those of you who were employed by the PTF have a choice. Form a new pack and come with me to stop Shedraziel, or travel north with Marc and maybe return to your old packs."

Tarlo stepped forward. He wore sweatpants and a T-shirt. His long black hair was pulled into a low ponytail. His close-set eyes found me over the beak of his nose. "How can we fight someone who turns us against ourselves?"

"That's why we're going to make a proper pack." I gestured to Marc. "The Colorado wolves were able to break free of Shedraziel's control because they had the support of their pack members to bolster them. You can do the same."

More muttering and foot shuffling.

"I can't force you to fight, and I wouldn't want to even if I could. I don't know if the alliance we were building with the PTF will survive the coming days. It may be broken already, but I intend to fight regardless. Those of you standing here answered my call once before. I'm asking you to do so again."

Sarah stepped forward first. "I signed up to serve and protect. That hasn't changed."

Faolan, the stocky man from Texas, and the Appalachian werewolf who'd fought in the gym what seemed like forever ago all came forward at the same time. The California siblings and "Old Bill" from Virginia were a step behind, followed by Xander and Jasmine.

Tarlo hesitated, then joined the others.

I opened my mouth to tell them how pleased I was that they'd all decided to join me. Then Gilbert stepped forward as well. My mouth stayed open, but no words came out.

Marc came up beside me. "Gil?"

The professor looked at Sarah, then back at Marc. "My place is with my mate."

"But you're not in the PTF," I blurted.

Gil lifted his chin. "A pack is about more than fighting, Alex. It's a family."

I closed my mouth.

Marc nodded. "Anyone else?"

The silence stretched for one long moment. Then Marc nodded again. "Everyone joining the new pack come with me. The rest of you stay here." Marc nudged my arm and tipped his head toward James, Emma, and the fae.

Following his lead, I said, "You guys wait here, too. Somehow, I don't think the werewolves want any fae observing their rituals."

Zee cocked her head to one side. "Are we not allies?"

Chase snorted and twisted to sit with his back to the werewolves.

"We'll wait," Kai said.

I patted James's arm. *Keep the peace.* Then I walked into the desert.

"THIS SHOULD DO." Marc indicated a wide bowl that created a sort of natural arena in the dirt. We were twenty minutes away from the road, the truck, and the rest of our people.

"So how does this work?" I asked, looking down into the earthen depression. "Tournament style? Or battle royal?"

"First"—he turned to the group who'd followed us—"Sarah, Xander, and Gil."

They came forward.

"You've been good and loyal members. I'm sad to see you go, but I wish you well." Marc shook hands with each of them, then took a step back and closed his eyes.

One by one, each of the three winced, gasped, and stumbled.

Marc opened his eyes. "You are pack no more."

They stepped back into the group.

Marc swept a hand over the bowl. "Let the sorting begin."

The werewolves shucked off their clothes, leaving them in piles on the dirt, dropped to all fours, and shifted. Some had smooth transitions, fur flowing seamlessly over reshaped muscles. Others grunted and groaned as their muscles stretched or contracted and their bones popped into place.

Once all the transformations were complete, they trotted down into the arena.

Marc sat down and crossed his legs.

I settled beside him.

He pointed to the wolves, who all seemed to be circling each other like participants in some complex square dance. "Now they will each vie for their position in the pack. Some have already clashed, and so know where they stand in relation to one another. Others will be able to tell instinctively that the gap between them is too great to question. But when wolves of near equal strength meet. . . ."

A gray wolf lunged for one with russet fur, clamping powerful jaws around its neck, and just like that, the dance was broken. Couples paired off with snapping fangs and swiping claws. Growls and whines shattered the silence of the night. Dust kicked up around scrambling paws. Bodies rolled together and sprang apart. Sometimes when two combatants came up, they moved away from each other, seeking new partners.

I cringed and winced with every blow as the werewolves tore into each other. "Will they even be able to fight after this?"

"They'll heal," was all Marc said. He followed the action with dedicated focus.

Soon after the battle began, a mottled brown wolf I recognized as Gil limped to the side of the bowl and lay down to lick his wounds. A moment later, a cream-colored wolf with a dark undercoat trotted over to sit beside him. Then a black wolf with a brown patch over part of its face left the fray.

One by one, the werewolves abandoned the fight, some limping and bloody, others seeming not to have taken much damage at all. They joined the circle forming along the far edge of the arena, always settling to the left of the last wolf in the line, until only four remained active. I recognized Sarah's tawny pelt and Faolan from when he attacked me in front of the PTF building, but the other two I wasn't sure about.

I leaned closer to Marc. "Do you know who's who?"

He pointed first to Sarah. "Sarah is fighting Noah there." He shifted to the other pair. "That's Faolan and Tarlo."

Sarah darted around sable-coated Noah, who was half again her size, using her speed and agility to make up for their difference in weight. Faolan and Tarlo—a golden-brown wolf with dark paws—were more evenly matched. They locked together, each with their teeth anchored in the other's pelt. They batted and scraped with their claws as they grappled, trying to throw the other off balance.

As the fights dragged on, I leaned closer to Marc and asked, "Who do *you* think would make the best alpha?"

"It's not up to me."

"Come on, you've gotta have an opinion."

He scratched a finger over the stubble on his jaw. His gaze never left the arena. "Sarah can be rash, but she's dedicated to justice and protecting the weak, which are good qualities in an alpha. I don't know much about Faolan or Tarlo. Noah is the most traditional choice, but he seems angry. I worry his ambition is fueled by fear rather than a desire to protect, but Kenma says he's solid."

I nodded. An endorsement from Kenma, alpha of the Appalachian pack, carried a lot of weight since he'd been the first to commit his wolves to fighting on the PTF's behalf.

The two brown wolves went down, rolling over one another. When the dust cleared, Faolan was on top, his teeth at Tarlo's throat.

Faolan placed a paw on the other wolf's chest, released his grip, then backed away. Tarlo got up and shook the dirt from his fur, then took his seat in line while Faolan paced, watching the remaining match to see whom he would fight next.

I leaned forward, squinting at the shapes still struggling under the starlight.

Noah lunged for Sarah, teeth flashing, but she deftly dodged the larger wolf and closed her jaws on the scruff at his neck, pinning his nose in the dirt. He thrashed for a moment, bucking and scrabbling, but he couldn't dislodge the smaller wolf. He flopped to his stomach then rolled onto his side, as far as he could with Sarah still holding him tight. He whined. Sarah gave one last jerk, then released him.

She took a step back, clearing a space for Noah to challenge Faolan. Her sides heaved. Blood flecked her coat. She seemed to be favoring her right hind leg.

Noah climbed to his feet. He looked at Faolan, who settled his weight, readying for the next attack.

Noah lowered his head and turned away. He trotted to his place at the head of the line.

Marc sat up a little straighter. "That's a surprise."

"You mentioned previous conflicts. When I was sparring with Sarah in the gym, I saw Faolan break up a fight between two other wolves who'd come to blows. Noah was one of them. Maybe that counts?"

He pursed his lips. "Being able to deescalate a conflict is a valuable trait for an alpha, but among the more traditional wolves, averting violence rather than confronting it head on could be seen as a sign of weakness. I'm surprised Noah would back down."

"You think Faolan should have joined the fight in the gym rather than sending them off with a verbal beatdown?"

"I'm saying *some* werewolves may think that."

"Still, assuming we can get back on track with the PTF collaboration when all this is over, 'bite first, talk never' isn't exactly the look we're going for."

"Perhaps not, but Faolan's apparent youth will make it hard for him to earn respect among humans. Sarah's gender may hinder her in the same way. Either one will have to face prejudices beyond their werewolf natures if they take the post."

I pulled my knees to my chest and wrapped my arms around them, thinking about how hard I'd been struggling to earn my title. "There is that."

Faolan and Sarah circled one another. Neither snarled nor made a move forward. They simply watched and walked, as though they were having a conversation with their eyes.

Both wolves stopped as one, mirror images of each other. They continued to stare from two feet apart.

"What are they doing?" I whispered.

"Assessing."

"Sarah and Faolan fought at the PTF building."

"Who won?"

"I think Zee knocked everyone out before either of them did."

The silence of the night stretched thin. My ears strained. My skin itched with the tension. I gritted my teeth. "Why don't they fight?"

"There's more than one type of fight," Marc whispered.

Faolan lay down, his sandy-brown pelt blending with the dusty ground. He rolled onto his back.

Sarah crossed the distance between them and placed her teeth against his neck. She didn't squeeze, and he didn't fight. The tableau lasted only a moment, then Sarah backed up, giving Faolan room to roll over. The wolves at the edge of the arena lifted their heads and voices as one, howling to the sky.

I jumped at the sudden, deafening noise and covered my ears. When the sound died away I looked at Marc. "That's it? I thought becoming alpha was all about brute strength. As much as I appreciate Sarah's badassery from our sparring sessions, she's injured. I feel like he could have beaten her if he'd tried."

"Perhaps, but a truly cohesive pack isn't just about who can hurt whom. A balanced pack requires mutual respect and an innate understanding of what's needed for the betterment of all. Physical aptitude is only one factor in deciding a person's rank. I believe Faolan saw in Sarah something that he himself lacked and chose to cede the fight."

"Like what?"

Marc shrugged. "Only Faolan and Sarah will know that. But I can tell you that Faolan will make an excellent second-in-command, and that can be just as important as choosing the right alpha."

Marc got to his feet. "Wait here."

He walked down the side of the bowl, sliding a bit on the loose dirt, until he stood beside Sarah. Faolan had taken his position beside Noah.

Sarah shifted. Animal whimpers became human groans as her body settled into shape. She was panting and sweaty, and she kept the weight off her right leg when she stood.

Marc set both hands on Sarah's shoulders and tipped his head so their foreheads met. "I, Marcus Howard, leader of the Front Range Pack, see you, Sarah Nazari, leader of the PTF Pack, and recognize you as my peer."

The wolves howled again, and again I covered my ears.

When the echoes died away, Marc released Sarah and stepped back. She turned and waved for me to join them.

I stood, dusted the dirt from my jeans, and scrambled down the hill. It was my turn. My hands were shaking. This demonstration wasn't just about being acknowledged as the PTF liaison. This was about convincing people to follow me into battle against Shedraziel. This was about making the strongest bond I could in this moment, and that was going to take a lot more than a simple parlor trick. Luckily, Marc had given me an idea when he mentioned how helpless being controlled had made him feel.

Sarah addressed the watching wolves. "Alex Blackwood requests to be acknowledged by the pack. I have fought beside Alex before. I have seen what she can do, and I accept her power. But I know not all of you have seen her in action. If any among you require proof of her strength, step forward now."

A moment passed. I exhaled. *Maybe I won't have to do this after all.*

Then Noah stood and took three paces forward. My heart sank.

Sarah looked at me and nodded. "Give him hell."

The night felt suddenly colder.

I licked my lips and took a step toward Noah.

His upper lip curled. A low rumble echoed out of his chest.

I lifted both my hands in a placating gesture. I kept my attention on Noah, but when I spoke, I addressed the whole group. "I'm not a werewolf. I can't fight like a werewolf. I'm a practitioner. I can cast magic." I glanced at Marc. "When I was told I'd have to demonstrate my power, the first thing I thought of was launching fireballs and shooting lightning from my fingertips. But you've all seen those tricks before, and a practitioner isn't all that I am. I'm also part fae, and if you'll allow me, I can show you something special."

I met Noah's gaze and waited.

He snorted and sat back on his haunches.

"Go ahead," said Sarah.

I took the final step to reach the shaggy black wolf and set my hand against the fur between his ears. The night grew still. The rest of the pack faded away.

I called up the rosy glow of my fae magic.

Doubt flooded me. I'd been thinking about trying this ever since I prevented the change in some of the victims from the PTF fight, but I wasn't sure I could affect a fully incorporated werewolf. If I failed, I'd look weak. I'd lose credibility. It was a risk, but there was too much at stake for half-measures. No one was going to *give* me authority this time. I needed to earn it. I couldn't afford to fail.

I settled my weight evenly across the soles of my feet and exhaled, unfocusing my eyes and my mind until I was looking beyond the physical world.

Noah's core was what I'd come to expect—a tangle of multicolored threads that mixed and merged to create the complex tapestry of his soul. There was a thrumming blue that hummed with power and purpose woven into his core that reminded me of my tether to James.

That must be the pack bond.

The darker threads that represented the werewolf infection were fused to the maroon of his human existence. They appeared completely inseparable, as I'd expected. Just as I'd been unable to completely separate James from his demonic influence, I would never be able to convert a mature werewolf back to human, but that wasn't my goal tonight.

I followed the dark threads, inspecting the places where they connected to and, in some cases, overwhelmed the maroon. I studied the pattern. Then I chose an intersection that seemed promising and pushed energy into the threads.

Magic danced between my fingers as I plucked at the strings of his soul, shifting the balance of color in favor of maroon. I didn't alter anything, I simply triggered a protocol that was already in place. Noah whimpered and shook his head, knocking my hand away, but I didn't need the physical connection anymore. I was already inside him.

Bones snapped and popped. Gasps and growls rang out around the arena.

I stepped away from the naked, panting human curled on the ground in front of me. I'd seen how freaked out Marc was that Shedraziel had forced him to change. I figured any werewolf would have to respect someone who could take that choice away.

Noah stared at me with wide eyes. His expression flickered between terror and awe. "Can you fix us?" he whispered. "Make us human?"

I shook my head, then lifted my voice to address the crowd. "One of the abilities of an alpha is to help control the change in a werewolf who cannot control itself." I gestured to Noah, who'd regained his knees but still seemed too stunned to stand.

Sarah came to my side. "Do any still doubt her strength?"

This time no one stepped forward. No one so much as twitched.

Sarah turned to me, set her hands on my shoulders, and pressed her forehead to mine. "Then I, Sarah Nazari, leader of the PTF Pack, see you, Alex Blackwood, halfer, practitioner, and pack friend, and recognize you as my peer."

A swell of energy tingled over my skin.

Another howl went up from the wolves. When the sound died down once more, Sarah led her new pack out of the bowl.

Chapter 19

WHEN THE TRUCK doors opened again, it was to full daylight. I rubbed my eyes, scraping loose a collection of crusty dust from my lashes. The other occupants of the truck, fewer now that Marc had taken his people north, filed past me. I stretched. My neck was stiff. The cuts I'd gotten from Faolan during the PTF fight, as well as the healing scar along my ribs, pulled and ached when I moved. My calf was tight as a spring. The last few days were definitely catching up with me. My stomach grumbled.

"Catch." James tossed an energy bar at me.

We both watched it hit my leg and tumble to the truck bed.

"Nice reflexes."

I picked up the bar and tore open the wrapper. "I'm not a morning person."

He glanced at the bright light streaming in through the open door. "It's not morning."

I grumbled, held the bar between my teeth, and stripped off my jacket. The temperature had to be at least in the eighties. I finished my breakfast in four bites and followed the werewolves out of the truck.

We were at a rest stop, though the definition was a loose fit at best. There were two benches with a trash can between them sheltered from sun and rain by a rickety wood-slat roof held up by four spindly poles. The structure looked like it could collapse at any second. There was also a single outhouse at the edge of the dirt area that marked the parking lot. Beyond the dirt was the cracked asphalt of the road we'd come in on and a sea of flat land covered with knee-high brown and gray brush. The only sounds besides our own were the wind and the occasional buzz of early-season insects. Shallow peaks rose in the distance. In the valley between them was a wall of sand.

"This is Quinn River Crossing?"

"Yep." Our driver stepped around the front of her cab. Heat waves shimmered off the hood. She raised a hand to shield her eyes and looked out over the desert landscape. "Not much to look at."

"I don't even see a river," I said.

"It's over that way." She pointed to the dust storm blocking the valley. "Not that it's much of a river, really."

The werewolves had spread out across the rest area, stretching their legs, snacking, relieving themselves. There didn't seem to be another living being for miles around.

I glanced up, shielding my eyes. The sun hung in the center of the sky. The moon trailed slightly behind, nearly invisible in the glow of her companion. I looked at Zee, who was also studying the sky. When she lowered her gaze and met mine, she said, "It's close."

I bunched my fists. We had to reach Shedraziel soon if we wanted to stop her next attack.

Sarah stepped up beside me. "Where are your fae?"

I winced. "I—"

Several of the werewolves growled and dropped into a fighting crouch. Everyone's focus seemed to be on the empty land at the far end of the parking lot.

A young woman stepped out of a shimmering ripple in the air. She was just over five feet tall, slim, and looked to be around sixteen years old. She wore a blue-and-white paisley dress that swished around her thighs and had a distinctive shock of short, silvery-white hair.

"Jynx!" Chase ran across the clearing and swept his sister into his arms. He spun her around twice, then set her back on her feet and stepped to arm's length. A scowl replaced his smile. "What are you doing here?"

Jynx glanced behind her.

A second girl emerged from thin air. This one looked to be in her early twenties with a long ponytail of bright-red hair. She wore a teal tank top, tan cotton shorts, and white sneakers smeared with mud.

I exhaled. Not only was Ava Jynx's wife, she was Targe's niece, with the same ability to form portals between locations. I trotted forward. "Did your uncle send you?"

Jynx stepped in front of Ava and planted her fists against her hips. "Nice to see you, too, Alex." She looked past me and pointed one accusing finger at Zee. "Is that dragon wearing my dress?"

I chuckled. "It's really good to see you, Jynx, and I'm looking forward to catching up." I glanced at the sky. "But not right now."

Ava squeezed Jynx's shoulder. "My uncle and the troops he's gathered are hiding in the mountains." She nodded toward the peaks. "He asked us to keep lookout and bring you when you arrived."

I nodded and waved Sarah over. She stopped a few paces away.

"We're going through a portal," I said. "Have your people line up."

Sarah looked Ava and Jynx up and down, then turned back to me. "Can't we just run there?"

Jynx crossed her arms. "You could, but it would take hours."

I shook my head. "We don't have that kind of time. Shedraziel's next attack could happen any minute now."

Sarah sighed and paced over to her pack, who were hanging well back from the fae. I veered off to address the non-wolves. James was standing near the edge of the weathered road with his face tipped toward the sun. Even weeks after his change, he still took every opportunity to bask in the sunlight that had been so long denied him. Kai, Zee, and Emma were chatting with the truck driver in the sliver of shade provided by the shipping container.

"Time to go." I offered the driver my hand. "Thanks for delivering us safely."

"It was my pleasure." Her grip was warm and firm. "For what it's worth, I hope you can salvage your alliance with the PTF."

I nodded and tugged Emma toward the waiting fae.

"I'll grab our bags," Kai offered.

"Emma!" Jynx bounded toward us.

I stepped in front of Emma, blocking the tackle I knew was coming in case she didn't have her "sight" turned on.

Jynx skidded in the dirt and cocked her head to one side. "What gives?"

Chase came up behind Jynx. "There were some developments while you were away." He met my gaze and jerked his chin toward Ava, who was now standing with her arms raised and a look of intense concentration on her face. "Go on, I'll see Emma gets through."

I patted Emma's hand, leaving her and Chase to bring Jynx up to speed.

The werewolves were standing in a loose line with Sarah at the lead. She stared at the slight shimmer in the air that marked Ava's portal with her arms crossed and her lips pressed to a thin white line.

"It's fine," I said as I passed the waiting people. "Just a couple steps and a little dizziness." I smiled reassuringly, but my forced cheer didn't ease the expressions on the werewolves' faces. Liam in particular seemed ready to snap, and Faolan watched him as though expecting to have to intervene. *Clever boy.*

Sarah clapped her hands. "Single file. Here we go."

She looked at me, and I took the lead. The desert scenery continued unbroken behind Ava's portal, but as I crossed the threshold there was a twisting sensation that left me momentarily breathless. When my foot came down, it was on rock rather than dirt. I stumbled a little on the uneven surface, then took a few steps to the side to make room for those behind me. Sarah was next, followed closely by Noah and Gil. Sarah and Noah seemed fine, though slightly ashen faced. Gil bent double and lost his lunch on the ground.

Jynx was the next one through. Her smile was gone. She found me and pulled me farther from the portal along the scree-covered slope. "We'd best get you to Targe. Ava will bring the rest."

I told Sarah where I was headed, then let myself be pulled along.

Jynx and I walked in silence for a moment. Then she shook her head. "I can't believe Emma's blind."

I nodded.

"And your father. . . ." She looked at me askance, as though she'd just realized she was holding a bomb.

"Yeah." Dry bushes clinging to the rocky slope scraped at my legs, hooking barbed branches into my pants. The air was hot and dry. Dust drifted on the wind, stinging my eyes and throat.

"And this deal you've struck with the PTF?" she asked. "How's that going?"

"It's . . . going. At least it was. Before Shedraziel."

"Targe said you got the fae from Crossroads released. That's how he was able to convince them to come back and help you."

"They shouldn't have been locked up in the first place."

"No argument here." She shook her head again. "It's hard to believe you're working for the folks that crashed my wedding."

We scrambled along a gravel-covered shelf of rock protruding from the hillside and rounded a bend that brought us in view of the fae camp. A rocky outcropping set partway up the hill created a crumbling windbreak on two sides. Hunkered on the scree amid the brush were about thirty fae, some of whom I recognized from my illegal visit to the fae cell block at the Genoa holding facility.

Sheltered as they were from human eyes, none were wearing glamour. Having come from a wide range of realms, the assembled fae looked like a who's-who quiz from one of my species identification books with tall, short, feathers, scales, and every color of the rainbow represented.

A shout went up when Jynx and I appeared, and Targe's fire-engine hair bobbed toward us from the far edge of the camp. He'd changed out of the prison pajamas I'd last seem him in and now wore a pair of olive-green corduroy pants, a black, long-sleeved shirt with the cuffs rolled to his elbows, and thick rope sandals on his hairy, hobbit-like feet.

"Glad to see you made it okay." He gestured to the group behind him, stretching the fabric of his shirt over his barrel chest. "Let me introduce you to your army. All with true names and ready to fight."

A few of the nearby fae dipped their heads in acknowledgment.

It was fewer than I'd hoped for but more than I'd expected. I patted Targe on one meaty, muscular arm. "I appreciate you rounding them up."

"I had my girls to help spread the word." He gestured to Jynx, who lifted her chin with pride.

I scanned the faces, looking for ashy complexions and amber eyes. "No shadow walkers?"

He shook his head. "Lord Dimitri has chosen to keep his realm neutral for the time being. We've mostly got shifters and illusionists. A few en-chanters."

I squashed my disappointment and nodded. The ability to pass in and out of shadows at will would have made even a single shadow walker a major asset in the coming assault, but even without them, thirty fae willing to fight was nothing to sneer at.

A tumble of rocks sounded behind me. I turned to see Ava leading Sarah and Zee around the bend. "We can add a few werewolves and a dragon to that."

Targe nodded. "Then it's time to talk strategy."

THE WEREWOLVES kept to the edge of the camp, unwilling to let them-selves be surrounded by fae. James stayed farther back still, clearly taking to heart Kai's comment that one of the fae might use this opportunity to rid the world of a vampire. Chase, Jynx, and Ava settled beside a dormant fire pit, content to let others handle the logistics. Emma, Sarah, Kai, Zee, and I joined Targe at the crumbling rocks that marked the far edge of camp. I looked down into the valley. The dust storm I'd seen from a distance raged just down the slope, blotting out the view. I squinted my eyes to narrow slits and pulled my shirt over my nose and mouth to keep from coughing.

"The storm is magical; it never stops." Targe propped his arms on the top of the outcropping, causing a shower of gravel to cascade off the far side. "The griffins carry it with them."

"You've seen them?"

He nodded. "They patrol the boundary at regular intervals, renewing the spell."

"Have you scouted inside at all?"

"A bit, but even the best fliers have trouble in a storm like that, and a ground scout would be an easy target." He pointed toward the heart of the storm. "We've managed to identify a structure that we believe is their head-quarters—an abandoned ranch house with several outbuildings. We think that's where the griffins reside when not on patrol."

"Do they ever come out of the storm?" Kai asked.

Targe shook his head. "Never."

I squinted into the storm, willing myself to see those buildings, but all I saw was dust. "Any sign of Shedraziel?"

He shook his head again. "If she's here, she's hidden at the heart of the storm."

Sarah crossed her arms and glared at the swirling dust. Her dark hair whipped around her face and shoulders. "If we charge across the plain, the griffins will pick us off from above while we're stumbling blind."

I nodded. "We need to take out their eyes in the sky if we want to reach the headquarters without sounding an alarm." I turned to Zee. "Any chance you could knock out the griffin patrols like you did the drivers during our ambush?"

"Doubtful. As I mentioned before, fae minds are more protected. Perhaps with enough time . . . but they would immediately become aware of the attempt, and we would lose any element of surprise."

"You said you have illusionists," Emma said. "Could they hide us?"

"Not such a large, moving group in such poor conditions," Kai said.

Targe nodded. "A handful at most."

"Then we need to take out those griffin patrols," I said.

"Look there." Targe pointed into the storm.

A large shadow streaked through the dust, sweeping past and banking north. I crouched lower, peeking over the rim of the rock.

"We're hidden here," Targe said. "Our illusions work fine on a set area. It's a moving target that's hard to cover."

I straightened, feeling foolish.

Emma's face was tipped up. She turned as though tracking the shadow through the swirling dust.

"Emma, can you see the griffin?"

She nodded.

Targe frowned. He leaned out over the rocks, squinting hard at the place where the dark splotch had disappeared. "Still?"

She nodded again. Then she raised a finger. We all waited, watching her watch the sand. I counted to twenty-six in my head before she finally lowered her hand. "It's gone."

I looked at Targe, an idea forming in my mind. "How long would it take to cast an illusion to hide an area?"

He shrugged. "About fifteen seconds."

"And it would hide anyone inside that area?" I asked.

"As long as they didn't leave it."

Kai perked up. "That's brilliant!"

"What is?" Sarah asked.

Kai grinned at her. "Emma can track the patrols through the storm."

"And with enough warning," I picked up, "illusions can be set to hide our group until the patrol passes."

Sarah looked at me, then at Targe, clearly uncomfortable about handing the safety of her pack over to the fae. "Will that work?"

He stared into the storm. "It might." He nodded. "It should. So long as she can give us enough warning."

I set my hand on Emma's shoulder. "What do you think? Can you see the griffins coming far enough away to give us twenty seconds?"

She bit her lower lip, worrying it back and forth, then gave one brisk nod. "I think so."

Sarah's lip curled. "You'd better be sure. If the griffins catch us blind, that valley will become a shooting gallery."

Emma's face set with determination. She covered my hand with hers and squeezed. "I can do this."

Zee placed a hand on Emma's other shoulder and looked at me. "We will remain here to practice while you arrange the rest of the troops."

Kai cleared his throat. "Not to be the naysayer, but what if Shedraziel is at the eye of this storm?"

Targe shrugged. "Isn't that what we want?"

My stomach flip-flopped as Kai's point slammed home. "Emma isn't protected from Shedraziel's power."

Kai nodded. "She needs to keep her distance or risk being used against you."

"But we need her," Sarah said.

I dug my fingers into my hair, snagging in the tangles twisted into it by the wind, wracking my brain for a solution. My gaze snapped to Targe. "You can portal her out once we're close enough."

He tipped his head, considering. "I can do that."

I exhaled and slapped him on the back.

He frowned at me.

I cleared my throat. "Let's tell everyone the plan."

TARGE HELD EMMA in the cradle of his arms. Her face was tipped up, but her eyes were closed against the beating sand carried on the wind. Apparently, she didn't need to have her eyes open for this new kind of "seeing." The dust that had been annoying on the mountainside was savage down in the valley, tearing into any exposed flesh like microscopic razor blades. My head was covered by a long scarf wrapped like a turban that left only a narrow slit for my eyes, which I had to keep nearly closed against the flying debris. Even with my shirt tucked into my pants, and my pants tucked into my socks, grit was getting *everywhere*. I perched on the balls of my feet, fingertips pressed to the ground, and strained my hearing against the raging wind and the flap and snap of cloth, waiting for confirmation that the shadow above had passed.

"Now." As soon as the word left Emma's lips I sprang up and charged forward, just as I'd done the last seven times. My shoes pounded against the hard-packed earth, scoured smooth by the constant wind. The bushes that had dotted the mountain were gone, leaving only a flat plain that faded into the obscuring storm at five paces in any direction. We were running blind, trusting Emma's magical awareness to steer us in the right direction. Even the highly attuned noses of the werewolves were useless in this gale.

I was near the front of the advancing force with Emma and Targe on one side of me, Sarah and Zee on the other. Clustered behind us were the fae Targe had recruited and the PTF werewolf pack. Sarah and the pack ran on four feet, their thick fur protecting them from the worst of the weather. The fae were mostly bundled like me, but a few, including Chase, wore the forms of animals with natural protection. Ten of them stayed in the very middle of the group, traveling in formation. When Emma raised her hand after five minutes of hard running, we all dropped where we stood. The ten in the center slammed their palms to the ground, hands overlapping, and murmured a chant I hadn't understood even when the winds had been low enough for me to hear it. A slight tingle spread over my body.

I looked up, squinting into the storm.

A shadow emerged in the dust, a darkening of the brown that grew larger and more distinct as its source drew closer. Eventually, I could make out the sweeping shape of wings and a long neck. A taloned claw with blue-gray scales flashed above me. I held my breath, willing my pulse to slow. The shadow continued on, fading from black to gray to brown until it was swallowed by the storm. We waited, poised to run.

"Now." Emma's voice cracked the monotonous drone of the wind like a starting gun, and we were off again.

Targe set a grueling pace despite carrying Emma. We ran until my injured leg cramped and a sharp pain throbbed in my side with every labored breath. None of the fae or werewolves complained.

After a shorter interval than our previous sprints, Emma spread her arms as though holding back a crashing wave. Targe stumbled to a stop.

"There are a lot of bodies ahead." Her words were barely audible. "Any closer and they'll see us."

Targe crouched, setting Emma down, and waved me over. Zee and Sarah joined us, and the five of us pressed our heads together. The tingle of magic spread over me again as the illusionists did their job. Sarah sneezed and pawed at her muzzle.

"What does it look like?" Targe asked.

"There's a bunch of hazy shapes that could be buildings. There are four people in that direction." She pointed to my left. "And three straight ahead. The other group is over there and farther away. I can't tell exactly how many."

"Can you tell if they're all griffins?" I asked. "Could any be Shedraziel?"

She shrugged. "Some of the shapes are definitely griffins, but some are too indistinct to be sure." She frowned. "One shape in the middle group is smaller than the others. That'd be my best guess for a non-griffin."

"All right," Targe said, setting one massive hand on Emma's shoulder.

"Time for you to head back. The rest of us will split into three groups, each with a mix of fae and wolves. The fae can keep the griffins grounded with magic. The werewolves will be responsible for finishing them off."

I thought of the chaos in front of the PTF building, allies turning against one another. "If Shedraziel is controlling the griffins like she did the people in Denver, we shouldn't kill anyone."

"Lives are at stake, Alex. Griffins are strong and proud. They will not go down easily. Don't hobble our chances of success by imposing unrealistic restrictions."

I pursed my lips. Targe was right. Insisting our people not take the lives of the griffins would put them in extra danger.

Targe waited a moment. When I didn't argue, he continued. "We should assume the griffins out on patrol will return as reinforcements."

"I will take care of the sky," Zee said. Unlike the rest of us, the only concession she'd made to the storm was to pull her lavender hair into a tight braid that was now pinned to her scalp, though wisps streamed from the edges. Apparently, her skin was hard as dragon scales even in human form.

"Then let's do this," I said.

Targe and Sarah took a moment to split the group into three teams of roughly even strength. Then Targe stepped back and spread his arms. He drew an arc in the air, touching the ground at two points roughly three feet apart. The dust between those points took on a shimmery quality, as though it were glitter and not simple dirt that blew by. He looked at Emma. "In you go."

Emma turned to me. "I wish I could be there when you bring that bitch down." Her voice strained with emotion.

I patted her arm. "We'll get her."

Emma vanished into the rippled air of Targe's portal. She'd wait at camp with James, Kai, Ava, and Jynx until the task was done.

Targe looked at the illusionists who were hiding us. Many had pinched expressions and shaking limbs. The strain of successive, sustained spells was definitely starting to show. "Your job's done, too." He looked at the rest of us. "The moment the illusion comes down, we're exposed. Move fast."

The illusionists sprang to their feet as one and raced toe-to-heel through Targe's portal. We were past hiding. It was time to attack.

I darted toward the central target while Targe and Sarah each led their own teams to a side. Chase, Faolan, the California siblings Marshal and Maddie, and six fae I hadn't learned the names of followed in my wake. As we got closer, the shape of an old farmhouse came into focus through the dust. A large creature was lying on the ground in front of a covered wooden porch that wrapped two sides of the white-washed, single-story building.

Chase quickly outpaced me, shifting mid-stride from the gray tabby I was familiar with to a form I'd only seen him take once before—a massive white tiger. He was easily as big as a werewolf with paws larger than my head that gobbled up the distance to the griffin.

The griffin's eagle head swiveled in our direction, drawn by the noise of our approach. It sprang to four taloned feet and snapped its wings open, but Chase was on it before it could launch into the air. He slammed into the griffin's side and tore at its wings. A strangled squawk passed its beak before Faolan, close on Chase's heels, snapped his jaws closed on the griffin's neck. Two of the fae—a sharp-featured sidhe and a short, wrinkled gnome with moss for hair—moved in to help contain the struggling beast.

From the far side of the building came an answering squawk. A second griffin launched skyward from behind the farmhouse.

A volley of fireballs shot after it from the fae woman on my right.

The griffin shrieked as the first bomb hit, searing its wings. It dropped a few feet, ducking under the next two projectiles, but managed to stay aloft.

A man with golden skin, an angular nose, and long black hair sprang into the air on my left, shifting mid-jump into a large black bird that darted toward the griffin. A second bird, a golden eagle, skimmed over my head from behind. The two birds scratched and clawed at the griffin's face while trying to avoid the snap of the other's much larger beak.

The griffin in the sky thrashed and spiraled while the one on the ground rolled in a tangled heap with my allies. I raced past the chaos and slammed through the front door of the farmhouse, searching for the third, smaller target.

The door crashed against the foyer wall, rattling the framed pictures hanging there. Marshall, Maddie, and two fae crowded in behind me, pushing me further into the house.

Pale-blue wallpaper faded with age covered the walls from the waist up, while the bottom sections were carved wooden panels. The floor was solid oak up the hallway and through the first opening on the right, which led to a kitchen large enough to cook for an army. A brass bar marked the line between the hardwood floor and the motley-brown carpet in the room to the left.

I drew my gun and peeked into the room. A couch with polished wood armrests and tiny pink flower patterns on its otherwise white upholstery sat under a large window in the far wall, directly across from a big-screen TV. A cast iron pellet stove that I couldn't imagine ever got used sat in one corner on a patchwork of slate tiles. The nearest corner contained a glass-fronted curio cabinet displaying an impressive collection of tiny crystal animals and sports memorabilia.

I shook my head and continued down the hall. A floorboard squeaked underfoot. I cringed despite the fact that the scuffle outside had surely raised an alarm by now. Five closed doors exited the hall at the rear of the house. I stopped at the first and motioned the fae to take the next two rooms, seeing as how the werewolves didn't have opposable thumbs at the moment.

Marshall bumped my thigh, nudging me enough to get in front of my door. He hunched like a coiled spring. Maddie joined the satyr at the next door, leaving the last fae—a woman with skin like month-old orange peel, rust-red hair, and sunset eyes—on her own on the other side of the hall. Everyone looked at me. I raised three fingers in silent countdown. When my last finger fell, I opened my door.

Olive-green bathroom fixtures and a sunflower shower curtain greeted me.

A deafening *boom* came from farther down the hall. I winced and ducked, simultaneously pivoting toward the threat. Maddie, the satyr, a collection of wood splinters I assumed were all that was left of the door he'd just opened, and what looked like shards of glass flew backward and crashed through the door across the hall.

Marshall reacted first, springing into the room the satyr had opened. The remaining fae and I were a step behind. Dust and debris were still falling from the doorway when I crossed the threshold, making me glad I hadn't unwrapped the scarf from my head.

A young woman stood in the center of the room. She was four feet tall and lithe, with blue-gray skin, emerald eyes that showed no white, a wide, flat nose, indigo lips, and black hair that draped her shoulders in loose curls. In contrast to her otherworldly appearance, she wore a pair of faded blue jeans and a thin yellow flannel with torn-off sleeves and the bottom tied under her breasts to create a baby tee that showed off her well-defined abs. Resting on her cleavage was a silver necklace set with the largest sapphire I'd ever seen.

Disappointment flickered through me, followed quickly by resolve. If Shedraziel wasn't here, I'd just have to make this woman tell me where she was. At least I could fulfill my deal with the Undine Lord, for surely this was her daughter.

The woman grabbed the lid off one of several large plastic barrels that lined the back wall of the room and flung the disc, Frisbee style, at Marshall.

He darted to the side, jumping onto the narrow bed pressed against the left wall. I ducked the barrel lid, and it clattered against the door frame.

The woman I'd come to rescue raised her arms and made a circling motion with one hand. A stream of water lifted from the topless barrel, moving through the air in mimic of her motions.

Marshall lunged.

The woman twisted and extended one empty hand in his direction.

The living water launched toward the leaping werewolf as though shot from a fire hose. The stream caught him in the chest and sent him tumbling into the wall above the bed. He hit with a *thud* and a whine, then fell to the mattress as she turned her water whip on me.

I tried to dodge the stream, but it redirected and slammed into me like an oak two-by-four across my chest. My hand opened involuntarily. I lost my gun.

As I stumbled back, my fae companion drew a pair of daggers that wrapped around her fists like brass knuckles and charged. The water gave me one last shove before switching targets. My back slammed against a tall wooden wardrobe hard enough to bruise. I struggled to inhale.

The fae with the punch daggers threw a flurry of blows at the other woman. A few scraped skin, but the water danced and swirled, knocking the blades aside at the last moment.

"Stop," I shouted, though my breath came in ragged gasps. "We don't want to hurt you." I fished for the pearl in my pocket.

The red-haired fae feinted to the left and snuck a thrust while the undine woman was distracted. The edge of the blade kissed her cheek, leaving a dark line in its wake.

The woman's expression contorted with anger. She pivoted low and slammed a roundhouse kick into her attacker's abdomen.

I jumped aside as my companion was thrown against the wardrobe, interrupting my search for the pearl.

The undine closed her hands on empty air and yanked down. The water followed, slipping around the top of the wardrobe and toppling the heavy furniture.

The orange fae hit the floor. The wardrobe followed her down, sandwiching her in place with a muffled shriek.

I drew my knife, not wanting to risk cutting the girl I was supposed to be rescuing with my iron-poisoned sword, and swung at the undine woman's exposed stomach, forcing her to skip back a step. She bumped into the empty barrel, losing her balance.

Marshall finally disentangled himself from the bed covers and slammed into the woman, a snarling ball of wet fur that rode her to the ground, scattering plastic barrels. He dug his claws into the woman's back. Saliva dripped from his bared teeth. He growled in her ear. The scent of wet dog filled the room.

The woman lifted one hand, but I stomped on her fingers before she could call her water to bear. "Stop fighting," I said. "We're here to rescue you."

The woman's gaze shifted from her trapped hand to my face. She burst out laughing.

I frowned and reached into my pocket. "Your mother sent us."

She jerked under Marshall's paws, sinking his claws in farther. "I'm not going back until the task is done."

I pulled out the pearl and held it pinched between my fingers for her to see. "Wanna bet?"

She squinted, then paled. "She's using you."

Alex!

I staggered, shaking my head at the sudden shout in my thoughts. *I shouldn't be able to pick up anything from James at this distance. . . .*

The lord's daughter yanked her hand free as my weight shifted.

Marshall opened his mouth to bite.

The water that had been hovering above the fallen wardrobe surged past my legs, knocking me down. I clamped my hand closed around the pearl. My head cracked against the bed frame. The water slammed into Marshall from beneath, lifting him into the air. He was pinned against the ceiling, kicking and snapping, in a bubble of gel-like liquid.

The woman ran.

I blinked, dazed, trying to clear the specks from my vision as she hurdled my legs and raced out the door.

"No." I rolled to my hands and knees, paused as a wave of nausea swept over me, then pushed to my feet.

Alex! James's demand for attention was even louder.

Not now. I sent the thought through our connection with the force of a bullet as I stumbled into the hall, knife clutched in one hand, pearl in the other. The Undine Lord's daughter—my best shot at finding Shedraziel—was halfway to the front door.

I raised the pearl above my head, aimed for the space right in front of her pounding feet, said a prayer, and let it fly.

The pearl plinked against the hardwood, bounced, and landed again, still whole. My heart sank. Then the undine woman's foot came down on top of it.

There was a *crack* and a *whoosh* as all the air in the building seemed to pull in toward that single point under the woman's foot. Then the direction reversed, and I was knocked on my ass by a sudden gale in the hallway. The wind carried with it the stench of decay. A dark pool spread across the floor, turning the polished wood into a watery abyss.

Tentacles sprang from the smooth surface and wrapped around the startled woman, who screamed and thrashed as though the slippery limbs were burning her.

My breath caught. My heart pounded. I'd assumed Annabrae would show up, or maybe the lord herself, not this putrid, writhing mass.

More tentacles surged up, squeezing the woman. Then they began to sink back into the depthless black, dragging the woman with them.

"Hey," I shouted, scrambling to my feet. "Wait a sec!"

The woman was already gone from the ribs down.

I charged up the hall.

"I still need her!"

The woman's scream cut off as her face vanished below the inky surface.

There was a *yelp* and a *crash* from the room behind me.

I hesitated at the sharp line between wood and water, then dropped to my knees at the edge of the pool. I leaned over but saw only my own reflection in its mirrored black surface. "What about our deal?"

The inky stain shrank as quickly as it had expanded, like a spilled drink recorded and played in reverse.

"Hey!" I dropped my knife and scrambled on hands and knees, clawing at the retreating liquid. My fingers slid over the surface, unable to breach the darkness.

The last drop vanished. The pearl sat on the polished wood of the hallway, cracked in two.

"Annabrae!" My shout echoed through the hall without response.

The daughter's last words ran through my head. *She's using you.*

I pounded my fists against the wood on either side of the broken pearl. Had I missed something in the deal with the Undine Lord, some loophole that let her screw me without lying? Did the lack of undine backup even matter if I couldn't find Shedraziel? My best lead had just been snatched out from under me, and I was out of time.

Chapter 20

THE FRONT DOOR of the farmhouse slammed against the wall just as it had when I'd entered, this time hard enough to knock one of the hanging pictures off its hook. The frame hit the floor in an explosion of glass that fell just short of reaching my fists. I looked up. James stood in the doorway. Dust and dirt blew in around him, ruffling his clothes. His black hair fell over his forehead, and he pushed it back from his wide blue eyes.

"James." I sat back on my heels. "What are you—?"

"We have to go." He took a step toward me and slammed the door, cutting off the desert storm that still raged outside. "Now."

He crunched past the broken glass and reached out a hand.

I knocked it aside, latching onto James as a target for my frustration. "If Shedraziel had been here and you—"

"I knew she wasn't."

I blinked up at him, my anger forgotten. "What? How?"

"Kai's magic bauble went off a minute ago. Bael's troops are in the mortal realm. They're engaging Shedraziel as we speak."

I sprang to my feet, wincing when my full weight landed on my still sore leg. "Where?"

"They tracked her to the Hoover Dam."

"So she *was* being literal."

A high-pitched yelp came from behind me. There was also a noise like wood scraping.

Turning away from James and the urgency in his expression was a struggle, but I had to help the people right in front of me first. I sheathed my knife and headed back down the hall.

The window in the room Maddie and the satyr had been thrown into was broken. The curtain whipped and snapped like one of the thrashing tentacles that had dragged the lord's daughter away. Dust sifted over everything. The satyr was sitting up in a pile of debris that might once have been a desk. He bled from dozens of holes and one of his eye sockets was a pulped mess. He looked as if he'd tried to play chicken with a Gatling gun. Maddie was on the ground beside him, also full of holes. She whimpered and twitched as the satyr extracted a long, thin piece of wood from her side.

Looking through the other door I found Marshall, in human form and soaking wet, struggling to lift the wardrobe as sections of it split and splintered. The fae trapped beneath grunted as a large chunk of the back collapsed.

James stepped around me and helped Marshall lift. Between the two of them they raised the mess high enough to reach the woman beneath. I tucked my hands under her armpits and pulled. She got one knee under her, but her other leg dragged like so much ground meat hanging off her hip.

As soon as she was clear, the guys dropped the wardrobe, and Marshall ran to the other room to check on his sister.

I got one of the woman's arms over my shoulder and tried to lever her onto the bed.

James reached out to help, but the orange-skinned woman pulled away and hissed between filed teeth. He lowered his hands and stepped back.

The woman flopped unceremoniously onto the bed, and I disentangled myself from her grip.

James cleared his throat. "We should go."

"But. . . ." I glanced over my shoulder at the other room.

Marshall looked up. He was cradling Maddie's furry head in his lap, gently stroking her muzzle as the fae continued to remove shrapnel. "Go," he said. "We've got this."

I hesitated a moment longer, but I was no healer. There was nothing more I could do here. I gave one brisk nod, found and holstered my gun, and headed for the front door.

My scarf had come loose during the struggle, so when I stepped onto the porch, the full force of the sand scraping against my skin made me shrink back. I lifted one arm and burrowed into the crook of my elbow, squinting over my sleeve. Those of my team who'd remained outside were standing guard over the two griffins we'd encountered, along with two others who must have shown up after I went inside, but most of their attention was focused out and up.

I glanced skyward. Shadows darted through the sand, coming together and breaking apart, sometimes vanishing altogether.

Hunching against the wind, I headed toward the barn. Targe would be my best chance to reach Shedraziel in time to help . . . though even he probably wasn't strong enough to create a portal over that kind of distance.

James walked at my elbow, leaning into the wind and covering his face just as I was. Rapid healing didn't make having your skin abraded any less painful.

There was a massive *thud* that I felt through the soles of my feet. A plume of dust kicked into the air a little ahead on my right. Then, all at once, the wind stopped.

The constant rush in my ears was replaced by a startling silence. I straightened and lowered my arm. Dust still flitted through the air, but the wind that had turned the grains into tiny daggers had vanished. I blinked and tipped my face up. Bright sunlight streamed from a clear blue sky, reflecting off the dust like glitter in a snow globe. I sneezed.

A shadow passed in front of the sun. Then the wind was back—not the steady battering of the storm but a series of pulses as Zee lowered herself to the ground. Her taloned toes gouged the dry earth.

Targe came out of the wide doors of the barn. Three battered griffins were hogtied behind him and guarded by his team.

I glanced in the other direction and spotted Sarah trotting toward us on bloodied paws. When everyone was within hearing range, I shouted, "Shedraziel is at the Hoover Dam."

Sarah shifted to two legs. She straightened, shook out her hair, and frowned at me. "That's nearly the whole length of Nevada. We can't possibly get there before she does whatever she's gone there to do."

"The drowned city." Zee's voice filled my head. I met the dragon's golden gaze.

I turned to James. "Call David. Tell him to get in touch with Bishop Silva. He should have the resources to evacuate the cities in the flood path."

James slipped his fingers into mine. "That's a lot of people. There may not be enough time."

"Then you'd better make the call." I squeezed his hand, then released him and turned toward Targe. "The rest of us need to get there somehow. Even if we fail to stop her, maybe we can slow her down."

Targe gestured to Sarah. "Your friend is right. It's too far."

I cringed and turned to Zee. "How long would it take to fly there?"

She swung her massive head from side to side. "She would be long gone."

James paused with the prepaid phone he'd just pulled from his pocket halfway to his ear. He lowered his hand and studied Targe. "Is your limitation with power or ability?"

I nearly choked. I'd learned early on in my dealings with the fae that questioning a fae's power, especially to his face, was a huge insult.

Targe pursed his lips and narrowed his eyes at James. The two stared at each other for a long moment. Then Targe settled back on his heels, crossed his arms, and said, "Power."

James nodded. "When we were out east, Alex needed to imbue many objects, more than she had the strength for. Kai set up a sort of . . . magic battery ritual to siphon energy from a group of people and feed it into her. Could we do that here?"

Targe's expression shifted from one of suspicion to consideration, but it was Chase who answered. He strolled forward on human legs, his long silver hair streaming like a ribbon behind him. "That should work." He glanced at Targe for confirmation.

"We might have enough juice between us to open a portal to Las Vegas, but I'll need Ava's help."

I frowned. "Why not take us straight to the dam?"

"I can't." He shrugged. "I've never been there."

"Fair enough." I rose to my tiptoes and planted a kiss on James's cheek. "Good thinking." I pointed at the phone in his hand. "Now make that call."

I SHADED MY EYES from the baking midday sun and looked out over the Black Rock Desert. Pale earth spread away from the ranch, a sea of sand that broke on the shores of the Jackson Mountains on the far side of the valley and stretched to the south until heat and distance obscured the horizon. Somewhere in that direction, Shedraziel was attacking the Hoover Dam.

Please let Rhoana hold the line.

"We're ready."

I turned toward Targe's voice. He and the rest of my allies were standing in the large clearing between the farmhouse where I'd fought and lost the Undine Lord's daughter and the large, whitewashed barn where all the griffins we'd incapacitated were now tied up. The ranch property was nestled among the first rolling hills leading into the mountains on the northern edge of the valley. The land was dotted with scrub brush and stunted pines that had been sculpted by the wind. Despite being so close, I hadn't been able to see the sparse greenery or inclining land until the dust from the griffins' storm had finally settled.

I walked over to the group who would accompany me through the portal, assuming Targe was able to make a stable connection. From among the werewolves, Old Bill, Maddie, and Xander had been too badly injured to keep fighting. They would remain behind with Gil and Noah and act as the pack's anchor against possession. Sarah, Faolan, Tarlo, Liam, and Jasmine would join me, along with Chase, Zee, and seven of the best fae fighters we had. James stood to one side, still on the phone with David. Everyone else was clustered together inside a circle scratched into the dirt that was lined with fae glyphs around the outer edge.

"Y'all ready for this?" I asked.

Sarah frowned, casting a sidelong glance at the fae who was going to "prep" the werewolves for travel. "Portals are one thing, but letting this fae transform us. . . ." She shook her head. "I don't like it."

"We've discussed this," I reminded her. "There's no other way to get you all there. Zee can't carry you as you are." I set my hand on her shoulder. "And he promises the spell won't have any adverse effects once you're turned back."

She grumbled, dropped to all fours, and sprouted fur like the rest of the wolves.

I turned my attention to James. His irritation was a tickle at the back of my mind. He was pacing a hole in the dirt. I moved closer, planting myself in his path. He lifted his gaze from the ground, met my eyes, and smiled, but the expression didn't ease the lines of worry etched on his features.

"David's still trying to get through to Silva. He's been suspended from his post pending an investigation into the transport ambush. Weatherly is stonewalling him."

I nodded. "Tell him to do whatever it takes. There are thousands of lives at stake."

"He knows." James lowered the phone from his ear. "I don't like the idea of being so far from you." He closed the distance between us. His arms were a comforting blanket wrapped around me.

"Neither do I." I rested my forehead against his chest, savoring the slow rise and fall of his breath. "But I have to go."

We stood in silence while the whole world seemed to pause around us, locking us into that single moment of contentment as we held each other. Then reality kicked in and it was time to go.

I raised my lips to his and breathed in deep, finding the spicy scent of him beneath the dry dust that tickled my nose.

His hand trailed down my arm. Our fingers locked for a moment. Then I took a step back. Our fingers parted, but the steady thrum of *I am here* continued to pulse through the bond in my soul. I smiled and turned away. No matter where I went, James would always be with me.

I waved to Emma, Jynx, and Kai, who stood in the circle of volunteers waiting to contribute their energy to Targe's spell, and called, "See you when this is over."

Returning to my position at the head of the travel team, I nodded to Targe, who looked at Ava.

Ava crouched beside the ritual circle. She set one hand against the glyphs, the other against her uncle's ankle, and closed her eyes. The symbols around the circle began to glow until the entire space sparkled with faint light.

Targe inhaled, held his breath, then let it out. He sketched a small circle in the air, barely a foot in diameter. His face contorted in concentration. He continued to trace the circle with one hand while marking the edge of it with his other. The air inside his whirlpool motion began to shimmer. Sweat beaded and dripped from Targe's brow. His jaw was locked. He grabbed the edge of the heat shimmer with both hands and stretched his fists apart.

One of the illusionists who'd provided cover on our first trip across the valley dropped to the ground.

Targe grunted. He continued to spread his hands. The shimmer expanded.

A second fae fell, then a third.

"Now." Targe growled the word through clenched teeth. His hands were shaking.

I glanced once more at James, whose gaze bore into me, and stepped through the portal.

There was a moment of now-familiar disorientation as my body was twisted then snapped back together. My foot came down on concrete.

Traffic rumbled and horns blared. A cacophony of chatter assailed my ears, making me cringe after the silence of the desert. Zee bumped my back, propelling me forward, and I used the momentum to reach the mouth of the alley we'd transported into. We'd emerged on a side street across from an artificial lake that was spraying fountains in a complex pattern combined with flashing lights and music. Palm trees lined the median of the main road. A replica of the Eiffel Tower straddled a building with Roman architecture on my left, and beyond that was a blue-and-yellow balloon with the word *Paris* scrawled across it. In the other direction was a massive glass-and-steel skyscraper. I smacked my lips, trying to work moisture into my dry throat. If anything, it was even hotter here than it had been in the barren desert.

Zee stepped up to my shoulder. I glanced at her bare feet on the hot sidewalk, but she didn't seem uncomfortable.

"Welcome to the city of light," I said, indicating the buildings around us. "If Shedraziel succeeds in breaking the dam, this place will lose all its power."

Zee took in the towering buildings and the elbow-to-elbow throngs of people. "You would mourn the loss of such a place?"

I looked around. Fifty-foot screens plastered to the sides of buildings cycled through advertisements for shows at the nearby casinos. Men and women thrust paper pamphlets at passing pedestrians, most of which were immediately dropped in the gutter. The overwhelming noise and motion of the place was already giving me a headache. "I prefer my quiet patch of mountain, but even places like this serve a purpose. Besides, more than the lights of this city will go out if Shedraziel wins here. A lot of lives will be lost, not to mention any hope of peace between the races."

"Then we had best ensure she does not succeed." Zee turned away from the sea of pedestrians. I followed.

The second-to-last of our group came through. I crossed my arms and glanced at the position of the sun as we waited for the final arrival.

Chase swore.

I looked at the portal and found James standing on the Las Vegas sidewalk. My jaw dropped. "What the hell?"

Kai emerged behind James, followed closely by Emma. The shimmer of the portal flashed out of existence. The last fae I was expecting was nowhere in sight.

James took a step toward me.

I backed up. "You shouldn't be here." I shifted my glare to Kai and Emma. "None of you should be."

"When I saw James bolt through the portal. . . ." Kai shrugged. "I thought you might need help containing him."

James laughed. "You think you can contain me?"

Kai turned on Emma. "I told you to stay put."

"I wasn't gonna be the only one left behind."

"You were *all* supposed to stay put," I yelled.

James shook his head. "I can't protect you from half a state away."

I bunched my fists, barely containing the urge to deck him. "With Shedraziel involved staying away is the only way you *can* protect me."

"I'll keep well back from the fight. She won't even know I'm there. But if you get into trouble. . . ." He shrugged. "We know I can hold out against her for a little while at least. Maybe long enough to get you clear."

I shook my head. There was no way James would be able to resist joining the fight if I was in danger, and I was definitely going to be in danger. "You're not coming."

"I'm not letting you go without me."

"People could die while we're wasting time arguing."

"But not you."

Zee moved behind James. She touched a finger to his temple.

James crumpled like a rag doll.

"As you said, arguing was wasting time." She stepped over James, walked calmly to the parking garage behind the nearest casino, and climbed the stairs. The rest of my team followed.

I stared at James, lying unconscious in the alley like a mugging victim, and sighed. *This is for the best.* I knelt to kiss his cheek then turned to Kai and Emma. "Take care of him." I raised a finger. "And keep him away from the dam."

Kai glared at James.

Emma saluted. "Good luck."

I trotted after Zee and the others. Only three cars had braved exposure on the bleached surface of the garage roof, leaving plenty of space for a dragon.

I turned to Sarah. "Ready?"

She growled and snorted but lay down on the sunbaked roof.

The fae who'd be performing the enchantment stepped forward so his leather boots were inches from her nose. He wore a brown tunic with a wide sword belt and dark leather pants, making him look like an extra from *Lord of the Rings*. He was short, barely clearing four feet, with thick lips, a bulbous nose, and flinty, close-set eyes. His reddish-brown hair hung nearly to his waist, contained by a series of complicated braids. He raised one hand and squatted until his palm rested against Sarah's forehead, right between her perked ears.

Her lip curled, but she didn't otherwise move.

The air around Sarah sparkled, then she changed. It wasn't the sinew-stretching, bone-popping shift of a werewolf, or even the candle-wax melt of a fae shifter. One moment she was a wolf, then *poof*, a small green snake was lying in her place.

I opened my backpack, which I'd emptied earlier in preparation for this, and held it wide. The fae scooped up snake-Sarah, who tried to strangle his wrist, and set her in the bottom of the bag.

The rest of the wolves followed suit. Some growled during the spell, some whimpered. As snakes, many of them tried to slither away, having lost all awareness of the situation. These weren't people in the forms of snakes, not with a basic enchantment like this. These were authentic snakes with no recollection of any other life. The enchanter set the spells one by one to ensure he didn't damage the pack bonds, but he'd assured me breaking the enchantment would be as simple as snapping his fingers to bring them all back.

Three of the remaining fae were also transformed into snakes, though none of them squirmed as much as the wolves had. The final two were natural shifters and quickly became the raven and eagle who'd attacked the griffin as it lifted off. Chase shrank to his tabby form, and Zee grew until she took up nearly the entire roof. I zipped the writhing mass of my companions into my pack and shrugged into it, then climbed onto Zee's neck. The enchanter settled behind me, much farther back than Kai had, and Chase curled in my lap. The birds perched in the space between Zee's wings and hunkered down, latching onto her scales with their claws.

I patted Zee's neck. "Ready when you are."

She hunched like a cat about to pounce.

I tightened my grip.

The force of her launch set off alarms on the three nearby cars, and it was to that cacophonous blare that we wheeled into the sky. I cast one last look at the alley and sent a prayer that James would stay safe.

The city of Las Vegas shrank beneath us. The chatter of crowds and the rumble of traffic was replaced by the rush of the wind. The petrol smells of the parking garage were replaced by the cool dry air of the desert, and the towering buildings fell away until only the endless stretch of the sky remained.

Zee banked toward the rocky red hills to the east. She sped through the sky on powerful strokes. I hunkered down to reduce the wind, but my eyes streamed, and my hair flattened to my scalp and slashed like whips against my neck. A dark line appeared near the horizon, stretching and growing wider as we closed the distance. Lake Mead extended for miles, tucked amid desert cliffs that framed the dark blue in contrasting colors.

So much water. If it's all released. . . . I tried to swallow but found no moisture in my mouth.

Zee dipped lower as we approached the southern end of the lake, rustling the scraggly sage clinging to the dust below. The first man-made structure I spotted was a massive bridge stretching from rim to rim across a canyon. Then we crested a ridge, and the bone-white arc of the Hoover Dam came into view. The dam was a smooth curve that bowed in toward the lake with four towers extending off the back. A road traced the top of the dam and climbed up the far hills in a series of switchbacks, one of which swung through a parking lot that nearly touched the thin white line that marked high tide. The road at the top of the dam was empty of traffic, but several people had gathered near the center.

I squinted at the tiny figures—a dozen or so fae in the brown-and-green livery of Bael's court. They formed a loose circle, facing out. I shifted my focus and found the pale glow of magic around them. The glow extended from their feet along the surface of the dam, encasing it in magic. Movement near the far edge of the dam drew my attention to another group of fae. They were locked in combat and too jumbled for me to make out clearly.

A resounding *crash* broke through the muffling effects of the wind. Zee swung slightly farther south, giving me a view of the front of the dam and the western rim. Half a dozen large shapes that were vaguely human but looked to be carved of clay or rock stood at the edge of one of the switchbacks.

Trolls or golems. Impossible to tell at this distance. I bit down on my chapped lower lip. *Bad news either way.*

One of the figures reached down and ripped a chunk of asphalt out of the already compromised road, hefted it over his head with both hands, and lobbed it at the dam. The boulder smashed against the concrete just below the area where Bael's troops stood. The magical glow flared, absorbing the impact. I glanced at the skirmish near the end of the dam then back at the area we'd just passed over, where a similar scene was unfolding.

They're trying to reach the enchanters protecting the dam.

I thumped my palm against Zee's side, pointed to the parking lot near the shore, and shouted, "Land there."

Zee came in fast, braking at the last moment by spreading her wings wide like a parachute. I slammed forward. Chase yowled, though the sound was muffled by my body.

I leaned back and swung my leg over Zee's neck, dropping to the dusty ground before her front legs touched down. I swung the bag off my back and unzipped it.

The fae enchanter landed beside me.

"Ready?"

He nodded.

I upended the bag near the ground. The snakes tumbled out in a pile. I took two steps back.

The stocky man waited until the snakes had spread out a little while Chase ensured none strayed too far. Then he made a series of shapes with his hands, mumbled something, clapped them together, and spread them wide.

There was distinct *pop*, followed by a puff of smoke that obscured the snakes for a moment. I coughed and waved a hand in front of my face to clear the acrid smell.

All the wriggling reptiles had returned to their original forms.

"Sarah?" I crouched in front of the dazed werewolf. "You okay?"

Her brown eyes, the same eyes she had as a human, focused on me.

I pointed to the near end of the dam where the fae were fighting. Her gaze followed. She growled.

"We need to stop those fae from breaching the dam. The ones wearing brown and green are on our side."

She yipped a short, sharp bark and surged forward, knocking me onto my butt. The rest of the wolves charged with her, spurred either by her command or her action.

I glanced over my shoulder at the opal dragon. "Did you see Shedraziel anywhere?"

"No." She stretched her long neck and scanned the area. "But she's here somewhere. I can feel her."

"You and the fae who can fly should head for the far bank. Maybe you can stop those big guys from throwing rocks."

She bobbed her long nose. The bird-fae sprang off her back and winged out over the water. Zee gave them a head start, then flattened me to the ground with her downdraft.

"Come on," I said to the remaining fae. "We need to get on that dam."

Chase shimmered and shifted into his tiger form and raced forward on powerful paws. The rest of us followed. Several of the fae prepared spells as they ran. I drew my gun.

Sarah and her wolves reached the skirmish well ahead of us, slamming into the exposed backs of the attacking fae and catching them in a vise of swords and claws. I could now see that the attackers ranged widely in species. Gnomes, eloko, pixies, satyrs, sidhe, pooka, panotti . . . Shedraziel must have conscripted soldiers from all over the fae realms.

A *splash* sounded behind me. I spun to see a column of water spurt from the lake and hit Zee in the belly.

No, not a column. . . .

At the center of the water was a writhing mass of tentacles. The leathery whips were such a dark green they looked almost black. Each sparkled wetly in the sun as they snapped around Zee's legs and wings, dragging her toward the surface of the water.

I reversed direction fast enough to wrench my ankle, charging toward the edge of the lake with no idea what I could do but every cell in my body screaming to act. Mist and rain showered around me, soaking my clothes and hair. My shoes squelched and slipped as dirt turned to mud.

Zee plunged beneath the surface.

Shouts, growls, and the clash of metal rang out behind me as the battle for the bridge continued, but I had to trust the werewolves would be enough to turn the tide of that battle.

As I scrambled past the low chain marking the edge of the viewing area a second surge of water erupted, this time right in front of me. The wave crashed over me, drenching me to my underwear, but water wasn't the only thing to emerge from the lake. A dozen fae stood on the shore.

I staggered to a halt, bracing to keep my balance as the receding water sucked at my feet. For a fleeting moment I believed the Undine Lord had kept her promise, that the horse-faced kelpie, shaggy bunyip, saucer-eyed kappas, and spear-wielding nereids were there to help. Then Shedraziel stepped out of the water behind them.

Chapter 21

SHE SLIPPED THROUGH the surface like a knife cutting butter, emerging dry when her bare toes reached the sandy shore. She wore swirling silks of green and blue that danced in the wind and caressed her cerulean skin like a lover's touch. Her long hair swirled around her shoulders and cascaded down her back, fading from teal near her scalp to indigo at the tips. When her emerald gaze settled on me, her dark lips curved in a satisfied smile.

"So glad you could make it."

"No you're not."

She raised one long-nailed hand to her chest and fluttered her lashes. "I couldn't say it if it wasn't true. I am a fae after all." She laughed. The sound rang like bells at Christmas. "For now."

I frowned, unsettled by her crazy.

A call went up among the fighters near the bridge. From the corner of my eye I saw some of my allies charge toward me. They'd seen Shedraziel and her reinforcements and were coming to help.

Shedraziel spread her arms wide. "This will all be so much sweeter with an audience."

I leveled my gun at her chest. "Your war ends here."

I squeezed the trigger.

A kappa darted sideways, taking the bullet I'd intended for Shedraziel.

"*My* war?" She *tsked* and waggled a finger. "This is *the* war. The only war. The endless war." Her smile stretched to a grin.

The fae around her advanced.

I squeezed off six more shots, emptying my gun.

A white streak brushed past my side. Chase crashed into a startled kelpie, tearing into her chest with razor claws that left her green-tinged skin hanging in ragged ribbons that mimicked her seaweed mane.

A shower of sparks arched overhead, sprayed from the fingers of one of the fae who'd accompanied me. Shedraziel waved a hand, knocking the embers away from her, but her soldiers weren't so fortunate. Where each particle landed, an arc of electricity jumped from body to body, causing the affected fae to convulse and in some cases drop to their knees.

Rather than waste time reloading, I holstered my gun and drew my knife. I opened myself to the energy around me, filled my reserves, bolstered my strength, and attacked. The stumpy-legged enchanter and two of the fae who'd traveled as snakes joined my charge.

An androgynous nereid with long, lithe limbs, kelp-green hair, and translucent skin thrust their spear at my abdomen. I pivoted and parried with my forearm, thankful for both the aikido lessons I'd taken before my non-human traits became too pronounced to hide and the more recent sparring sessions with Sarah that had taken their place. I rolled along the weapon's shaft and lifted my elbow, catching the fae in the face. They stumbled to the side then swung the spear butt at my ankle. I jumped the sweep, but when I landed, the ache in my calf from my gunshot wound flared like knives through my nervous system. I dropped to one knee with a gasp.

The flint-tipped end of the spear arced toward me.

I rolled clear, came up in a ready stance, and jabbed my knife into the nereid's exposed thigh.

The spear butt swung up and caught me on the chin.

I fell back, losing my grip on the knife.

Before either of us had a chance to make the next move, a monkey-like form slammed into the nereid's back. The momentum yanked the nereid off balance, and the two of them tumbled away from me, taking my embedded knife with them.

I stood, wiped my chin, and caught a glimpse of Chase, snapping and clawing at Shedraziel near the shore. I drew my sword and took a step in that direction. *If we stop her, the rest of the fae should fall into line.*

A ball of brown fur barreled into my chest. My back slammed against the soggy ground, but the mud didn't lessen the impact. I tucked my chin to keep from cracking my head and gasped as the air was forced from my lungs. I barely managed to keep hold of my sword. I struggled to rise, but powerful arms covered in stringy hair pinned my shoulders to the ground. The bunyip leaned down, sinking me further into the mud. He had a flat, triangular face with wide-spaced eyes, flared nostrils, and protruding fangs. When he exhaled, I nearly choked on the stench of swamp and rot.

I took a deep breath through my mouth, trying to clear my head of the panic shouting from the corners of my mind. My thoughts jumped to the werewolves battling for alpha in the desert. *Large, strong people tend to rely on their weight to win. Sarah beat Noah by outmaneuvering him.*

I tightened my grip on my sword but kept the blade flat at my side. Then I tucked one leg, slammed my fist into the bunyip's elbow, and bucked my hips. My opponent's weight shifted. We rolled. I rose to the top, but our momentum kept us going as he sought to reclaim the higher ground.

As our center of gravity shifted again, I kicked against his thighs with both feet. The bunyip's weight lifted. Not enough to knock him loose, but all I needed was a little space. I twisted my sword and braced the hilt against my side to hold it steady. My back and arm impacted. I felt the hilt lodge in the mud. The bunyip came down on top of me.

As his weight settled, a mouth full of fangs shrieked into my face. His claws shredded my sleeves, but the movements were too erratic to dig deep. He flailed and thrashed, but the six inches of bloody iron-tainted silver protruding from his back held him in place. The scent of burning flesh—a smell I had become entirely too familiar with—filled the air.

He jerked to the side and I let him roll off me, pulling the sword free. He flopped and squirmed, all the while wailing in anguish. Tufts of shed hair littered the ground, dark and shriveled as though they'd passed too close to a flame. A four-inch circle of blackened flesh surrounded the wound in his torso, and the darkness was spreading.

I'd hoped to save my iron edge as a surprise for Shedraziel, but a secret weapon wouldn't do much good if I died before I got the chance to use it.

The bunyip collapsed with a gasp. His glassy eyes rolled up in his head. A trickle of saliva dripped from his open mouth.

My stomach heaved. I clamped a hand over my mouth and turned away, suddenly not so proud of the results of my imbuing.

A splash drew my attention to the lake. My heart thrilled for a moment to see Zee break the surface, but the triumph was fleeting. She thrashed in the water, unable to free herself from the glossy tentacles that continued to pull her down. She tore at the leathery limbs with her teeth and claws, but for every section she severed another sprang up to take its place, wrapping her tight and dragging her under.

My gaze shifted to the dam behind her, and my heart sank even further. The fae from the far shore had breached the upper road and were cutting down Bael's enchanters. The shimmer of magic protecting the dam was gone. The next boulder that slammed into the dam took a sizable chunk out of the concrete. Several of the enormous creatures on the far bank lumbered forward, clearly intent on a direct assault. A shout went up on the near shore. Shedraziel's troops redoubled their efforts to break the line of defense, spurred by the success of their companions.

I pulled my attention away from the massacre on the bridge and scanned the nearby shore, searching for the cause of all this death. Half a dozen fae lay unmoving on the ground, getting trampled by those still fighting. Chase was now near the edge of the battle fending off two spear-wielding kelpie. Blood streaked his white fur. A flash of indigo drew my attention. The fae who'd thrown sparks over my head collapsed to her knees in front of Shedraziel. The woman's head had been wrenched entirely around. Her clouded eyes stared behind her as she fell to the mud.

Shedraziel's gaze met mine. Light and laughter danced in her emerald eyes. She strode forward as though navigating a party rather than a battlefield.

I checked my magic was still primed and raised the tip of my sword.

She glanced at the charred bunyip. Her jaw stiffened. I'd lost the element of surprise.

She took another step toward me. I stepped back.

I needed to get closer to strike, but I couldn't stop my body from retreating. She wasn't controlling me, she wasn't even trying, but the look in her eyes scared the shit out of me.

I licked my cracked lips.

"Everyone knows you're behind this," I said. The words gave me courage, and I found I could hold my ground. "Even if you manage to drown a few cities, the PTF will know it's just you. They won't go to war with the fae."

She continued to advance.

"And the fae know you're behind this, too." I tipped my chin toward the liveried troops. "Bael is honor-bound to stop you."

She showed me her teeth, perfect white triangles locked together. "Bael has lost his stomach for war. He grows old and feeble upon his iron throne."

I swallowed. "Is that why you broke ties with him? You think you can overthrow him by taking over the mortal realm when he failed to do so?"

She laughed. The sound simultaneously made me want to close my eyes to listen and sent shivers down my spine. "How do you function with such a pitiful intellect? A throne is but another form of prison." She gestured absently. "See what it has done to Bael." She shook her head. "No, I would not rule a realm. My ambitions have grown beyond that."

"What then?"

She shook her head. "I've already told you. I cannot help if you are too deaf to hear."

She slipped her hand beneath the rippling fabric of her dress and unsheathed a long, thin, silver blade hidden among the folds.

She lunged without warning, without even shifting her weight. I stumbled back, raising my sword in a sloppy block that sent shock waves through my arm. Her next strike nicked my thigh, then my shoulder, then my wrist. Each blow I managed to deflect twisted into a new move too fast for me to follow. This wasn't like sparring with Kai, or even fighting the more experienced Hortense who'd once handed me my ass while wearing ten pounds of formal wear. Shedraziel was ancient. She was a warrior, a general, a killer. She was playing with me.

I dodged and weaved, deflecting what attacks I could as she continued to press me back. I never got the chance to counter.

A slice opened up on my arm, my calf, my hip, my cheek, none deep enough to draw more than a trickle of blood, but each a burning badge of shame and pain. Death by a thousand cuts. Shedraziel's expression became exultant as she danced past my defenses, delivering blow after humiliating blow.

I scrambled up the embankment, trying to clear my mind but constantly brought back to my body as another searing line split my skin.

She's too close.

I was breathing hard. My pulse was an erratic drumbeat in my ears.

Too close.

Her blade nicked my lip, barely missing my nose on the upsweep.

Her arm was up. Her torso exposed. But my blade was too low to make the strike before she recentered.

I spread the fingers on my left hand, which had come up instinctively, and channeled all my stored energy into a single shot. I didn't have the clarity of focus to shape the spell, just the overwhelming desire to create some space between us.

My magic went off with a bang—a sudden rush of light, noise, and force. I cringed, momentarily blinded by the flash, and swung my blade recklessly toward the shout of surprise on the other side of the explosion.

My sword struck solid matter.

There was a hiss, then Shedraziel's backhand hit me full in the face like a bag of bricks.

I cartwheeled sideways, rolled over twice, and skidded to a stop against an outcrop of slick rocks worn smooth by higher tides.

I blinked, trying to clear the sparkles dancing in my vision. My sword was gone, lost in the tumble. My magic had scattered with that one wild spell, and my focus was shot. I tried to rise, but a sharp pain lanced through my arm when I pressed my hand to the ground. I fell back and glanced down. My wrist was splotched with purple and starting to swell.

I twisted onto my side and looked along the shore. Shedraziel stalked toward me. Her smile was gone. Smoke rolled off her charred clothing. Soot streaked her cerulean skin. Blood oozed from a deep gash in her right shoulder, the edges black and burned.

A tiny insane voice at the back of my mind jumped for joy—*I landed a hit!*—while the more rational part of me realized that it didn't matter because I was about to die.

Shedraziel raised her sword. Her bared teeth no longer resembled a smile, and the light in her eyes gave the impression she was looking at something beyond me.

An ear-splitting *CRACK* reverberated against the canyon walls, momentarily drowning out the sounds of battle. Everyone turned to look. It was as if the sound had cast a spell, forcing our attention.

Some of the giant rock fae had taken the place of the defending enchanters at the center of the dam. A wide crack now split the cement wall from the road where they stood to the surface of the lake. Only Zee's thrashing and the slap of tentacles against the water broke the pregnant silence as attackers and defenders alike held our breath. Then the dam began to crumble, and all my hope rushed out like the water breaking free.

Once the water started moving, larger sections of the structure tore loose. The fae who'd braved the top of the dam fell into the surge of current.

Shedraziel tipped her head back and laughed at the sky.

Freed from my trance, I scooted backward and got my feet under me, clutching my injured wrist to my chest and skidding on the slick rocks. I glanced around for my sword. A glint of silver sparkled near the water's edge.

Shedraziel's laughter suddenly cut off.

I jerked my attention back to her, expecting to see the edge of her blade falling toward me. Instead I found her staring at the surface of the lake. A grim frown creased her features. The noise of the torrent had vanished save for the clatter of falling debris as it ricocheted off the canyon walls. The water that had been gushing through the dam, eroding the man-made barrier, while clearly still liquid, had frozen in place.

Zee and all the dark tentacles entangling her suddenly vanished from the near side of the dam, replaced by a massive bump of iridescent scales that slipped out and back into the water, spreading ripples across the place where Zee and her attacker had disappeared.

I gulped, recalling the endless coils of the sea dragon who'd circled the undine city.

The creature dropped out of sight, never revealing a beginning or end. A second later, Zee thrashed to the surface and began paddling for the far shore, her wings streaming behind her like saturated cloth. The black tentacles that had tried to drown her did not return.

Shedraziel *tsked* and glared at the water.

I took two careful steps in the direction of my sword, but froze again as a figure rose from the center of the lake.

The Undine Lord had coiled her hair into tight braids. She wore a gold-and-silver breastplate with matching bracers and held a three-pronged scepter. The image brought to mind paintings and sculptures I'd seen of Poseidon wielding his trident, and I wondered if those Greek artists had witnessed something similar.

The lord's jellyfish-like tentacles rippled over the surface of the water, carrying her forward. She did not spare a glance for the shattered dam, me, or anyone else on the battlefield. Her attention was for Shedraziel alone. "This ends between us today."

Shedraziel's smile was back. "I'd like nothing better."

A tidal wave surged onto the shore, soaking everyone except Shedraziel, who raised a hand to split the water around her. The wave, coupled with the slippery rocks, knocked me off my feet. Gravel scraped my back and side as I curled around my injured arm. My ankle slipped into a crack and caught fast. I shrieked a stream of bubbles as the force of the water pressed me against the stone. When the wave subsided, I gasped for breath and wiped the droplets off my face. The rest of the combatants had been pushed back from the shore.

I spotted Chase at the far edge of the parking lot. He lifted his head, looking none too happy with his wet fur slicked down to his bones. He tried to stand but wobbled and dropped. Blood stained the fur along his side and back leg. Other fae scattered by the wave began climbing to their feet. Some stumbled, disoriented. Others took the opportunity to land attacks on vulnerable enemies. I tugged at my ankle and grunted as the spurs of rock wedging it in place scraped against my skin.

Annabrae and twenty undine soldiers swarmed the shore on the tail of the wave. They came in a variety of shapes, but all wore blue-and-silver-scale armor, wielded daggers, and had small, round shields strapped to their arms. The remainder of Shedraziel's fae were pressed back, higher up the slope, as they struggled to survive the onslaught.

Metal sparked against metal nearby, and I turned my waterlogged attention back to the fae nearest me. Aside from myself, the observation area had been cleared of all but Shedraziel and the Undine Lord, who were now locked in combat.

While Shedraziel's rapier was long and thin, giving her a greater reach and snapping through the air like a whip, the lord's sword was wider and curved like a kopis. The two came together again and again, clashing blades then springing apart. Their movements looked more like a choreographed dance than a fight. The lord's tentacles writhed on the sand, lashing out at Shedraziel's legs. Shedraziel stumbled, and the thicker blade carved a line across her abdomen, shearing free several strips of cloth and staining those that remained with her blood.

She skipped out of reach and clamped a hand to her wound. She met the lord's gaze and grinned, panting slightly. "You've improved."

"So have you." The lord's chest was heaving with exertion, but her voice was firm.

"I found the secret." Shedraziel moved as she spoke, circling the less mobile lord. "How they did it."

The lord blanched, her purplish-gray skin turning nearly white. "That's not possible."

Shedraziel's gaze flicked past the lord's shoulder and found me struggling to free my leg. She smiled. "Do you know how the first fae were formed, Alex?"

"Don't." The lord slashed at Shedraziel, who danced away again.

"It's a truth long buried. A truth your mortal Church guessed from the very beginning. A truth you've fought so hard, and so pointlessly, to prove wrong."

Laughter coated her words and bubbled out as she crossed blades with the lord again.

"They came from the Rift—the energy that flows between and through all the realms, endless and unbridled—but they chose to limit themselves." She caught the lord's blade against her own and twisted them together, locking them in place long enough to land a kick on the lord's chest. "To this." Shedraziel gestured to the lord as she stumbled back, one hand braced over ribs that were surely broken.

I glanced up the hill. The fighting in the parking lot was over. Those who remained standing watched the battle between the two women from a safe distance. I wanted to scream at them to help their lord; surely Shedraziel wouldn't stand a chance if they attacked together, but I knew they wouldn't. Duels were more than a matter of honor for the fae. If the lord's subjects had to intervene, she would prove herself weak, unfit to rule. Even if she won, she would lose.

"Perhaps you are content to live within the cage created for you." Shedraziel stalked around the perimeter of their makeshift arena, playing to the crowd. "You always were easily controlled. But I will become what our species was always meant to be." She spread her arms wide, a wild light dancing in her eyes. "A god."

The lord straightened and raised her sword once more. "As usual, your ambitions overshadow your sensibility . . . if you even possess such a thing." She closed her left hand on air, and from her fist flowed a stream of crystal-blue water. She flicked her wrist. The water snapped like a whip.

Shedraziel snarled, hatred twisting her features.

She lunged forward. The lord moved to meet her, knocking the first thrust aside with her whip. The two were evenly match in strength and speed, and with the liquid chain at her command the lord could now compete with Shedraziel's reach. I continued to work my ankle free as the women rained blows on each other. Water cracked like snapped leather. Metal sang. Both women were breathing hard—the only ones who dared until the outcome was known. Bael's troops, those who hadn't been swept away in the now-frozen flood, joined the undine as they watched their lord struggle. The werewolves sat apart, licking their wounds. Sunlight turned the surface of the lake to diamonds as Zee finally pulled herself onto solid ground.

My ankle came free of the stony crevice, scraped raw by the process. Clutching my injured wrist tight to my side, I stood and tested my ankle. Bruised, but it would hold my weight.

Shedraziel slashed. The lord's whip caught the tip, redirecting it, and the wider blade found an opening in Shedraziel's guard. The metal bit deep, protruding a full inch out of her back.

Shedraziel stumbled. The lord's blade slid free. Blood flowed like a river over Shedraziel's abdomen. Her rapier clattered to the rocky ground.

The fae circling the area did not cheer or run forward to congratulate the victor. They simply waited and watched.

The Undine Lord regarded Shedraziel, her face twisted with sorrow.

I stared at the woman who'd kidnapped and tortured children, who'd tried to start a war, who'd killed untold people and enjoyed every moment of it. Even now the light of laughter still danced in her eyes, but her skin had taken on a strange, translucent quality. Particles of glitter shed from her body as she began disintegrating right before my eyes. The shimmering dust was snatched by the breeze and carried over the sparkling lake.

Kai had told me once that the fae didn't leave bodies behind, that the magic holding them together simply broke apart and they faded to nothing, but I'd never seen the process myself. The first fae I'd killed . . . well, I hadn't been aware of much after that fight, and Kai had purified the area immediately after. It never occurred to me to wonder how long the body would have lingered if he hadn't done that.

I glanced at the corpses strewn about the parking lot. Not all were enemies. I spotted the short, bulbous-nosed enchanter who'd answered Targe's call and followed me into battle. I could clearly make out the ground beneath his fading form.

The Undine Lord bowed her head. "May the Summerlands welcome you home."

"I came from the Rift." Shedraziel raised one hand, staring at her translucent palm with wide eyes. "And it's to the Rift that I will return." She met the gaze of the Undine Lord through her diaphanous fingers and said, "I never loved you."

The fading sparks turned to smoke, black as the coal from my forge. Magic built around her, crackling through the air.

The lord gasped and took a step back, as though Shedraziel's words had pierced her heart as surely as a sword. She was nearly level with me on the shoreline and close enough for me to make out the flicker of fear in her jet-black eyes.

Shedraziel coiled like a track star on the starting block, then burst forward at a speed that would have made James proud.

Shouts rang out from the crowd, but the others were too far back to do any good.

I didn't think, I just jumped.

My shoulder slammed against the Undine Lord's side, sending a shock wave through my body. Then Shedraziel's weight hit me and changed my trajectory. I braced for impact with the ground, or possibly the water if her momentum carried us that far, but before I hit anything, there was a sound like tearing paper, and I was overwhelmed by the gut-wrenching sensation of being twisted inside out.

Color bled out of the world. Not the localized desaturation of a waste that came from draining a place of magical energy, but a uniform bleaching of everything I could see, as though I were looking through a lens that neutralized color. The sky turned white, the water gray, and where the ground should have been . . . it wasn't. Clouds of darkness rolled across my vision. My back passed through the level of the ground as I continued to fall. Only one small strip of light remained—a tear in space through which I watched my world slip away. Then the darkness closed around me.

The twisting sensation grew worse, as though every cell in my body was being ripped apart. My skin was on fire. There was no up, no down, no form or matter in this place. I was adrift in pain, and even my screams failed to carry.

"Not what I'd hoped for." Shedraziel's voice came from everywhere and nowhere. It was inside my head and miles away. I writhed and strained, searching the darkness. Shapes moved in the mist, lighter or darker patches that swirled and scattered.

"Still . . . I suppose you'll do for a consolation prize."

"It's to the Rift that I will return." That's what she'd said. Could she have taken us into the Rift? But people can't enter the Rift. It's pure energy. I couldn't hold on to my fractured thoughts. I couldn't even tell if I had a body anymore. There was nothing but pain.

Shedraziel's silver-bell laughter filled my awareness. "Enjoy eternity."

I strained, waiting for another word, another sound, anything to anchor me—to hold my consciousness together as my cells dissolved into the chaos around me. A low hum of white noise was all I found, as though dozens, maybe hundreds of voices were mumbling and muttering in an incomprehensible monotone. The hum buzzed inside my skull, vibrating my mind to jelly. I twisted and tumbled, rolling through the cloudy gray emptiness. I felt as if I was drowning, or burning, or maybe just fading away.

A light flashed somewhere to my right.

I tried to turn toward it, to find it again, but there was no direction in this place. No texture to let me know I was moving. I thrashed what I thought were my arms as though swimming. Gray and black swirled around me. The bright speck was suddenly in front of me, but it wasn't a speck. It was a gash. A line of light in the darkness.

I flailed, struggling to reach it with every fiber of my being.

I didn't move, but the light suddenly surrounded me; then I was falling forward.

My hands and knees struck solid ground. My wrist crumpled. I shrieked, fell to my side, and curled into a ball. Tears streamed down my cheeks. My pulse thumped like the chugging wheels of a runaway freight train. I took deep, shuddering breaths and sobbed on the exhales as my body remembered what it meant to exist.

When I dared open my eyes, the darkness was replaced by a uniform gray. I was on a bed of moss in a clearing lined with bushes and trees, but the plants, the ground, even the sky were all shades of the same flat gray. I tasted the air and found it stale as a sealed tomb. Nothing moved. The stillness reminded me of the static prison where, until recently, Shedraziel had been trapped. A cold sweat broke out across my body.

I sat up. I ached all over. My wrist was definitely broken. My nerves were smoldering coals, ready to burst into flame at the slightest touch. I sniffled, wiped my eyes, and twisted to look behind me. The same monochrome landscape greeted me. I could feel the warmth and hope draining out of me, turning me the same pale gray as the lifeless world into which I'd tumbled.

I can't stay here.

The thought spurred me like a command. I touched my magic, shifted my perception, and found a shimmering, barely visible line in the air, like a single strand of spider silk hanging in space. I reached for the tear through which I'd arrived. My fingers passed through the shimmer to no effect.

I swore and tried again. Same result.

The weight of the silence and the stillness around me was smothering. I couldn't breathe. I couldn't think. I charged a handful of magic and forced it into the crack in the world. My hand passed through. I had a split second of elation, then the wrenching pain of being unmade set my fingers on fire. I screamed and fell back, gasping against the gray ground.

I can't do it. I can't go back. Even if I get it open. I can't go through that again. I panted into the colorless moss as my will to fight leached away.

Chapter 22

THE WHISPERS STARTED on the second night—despite the uniform blankness of the sky, there was a day-night cycle, or something like it. At first I'd thought Zee was trying to reach me through my dreams, but by the fourth day I'd come to the conclusion that the whispers in my head were a symptom of frayed nerves and my dwindling grip on reality. Sleep deprivation and starvation could do that to a person.

I dug my fingers into the hair at my temples and bunched my hands into fists, trying to anchor myself as the incessant hum grew louder. The rough splint I'd tied around my broken wrist scraped my cheek. The whispers weren't a sound exactly, more like the buzz of a million hornets vibrating my skull, but when the noise was at its strongest, I swore I could almost make out a voice.

I scrunched my eyes closed and shouted to chase that voice away. The hum inside my head eased. It never faded entirely. I took a deep breath and lowered my hands. I stared at my pale palms. They were the same gray color as the grass.

This place is killing me.

I'd repeated that thought a hundred times. Every day, every minute, every second I spent in that realm drained a little more out of me. This enervating effect, plus the bleached environment, made me think I'd landed smack in the middle of a waste—one of the magical dead zones created during the Faerie Wars. Except I'd never heard of a waste this big.

I'd walked a full day out and back in every direction from the clearing that was my only link to home. I hadn't found a single sign of life. No birds. No game trails. No smoke. Hell, I would have jumped for joy to get a bug bite. There was nothing. The gray landscape stretched to the gray sky no matter where I looked. In the six days since my arrival, the wind never stirred, the sun never shone. The only movement I'd found was the lethargic trickle of water along a narrow creek bed. I'd nearly tripped over the bank before I noticed the muted burble, and when I brought the liquid to my lips, it was somehow as stale and lifeless as the air. I'd never realized how much flavor water had until it wasn't there.

I slunk over to that stream now, splashed my face, and slurped several handfuls of water with my uninjured hand. Normally, I would have worried about giardia or worse drinking unfiltered water, but nothing lived in this place. When I sat back, my gaze settled on the snowy peaks in front of me. I'd scouted the foothills but hadn't climbed to the summit. That peak represented my last hope . . . and the last of my energy. If I couldn't see an edge to this waste from up there, there likely wasn't one.

I'd put off moving too far from where I'd landed in the hopes that my friends would somehow find a way to rescue me, but those dreams had faded with each passing day, twisting to darker thoughts.

Maybe stopping Shedraziel wasn't enough. Maybe Anderson and Weatherly bombed the Colorado Reservation anyway, and my world is being torn apart by war. Maybe everyone I care about is dead.

I pulled my knees to my chest, wrapped my arms around them, and imagined James was holding me tight, but even the unbreakable link between us seemed to be gone. I snuffled and curled tighter around the emptiness inside me.

"Moping never got anyone anywhere," I scolded myself.

I wiped my nose and looked again at the distant ridge. The hunger pains of the first few days had passed, but my energy reserves were fading. "It's now or never."

I glanced over my shoulder. I'd spelled my name in river rocks in the clearing where I'd first arrived in case anyone came looking while I was away. I closed my eyes and shook my head. *No one's coming.*

I took one last drink, then stood.

Between my bruised ankle and still-healing bullet wound, I walked with a bit of a limp, but the tree limb I'd found on my third day made a decent crutch. I moved slowly, conserving as much energy as I could. *Hopefully, the tortoise can win this race.*

Unlike Shedraziel's prison, the plants here were not carved from stone. They bent and broke as I bushwhacked my way through them. I'd tried digging up the roots of a few for sustenance on the second day, but they'd turned to dust in my mouth.

I marched to the drumbeat of my pulse and the huff of my breath. The only other sounds were the whispers scratching at my mind, looking for a way in.

Halfway up the first major slope, a twinge in my chest made me gasp. I braced my foot against the pale scree and rubbed my sternum. The sensation eased. I took three more steps. The twinge came back, stronger.

I stumbled to a stop, panting for breath. Loose rocks skidded down the slope below me.

What the hell? I know I've lost some muscle mass, but I've barely started. I looked at the distant peak. Despair sat heavier on my shoulders than any pack I'd ever carried. *I'll never make it if I'm wearing out already.*

I arched back and took a deep breath, trying to stretch out the tightness.

Alex.

I froze, staring at the whitewashed sky. I lowered my gaze and turned in a circle. Gray trees, gray bushes, gray moss, gray rocks. Nothing moved. I shook my head, wondering if the whispers had finally driven me mad.

I'm here.

My bond to James, quiet since I arrived, slammed into my awareness. I stumbled and dropped to one knee, splitting the skin against a jagged stone. My heart raced, pumping blood so fast I grew dizzy. I looked down at the valley, searching.

It's a trick. It has to be a trick. I shook my head, trying to clear the constant buzz that plagued me. Warning myself not to hope, I thrummed the thread anchored in my heart and held my breath.

The response was immediate and an eternity in coming: *I am here.*

My muscles turned to liquid as relief washed over me. Tears blurred the monochrome world.

He's really here. Somehow, impossibly, finally, he found me.

I huddled there on the ground shaking from the wash of emotion. Then another thought broke into my awareness. *I'm not home yet.*

My feet were moving before I realized what was happening. I slid down the slope in a mini-avalanche and crashed through the underbrush, speeding full-tilt downhill, my walking stick abandoned. The connection grew stronger with every step.

Please let this not be a dream.

I splashed through the sorry excuse for a stream, soaking my shoes, and scrambled up the opposite bank. My heart was pounding. My lungs strained. My leg screamed as every other step sent pain jolting through my still-healing wounds.

Hurry, Alex.

I pushed harder, spurred by the hope of rescue . . . and the fear of missing it.

I jerked to a stop at the edge of the clearing where I'd first entered this realm and stared at the smeary shape standing at its center—a shape I would have recognized even with my eyes closed. The bond between us was practically singing. The hollow ache in my chest was filled to bursting as his relief swelled to match my own.

"Alex!" James extended one arm, reaching for me.

I opened my mouth but choked on the words that rushed to get out. I staggered forward with the last of my strength. Each step threatened to drop me. When I was an arm's length away, I reached out and set my hand against his chest. His immortal heart thumped under my palm, devastatingly solid. I choked back a sob as the last of my doubts vanished.

James pulled me closer and squeezed until I couldn't breathe. I wrapped my arms around him and dug my fingers into his back, heedless of the pain in my broken wrist. His lips found mine. Our kiss tasted like salt.

When I finally broke for air, I pressed my forehead to his collarbone and babbled. "You're really here. You found me. I'd given up, but you came. You're really here."

"Alex." James ducked his chin and tipped his head, trying to get into my field of vision without releasing me. "We need to go."

I exhaled a shaky breath and nodded, chiding myself. *It's not time to fall apart yet.*

I glanced down and frowned. James was only hugging me with one arm. His other was extended behind him. I leaned to the side and saw that his arm stopped abruptly at the elbow, marking the place where reality split.

I gasped and tried to step back, but James held me in place.

He caught my gaze, forcing me to focus on his face. For the first time I noticed that his expression, though clearly happy to see me, was contorted by pain. Sweat glistened on his skin. The color he'd gained from so much time in the sun seemed to have drained away, and deep lines scored the corners of his narrowed eyes.

"What's going on?"

He winced in silent apology. "We have to go back through the Rift."

I glanced at his missing hand, recalling the agony of that place. My mouth went dry. I shook my head. "We'll be ripped apart."

A sensation similar to what I'd felt in the Rift rippled through our connection. "Vampires carry a piece of the Rift inside us. That's the price we pay for what we are, but it gives me a certain tolerance. I'm stretched across the Rift right now, anchored on the far side. You'll only be in it for a moment."

Bile rose in my throat. The idea of being spread across dimensions, with part of me trapped in that in-between place, being ripped apart at a cellular level. . . . I shuddered. The longer I delayed, the more pain I was causing him. "Let's go."

"Take a deep breath and hold on tight."

I wrapped my arms around his neck, inhaled, and closed my eyes.

James stepped back, taking me with him.

The moment I passed through the tear into the Rift was marked by the twisting sensation of moving between realms. My body was unmade one molecule at a time. I clung to James as my nerves were frozen, set on fire, smashed, slashed, and electrocuted all at the same time.

As abruptly as the sensations began, they vanished, though the terrifying memory of that agony lingered like an echo in my mind.

I peeked through the lashes of one eye, then the other, and finally opened them fully to take in the scene around me. James's second arm, hand and all, was now wrapped around my waist. Emma stood a few inches away. Her face was pale. Her eyebrows were drawn together with worry.

She threw her arms around James and me both and started to cry in jerky, hiccupping sobs. "We thought we'd lost you."

Behind her, Kai, Chase, Sarah, and Zee wore matching looks of disbelief. The rocks they stood on were red and brown. The sky was blue. The wind lifted my hair and tickled my neck. But the biggest difference was the silence in my head. The whispers that had plagued me were gone. That more than anything convinced me I was home.

I coughed to clear the wad of emotion blocking my throat and said, "Thanks for not giving up on me." My voice cracked, but at least I got the words out.

Zee stiffened and looked away. The rest of the group didn't so much as bat an eye at my gratitude. They wouldn't demand the compensation of debt that fae custom dictated. They were my friends.

Emma straightened. She tipped her head toward James. "As if this guy would let us. He's been a maniac since you disappeared."

Setting my hand against James's stubble-covered cheek, I met his cornflower gaze and mouthed, "Thank you."

He smiled and closed his eyes, leaning into my hand. The lines of tension in his face eased.

I still wasn't sure how much of him was the man I'd known for the past few years and how much was the vampire he'd once been, but at that moment I didn't care, because they both loved me. I could feel that through and through as the threads of our connection reestablished themselves.

I finally stepped away from James, but I caught his hand and held it tight, not willing to break the physical connection just yet. "What happened after . . .?" I stumbled on the memory.

Kai gestured to something behind me. "See for yourself."

I turned. The first thing I noticed were the werewolves, all in fur form, gathered in the shade of a rocky overhang just past the parking lot. *I can't believe they all stuck around this long.* Then I spotted Annabrae and Rhoana, both still wearing their armor, standing by the lake. I blinked and squinted at the lake. My jaw dropped.

The water that had broken through the dam was gone. The lake stopped in a curved line that mimicked the arc of the man-made structure, leaving a gap half as wide as the dam was tall between the broken concrete and the wall of water where the lake now ended. The two sides of the dam reaching out from the canyon walls ended in ragged edges that created a wide "V" through which I could see the cliffs on the far side.

I squeezed James's hand and gave it a tug. He matched my pace as I walked to the shoreline, quietly supporting me as I willed my legs to stop shaking. The rest of my friends followed.

The two fae captains stood a safe distance apart, outwardly relaxed . . . but that could change in an instant. Both turned at my approach. Annabrae's expression was inscrutable, but I caught the faintest flicker of relief in Rhoana's eyes. I stepped between them and looked over the suspended water. Dark coils moved in the depths but never broke the surface.

"Incredible," I whispered. "He's been holding the water in place for six days?"

James's grip tightened, pinching my fingers. Confusion rolled through our connection.

Annabrae frowned at me. She shifted her gaze to my companions, Rhoana, then back to me and said, "You've been gone barely an hour."

I opened my mouth, made a choking sound as words failed me, and closed it again.

James's second hand closed over our already twined fingers. "You felt you were gone for a week?"

I blinked, my mind racing. I nodded.

"The effect of a time difference between realms." Kai's voice was tight.

Emma's hand found my shoulder. "We got to you as fast as we could."

I patted her hand awkwardly with my splint and said, "I know," but inside I was screaming. *I'd given up, convinced that my friends had already tried and failed to reach me. If I'd crossed that ridge, would I have felt James? Would I have been trapped in that realm forever?*

My chest cramped with panic. Even knowing I was home, even touching James with one hand and Emma with the other, the fear of being trapped in that dead place, with that endless whisper whittling away my sanity, stole the air from my lungs.

"I will always find you, Alex." James pressed his free hand over my heart. I could feel my pulse racing against his palm, reflecting back through our bond like an echo. He rested his forehead against mine. "Always."

His solid presence poured into me, grounding me. My anxiety eased.

I took several deep breaths then set my hand over his heart in mirror of his pose. The two of us would discuss our experiences of the last few days . . . or hours. We would fall apart in each other's arms and find comfort there, but this was not the time. Not when we had an audience.

I don't care who's watching. His thought barely reached me before his lips were on mine, chasing away the memories of loneliness.

I melted against him for a moment, savoring the contact. *But I do.* I pulled back. Much as I wanted to pretend it was only the two of us, the outside world was waiting.

He gave me a look that said the rest of the world could go screw itself, but remained at arm's length.

I gestured to the gap between the lake and the dam. "How long can he hold it like this?"

"We will remain until another solution can be found . . . as a show of good faith to your PTF." Annabrae cast me a sidelong glance. "It seemed the least we could do after you sacrificed yourself for our lord."

"A brave but foolish act." Rhoana spoke through clenched teeth. "Had you died—"

"But I didn't." If I started thinking about what-ifs again, I'd lose it. I frowned, thinking back to the enchanters on the dam during the battle. "Were there many casualties?"

"Eight were lost when the dam broke. Seven in the fighting on the shore." A breeze blew off the reservoir, ruffling the strands that had pulled loose from Rhoana's long braid. Her forest-green cloak swished behind her. A long tear ran up one side. The hem was stained with blood. Her angular profile turned toward me. Silver specks danced in her indigo eyes. "I trust this clears Lord Bael of responsibility in this matter?"

I pursed my lips. Bael was still responsible for Shedraziel's actions, whether through intent or neglect . . . but pursuing the matter would do nothing but alienate us further and complicate our future interactions. Right now the most important thing was to ease the tensions left in Shedraziel's wake, and casting blame never ended a conflict. I sighed. "He didn't break his word. Without you and your troops, the dam would have fallen uncontested, and Shedraziel would still be loose."

I recalled her mocking voice during those first terrible moments in the Rift, and a horrifying thought struck me. "She is gone . . . isn't she?"

The gathered fae exchanged unreadable looks. Finally, Annabrae said, "We're not sure."

The world tilted. "What do you mean you're not sure? How can you not be sure? She got stabbed. She died."

"She didn't die as a fae dies," Rhoana said. "She didn't return to the Summerlands. She . . . changed."

All the fae looked uncomfortable. No one would meet my gaze.

"They think she turned into a demon," James said. "In which case, she could still exist somewhere within the Rift."

I thought about the way Shedraziel's glittering particles had turned to smoke right before she charged the Undine Lord. "How?"

"She lied." Rhoana flipped her cloak behind her shoulder, looking agitated. "Not a half truth or omission, but an outright, intentional lie."

I gulped, stunned by the realization of what truly prevented the fae from lying.

"Now if you will excuse me, I shall return to Lord Bael and relay the news of our victory." She placed two fingers to her lips and blew out a shrill whistle, then pivoted with military precision and strode to the center of the parking lot.

A deep-throated neigh drew my attention to a large, brown elk-like creature as it crested the ridge to my left, trotting across empty air. The gaala's six legs touched down lightly on the asphalt, and Rhoana vaulted to its back. She raised a hand in farewell. The gaala raced forward, climbing higher with each step as though running up an invisible incline.

I watched until Rhoana and her mount became a speck on the horizon, then turned back to Annabrae. I studied her calm expression. "After the way the girl in the desert disappeared when I broke the pearl, and then Shedraziel having so many undine fae on her side . . . I honestly didn't think you were going to come."

She arched an eyebrow. "Perhaps you didn't notice, but we had a civil war on our hands." She gestured to the viewing area where the battle had taken place. "Those here were not the only ones among our subjects who'd fallen in line with Shedraziel's plan to dethrone the lord. We had to set our own house in order first, lest we return to a coup."

"I get it," I said. "I just wish you'd given me some kind of heads-up."

She frowned.

"A warning. A clue as to what you were planning," I clarified.

"I will bear that in mind for the future." She glanced at me, then away. "I'm pleased you survived. It seems Bael has finally produced something worthwhile."

I smiled and stared out across the water.

After a long stretch of silence, Emma asked. "What happens now?"

I took a deep breath and let it out slowly. "Now it's time for someone else to take the lead."

FOUR DAYS LATER, washed, fed, and relatively well rested, I walked through the sliding-glass doors into Saint Joseph Hospital. It was my first trip out of the house since the bureaucrats had taken over. James had called David, who'd called Silva, who'd managed to talk Anderson down from his suicidal plan before southern Colorado became a smoldering crater. The werewolves made themselves scarce before the first helicopter arrived, as did Zee, Chase, and Kai.

The trip home had been a bit of a blur. I remembered lots of shouting, an IV, and James by my side. There'd been several hours of interrogations and threats, during which I lost count of the number of times I was asked to repeat what had happened. Eventually, I was put back under house arrest, which had suited me just fine since home was exactly where I wanted to be.

James had claimed the need to stay with me for medical reasons, and I guess I must have looked even worse than I felt because no one argued.

I'm sure Anderson would have preferred my head on a plate, but fear that the undine fae might release the waters of Lake Mead before the dam repairs were complete was doing wonders for interspecies relations. As it was, the only real inconvenience was that the guards at the end of my driveway had moved up to camp on my lawn.

As I passed the nurses' station in front of the ICU, I wondered if my luck would hold out. One way or another, today's summons was going to change everything.

I reached for the handle to Harris's hospital room. The door swung out of reach. I pulled back and looked into the angry brown eyes of Peter Weatherly. He bared his teeth in a laughable impression of a werewolf's snarl and brushed past me, stalking down the white hall without a word.

That's a good sign.

Everly Harris was sitting up in her bed. A bandage still wrapped her head, and she was paler than normal, but her eyes were open. She was looking at a robin perched in the bud-covered ash tree outside her window.

I closed the door behind me. "How are you feeling?"

"Better than Weatherly wishes." She turned her dark gaze on me. "How are you holding up? Happy to be out?"

I lifted one shoulder in a half-shrug. "I was kind of enjoying my house arrest this time around."

She smiled. "Too bad. I need you back at your post."

"You're reinstating me?"

"With a few tweaks to your job description."

I glanced at the closed door. "No wonder Weatherly was mad." I narrowed my eyes at her. "What kind of tweaks?"

"That deal you made with Bishop Silva?"

I nodded.

"He followed through."

I stared at her for a moment while my brain caught up to the conversation. "He actually convinced the Church to back our actions? To offer their support of paranatural inclusion?"

"Not only that, he's convinced them to pressure the PTF into negotiating a new treaty with the fae . . . assuming we can convince them to deal." She arched an eyebrow at me.

"Ah. That's my new job?"

"I can't think of anyone better, and the Church agrees. The way you brought everyone together to stop Shedraziel was impressive."

"And totally illegal."

She nodded. "In light of the outcome, the PTF board and related governing bodies have agreed to grant you and your allies clemency. Consider yourself pardoned."

"And the paranatural partnership experiment?"

"Still running," she said.

I exhaled and looked out the window. David had called me the night I got back to tell me the One Earth protesters had not only clogged the streets of Denver for an entire day but had flocked to southern Colorado to sit in solidarity around the fae reservation after hearing about Anderson's plan. There would always be people who opposed change and the inclusion of those who were different, but there were also those who embraced it, and our influence was growing. But was I the right person to spearhead that movement?

"I'm tired of fighting," I muttered, not realizing I'd spoken the words out loud until Harris responded.

"The only way out is through."

I grimaced.

"Like it or not, you're much more than an artist now. You're the spokesperson for interspecies tolerance."

"Maybe, but I'm not a PTF Director." I shook my head. "Let's face it, I never really was."

She frowned. "What are you saying? After all you've done to get us to this point, you won't help with the final push?"

"Oh I'll help. If this experience has taught me anything, it's that I can't walk away from this mess. But I'm not an administrator. Garrett and Sarah will handle the liaison work better than I ever could."

"A consultant then. Duties to be agreed upon as needed." She extended her hand.

I studied her palm, weighing my options, then reached out and grasped it. "I can live with that."

"I suggest you take advantage of your free time while you have it." She settled back against her pillows. "There are a lot of hoops to jump through before we can move forward with a project this monumental, but once we do, you're going to be so busy your head will explode."

"Can't wait." I opened the door but paused before passing through. "I'm glad you're back, Everly."

She winked at me. "Likewise."

Want more?
Continue the adventure with
Lies and Illusion
Book 7 of The Magicsmith series.

Acknowledgments

First and foremost, I have to thank my husband, David. His support lets me pursue this career during these uncertain times of getting myself established as an author. He is also the voice of reason and encouragement when my doubts get the better of me. He is my partner in all things, and I love him.

Thanks as well to my daughter, Alice, who is now old enough to understand what I do and is both encouraging and proud of her "famous" mother. You are the light of my life.

Thanks to my parents and in-laws who've not only been incredibly supportive of my writing endeavors, but also acted as babysitters while my husband and I ran tables at various conferences and conventions. And a special thanks to Connie, who has beta read every one of my books and short stories to help me get the cleanest copy possible.

Thanks to Debra Dixon and the team at Bell Bridge Books who've worked with me since book 1 to build and promote the amazing *Magicsmith* series. Every time I get my manuscript back for revisions I know the story is going to be so much stronger thanks to your thoughtful insights. From collaborating on cover designs to commiserating about delays, you've been a joy to work with.

About the Author
L.R. Braden

L. R. Braden is a bestselling, multi-award-winning author of dark-yet-hopeful urban fantasy stories. Her published works include the *Magicsmith* series, the *Rifter* series, and several works of shorter fiction. A bit of a recluse, she enjoys collecting skills that may (or may not) prove useful in the event that she is suddenly transported to an inhospitable alternate reality. Since that hasn't happened yet, she mostly spends her days weaving fantastic tales, playing with her family, and getting lost on purpose. Her writing has won many awards, including the Eric Hoffer Book Award for Sci-fi/Fantasy, the Next Generation Indie Book Award for Paranormal Fiction, and the Imadjinn Award for Best Urban Fantasy.

Connect with her online at lrbraden.com

www.ingramcontent.com/pod-product-compliance
Lightning Source LLC
Chambersburg PA
CBHW021007260626
47169CB00006B/1992